DO DREAMS
ALWAYS END . . . ?

Kate looked into his eyes. "I don't know how to say this, Nick. It sounds so ungrateful. My son was thrilled with the pony you gave him. It's like a dream come true. *You're* like a dream come true. Maybe that's what's bothering me though . . . what I'm trying to say. I don't want all of this to be just a dream. And maybe if . . ."

"Maybe if I just vanish, then where will you both be? Is that it, Kate?" He looked as though he understood all that she felt.

"I guess that is it, Nick. What would happen if suddenly you weren't here any more? One minute ponies and promises of Disneyland, and the next . . ."

"I'm going to be here, Kate. For a long, long time. As long as you'll let me be here. I'm not going anywhere."

It was just what Tom had said.

But life wasn't like that.

She knew better now. . . .

DELL BOOKS BY DANIELLE STEEL

PASSION'S PROMISE

NOW AND FOREVER

THE PROMISE

SEASON OF PASSION

SUMMER'S END

TO LOVE AGAIN

LOVING

SEASON OF PASSION

Danielle Steel

A DELL BOOK

Published by
Dell Publishing Co., Inc.
1 Dag Hammarskjold Plaza
New York, New York 10017

Dell ® TM 681510, Dell Publishing Co., Inc.

ISBN: 0-440-17703-0

Printed in the United States of America
First printing—February 1979
Second printing—March 1979
Third printing—April 1979
Fourth printing—May 1979
Fifth printing—November 1979
Sixth printing—March 1980
Seventh printing—August 1980

*To Bill, Beatrix, and Nicholas
with all my love.
And with special thanks
to Nancy Bel Weeks.*

"How arrives it joy lies slain,
And why unblooms the best hope ever sown?"
"Hap" by Thomas Hardy

"Sweet are the uses of adversity,
Which, like the toad, ugly and venomous,
Wears yet a precious jewel in his head."
William Shakespeare

PART
ONE

CHAPTER 1

The alarm went off just after six. She stirred, reached an arm out from under the covers, and turned it off. She could still pretend that she hadn't heard it. She could go back to sleep. She didn't have to go . . . it wasn't as if . . . and then the phone rang.

"Damn." Kaitlin Harper sat up in bed. Her long brown hair hung over her shoulders in the braids she had worn the day before, and her face was brown from the sun. The phone rang again, and with a sigh she answered it, crushing a yawn between her teeth. She had a delicate mouth, which smiled abundantly when she was happy, but today her green eyes already looked too serious. She was awake now. It was so much easier to sleep and forget.

"Hi, Kate." She smiled at the familiar voice. She had known it would be Felicia. Nobody else knew where she was.

"What are you doing up at this hour?"

"Oh, the usual."

Kate broke into a broad grin. "At six o'clock? Some usual." She knew Licia better than that. Felicia Norman could barely make it out of bed by eight, and at her office her secretary was carefully instructed to shield her from any undue shocks until at least ten. Six o'clock in the morning was hardly her hour. Except for Kate. For Kate, she would even get herself up

11

at that ungodly hour. "Don't you have anything better to do than check on me, Licia?"

"Apparently not. So what's new?" You could almost hear Felicia trying to force herself awake. The well-cut blond hair, which hung straight to her shoulders, now lay flat on her pillow as a carefully manicured hand covered the ice-blue eyes in her chiseled face. Like Kate, she had the face of a model, but she was older than Kate by twelve years.

"Nothing's new, silly. And I love you. But I'm fine. I promise."

"Good. I just thought maybe you'd like me to meet you there today." There. An anonymous word for an anonymous place. And Felicia was willing to drive for two hours just to meet her friend "there." And for what? Kate had to do it alone now. She knew that. You couldn't go on leaning on people forever. She'd done that for long enough.

"No, Licia, I'm okay. Besides, the store will end up divorcing you if you keep running off in the middle of the day to baby-sit for me." Felicia Norman was the fashion director of one of San Francisco's most elegant stores, and Kate had met her when she was modeling.

"Don't be silly. They don't even miss me." But they both knew that was a lie. And what Kate didn't know was that Felicia had the Norell show to oversee that afternoon. The whole winter line. And Halston in three days. Blass next week. It defied the imagination. Even Felicia's. But Kate was removed from all that now. She wasn't thinking of seasons and lines. She hadn't for months.

"How's my little friend?" Felicia's voice softened when she asked, bringing a smile back to Kate's eyes. A real one this time, as she ran a hand over her full stomach. Three more weeks . . . three weeks . . . and Tom . . .

"He's fine."

"How can you be so sure it's a boy? You've even convinced me." Felicia smiled at the thought of the stack of baby clothes she'd ordered on the seventh floor last week. "Anyway, it better be!" They both laughed.

"It will be. Tom said—" And then a silence. The words had slipped out. "Anyway, love, I don't need a baby-sitter today. I promise. You can stay in San Francisco, get another two hours sleep, and go to work in peace. If I need you, I'll call. Trust me."

"Where have I heard that before?" Felicia laughed a deep soft laugh into the phone. "If I waited for you to call, I'd die of old age. Can I come down this weekend, by the way?"

"Again? Can you stand it?" She'd been there almost every weekend for the past four months. But by now Kate expected her; Felicia's inquiry and Kate's response were only a formality.

"What can I bring you?"

"Nothing! Felicia Norman, if you bring me one more maternity anything, I'll scream! Where do you think I wear that stuff? To the supermarket? Lady, I live in a cowtown. You know—the men wear undershirts and the women wear housecoats. That's it." Kate sounded amused.

Felicia did not. "That's your own goddamn fault. I told you—"

"Oh shut up. I'm happy here." Kate was smiling to herself.

"You're nuts. It's just this nesting instinct you've got from being pregnant. Wait till the baby comes. You'll come to your senses." Felicia was counting on it. She was even keeping an eye out for available apartments. There had already been two or three gems in her neighborhood on Telegraph Hill. Kate was

13

crazy to stay down there. But she'd come out of it. The furor was already dying down. Another couple of months and she could come back in peace.

"Hey, Licia"—Kate looked over at the alarm clock—"I'd better get moving. I have a three-hour drive ahead of me." She stretched gingerly in her bed, hoping her legs wouldn't cramp and send her leaping out of bed—as best she could "leap."

"And that's another thing. You could stop going up there for the next month, at least until after the baby. There's no point—"

"Licia, I love you. Good-bye." Very gently, Kate hung up. She had heard that speech before. And she knew what she was doing. It was what she had to do. What she wanted to do. Besides, what choice did she have? How could she stop going now?

She rolled slowly to a sitting position at the edge of the bed and took a deep breath as she looked at the mountains beyond her window. Her thoughts were years and miles away. A lifetime away.

"Tom." She said it gently. Just the one word. She wasn't even aware she'd said it aloud. Tom . . . how could he not be there? Why wasn't he running his bath, or singing from the shower, teasing her from the kitchen . . . was he really gone? It had been so little time since she could just call his name and hear his voice. He had been right there with her. Always. Big, blond, beautiful Tom, full of laughter and hugs, and a gift for making wonderful moments. Tom, whom she had met during her first year in college, when the team happened to be in San Francisco, and she happened to go to the game, and then happened to go to a party, and someone knew someone on the team . . . madness. And luck. She had never done anything like it before. She had fallen in love with him on the spot, at eighteen. And with a football player? The idea had seemed funny to her at first. A football player. But he wasn't just that. He was special. He was Tom Harper. Loving, warm, thoughtful in infinite ways. Tom, whose father had been a coal miner in Pennsylvania, and whose mother had worked as a waitress to help put him through school. Tom, who had worked nights and days and summers himself to get to college, and then had finally made it after all on a football scholarship. He had become a star. And then a pro. And then a real star. A kind of national hero. Tom Harper. And that was when she had met him. When he was a star. Tom . . .

"Hello, Princess." His eyes had run over her like a trickle of warm summer rain.

"Hello." She had felt so foolish. Hello . . . it was all she could think of to say. She had nothing to say to him really, but something small and tight had turned over in the pit of her stomach. She had had to look away. His bright blue eyes were too much for her, the way he searched her face, the way he smiled. Meeting those eyes was like trying to stare into the sun.

"Are you from San Francisco?" He had been smiling down at her from his immense height. He was a huge, powerfully built man, with the classic shape required for his profession. She was wondering what he was thinking about her. He probably thought she was ridiculous. A groupie, or just a kid.

"Yes. I'm from San Francisco. Are you?" And then they both laughed, because she knew he wasn't. Everyone knew where Tom Harper was from. And the team was based in Chicago.

"Why so shy?"

"I . . . it . . . oh damn." And then they had laughed, and it was better after that. They had slipped away from the party and gone out for hamburgers.

15

"Will your friends be upset?"

"Probably." She sat at the counter on a stool next to him, swinging one long leg, and smiling happily over her dripping hamburger. She had had a date, somewhere, back there at the party. But not anymore. She was out with Tom Harper. It was hard to get used to the idea. But he didn't seem to match the legend she had heard about. He was just a man. She liked him. But not because of who he was. Just because he was nice. No . . . more than that . . . but she wasn't quite sure what it was. She only knew that a strange tiny butterfly was soaring happily through her gut. It happened every time she looked at him. She wondered if he could tell.

"Do you do this often, Princess? I mean, ditch dates at parties." He looked at her sternly for a moment, and they both laughed again.

"Never. Promise."

"Better not do it to me."

"No, sir."

It had been a night of teasing and laughter, and she had instantly felt close to him, yet humbled at the same time. He could make her feel like a little girl, but he also made her feel safe, as though she had waited all her life for him to protect her. It was a strange feeling, but she liked it. They had driven to Carmel after the hamburgers, and walked along the ocean, but he hadn't tried to make love to her. They had only walked, and held hands, and talked until the sun came up, exchanging the secrets of childhood and youth . . . "and wait till I tell you about . . ."

"You're a beautiful girl, Kate. What do you want to be when you grow up?" She had laughed at the question and delicately slid a handful of sand down the back of his shirt. He had retaliated in kind, and she wondered if he would kiss her, but he didn't. And she wanted desperately to kiss him. "Stop that. I'm serious. What do you want to do?"

The question made her sit back with a shrug. "I don't know. I just started college. I think maybe I want to major in political science, or maybe literature. You know, useful stuff like that. Who knows? I'll probably graduate and get a job selling cosmetics at Saks." Or run away, or be a ski bum, or teach school, or be a nurse or a fireman or . . . hell, how did she know? He was silly.

He was smiling at her again, that rich blue-eyed smile that melted the seat of her pants. "How old are you, Kate?" He was full of questions, and he looked at her again and again as though he had always known her. The questions seemed only a formality. Somehow she thought he already knew the answers.

"I was eighteen last month. And you?"

"Twenty-eight, m'love. Ten years older than you are. I'm almost over the hill. In this business anyway." His face tightened as he said it.

"And when you retire?"

"I'll join you selling cosmetics at Saks." She laughed at the thought. He was easily six feet four or five. The idea of Tom Harper selling anything smaller than a battleship was absurd.

"What do retired football players do?"

"Get married. Have kids. Drink beer. Get fat. Sell insurance. The good things in life." He sounded half ironic, half scared, and very serious.

"Sounds terrific." She was smiling gently and looking out to sea as he put an arm around her shoulders.

"Not really." He was thinking of the part about selling insurance, and then he looked at her. "Do marriage and kids sound terrific, Kate?"

She shrugged. "I guess. That stuff seems a long way off to me."

"You're young." He said it so soberly that it made her laugh.

"Yes, grandfather."

"What do you really think you'll do after you graduate?"

"Honestly? Go to Europe. I want to spend a couple of years over there. Kicking around. Working. Whatever comes up. I figure I'll be pretty fed up with the discipline of school by then." All that was still three years away.

"So that's what you call it. 'Discipline.' " He grinned to himself, thinking of the slightly rowdy crowd of rich kids he had watched her arrive with at the party. They all went to Stanford. They all had money, and fancy clothes, and there had been a Morgan and a brand-new Corvette parked at the curb. "Where in Europe?"

"Vienna or Milan. Maybe Bologna. Maybe Munich. I haven't decided yet, but someplace small."

"Tsk."

"Oh shut up." The urge to kiss him was overwhelming again. It made her smile quietly in the night. Here she sat, virtually in the arms of Tom Harper. Half the women in the country would have drooled at the thought. And there they sat, like two kids, with his arm around her, and talking easily. Her parents would *not* have been thrilled. She almost laughed at the thought.

"What are your folks like?" It was as though he had read her mind.

"Stuffy. But nice, I suppose. I'm an only child and they had me a little late. They expect a lot."

"And you deliver?"

"Most of the time. I shouldn't though. I've given

18

them bad habits. Now they expect me to toe the line all the time. That's part of why I want to go away for a couple of years. I might even do my junior year abroad. Or go next summer."

"Subsidized by Daddy, of course." He sounded smug, and she turned to look at him with anger in her green eyes.

"Not necessarily. I make my own money too. Actually, I'd rather pay for my own trip. If I can get a job over there."

"Sorry, Princess. I just figured. I don't know . . . that whole group you came in with tonight looked pretty well-heeled. I knew the type when I was at Michigan State. All of them were from Grosse Pointe, or Scottsdale, or wherever. It's all the same thing."

Kate nodded. She didn't disagree with him, she just didn't like being tossed into the same basket with all those other kids. But she knew what he meant. Even though she had never rebelled, that way of life didn't appeal to her much either. Everyone seemed to have so much of everything. And no texture, no pain, no questions, no qualms. They all had so much. And Kate was no exception. But at least she knew it.

"What do you mean, you make your own money?" He looked amused again.

She looked annoyed. "I model."

"You do? For magazines or what?" Now that was a surprise. She had the looks for it, but he just figured she didn't work. But modeling was a nice gig. He was almost impressed. He turned to look at her and the anger in her face softened.

"All kinds of stuff. I did a commercial last summer. Most of the time I just get called to do fashion shows at I. Magnin, Saks, stores like that. It's kind of a pain to go into the city just for that, but it pays decently and it gives me a little independence. And it's sort of fun sometimes." He could just see her going down the runway, half colt, half doe, tall and thin in some five-hundred-dollar dress. Or maybe they didn't have her modeling stuff like that. But she had the style to pull it off. And though Tom knew little about fashion, he had guessed correctly.

"Is that what you're going to do in Europe when you finish school? Model?" He looked intrigued, as he kept a warm arm around her shoulders. She was comfortable there.

"Only if the alternative is starvation. I really want to do other things."

"Like what?" He pulled her closer. He seemed older and yet not older at all. And for the first time in her life, she wanted a man to make love to her. That was crazy. She was a virgin, and she didn't even know him. Not yet. But he was the kind of man you'd want to be first. She couldn't imagine him being anything but gentle and kind. "Come on, Kate, what kind of 'other things' do you want to do in Europe?" He sounded a little bit teasing, and it made her smile. She had always wanted a big brother who would sound like that.

"I don't know. Work for a newspaper maybe. Or a magazine. Be a reporter. Maybe someplace like Paris or Rome." Her face lit up and he rumpled her hair.

"Listen, kid, why not settle for modeling and live like a lady? What do you want to chase around after fires and murders for? Christ, you can do that over here. In English."

"My father would have a nervous breakdown." She giggled.

"So would I." He held her close again, as though to keep her safe from unseen evil.

"You're a party pooper, Tom Harper. I'm a damned good writer. I'd be a good reporter."

"Who says you're a good writer?"

20

"I do. And one day I'm going to write a book." Damn. She'd said it. She looked away and stopped talking.

"You're serious about that, aren't you, Kate?" His voice was as soft as morning, and she nodded silently. "Then maybe one day you will." He tiptoed gently, trying not to step on any of her dreams. "I used to want to write a book too. But I gave up the idea."

"Why did you do that?" She was horrified, and he tried to keep his face serious. He loved her intensity.

"I gave up the idea because I can't write. Maybe one day you'll write one for me." They sat quietly for a while, looking out to sea, enjoying the night breeze on their faces. He had lent her a spare parka, and they huddled together on the beach. It was a while before either of them spoke again.

"What do your parents want you to do?" he asked.

"Later?" He nodded. "Oh, something 'pleasant.' A job in a museum, something at a university, or graduate school. Or best of all, find a husband. Boring stuff. What about you? What are you going to do after the newspapers stop telling us all what a fabulous football player you are?" She looked like a kid as she lay on the sand, but there was a woman lurking in her eyes, and Tom Harper saw her.

"I told you. I'll retire, and we'll write that book." She said nothing more, and they sat in silence and watched the sun come up, and then drove back to San Francisco.

"Want to have breakfast before I drop you off?" They were in Palo Alto and he was already nearing her street in the little British sports car he had rented for his stay in the city.

"I should probably get back." If her mother called and learned she'd been out all night, she'd have some very fancy explaining to do, but the girls would probably cover for her. She covered for them. Two of the four were no longer virgins. And the third was doing her damnedest to change her status. Kate didn't really care—or she hadn't anyway, until Tom.

"What about tonight?"

She looked crestfallen. "I can't. I promised my parents I'd have dinner with them. And they've got tickets to the symphony. Afterwards?" Damn, damn, damn. And then he'd be leaving town and she'd never see him again.

There was something suddenly sad in her face and he wanted to kiss her. Not like a kid. Like a woman. He wanted to hold her close to him and feel her heart pounding against him. He wanted . . . he forced the thoughts from his mind. She was too young.

"Can't make it afterwards, Princess. We play tomorrow. I have to be in bed by ten. Don't worry about it. Maybe we can grab a few minutes together tomorrow before we fly out. Want to come to the airport with me?"

"Sure." The look of despair started to fade.

"Want to come to the game tomorrow?" And then he laughed at something he saw in her face. "Oh, baby, tell the truth. You hate football, right?"

"Of course not." But she was laughing. He was onto her. "I don't hate it."

"You just don't like it much, right?" He laughed as he shook his head. It was perfect. A kid, a college girl, from some uptight fancy family. It was crazy. Totally crazy.

"Okay, Mr. Harper. So what? Does it matter if I'm not the world's hottest football fan?"

He looked down at her with a broad grin and shook his head. "Nope. Not a bit." In fact, the idea amused him. He was sick to death of groupies. And then, suddenly, they were in front of her house, and it was over.

"Okay, kiddo, I'll call you later." She wanted to make him promise, to ask him if he was sure he'd call, to tell him she'd cancel the dinner with her parents. But hell, he was Tom Harper, and she was just another girl. He'd never call again. She pulled a thin cloak of indifference around her, nodded, smiled easily, and slid out of the car. She was stopped before her feet touched the street. Tom Harper had a crushing grip on her arm. "Hey, Kate. Don't go off like that. I told you I'd call you. And I meant it." He understood that too. He understood everything. She turned to him with a smile of relief.

"Okay. I just thought . . ." The grip on her arm eased, and he ran a hand gently over her cheek.

"I know what you thought, but you were wrong."

"Was I?" Their eyes held for a long moment.

"Yes." It was the softest word she had ever heard. "Now go get some sleep. I'll call you later."

And he had. He called twice that morning, and once late at night, after she got home from the evening with her parents. He had been in bed, but couldn't sleep. They made plans to meet after the game the next day. But it was different this time. Too hurried, tense. They had won the game, and he was all keyed up, Kate was nervous. It wasn't the beach at Carmel, and it wasn't dawn. It was the whirlwind of Tom Harper's career, and a crowded airport bar before he flew to Dallas for another game. Other men from the team came and went, waved at them, two women wanted his autograph, the barman kept looking over and winking, and there was a constant turning of heads, whispers, nodding . . . over there . . . Tom Harper? . . . yeah? . . . hell, yes! . . . Tom Harper! It was distracting.

"Want to come to Dallas?"

"Huh?" She looked shocked. "When?"

"Now."

"Now?"

He grinned at the look on her face. "Why not?"

"You're crazy. I have to . . . I have exams . . ." A frightened little girl darted into her eyes, and suddenly he understood something else. Driving to Carmel with him had been an act of faith, of bravado, of something. She could handle that. But a trip to Dallas—that was something else. Okay. Now he understood. He would walk softly. This was a very special girl.

"Relax, Princess. I'm just kidding. But what about meeting me somewhere else, sometime after exams?" He said it very gently and prayed that no one would turn up for an autograph, or to congratulate him on the day's game. No one did. He held his breath as she looked at him.

"Yeah. I could do that." She was trembling inside, but it was a beautiful feeling.

"Okay. We'll talk about it." But he didn't press the point. And it was laughter and teasing all the way to the gate. They stood there for a moment and she wondered if he would kiss her or not. And then, with a slow, gentle smile, he bent down and kissed her, softly at first, and then as her arms went around him, he took her tightly in his and kissed her hard. It took her breath away and her head reeled. And then it was over, and he was gone, and she was alone at the gate.

He called that night. And every night, for a month. He invited her to various places where he was playing, but she couldn't get away, or his schedule was too tight, or she had a modeling job, or her parents wanted to do something with her, or . . . and she wasn't really sure if she wanted to "do it" yet. She thought so, but . . . She never explained that to him. But he knew.

"What are you telling me, Princess? That I'm never going to see you again?"

"Of course not. I just couldn't till now. That's all."

"Bullshit. You just get that skinny little ass of yours on a plane to Cleveland this weekend, or I'm coming out to get you myself." But there was always laughter in his voice, always that gentleness that let her know she was safe. He was the gentlest man she had ever known. And he was beginning to seem a little spoiled too. He kept insisting that he wanted her to come to him. But there was a reason for it. He wanted her away from home ground. Away from roommates and parents and guilt. He wanted to give her not just a night, but a honeymoon.

"Cleveland, this weekend?" Her voice held a quaver.

"Yes, love, Cleveland. Not Milan. Sorry."

"You should be."

But she had gone. And Cleveland had been hideous, but Tom was a dream. He had been waiting for her at the gate when she got off the plane, with the happiest smile she'd ever seen. He stood there, watching her walk toward him, and carrying one long-stemmed coral rose. And he had borrowed a house from the cousin of someone on the team. It wasn't a luxurious house, just a warm friendly one. It was what Tom was, unpretentious, tender, loving. And that was what he had been to her. He had deflowered her so gently that she was the one who wanted the second time. That was how he had meant it to be: he wanted her to want him. And from that moment on she was his. They both knew it.

"I love you, Princess."

"I love you too." She had looked at him shyly, with her long brown hair lying damp and soft over one shoulder. She was surprised at how unembarrassed she was with him, right from the first moment.

25

"Will you marry me, Kate?"

"Are you kidding?" Her eyes opened wide. They had been lying naked on the bed, watching the fire die in the grate. It was almost three in the morning and he had a game the next day. But this was the first thing in his life that had been more important than the game.

"No, Kate, I'm serious."

"I don't know." But there was a spark of interest in her eyes. Just enough. "I've never thought about anything like that. That always seemed like such a long way off. I'm only eighteen, and . . ." She looked up at him with a mixture of gravity and mischief. ". . . my parents would freak."

"Because of me, or your age?" But he knew, and she hesitated, looking for the right words. "Okay, I read you." He smiled, but he looked hurt too, and she quickly threw her arms around him.

"I love you, Tom. And if we did get married, it would be because I love you. I love who you are and what you are—I mean because you're Tom, not all the other stuff. And I wouldn't give a damn what anyone thought. It's just that . . . well, I've never thought of it. I kind of figured I'd float for a while."

"That's bullshit, my love. You're not a floater." And they both knew he was right. But this was crazy. She was the one who was supposed to want to get married, and here he was, offering it to her on a silver platter. For a brief moment, there was a marvelous feeling of power. She was a woman now. And more than that, she was Tom Harper's woman.

"You know something, sir? You're terrific." She lay back against him, and smiled with her eyes closed. And he smiled down at the delicately etched face.

"You're terrific too, Miss Kaitlin."

She made a face. "I hate that name."

But when he kissed her, she forgot all about it. And then he suddenly bounded out of bed, and went to the kitchen to get himself a beer. She watched the broad shoulders and trim hips and long legs, as he walked easily across the room in all his natural splendor. He was an extraordinary-looking man, and then she found herself blushing and embarrassed when he turned and smiled at her. Her eyes darted away to the fire. She kept them averted, but the blush still hovered on her cheeks.

He sat down next to her on the bed, and kissed her. "You don't have to be afraid to look at me, Princess. It's cool." She nodded, and took a sip of his beer.

"You're beautiful." She said it very softly, and he ran a hand slowly down her shoulder, gazing at her breasts.

"You're crazy. And I just had a wonderful idea. You don't want to get married yet, so how about if we live together for a while?" He looked pleased with the thought, and Kate, at first surprised, suddenly smiled.

"You know something? You're amazing. I feel like you're offering me the moon on a blue satin ribbon." She held his eyes with her own.

"You wanted red velvet?"

She shook her head.

"Well, then?"

"Can we wait a little bit?"

"Why? Kate, we have something very rare and we both know it. We know each other better than either of us knows anyone else. We've spent the last month on the phone, sharing every thought, dream, hope, fear, that either of us has ever had. We know all we need to know. Don't we?"

She nodded, feeling tears start to her eyes. "What if things change? What if . . ." And then he knew what was troubling her.

"Your parents?" She nodded. He'd find out soon enough.

"We'll handle it, Princess. Don't worry about it. And if you want to grow into it for a while, then you do that. Why don't we just relax till you finish the semester at school?" It was an easy wait. He had only another six weeks till the end of her first year. Then there was the summer. He knew it was settled. And secretly, so did she. And then quietly, gently, slowly, he let his lips run from her mouth to her neck, and play games with her nipples, his tongue darting around them and making her writhe slowly beneath his hands. He was afraid to try for a third time that night—he didn't want to hurt her. So, with all the tenderness he showed her in all things, he ran his tongue along the inside of her thighs, until he heard her begin to moan softly. It was a night she remembered with tenderness always.

She cried on the flight back to San Francisco. She felt wrenched away from him, torn from her roots. She needed him. She was his now. And when she got back to the house in Palo Alto, there were roses waiting for her, from Tom. He took care of her the way even her parents never had. They were so distant and aloof, so cool, so unaware of her feelings. Tom never was. He called two or three times a day, and they talked for hours. He seemed to be with her constantly. He flew back to San Francisco the weekend after Cleveland, and borrowed another apartment from a friend on the team. He was always careful and discreet. He wanted to shield Kate from reporters. And when school ended, she knew that she had to be with him. They had both zigzagged across the country for six weeks, and it was an insane way to live. The week after school ended, he was traded to San Francisco. It was perfect. Now they could rent an apartment in San Francisco, and she could travel with him all the time. They would always be together. She was sure. He was the most important thing in her life. She could always finish school later—hell, maybe in a year or two she'd go back. This was only a hiatus. Maybe until Tom retired from the team. School was no big deal.

That was not, however, how her parents viewed it.

"Are you out of your mind, Kaitlin?" Her father stared at her in disbelief from his traditional stance near the fireplace. He had been pacing back and forth and had finally stopped there, with a look of desperation in his eyes. "Leave school and do *what?* Live with this man? Have a baby out of wedlock? Or maybe someone else's baby—I'm sure there are other men on his team who'd be glad to oblige." His eyes flashed as he went off on his own private tangent, and Kate saw Tom tense across the room.

"Daddy, that's not what we're talking about. I'm not having anyone's baby." Her voice trembled.

"No? How can you be so sure? Do you have any idea what kind of a life you'll lead with this man? What kind of raucous, low-class, miserable life athletes lead? What exactly are you aspiring to? Sitting around in bars watching football on television and going bowling on Tuesday nights?"

"For God's sake, Daddy, all I told you is that I'm leaving school for a semester and I'm in love with Tom. How can you—"

"Very easily. Because you don't know what you're doing." His tone held only condemnation, and her mother nodded silent agreement as she sat stiffly in her chair.

29

"May I interject a word, sir?" It was the first time Tom had spoken since they'd begun. He had accompanied Kate only to provide emotional support: he knew that the matter had to be handled between Kate and her parents. He had wanted to bolster her, not interfere, but there was no way to avoid interfering now. Kate's father was getting way out of hand, and enjoying it. It showed in his eyes.

Tom turned to her father now with a look of quiet concern. "I think you have a somewhat frightening view of what my life is like. True, I don't work as a lawyer or a stock broker, and there isn't anything very intellectual about playing football, but that's my life. It's an all-out, hard-working, physical job. And the people in it are like any other kind of people, there are good men and bad men, stupid ones and smart ones. But Kate's life will not be spent with the team. I lead an extremely quiet private life, and I'd be very surprised if you could take exception to—"

Her father cut him off with a furious glare. "I take exception to *you*, Mr. Harper. It's as simple as that. And as for you, Kaitlin, if you do this, if you leave school, if you dare to disgrace us in this way, you're finished. I don't want to see you in this house again. You may take whatever personal items you want now, and you may leave. I will have nothing more to do with you, nor will your mother. I forbid it."

Kate's eyes filled with tears of pain and anger as she looked at him.

"Do you understand?" She nodded without taking her eyes from his. "And you won't change your mind?"

"No. I won't." She took a breath. "I think you're wrong. And I think you're being . . . very unkind." Her voice caught on a small sob lodged in her throat.

"No. I'm being right. If you think I have waited these eighteen years to banish my own daughter from my house, to stop seeing my only child, then you are greatly mistaken. Your mother and I have done everything we could for you. We have wanted everything for you, given everything to you, taught you everything we know and believe. And now you have betrayed us. It tells me only that we have had a stranger in our midst for these eighteen years, a traitor. It is like discovering that you are not ours, but someone else's child." As Tom listened with growing horror, he suddenly agreed. She was someone else's now. She was his. And he would love and cherish her even more after this day. What bastards they were. "You are no longer ours, Kaitlin. We could not have a daughter who could do these things." He said it with ponderous solemnity, and a burst of almost hysterical laughter escaped from Kate's constricted throat.

"Do what things? Drop out of school? Do you have any idea how many kids do that every year? Is that the big deal?"

"I think we both know that's not the issue." He glared at Tom. "Once you have besmirched yourself, as you so determinedly plan to do, it will not matter whether you go to school or not. School is only part of it. It's a matter of your attitude, your goals, your ambitions. Where you are going in your life . . . and where you are going, Kaitlin, seems to have nothing to do with us. We are finished. And now"—he looked away from her to her mother—"if you want to get some of your things, please do so quickly. Your mother has been through enough." But her mother didn't look exhausted or shaken, she looked glazed and indifferent as she sat there, staring at her only daughter. For a moment Tom wondered if she was in shock. And then she stood up with an icy expression, and opened the living-room door, which had been carefully closed so the maid wouldn't overhear the exchange. In the doorway she turned to look at Kate, who was rising slowly and almost painfully from her chair.

"I'll wait while you pack, Kate. I want to see what you take."

"Why? Are you afraid I'll take the silver?" Kate looked at her mother, stupefied.

"Hardly, it's locked up." She swept from the room then as Kate started to follow. And then Kate stopped. She looked at Tom, and then back at her father with an expression of revulsion on her face.

"Forget it."

"Forget what?" For once, her father seemed at a loss.

"I don't want anything from you. I'll go now. You can keep whatever is in my room."

"How kind of you."

And then, without another word, Kate walked slowly from the room. Her mother was waiting for her in the hall, with her face set in hard, angry lines.

"Are you coming?"

"No, Mother, I'm not. I think I've had about enough." No one said anything for a long moment, and then pausing for a last moment by the door, she turned to look at them and said only one word: "Goodbye." She was out the door as soon as she said it, with Tom next to her and his arm tight around her shoulders. What he really wanted to do was go back and kill her father and slap her mother so hard her teeth would jangle in her throat. My God, what was wrong with those people? What were they made of? How could they do this to their only child? Memories of his own mother's love for him brought tears to his eyes as he thought again about what Kate had just been through. He pulled her close to him as they reached his car and for a long, long time he just held her, as tightly as he could, letting his arms and his heart and the warmth of his body tell her what he could barely find words to say. He would never let her go through anything like that again.

"You're all right, babe. You're just fine, and you're beautiful and I love you." But she wasn't crying. She was only trembling very slightly in his arms, and when she looked up at him, the much too serious eyes reached out to him as she tried to smile.

"I'm sorry you had to see that, Tom."

"I'm sorry you had to go through it."

She nodded silently and pulled slowly away from his arms. He opened the car door for her and she slipped inside.

"Well"—it was a tiny voice as he slid into the car next to her—"I think that means it's just us. My father said he never wanted to see me again. He said I'd betrayed them." She sighed deeply. Betrayed them. By loving Tom? By leaving school? Stanford was a tradition in her family. And so was marriage. "Shacking up," as her father had called it, was a disgrace. So was loving a "nobody." A coal miner's son. She was forgetting who she was, who her parents were, who her grandparents had been . . . all the right schools and right clubs and right husbands and right wives. Her mother was then the president of the Junior League, and her father was senior partner of his law firm. And now she sat in the car next to Tom, looking stunned. He glanced at her again worriedly. "He'll change his mind." He patted her hand and started the car.

"Maybe he will. And maybe I won't."

He kissed her very softly and stroked her hair. "Come on, baby. Let's go home."

Home that week was the apartment of another player on his new team. But Tom had a surprise for Kate the next day. He had been busy all week. He had rented a flat in a beautiful little Victorian house on a hill overlooking the bay. He drove her to the door, put the key in her hand, and carried her easily up three flights of stairs and over the threshold, while she laughed and cried. It was like playing house. Only better.

And he was good to her, always, even more so after they realized she would never again hear from her parents. Tom couldn't really understand what they were doing to her, or why. To him family was family; that meant love, and roots that couldn't be destroyed, bonds that couldn't be severed, people who never deserted you, no matter how angry they were. But Kate understood. Her parents had counted on her to be everything they were, and more, to be "one of them." She had committed the unpardonable error of falling in love with someone different, and daring to be different herself: daring to betray the rules, daring not to be bound by their restrictions or tiny hopes. She had hurt them, so they were hurting her. They would justify and inflate and dignify their actions until they were convinced her sins were beyond repair, until they wouldn't have to admit even to each other how much the loss of their daughter had hurt them. And if for a moment they doubted, her mother could speak to her bridge friends, or her father to his partners, and there would be instant reassurance: "It's the only way . . . you did the only thing you could do." Kate knew. So now Tom was everything to her—mother, father, brother, friend—and she flourished in his hands.

She traveled with Tom, she modeled, she wrote poems, she took beautiful care of the flat, she saw some of her old friends now and then, though less and less often, and she came to like a few of the players on Tom's team. But mostly Kate and Tom were alone, and her life centered increasingly around him. About a year after they moved in with each other, they were married. Two minor happenings threatened to mar the event, but nothing really could. The first was that Kate's parents refused to attend the wedding, but that came as no surprise. And the second was that Tom got wound up in a heated discussion in his favorite bar and knocked a guy cold. He had been under a lot of pressure at the time. The San Francisco team was not what his old one had been, and he was one of the "old men" on the team. Nothing came of the incident in the bar, but the papers made it sound ugly. Kate thought it was silly, Tom laughed it off; the wedding took precedence over everything.

One of his teammates was their best man, one of her roommates from Stanford was her maid of honor. It was a strange little wedding at city hall, and *Sports Illustrated* covered the story. She was Tom's now, entirely and forever. And she looked exquisite in a dress that was layer after layer of white organdie, with delicate embroidery and a little-girl scooped neck and huge, puffed, old-fashioned sleeves. It had been a present from Felicia, who was growing increasingly fond of the doe-like young model oddly paired with one of the country's heroes. For Kate she had chosen the cream of the store's spring line.

Kate looked like a beautiful child at the wedding, with her long hair swept up on her head in a gentle Victorian style, threaded with lily of the valley. She carried a bouquet of the same tiny fragrant white flowers. There were tears in her eyes and Tom's as they exchanged wide gold rings and the judge pronounced them married.

They spent their honeymoon in Europe, and she showed him all her favorite spots. It was his first time abroad, and turned into an education for both of them. He was growing in sophistication, and she was growing up.

The first year of their marriage was idyllic. Kate went everywhere Tom did, did everything Tom did, and spent her spare time writing poetry and keeping a journal. Her only problem was that she didn't like being financially dependent on Tom. Felicia's position enabled Kate to get all the work she wanted, but her constant traveling with Tom made it hard for her to model as much as she felt she should. There was still the tiny income from a small trust her grandmother had left her, but that was barely enough for pocket money; it was impossible to reciprocate the lavish gifts Tom constantly gave her. On their first anniversary Kate announced that she had made a decision. She was giving up traveling with him to stay home and model full-time. It made sense to her. But not to him. It was hard enough traveling with the team he worked for now, without having to do it alone. He needed Kate with him. But she thought he needed a financially independent wife. He put up a fight, but he lost. She was firm. And three months later, he broke his leg in a game.

"Well, Princess, looks like the end of the season." He was good-humored about it when he flew home. But they both knew that it might be the end of his career. He was over thirty, the deathly magic number. And it was a bad break; the leg was a mess. He was getting tired of the game anyway, or at least that was what he said. There were other things he wanted more, like children, stability, a future. The move to the San Francisco team had made him professionally insecure; it was something about the chemistry of the team, or maybe the constant underlying threats of the manager, who called him "old man." The man's attitude drove Tom nuts, but he lived with it, hating the manager every inch of the way.

He also worried about leaving Kate when he traveled. She was twenty years old; she needed a husband around more often than he could be. He'd be home with her now, though, because of the leg. Or he thought he would be. As it turned out, *he* was home. Kate wasn't. She was getting a lot of modeling work, and she had signed up for a class on women in literature, at State. She went twice a week.

"And there's a super creative writing class next term."

"Terrific." She looked just like a kid when she talked about the courses. And he felt like what they called him on the team. Old man. A very bored, nervous, lonely old man. He missed the game. He missed Kate. He felt as if he were missing life. Within a month, he punched out a guy in a bar, wound up in jail, and the story was all over the papers. He talked about it constantly, he had nightmares about it. What if they suspended him? But they didn't. The charges were dropped, and he sent the man a big check. The leg still hadn't healed, though, and Kate was still out modeling most of the time. Nothing had changed. And a month later, he decked another guy in a bar, breaking the man's jaw. This time the charges stuck and he paid a whopping fine. The team manager was frighteningly quiet.

"Maybe you should go into boxing instead of football, huh, sweetheart?" Kate still thought Tom's antics were funny.

"Look, dammit, you may think it's amusing, kiddo, but I don't. I'm going goddamn nuts sitting around here waiting for this fucking leg to heal." Kate got the message. He was desperate. Maybe about a lot of things, not just the leg. The next day she came home

with a present. After all, that was why she modeled—
so she could offer him gifts. She had bought two tickets
to Paris.

The trip was just what he needed. They spent two
weeks in Paris, a week in Cannes, five days in Dakar,
and a weekend in London. Tom spoiled her rotten,
and she was thrilled with having bought him the
trip. They came back restored, and Tom's leg had
healed. Life was even better than before. There were
no more bar fights and he began practicing with the
team again. Kate turned twenty-one, and for her birthday he bought her a car. A Mercedes.

For their second anniversary Tom took her to Hono-
lulu. And wound up in jail. A fight in the bar of
the Kahala Hilton resulted in a bad story in *Time*
magazine and a worse one in *Newsweek*. And cover-
age in every newspaper in the country. Jackpot. Only
the story in *Time* told Kate why the fight had really
happened: apparently there had been a rumor that
Tom's contract wasn't going to be renewed. He was
thirty-two. He had been playing pro ball for ten
years.

"Why didn't you tell me?" She looked hurt. "Is it because of the fighting?" But he only shook his head
and looked away, as the lines tightened around his
mouth.

"Nope. That schmuck who runs the team has this
mania about age. He's worse than anyone else in the
business. The fights aren't such a big deal. Everyone
fights. Rasmussen kicks ass on more people in the
streets than he does on the field. Jonas had a drug
bust last year. Hilbert's a fag. Everyone's got something. But me, it's my age. I'm just too old, Kate. I'm
thirty-two, and I still haven't figured out what the
hell to do with myself after football. Christ, this is

all I know." There were tears in his voice and in her eyes.

"Why can't you get yourself traded to another team?"

He looked at her finally and his expression was grim. "Because I'm too old, Kate. This is it. Last stop. And they know it, which is why they hassle me all the time. They know they've got me."

"So get out. You could do all kinds of other things. You could be a sportscaster, a coach, a manager . . ." But he was shaking his head.

"I've been putting out feelers. It all comes back no."

"Okay. So you'll find something else. You don't need a job right away. We could go to school together." She tried to look cheerful. She wanted him to be happy, to share her youth with him, but her efforts only made him smile ruefully.

"Oh, baby, I love you." He folded her into his arms. Maybe it didn't matter. Maybe all that mattered was what they had. And her support did help, for a while. A year, more or less. But after their third anniversary, things seemed to get worse. Tom's contract was under negotiation, and he started getting into fights again. Two in a row, and this time two weeks in jail and a thousand dollar fine. And a five thousand dollar fine imposed by the team. Tom sued for causes of injustice. He lost. He got suspended. And Kate had a miscarriage. She hadn't even known she was pregnant. Tom drove himself nuts. In the hospital, he wept more than she did. He felt as though he had killed their child. Kate was stunned by the sequence of events. The suspension would last for a year, and now she knew what was in store—bar fights, fines, and a lot of time in jail. And yet Tom was so good to her. So sweet, so gentle. He was all she'd ever dreamed of in a man. But she could see only trouble ahead.

"Why don't we spend the year in Europe?"

He had shrugged disinterestedly at her suggestion. He moped for weeks, thinking about the child they had almost had. But what really frightened him was what was happening to his career. When the suspension ended, so would his career. He was too old to make a recovery.

"So we'll start a business." Kate was still so damn young, and her optimism only depressed him more. She didn't know what it was like—the terror that he'd be a nobody, have to drive a truck, or even work in the mines like his father. He hadn't invested his money well and he couldn't count on that income. What the hell was he going to do? Commercials for underwear? Pimp for Kate's modeling career? Have her ghost-write his memoirs? Hang himself? Only his love for Kate kept him from the bleakest possibilities. The bitch of it was that all he wanted to do was play football. And none of the colleges were considering him as coach. He had earned himself a stinking reputation with all the fighting.

So they went to Europe. They stayed a week. He hated it. They went to Mexico. He was equally miserable there. They stayed home. He hated that too. And he hated himself most of all. He drank and he fought, and reporters bugged him everywhere. But what did he have to lose now? He had already been suspended and they probably wouldn't renew his contract anyway. The only thing he knew for certain was that he wanted a son. And he'd give his son everything.

Just before Christmas, they found out that Kate was pregnant again. This time they were both careful. Everything stopped. Kate's modeling, his drinking, the fighting in bars. They stayed home together. There was nothing but tenderness and peace between them, except for her occasional bouts of temper or tears. But neither of them took that very seriously; it seemed to be part of the pregnancy, and if anything, it amused Tom. He didn't even give a damn about the suspension anymore. To hell with them. He'd sit it out, and then he'd force them to renew his contract. He'd beg them. All he wanted now was one more knock-out year, so he could put the money away and take good care of his son. The next year he played would be for the baby. For Kate, he bought a mink coat for Christmas.

"Tom, you're crazy! Where'll I wear it?" She modeled it over her nightgown with a huge grin. It was heavenly. But she also wondered what he was trying to hide. What wasn't he facing? What didn't she know?

"You'll wear it to the hospital when you have my son." And he had bought an antique cradle, a four-hundred-dollar English pram, and a sapphire ring for Kate. He was crazy, and madly in love with her, and she was just as in love with him. But deep inside, she was afraid. They spent Christmas alone in San Francisco, and Tom talked about buying a house. Not a big house. Just a nice house in a good area for bringing up a kid. Kate agreed, but wondered if they could really afford a house. As New Year's approached, she had an idea. They'd spend the holiday in Carmel. It would do them both good.

"For New Year's? What do you want to do that for, sweetheart? It's foggy and cold. Pizza, sure. Tacos, okay. Strawberries, what the hell. But Carmel in December?" He grinned at her and ran a hand over her still flat belly. But soon . . . soon . . . the thought made him warm inside. Their baby . . . his son.

"I want to go to Carmel because it's the first place we ever went together. Can we?" She looked like a little girl again, although she was going to be twenty-three soon. They had known each other for five years. And of course he gave in to her wish.

"If the lady wants to go to Carmel, then Carmel it is." And Carmel it was. The best suite at the best hotel, and even the weather smiled on them for the three days they were there. Kate's only worry was that Tom bought everything in sight for her and the baby, whenever they wandered past the shops on the main thoroughfare. But they spent a lot of time in their room, drank a great deal of champagne, and the worry faded.

"Did I ever tell you how much I love you, Mr. Harper?"

"I love to hear it, Princess. Oh Kate—" And then he swept her up in a giant hug and held her close. "I'm sorry you've had such a stinking time. I promise I'll shape up now. All that bullshit is over."

"Just so you're happy." She looked so peaceful lying in his arms, and he had never thought her more beautiful.

"I've never been happier." And he finally looked it.

"Then maybe this would be a good time to quit."

"What do you mean?" He looked shocked.

"I mean football, my love. Maybe now, we should just take the money and run. No more hassles, no more crap about your being an 'old man.' Just us, and the baby."

"And starvation."

"Come on, sweetheart. We're nowhere near starving yet." But she was startled. If he was so concerned about money, why the mink coat, the ring?

"No, but we don't have a real, solid nest egg. Not enough to do right by the baby in five or ten years.

42

Another good year on the team will make all the difference."

"We can invest my modeling money."

"That's yours." His voice sounded cold for a minute. "You wanted that, and you earned it. I'll take care of you and the baby. And that's it. I don't want to talk about it."

"Okay."

His face had softened then and they had made love in the soft light of dusk. Kate was reminded of their first "honeymoon" in Cleveland. But it was Tom who fell asleep this time, as he lay in Kate's arms, and she watched him. She watched him for hours, thinking, hoping this year would be different, that they'd be decent to him, that the pressures wouldn't get to him as cruelly as they had before. That was all she wanted now. She was growing up.

The day after they went back to San Francisco there was a story in the papers that reported that Tom Harper was "through." It was carried by every major paper in the country. Through. He went crazy when he read it, and a little careful digging brought him the information that the story had been planted by the team . . . by the team . . . the team . . . the Old Man. . . . He had slammed out of the house without a word to Kate, and she hadn't seen him until six that night. On the news.

He had gone to the home of the owner of the team and threatened his life, then he had gotten into a fight with the team's manager, who had walked in on the scene. Both men had realized that Tom was drunk and wildly irrational, and the owner claimed that Tom had been like a madman, raving about what they couldn't do to his son. In a careful monotone the newscaster explained that Tom Harper didn't have a son;

he didn't need to add the conclusion that Harper was obviously crazy. And as Kate watched, her heart rose to her throat. The newscaster went on to explain that the two men had "tried to subdue Harper as he ranted and swung wildly at them both. But unexpectedly, Harper had pulled a gun out of his pocket, taken aim at the owner of the team, and then swung wildly on the manager and fired a shot. Miraculously, he had missed, but before anyone could move, he had then pointed the gun at himself, taken erratic aim, and fired twice. But this time he didn't miss. The manager and team owner were both unharmed, but Harper himself had been hospitalized in critical condition." The newscaster stared somberly from the television for a moment and gravely intoned, "A tragedy for American football."

For the tiniest moment Kate had the insane feeling that if she jumped up and changed the dial, none of it would have happened; all she had to do was switch channels and someone else would say it wasn't true. It couldn't be true. Not Tom . . . oh please, not Tom . . . please . . . she was whimpering softly as she turned around and stared at the room, wondering what to do. They hadn't said what hospital Tom was in. What was she supposed to do? Call the police? The team? The television station? And why hadn't anyone called her? But then she remembered—she had taken the phone off the hook for two hours while she took a nap. Oh God . . . what if . . . what if he was already dead? Sobbing, she turned off the television and ran to the phone. Felicia . . . Felicia would know . . . she would help her. Without thinking, she dialed Felicia's private line at the store. She was still there.

Felicia was stunned by the news and ordered Kate not to move. As she had her assistant call for a cab on one line, she called the police on another, and got the information. Tom was at San Francisco General. He was still alive—barely, but he was alive. Felicia fled from her office at a run, wondering for a moment why Kate had called her. Surely there was someone else. Her mother, a closer friend, someone? She and Kate were good friends through their work, but they'd never seen much of each other socially. Kate was always too busy with Tom. The hub of that girl's life was the man who lay dying at San Francisco General.

When Felicia arrived at the apartment, Kate was incoherent, but dressed. The cab was still waiting downstairs.

"Come on, put your shoes on."

"My shoes." Kate looked blank. "My shoes?" Tears filled her eyes again and she looked grayish green. Felicia found the closet and a pair of black flats.

"Here." Kate slid her feet into them and left the apartment without handbag or coat, but Felicia slipped her own coat over the girl's shoulders. She didn't need a bag, anyway, because she was in no condition to go anywhere alone. And she didn't have to. Felicia stayed with her day and night for four days, and at the end of that time Tom was still alive. He was in a coma, and the prognosis was poor, but he was alive. He had done a fairly thorough job when he fired, though. He would never walk again, and there was no way to tell yet how extensive the brain damage was.

When Felicia went back to work, Kate carried on like a machine, moving from Tom's bed to the corridor to his bed to the corridor, to cry alone. It was a treadmill which Felicia joined her on when she could, but there was no getting Kate away from the hospital. She was mourning for Tom. She just sat there, staring, or crying, or smoking, but she wasn't really there, and the doctor was afraid to give her anything, in case the medication hurt the baby. Felicia was amazed that she hadn't lost it.

While the newspapers tore Tom apart, Kate tore herself apart. Why hadn't she seen some sign? Why hadn't she known? Could she have helped? Did she take his worries about the future—followed by those spending binges—seriously enough? It was all her fault. It had to be. With the egotism of grief, she tormented herself day after day. Football. It had been his whole life, and now it had killed him. The thought that he'd almost killed two other men was even more terrifying, but she didn't believe he could have done that. Not Tom. But what he had done was bad enough. He had destroyed himself. Poor gentle Tom, driven berserk at the idea of losing that last year of security he wanted for his son. Kate didn't let herself think about the baby though. Only about Tom. It was a nightmare that went on for seven weeks, while Kate paced and cried and was constantly haunted by reporters. And then he came to.

He was weak, broken, and tired, but little by little he grew stronger. He would live now—what was left of him—they were sure of it. He would never walk again, but he could move. He could talk. And he could think. Just like a child. The long weeks of coma had moved him backward in time and left him there, with all his sweetness and tenderness and love intact. He was a little boy again. He remembered nothing of the shooting, but he recognized Kate. He cried in her arms as she stifled silent sobs which shook her tall, terrifyingly thin frame. The only thing he truly understood was that he belonged to her. But he wasn't sure how. Sometimes he thought she was his mother, sometimes his friend. He called her Katie. He would never call

46

her Princess again. . . . Katie . . . that's who she was now.

"You won't leave me?"

Gravely, she shook her head. "No, Tom."

"Never?"

"Never. I love you too much ever to leave you." Her eyes filled with tears again, and she had to force ordinary thoughts into her head. She couldn't let herself really think of him when she said the words, or it would kill her. She couldn't let herself cry. She couldn't do that to him.

"I love you too. And you're pretty." He looked at her with the bright, shiny eyes of a seven-year-old boy, and the wan, tired face of an unshaven, desperately sick man.

After a few weeks, he looked better again, healthy and whole. It was strange to see him, the ersatz Tom. It was as though Tom had left, and sent in his stead a small boy who looked like him. It would be that way forever. But Tom's condition settled the legal aspects of the case permanently. There was no case. Tom Harper was no more.

Three months after what Kate and Felicia called "the accident," Tom was moved to a sanatarium in Carmel. Photographers had lunged at the ambulance as he was being wheeled inside. Tom had wanted to wave at them, and Kate had distracted him while he held tightly to her hand. She was used to them now. Some of the faces were even familiar. For three months they had torn her apart in story after story, exploded flashbulbs in her face, and crawled over the roof of their house to get a better view into the apartment. She had no one to turn to, to defend her. No family, no man. And they knew it. They even ran stories about how her family had disowned her years before because of Tom, and how they thought of her as dead. And she had lain in bed at night, sobbing, praying that the press would go away and leave her alone. But they didn't. Not for one day. Until he was moved to Carmel. And then, magically, it was as though they forgot. As though Tom no longer existed, or Kate, his wife. The two of them had left the magic circle. At last.

When Tom left San Francisco, so did Kate. The house was already waiting. Felicia had seen the ad, and the place turned out to be perfect. The owner lived in the East; his mother had died, leaving him a house he didn't need and didn't want to sell. One day he would retire there, and in the meantime it was Kate's hideaway, nestled in the mountains north of Santa Barbara. It was a three-hour drive from Tom's sanatarium in Carmel, but Felicia assumed that Kate would be back in San Francisco as soon as things calmed down, right after the baby was born. It was a pretty house, surrounded by fields and trees, with a little brook just down the hill from the house. It would be a good place to recover. It would have been a wonderful place to share with Tom. Kate tried not to think of that as she signed the lease.

After four months she was used to it; it was home. She awoke at dawn when the baby kicked and stirred, hungry for more space than she had to give him. She lay quietly, feeling him pound inside her, wondering what she would tell him one day. She had thought of changing her name, but decided not to. She was Kate Harper. No one else. She didn't want her father's name anymore. And Tom's baby would be a Harper. Tom didn't understand now about the swollen belly, or maybe he just didn't care. Children didn't, Kate reminded herself, as long as nothing changed for them. Nothing had. She went on visiting him, often at first, and only slightly less frequently as the pregnancy progressed. Nowadays it was twice a week. She was always there. She always would be, as he had been for her. There was no question of it. This was her life now. She had accepted it. She understood, as much as one can. "Always," whatever that meant. "Forever," whatever that was. It meant that each time she saw him, he was the same, always would be. Until one day, when he would quietly die. There was no way to say when. The doctor said he might live to be "considerably older," though not what was normally thought of as old. Or it might all end in a year or less. At some point, Tom's body would simply fade and die. He would just let go. Unconsciously, but he would. And Kate would be there, for all the time in between, loving him. He still looked like Tom, and now and then there was still that magical light in his eyes. It allowed her to pretend that . . . but it was a futile game. Now she held him as he once had held her. She didn't even cry anymore.

Kate stood up after her call from Felicia, pushed open the window, and took a deep breath of summer air. She smiled to herself. There were new flowers in the garden. She would take him some. She could still love him. She could always love him. Nothing would change that.

The clock on the bedside table said six twenty-five. She had half an hour to get on the road if she wanted to be there before ten. It was a hell of a drive. A hell of a way to grow up—but she had. Kate Harper was no longer any kind of child. And the baby stirred in her belly as she slipped off her nightgown and stepped into the shower. She had a long day ahead.

CHAPTER 2

The dark blue station wagon shifted easily into gear and Kate turned swiftly out of the gravel driveway. The little Mercedes Tom had given her was gone. She didn't need it anymore. This car suited her life now. The hills rolled away toward the horizon; they were still lush even this late in the summer. Here and there she noticed a brown patch, but there had been enough rain through the summer to counteract the heat. And there was a majesty to the scene that always took her breath away as she stood with the mountains at her back and the hills rolling ahead, blanketed with wild flowers and dotted with clumps of trees. She could see livestock grazing in the distance. It was the kind of scene you read about in storybooks, and it would be a beautiful place to bring up her child. He would grow strong here, he would feel free, he would play with the children of ranchers and farmers. He would be healthy and alive, not twisted like her parents, or tormented like Tom. He would run barefoot in the meadow near the house, and sit dangling his toes in the brook. She would make him a swing, would buy him a few animals, maybe one day a horse. It was what Tom would have wanted for his son. And if the child was a girl, she would benefit from the same life. And when she was older, she could go back to the world if she chose, but Kate wasn't

50

going back. Let them forget. They would never touch her again. Not the press, not her parents, no one. This was her home now. She had carved out a place for herself, she had chosen her role. The Widow Harper. It sounded like something in a bad Western, and it made her laugh as she flicked on the radio and reached for a cigarette. It was a rich summer morning, and she felt surprisingly good. Pregnancy wasn't as hard as she had expected it to be, but then, she'd had so many other things on her mind, so many decisions to make, changes to think out. Who had time to worry about heartburn and leg cramps and pains? But still, she had had surprisingly few of those. Maybe it was the easy life she led now in the country. And it was easy, except for the long drives to see Tom. And the way she felt afterward.

The radio throbbed with the soft beat of ballads alternating with rock and roll, and the early morning announcer purred comments and snippets of news. It was summertime. Everyone was on vacation, taking trips, visiting, going to the beach. It was hard to remember that life now. Kate's life consisted of visiting Tom, then going home and writing. Sometimes she went into the nursery and sat in the rocking chair, wondering what it would feel like to hold the baby in her arms. Would it feel strange, or would she instantly love it? Being a mother was hard to imagine, even with the baby packed so tightly inside her. That she understood, but seeing it would be different . . . holding it . . . she wondered if it would look like Tom. She wanted it to. His name would be Tygue if a boy, and Blaire if a girl. She wanted an unusual name. She had wanted to pick something pretty, something special. Tom would have . . . a small sigh escaped as she put out the cigarette and turned the radio up louder. She'd had enough of her own thoughts. She rolled down the window and let the early morning wind play with her hair. She hadn't bothered with the braids today. Tom had always liked her hair loose. And the denim jumper was too tight now, but he wouldn't notice. The seams seemed to beg for release the way her own skin did now. But there was no give left in either her or the dress. She patted her stomach softly with one hand, as she turned onto the freeway and stepped on the gas. The baby was moving again, almost like a puppydog squirming in her lap. It made her smile as she edged the station wagon up to eighty-five. She wanted the drive to go faster. She wanted to see him now.

After another two and a half hours on the freeway, she knew the turnoff was near. All the signals were familiar now. A big green billboard advertising the restaurant another ten miles down the road. A white clapboard house with blue shutters. A sad-looking little motel, and then the turnoff. She automatically slid into the right lane and eased down her speed. Nervously she flicked off the radio, lit another cigarette, and waited at the first crossroads for the traffic to pass. Another fifteen miles and she'd have been in Carmel. This area was more rustic, but prettier in its own way. It was inland from Carmel, but you could see the gulls overhead, endlessly looking for food.

Kate stepped on the gas again, and turned onto the first narrow road on her right. It led her onto another smaller road, more like a lane, overgrown with bushes and small trees. Here and there she could see berries ripe on the bushes, and she longed to get out of the car and pick some; she had done that as a child. But she didn't have time, she had to get there. She looked at her watch. It was already nine-thirty. He would be sitting outside now, or maybe just lying in his hammock, thinking. He did that a lot. She wondered what he thought. He never said. He just laughed when she asked, and sometimes he would look like Tom again, as if he still had things to think about. It was strange to see him that way, as though he were teasing, as though any minute he would stop the game. It made her love him even more; there was such sunlight in his eyes, such joy in his face. He was a beautiful boy.

The main building looked like any large well-kept house. It was painted a crisp white with freshly tended yellow trim, there were flower boxes at almost all the windows, and beautiful flowers planted at the edge of the lawns. A narrow, winding walk led to the front door of the main house, which bore a small brass plaque, carefully engraved. Mead Home. Only two words. They didn't need to say more; anyone who came there knew what the place was. There were several smaller houses visible nearby, all painted in the same yellow and white, and farther from the main cluster were a dozen small, cozy-looking yellow cottages, surrounded by flowers and adorned with white trim. The cottages were the more exclusive accommodations. Some were fitted for two residents, others for only one. And each cottage had its own resident attendant to care for his or her charge. Tom lived in one of the cottages, with a quiet older man in attendance— Mr. Erhard, who discreetly disappeared when Kate visited. The enormous insurance Tom had had as a member of the team miraculously covered his stay at Mead, and would continue to do so for ten or twelve years. After that, Kate was going to have to make other arrangements, but by then . . . who knew . . . the doctors said he could go on for years the way he was.

The grass felt damp on her sandal-clad feet as she walked toward Tom's cottage. She didn't have to check in at the main house anymore. The residents were carefully protected, but she was familiar now. They saw her arrive from the ever-watchful windows of the main house, and she could come and go as she pleased. She simply arrived and went to find Tom. He was easy enough to find. But today when she reached the cottage, he wasn't there.

"Tom?" There was no answer to her knock. "Mr. Erhard?" The attendant seemed to be gone too. Gingerly, she opened the door and looked around. The room was neatly kept and as bright and pretty as the rest of the facilities. It was why she had chosen Mead Home for Tom. She had been to see a number of places like it within driving distance of San Francisco, and all of them had looked bleak, full of despair. Mead had an aura of hope and sunshine about it. It was a place that time no longer touched, the way it no longer touched Tom. It was safe, tucked away. And it looked more like a school than a sanatarium; Kate always expected to hear children singing, or see them running off to play baseball.

"Tom?" She wondered where he had gone, as she sank into a chair for a minute to catch her breath. She was breathless today, more than she had been. The baby was crowding her increasingly. And she had driven the three hours straight through without stopping, despite her doctor's orders. But stopping took too much time. She always figured she could get the kinks out when she got to Mead. She stretched her legs for a minute, enjoying the comfortable rocking chair. It was upholstered in a bright print with little red flowers, and the quilts on the two beds matched the chair. The curtains were airy white dotted Swiss, and there was a small jar crammed full of bright yellow flowers on the table near the window. She knew Tom had picked them. Some of his drawings were tacked to the walls, and his hand still had the maturity his head no longer had. There were delicate watercolors of flowers and birds. She had never known that he could draw until he had come to Mead. He had never done anything like it before. Only football. Now he didn't even remember he had played. It was as though he had had to go all the way back to childhood to get rid of it. But at last he had.

Actually this was the perfect cottage for anyone, sick or well, adult or child, and Kate liked knowing he was happy there. And he could get around easily in his wheelchair. Outside there was a hammock Mr. Erhard helped him into when Tom was content just to lie and watch the birds. Sometimes he even let him lie there for a while at night, covered with blankets, looking up at the stars. Mr. Erhard was good to Tom. He had been one of his fans for years, and he was pleased with the special assignment when Tom arrived at Mead.

There was a rustle outside as Kate pushed herself out of the chair, and then she heard Mr. Erhard's rich baritone, telling Tom a story. There was a pause for a moment, when he must have noticed the door to the cottage was slightly ajar. She heard his step on the narrow flagstone path, and in a moment the white mane of her husband's attendant was visible in the doorway.

"Yes?" It was a stern sound, and he looked like a man who brooked neither nonsense nor intrusions. But his face softened instantly when he saw Kate. "Well, hello there. How are you feeling?"

"Fine. Fat." They both laughed. "How's our friend?"

Mr. Erhard nodded, with a satisfied look. "Doing fine. He did a whole batch of new drawings yesterday, and we picked some flowers this morning. He'll tell you all about—"

"Hey! Andy!" It was Tom's voice from outside. The chair was stuck in the grass. "Hey!"

"Coming, son." Erhard was quick to leave the cottage and Kate was right behind him. It was crazy, that smile bursting into her eyes and onto her lips. Why did she still feel like this? As though he were still the old Tom, as though . . . she always felt the same thrill, the same excitement, the same pleasure in just looking at him, touching him, holding him, just knowing he was all right and still hers.

"Katie!" It was a burst of delight as Tom saw her coming toward him. His eyes danced, and his smile went on forever as he reached out his arms.

"Hi, sweetheart. How you be today?"

"Terrific! Wait till you see what we found!"

Mr. Erhard's wise old eyes twinkled as he rolled Tom gently toward the cottage and then inside. He was already gone when Kate turned around.

"Your new drawings are so pretty, love." But she wasn't looking at the drawings, she was looking at him. He looked brown and strong and happy. The Tom Sawyer of Mead Home. And then he wheeled right up to her and she quickly bent down and took him in her arms. It was a good, clean, warm hug. That was all he understood now, but it carried with it the strength of everything she felt for him.

"You look pretty, Katie." He looked almost embarrassed as he pulled away, and then wheeled his chair quickly to the table. He picked up the jar with the yellow flowers and then wheeled quickly back. "I picked these for you." Tears sprang to her eyes as she smiled at him and took the jar. But they were happy pregnant tears, not tears of grief.

"They're beautiful." She wanted to hug him again, but she knew she had to wait. It would make him un-

56

comfortable if she overdid it. He would come to her in his own time. "Want to go for a walk?"

"Okay."

She tossed her handbag aside and started to push his chair. It was heavier than she had realized, or maybe she was just exceptionally tired. The baby seemed to weigh a thousand pounds today. But Tom helped her as they got onto the walk. He guided the wheels with his hands, and they quickly found one of the smoother walks.

"Want to sit by the lake?" He looked back at her and nodded happily, and then he started whistling to himself.

The lake was tiny but pretty, like everything at Mead. Kate had brought him a model sailboat to use on the water, and he went there often. Mr. Erhard said it was one of his favorite things to do. But they had left it at the cottage. Gently, she turned the chair around, and sat down heavily on the grass.

"So, what've you been up to all week?"

"How come you didn't come to see me this week?"

"Because I was too busy being fat." There was still this foolish compulsion to talk to him about it, as though she could jog his memory, as though he would understand that the baby was his, or even that there was a baby at all.

"I bet it's hard to run." He said it with a broad grin and a barely suppressed chuckle that made her laugh too. She reached for his hand, and the clear sound of her laughter rang out over the small lake.

"It sure is. I look like an old mother hen waddling along." He laughed too then, and kept hold of her hand. They sat smiling for a long time and then he grew serious.

"How come I can't come home with you, Katie? I

can do the chair myself. Or maybe we could take Mr. Erhard. Huh?" That again. Dammit.

Kate slowly shook her head, but continued to hold his big hand in hers. "Don't you like it here, Tom?"

"I want to go home with you." He looked so wistful that she had to swallow the tears in her throat. She couldn't discuss that with him. Not again. He didn't understand. He made her feel as if she were abandoning him.

"That would be kind of hard to do right now. Why don't we just leave it like this for a while, and then we can talk about it another time?"

"You won't let me then either. I promise I'll be good." There were tears in his eyes now, and all she could do was rise to her knees on the grass and put her arms around him to hold him close.

"You are good, and I love you. And I promise, darling, if it's possible at all, one day I'll take you home." There was a long sad silence, as they both held tightly to their own thoughts, worlds away from each other and yet never closer. "And in the meantime, I'll visit and we'll play, and Mr. Erhard will take good care of you, and . . ." It was impossible to go on as she choked back the tears. But Tom had already lost the thread of the conversation.

"Okay. Oh, look!" Excitedly, he pointed upward and she leaned back to look into the sun, wiping the dampness from her eyes. "Isn't he pretty? I forget what you call it, Mr. Erhard told me yesterday." It was a blue and green bird with a yellow tail and shimmering wings. Kate smiled slowly at Tom and sat down on the grass again.

"I brought you a picnic. How about that?"

"For real?"

She held up a solemn hand. "For real. I promise." It was fun doing things for him, even if it was only making a picnic lunch. She had brought salami sandwiches, and big fresh country potato chips, macaroni salad, beautiful peaches and a basket of cherries. And there was a thermos of lemonade and a slab of chocolate cake. He even ate like a kid now.

"What's it got?" His eyes were dancing again. The wanting to go home with Katie was already forgotten. For now.

"You'll see what's in the picnic when you get hungry for lunch." She waggled a finger at him, and he caught it. It was a game they had played since they met. They still played it. It was one of the things that allowed her to pretend, for a moment, a minute, the flash of an eyelash, that everything was the same.

"I'm hungry."

"You are not. You just want to see what's in the picnic basket." She lay on the grass, feeling like an overturned whale, and grinned up at him.

"Honest, I'm hungry!" But he was laughing again, they both were.

"How can you be hungry? It's ten-thirty in the morning."

"Mr. Erhard didn't give me any breakfast." But the laughter danced right out of his eyes and he couldn't keep a straight face.

"Baloney. You fibber."

"Come on, Katie, I'm starving."

"You're impossible." But she pushed herself up to a sitting position and thought about getting the basket. If he was hungry, why not? "I brought you a present, by the way."

"You did? What?"

"You'll see."

"Oh, you're so mean!" He said it with the outrage of childhood, and a fierce impatience for both the picnic and the gift. And with another slow smile, Kate got to her feet and then bent down to kiss the tip of his nose. "Don't do that!" Gently, he swatted her away.

"Why not?"

"Because you're a meanie, that's why!" But his arm went around her waist, and for a moment they stayed there, he in his chair and she standing next to him. This time she moved away first.

"I'll go get the stuff." There was smoke in her voice, and they still had the day ahead of them.

"Want me to help?"

"Okay. You can carry the picnic basket." He wheeled himself to the car as she walked along slowly beside him in the sunshine. They chatted, and he told her what he'd been doing, about the drawings, about a new game she'd brought him the week before, about a nurse he hated at the main house, and "the best dinner I've ever had," while Kate listened as though it were all true, as though it mattered.

When they got to the car, she lifted the picnic basket carefully onto his lap, and reached in beside it for a red- and white-striped package tied with a big bow.

"For you, my love." She closed the car, and pushed him slowly back up the walk.

"Hurry up!"

"We have a problem?" She'd need Mr. Erhard for that. Tom was far too heavy for her to cope with when he needed to relieve himself.

"No, dummy, I want to open my present!" He was holding it close, and had already dug a hand into the picnic basket and come up with a handful of cherries and a little tiny piece of the cake.

"Stay out of that, Tom Harper, or I'll—"

"No, you won't, Katie, you love me too much."

"You're right." They both smiled then, and Kate

settled him under a tree outside his cottage. The grounds were fresh and bright. In time he might tire of them. But not yet.

"Can I open it now?" He looked at her for approval and she nodded, as he quickly tore off the paper. It had been a foolish thing to buy him, but she hadn't been able to resist when she'd seen it. And she'd bought one for the baby's room too. "Oh, I love him! What's his name?" Tom held the big brown bear close, and squeezed it tight. Kate was surprised and pleased at his instant delight.

"I don't know his name. You tell me. I think he looks like a George myself."

"Yeah. Maybe." Tom looked him over thoughtfully.

"Lucius?" Kate was smiling again. She was glad she'd bought it for him after all. So what if it was silly? What difference did that make now, if it made him happy?

"Not Lucius, that's horrible. I know! Willie!"

"Willie?"

"Willie!" He leaned over with his arms held out and Kate gave him a hug, and a little kiss on the forehead. "Thank you, Katie, he's beautiful."

"He looks like you."

He swatted her with the bear then and they both laughed.

"Want to sit in your hammock? I'll get Mr. Erhard if you want."

"No, this is nice." He was already elbow deep in the picnic basket and he stayed that way for the next half hour, with Willie sitting contentedly on his lap.

They rested quietly for a while after lunch, and Kate almost fell asleep in the warm summer air. There was the tiniest breeze ruffling her hair as she lay near

Tom's wheelchair, and the baby was finally still for the first time all day. They passed the basket of cherries back and forth, shooting pits at the trees and then laughing.

"One day there will be a whole field of cherry trees here and no one will know why."

"We will. Right, Katie?"

"Right."

His voice was so soft, almost wistful, that she thought he must know. But what was the point of his knowing? It was the one thing that always stopped her from trying to jolt him into remembering. If he ever returned to what he had been, he would have to stand trial for assault or attempted murder or whatever they decided to call it. He was better off in Mead Home, the way he was, than in a different kind of prison. There was no way to "jolt" him back anyway. The doctor had explained it to her often enough. But the temptation was always there. Sometimes, just for a second, he sounded so much like himself, like the old Tom, that it was hard to believe the bullet had destroyed as much as the doctors said it had. It had been hard to give up hope, to stop trying.

"Katie?"

"Hm?" She looked up at him, a twig of cherries still in her hand; she had forgotten them for a moment.

"What were you thinking?"

"Oh nothing much. Just lying here, feeling lazy."

"You look pretty when you think." And then his eyes slid politely to her belly. He was sorry she was so fat, but it didn't matter much. He loved her, no matter what.

"Thank you, Tom." She poured him a glass of lemonade, and lay back on the grass. There was a tall tree overhead, shading them from the bright sun, and in the air the wonderful stillness of a summer afternoon. The only thing missing was the squeaking of a screen door, somewhere in the distance, and then the banging of it as a child went in for a glass of cold water. "It's pretty here, isn't it?" He nodded happily in answer and shot another cherry pit in the direction of the cottage.

"I need a slingshot."

"My eye you do."

"Not to hurt anyone with"—he looked offended—"just for things like cherry pits. Or paper clips. You know—to shoot at trees." But he was grinning again, the irrepressible, mischievous grin.

"How do you even know about those things anyway? They went out of style years ago."

"I saw one on TV."

"Terrific."

"Maybe I could make one." But she wasn't listening to him. The baby had just delivered a ferocious kick to her ribs. She took a deep breath, let it out slowly, and wondered if it was time to call it a day. She still had the long drive home, and it was almost two. She had been there for four hours. It wasn't long, but right now it was about all she could manage. She looked at Tom taking careful aim with another cherry pit. He still had a smudge of chocolate cake on one cheek. She sat up and wiped it off gently, then looked toward the cottage. She had seen Mr. Erhard go inside almost an hour before.

"I'm going to go inside for a minute, love. Want anything?"

He shook his head happily. "Nope."

Mr. Erhard was waiting, reading the newspaper and smoking a pipe. It seemed a wintry pastime for such a warm, sunny day.

"Ready to go?"

"I think I'd better."

"I'm surprised your doctor even lets you come up here." And then he smiled a fatherly smile. "Or don't you ask him?"

"Well, let's just say we compromise on it."

"You know, you really could skip a couple of weeks. I'll keep him busy. He may complain about it when you get back, but he won't notice it while you're gone." It was depressing to realize Mr. Erhard was right.

"I don't know. I'll see how I feel next week."

"Good enough."

After another quick stop at the bathroom, she went outside and he followed her, walking toward Tom, waving his pipe in a greeting.

"So you're the one who's been pelting the house with cherry pits all day, is that it?" But he was grinning broadly and Tom laughed with delight. "I'll bet you can't hit that tree." But he was wrong. Tom hit it and squarely.

"You'd better watch out, Mr. E., he wants a slingshot."

"Remember? Like the one on that show the other night? The one when the boy . . ." The tale was long and garbled, but Mr. Erhard fell into the discussion with ease, and Kate watched him for a silent moment. She hated leaving him. She always hated leaving him. It should have been a relief, but it wasn't. Getting there was a relief, seeing him was, leaving him still tore at her heart.

"Okay, love, I'm going to go now, but I'll be back soon."

"Okay, Katie, so long." He waved nonchalantly, and the discussion of the morning was long since forgotten. This was more home to him now than anywhere else. He didn't even flinch at her departure.

64

She stooped to kiss him on the cheek and squeezed his shoulder.

"Take good care of Willie, my love." She walked away with a wave and a smile and a rock settling on her heart, as he sat in his chair holding the teddy bear. She could still see him as she backed the car slowly out of its space. She rolled down the window for a last wave, but he was already engrossed in his talk with Mr. Erhard. "Good-bye, Tom. I love you." She said it to herself in a whisper as she drove away.

CHAPTER 3

The drive home seemed longer than it ever had before. She kept seeing Tom with the teddy bear, and thinking of things he had said. She finally forced the visit from her mind, and flicked on the radio. She had cramps in her legs, and suddenly all she wanted was to get home. It had been too long a day, and she had that desperate feeling of exhaustion that swept up on her so quickly now, as though she hadn't the strength for another step. Maybe Mr. Erhard was right. Maybe she should stop coming for the next few weeks. It was only going to be three more weeks till the baby came. She didn't even let herself think of that though. Not the baby, not Tom. All she could think of was her bed, and getting out of the clothes that seemed to be strangling her whole body. It seemed a thousand years later when she finally pulled into her own driveway. She was so tired she didn't even see the little red Alfa Romeo parked at the side of the house. She just slipped out of the car, stood next to it for a minute, steadying herself and rubbing her calves, and then began to walk slowly and stiffly toward the front door.

"You look like you're in great shape." It was the deep, cynical voice of Felicia Norman, and Kate jumped a foot. "Hey, lady, take it easy. I'm a miserable midwife." And then Kate looked up and laughed.

"You scared the hell out of me, Licia."

"I'm surprised you've got enough energy left to be scared. What do you think you're doing to yourself?" She took the basket out of her friend's hand and they walked slowly toward the house.

"Never mind that. What are you doing down here early?"

"I decided I needed a vacation and you needed a guest."

"A vacation?"

"Well, a long weekend. I took four days." And she was glad she had come. Kate looked wiped out, and if that was what going up to see Tom did to her, maybe she could stop her from going for a while, or at least drive her up there. But this was lunacy.

"Do you realize what a miracle it is that you haven't been fired yet, thanks to me?" But Kate was grinning. It was so good to see her.

"They're just goddamn lucky I don't quit. If we do one more show this month, I'm going to have a nervous breakdown." And so would her assistant. In order to be with Kate, Felicia had foisted all the week's shows onto her assistant again. That was going to cost her another Gucci bag, and a fat lunch at Trader Vic's, but she had had this feeling . . . she had to come down to see Kate. And she was glad that she had. She shoved the picnic basket onto the kitchen counter and looked around. It really was a pleasant house. It had been a good choice. "So how's Tom?"

"Fine. Happy. Nothing new." Felicia nodded solemnly and sat down in a chair. Kate followed suit.

"You know, Licia, you look worse than I do, but then, you drove further. Want the leftover lemonade?"

Felicia made a horrible face. "Darling, I love you, but lemonade is not me. God, what a horrible thought."

Kate looked at her with an apologetic smile. "I don't have anything more interesting to offer you, I'm afraid."

"The hell you don't." Felicia grinned wickedly and walked toward a cupboard with glee. "I left some vermouth and gin here last week. And I brought onions and olives." She pulled the little jars out of her bag with a broad smile.

"You'd make a fabulous Girl Scout."

"Wouldn't I though?" She retrieved her bottles and mixed herself a professional-looking martini, as Kate sat up a little straighter in her chair. "Heartburn again?" Felicia knew the look on her face. She had been around enough to know all the looks, better than Kate herself did. Everything from heartburn to hysterics. And this looked like heartburn.

"I think I ate too many cherries at lunch. It feels more like indigestion than heartburn." And cramps. Jesus, that was all she needed, a bellyache to go with her big belly. Poor baby, how could she have done that to him, and herself? Thinking of it made her giggle. "Maybe I just need a martini." But they both knew she didn't mean it. She hadn't had a drink in months.

"Why don't you go lie down? I'll have a shower, and then I can throw some dinner together." Felicia looked matter-of-fact and very much at home.

"You came down here to cook for me, yes?"

"Yes. Now go get out of your dress and lie down."

"Yes, mother."

She felt better though when she had. And after a shower, she felt wonderful. She could hear Felicia starting to rattle around the kitchen, and she stopped in the nursery for a minute, and there it was. Willie.

The same bear as Tom's. She wondered how his Willie was doing just then, if Tom was holding it, loving it, or had already forgotten it. She touched the bear gently and then left the room.

"What are you up to?"

"Spaghetti okay with you?" It was one of three things Felicia could cook. The other two were fried eggs and steak. Kate nodded.

"Wonderful. Spaghetti ought to be worth another five pounds, but at this point, what the hell."

They ate dinner by candlelight, looking at the view, and it was refreshing to have someone to talk to. Kate was growing too used to silence, and to seeing only Tom. She needed Felicia to add a little pepper to the cream soup of her life. Felicia added lots of it. Pepper supreme. She was in the midst of regaling Kate with the week's gossip from the store—who was screwing whom, being promoted, getting fired, or had turned out to be a fag after all. But Kate wasn't listening as intently or laughing as hard as she normally would have.

"What's the matter, love? You look kind of green. My spaghetti?"

"No. I think it's those goddamn cherries again." It was that same gnawing, grinding feeling she'd had before dinner, only slightly worse.

"Cherries, my ass. You wore yourself out. Why don't you lie down on the couch? Or do you want to go to bed?"

"I'm not really tired." In fact, she felt jumpy, but she had felt like that before, just after seeing Tom. She lay down on the couch anyway, and then started to joke with Felicia again. "Maybe it *is* your lousy spaghetti."

"Up yours, lady. I happen to make the best spaghetti in the West."

"Mama Felicia."

Felicia concocted herself another martini and the two women bantered and laughed. But the indigestion grew worse rather than better.

"Maybe I'll go to bed after all."

"Okay. See ya." Felicia grinned as Kate went off to her room. The dishes had already been done. Kate had meant to say something about being glad her friend was there, but she had told her so many times before that she was no longer sure how to say it.

Kate was asleep before nine o'clock, and Felicia tucked herself onto the couch with a book. She wasn't tired and it had been a rough week at work. It was nice just to sit and unwind, nice to get away. She got engrossed in the novel and it was almost one o'clock when she heard Kate stirring in her room. She listened for a minute to be sure, and then she saw a gleam of light under the bedroom door.

"You okay?" Felicia was frowning as she called out. But the voice came back quickly.

"Yeah." She did sound all right.

"You still have that bellyache?"

"Uh huh."

It was two minutes later when Kate came out of her room, and stood in the doorway in a long pink and white nightgown. She looked like a strangely swollen child, and on her face was a bright wide-eyed smile.

"Felicia . . ." The smile broadened.

"Yeah? What's up?" Felicia didn't know what to make of the look on Kate's face. She looked ethereally happy, and Felicia had never seen her look like that before.

"I don't think it's a bellyache. I think maybe . . . it's the baby." Kate almost laughed. She felt elated. It was crazy—she was scared, and it was too soon, but

70

she was excited. The baby! It was coming at last!

"You mean you're having it?" Felicia suddenly looked gray.

Kate nodded. "Maybe. I'm not sure."

"Isn't it early?"

Kate nodded again, but she didn't look upset. "I think eight months is safe. And it's been almost eight and a half."

"Did you call the doctor?"

Kate nodded again solemnly, with a look of victory. She was going to do it. She was going to have the baby. Maybe tonight. She didn't have to wait anymore. It was over! It was beginning! "He said to call him back in an hour, or if the pains got much harder."

"You're having pains?" Felicia squeezed the book in her lap and stared at her friend.

"I guess so. I thought it was just indigestion, but they keep getting stronger, and then every now and then . . ." And then, as though impatient with talking, she sat down suddenly and reached for Felicia's hand. "Here, you can feel it."

Without thinking, Felicia let Kate put her hand on the bloated belly. She could feel its hardness and tightness. It didn't even feel like a belly. It felt like a wall, a floor, something that could be cracked open, not squeezed.

"My God, how awful. Does it hurt?"

Kate shook her head, with that same excited look in her eyes, but there was a thin veil of sweat on her forehead. "No, it doesn't hurt. It just feels very, very tight."

"Can I get you something, love?" Felicia's hands were trembling and Kate laughed.

"No, and if you fall apart now, I'll kick your ass. I'm glad you're here."

71

"So am I." But she didn't look it and Kate laughed again.

"Relax."

"Yeah." Felicia sighed deeply and sat back against the back of the couch. "I can handle almost any crisis. But babies have never been my thing. I've never been to one before, I mean . . . oh damn. I need a drink." The unrufflable Felicia Norman was ruffling badly, and Kate was strangely calm. This was what she had waited nearly nine months for.

"You don't need a drink, Licia. I need you." That was a sobering thought and Felicia looked at her. Kate didn't look as though she needed anyone.

"You mean it?"

"Yes." Her voice was tight again, and Felicia watched her. She knew what it was now.

"Another pain?"

Kate nodded, with a vague look, as though she were thinking of something else, and Felicia silently held out her hand. Kate took it and squeezed hard. The pains were starting to hurt.

CHAPTER 4

The pains were rising to a rapid crescendo now, and there was barely a moment to breathe between them. Felicia sat tensely in a chair near the bed in the bleak little hospital room. She was holding Kate's hand. The sun was just peeking over the hills with a golden halo around it.

"Want another piece of ice?" Felicia's voice was harsh in the quiet room, but Kate only shook her head. She couldn't speak now. She just lay there, panting determinedly as she had learned to do in the classes she had taken two months before. "Aren't you tired of doing that?" Kate shook her head again, closed her eyes, and for ten seconds the panting stopped. She hardly had time for one normal breath before the pain crashed through her consciousness again. Her hair lay damp and matted around her face, and for what seemed the thousandth time that night Felicia stood up and wiped her forehead with a damp cloth. The exhilaration was gone from Kate's face. The only thing visible there now was pain.

"Hang in, love, it can't be much longer." Kate showed no sign of having heard. She was panting again, and then suddenly she stopped and a soft moan gave way to a short startling scream. Felicia jumped in surprise, as Kate began to thrash in her bed and move her head from side to side.

"Licia . . . can't . . . I can't . . . anymore . . ." But even the time it took to say those words was too long. Already the pain was tearing through her again, and another moan escaped her, quickly capped by another scream.

"Kate . . . hey, baby, come on . . ." Jesus. She wasn't prepared for this. It was worse than anything she'd seen in the movies. Frantically, Felicia rang for the nurse, and Kate began to cry.

It was less than a minute later when the nurse opened the door and stuck her head inside. "How's it going, girls?" Felicia looked at her in icy fury.

"How does it look like it's going?" She wanted to kill her. Why the hell wasn't she doing something for Kate? The girl was in agony for chrissake. People died like that—didn't they?

"Looks just fine to me." The nurse's eyes seemed to shoot sparks at Felicia. She walked quickly to Kate's bed and took the girl's hand. "You're almost there, Kate. This is the hard part. You're in transition now. After this it gets lots easier, and pretty soon you can start to push." Kate turned her head from side to side again, in a sharp frantic motion, and her tears mixed with the sweat running into her hair.

"I can't . . . I can't . . ." She retched as though to throw up, but nothing came.

"Yes, you can. Come on, I'll breathe with you." And quickly, the nurse started the panting, holding firmly to Kate's hand. "Come on, now, Kate . . . now . . ." She could see the pain starting to tear at Kate's face again. "Now . . . there . . ." The panting was driving Felicia nuts, but Kate looked less panicky. Maybe she would make it after all. God, it was awful though. Christ, why would anyone go through that? Another soft moan, and then a sharp little scream burst in on her thoughts again, and the nurse's soft purring continued. She wondered how Kate stood it; she had always seemed so frail. No child was worth this. No man. No one. Felicia felt tears burn her eyes, as she turned to look at the rising sun. She couldn't bear to see her friend suffer anymore. She had already been through too much, and now this. When Felicia turned from the window, she found the nurse's eyes meeting hers, this time more gently. "Why don't you get a cup of coffee? The coffee shop should be open by now."

"No, it's all right. I—"

"Go on. We're doing fine." And she was right, Kate did look better. There was still that dogged look of pain in her eyes, but she was back in the fight again. And probably working too hard to care whether Felicia left for a few minutes. This was labor, in the real sense of the word.

"Okay. But I'll be back soon."

"We'll be here." The nurse smiled cheerily and went on breathing with Kate while timing contractions. And for the first time, Felicia felt left out. She wondered if that was how fathers felt as they watched their wives writhe in pain, straining toward a goal a man could see but never feel. Felicia knew she would never feel that pain. She would never love anyone enough for that. Not the way Kate had loved Tom. Thinking about it tore at her again, as she walked soberly toward the coffee shop. She didn't even want a drink now. What she really wanted was to know that it was over, and go home to shower and sleep. The long drive of the day before and the long sleepless night were beginning to catch up with her.

"How's Mrs. Harper doing?" A fat matronly nurse at the desk glanced up at Felicia. It was a very small town. Felicia wondered if the woman at the desk remembered everyone's name.

"I don't know. It looks awful to me."

"Ever had a baby?" Felicia shook her head expressionlessly. Funny to be answering these questions for a stranger. The woman nodded. "She'll forget all about it in a couple of days. She may talk about it a little, but she'll forget. You'll remember it longer than she will."

"Maybe so." For no reason she could fathom, she paused for a moment at the desk, as though expecting the nurse to say more. Just talking to someone was comforting. "I hope it won't be much longer."

"Might be. Might not. Hard to tell. It's her first one, isn't it?" Felicia nodded. Then that meant more pain, did it? The first one. And maybe her last. Poor Kate . . . "Don't look so sad. She'll be just fine. You'll see. As soon as the baby's born she'll be laughing and crying, and she'll call her folks and tell everyone she knows." The woman's face clouded momentarily as she looked at Felicia. "She's a widow though, isn't she?"

"Yes."

"That's an awful shame. At a time like this. What did he die of?"

"Of . . . in an accident." Felicia's face closed quietly. Like a door. They had said enough.

"I'm sorry." The nurse had sensed it, and sat silently for a moment, as Felicia gave her a small mechanical smile and walked away. The coffee would do her good.

She spent only five minutes in the coffee shop. She would have stayed for days if she could have, but she didn't want to leave Kate alone. She swallowed the hot coffee as quickly as her mouth could stand it, and considered an order of toast. But that seemed excessive. Kate was in agony, and she was going to eat toast? The thought of it made her feel sick. And then, suddenly, as she waited for her check, she found herself thinking of Tom. She wondered if Kate was thinking of him too, or only of her pain. Tom. He should have been here for this. It was incredible to realize that he would never see his child. He would never understand that he had one. The girl behind the counter slipped the check under Felicia's empty cup, and Felicia glanced at it and absentmindedly left two quarters on the counter. She had to get back to Kate. She didn't have time for this kind of thinking.

The black espadrilles she had worn the day before whispered silently down the corridor, and she looked down at how rumpled she was. The black cotton pantsuit she'd picked up on the third floor earlier in the week looked like she'd slept in it, and the heavy Indian silver bracelet was leaving a long red furrow on her arm. She wondered how much longer this waiting would go on, and how much more Kate could take. She had been in labor since a little after midnight, and it was now just after seven in the morning. But when Felicia gently pushed open the door, things had changed in the room. Kate's face was wet with sweat now, not just damp—she looked as though she had been standing under the shower. The blue hospital gown clung to her body, and her hand kept a white-knuckled grip on the nurse. But her eyes were brighter, her face was alive, and the rhythm of her movements had changed; it was as though she had moved from an agonized painful trot to a full-blown gallop. It was hard to tell if the pain had lessened, and even the nurse couldn't take time to talk to Felicia now. She was telling Kate about "cleansing breaths" and giving orders with military precision. But Kate seemed to be totally absorbed in what she was saying. And then Felicia noticed the nurse's free hand go quickly to the buzzer and press three times.

Felicia stood by, feeling useless, not knowing if

things were going badly or well, and afraid to interrupt Kate's concentration by asking questions. But something had changed. Everything had. There was a light in Kate's face that Felicia had never seen before in anyone's face. It made her want to work too, want to help, want to run the race along with her and feel the winner's ribbon give way on her chest as she crossed the finish line and won. She was winning now. You could feel it in the room. She even smiled once, briefly between two mammoth pains. The smile darted away, but its aura remained.

The nurse buzzed again, and this time the door opened quickly and two nurses in what looked like blue pajamas appeared with a gurney. "Doctor's waiting for us in two. How's she doing?" They looked relaxed and unconcerned, and for a moment their attitude reassured Felicia, but Kate seemed not to notice them at all. The nurse at her side waited between pains to look at the two nurses in blue, and then gave them a wide, easy smile.

"We're ready. Very ready. Right, Kate?" Kate nodded, and for the first time in a while, her eyes searched for Felicia. She found her quickly, and started to talk. But she had to wait for another pain to pass before she could speak, and then the two nurses used the few seconds they had between pains to shift her to the gurney. But she was anxious for Felicia, who was quick to step to her side.

"Come with me . . . please, Licia . . ."

"Now?"

"I want you . . ." It was suddenly much harder to speak. As though all her air were cut off during the pains. Fresh rivers of sweat broke out on her face and ran down her neck, but she wouldn't let go of Felicia. "Please . . . when the baby comes . . . you too." Felicia understood. But oh God, why her? The nurses were with Kate, they knew what they were doing. They could help her more than she could. But there was no denying that look in Kate's eyes.

"Sure, love. You just keep busy with what you're doing, and I'll be right with you holding your hand." She was already walking beside the stretcher, as it was rolled down the hall. The nurse striding quickly beside Kate raised an eyebrow in Felicia's direction.

"Are you planning to be in the delivery room?"

There was only the tiniest second of hesitation, and then her answer was firm. "Yes." Oh Jesus. Her stomach turned over again, but she couldn't let Kate down.

"Then you'll have to scrub and change your clothes."

"Where?"

"In there." The nurse nodded at a door. "The nurse on duty will help you. Meet us in delivery room two."

"Two?"

The nurse nodded distractedly as Kate arched her back in pain and forgot Felicia's presence. "Hold on, honey, we're almost there. Not yet. Not yet. Just as soon as we get you on the table." And then she was gone, and Felicia disappeared into the appointed door to scrub and change.

She emerged less than three minutes later in sterilized blue pajamas and rubber-soled "grounded" shoes, and ran nervously down the corridor toward delivery room two. The nurse in the scrub room had told her where it would be. She pressed a floor buzzer and the door automatically swung open. She was careful to keep her hands and arms away from contact with any surfaces, as she had been told. Once in the delivery room she could hold Kate's hand, but she couldn't touch anything before that, or she'd have to scrub again, and she didn't want to keep Kate waiting that long. It had already seemed like hours. She caught

79

a glimpse of herself in a narrow glass panel and almost grinned. She looked like a character in one of the medical shows on television, her hair tightly wound into a knot and covered with a blue cap that looked like a shower cap. She even wore a little mask. Christ, what if someone took her for a nurse? It was a horrifying thought as she walked into the delivery room, and then she realized that no one could take her for anything but a tourist. The pros were busy getting organized, and Kate was already draped with white sheets. Her legs had been strapped high in the air. To Felicia it looked primitive and cruel, but Kate didn't seem to notice. She kept lifting her head now, as though there were something to see. And for a moment, Felicia felt a small thrill run through her as she realized that maybe there was. This wasn't just Kate's ordeal anymore. It was an event, a happening, a birth. In a few minutes a baby would be born, and the horror of it would be over for Kate. But Felicia had to admit that even now there seemed to be no "horror" for Kate. For the first time in hours, Kate turned her head toward her and her eyes seemed to be laughing.

"Hi, cookie." Felicia tried hard to sound more at ease than she was.

"You look ridiculous, Licia." She could talk again. Felicia felt so relieved she wanted to hug her, but knew she couldn't. Instead, she started to reach for Kate's hand, and then realized that Kate's hands were busy now, pulling at two straps to give herself the leverage she needed to push. The doctor was at the foot of the delivery table, gowned and masked, and his eyes looked kindly behind horn-rimmed glasses.

"Okay, Kate, a nice big one now . . . steady . . . there . . . that's it . . . a little more . . . come on, girl, harder . . . there . . . okay. Rest for a minute now." For a moment Kate's face had been contorted with the effort, and the damp pallor gave way to a hot flush of bursting effort. She was breathless from the strain, and let her head fall back on the pillow, with a quick look at her friend.

"Oh Licia, I can't . . . help me." Felicia looked frightened and helpless for a moment and a nurse came rapidly up to the head of the table where she stood.

"If you'd support her shoulders while she pushes, it would help a lot."

"Me?" It was the only word Felicia could think of, but Kate was looking like a tired child again—the joy and anticipation had gone. She was exhausted. And then another pain roared through Kate, and everyone seemed to tense with anticipation as the doctor did something between her legs.

"Licia . . ." Without thinking, Felicia gently scooped Kate's shoulders into her arms, and held her as the laboring girl shook with the effort. She had never worked as hard at anything in her life. "I can't . . . it won't . . ."

"Harder, Kate! Come on, now!" The doctor sounded urgent and firm, the nurses seemed to be doing a lot of running and clattering, and Kate was starting to cry again.

"I can't . . . I . . ." Felicia felt sweat begin to run down her own face as she continued to support Kate's shoulders. Even that was almost too much effort, and she knew it was nothing compared to what Kate must be feeling. Why the hell didn't they give her something to speed it up, or use forceps, or *something* dammit?

"Push harder!" The doctor sounded merciless, and Felicia hated him as she watched Kate's face contort with what she thought was pain. It was more work than pain, but Felicia couldn't know. And then suddenly the nurses were buzzing around them again.

"Come on, Kate. You can do it now. Just one more good hard push. That's it . . . come on . . ." There was no respite, and then suddenly Felicia realized the tension in the room had heightened. As she glanced at the doctor she saw a different look in his eyes, and one of the nurses was checking a monitoring system they had looped to Kate somewhere. And then Felicia heard it, softly, at the other end of the table. She prayed that Kate was too distracted to hear. "Fetal heart monitor, Doctor."

"Slowing?"

"Irregular."

He nodded in answer, and another pain ripped into Kate.

"Okay, Kate, this is it. I want one nice big push from you. Now!" But this time she only flinched at the command, and fought against Felicia's arms behind her. She let her head fall back, and an endless sob burst from her.

"Oh Licia . . . Tom . . . Tom! Oh Tom . . . please . . ."

"Kate. Please, baby. Please, for us. For Tom. Just one more try." Tears had begun to pour down Felicia's cheeks now and into her mask. She was blinded by them, as she held the frail shoulders in her trembling arms, and prayed that the ordeal would end. It had to. Kate couldn't take any more. Felicia knew that. But maybe for Tom . . . "Please, baby, I know you can do it. Push as hard as you can." And then a riot of sounds, the clattering of instruments, a grunt from the doctor, a little cry from a nurse, sudden silence from Kate, and a long, cackling little wail.

"It's a boy!" The doctor slapped him firmly on the bottom and Kate lay back with tears streaming from her eyes and smiled up at her friend.

"We did it."

"You did it, champ!" Tears poured from Felicia's eyes too. "Oh and he's so beautiful." He was small and round and his face was an angry red as he wailed on, and then suddenly he stuck a tiny thumb in his mouth and the crying stopped as Kate laughed, watching her son. Felicia had never seen anything as beautiful as the way Kate looked. She couldn't stop crying, and Kate just grinned, silent and proud. And then without another word, they wrapped him carefully and handed him to his mother. The cord had been cut. He was free now. And he was hers.

Kate lay there with her son in her arms, tears still flowing from her eyes, and she looked up at Felicia again. And Felicia understood. She had seen it too. Tiny as he was, he looked just like Tom.

"What's his name?" The nurse who had been with Kate the longest came to look at the tiny pink face snuggled in his mother's arms. He was a big baby, just under nine pounds.

"His name's Tygue." And then in the lull of activity, as the doctor looked on and smiled, Kate laughed a long happy laugh. She sounded like a girl again, and she picked up her head and looked around the room. "Hey, everybody, I'm a mom!" They laughed with her, and Felicia couldn't stop laughing despite the tears still in her eyes.

CHAPTER 5

"You're sure you'll be all right?"

Kate grinned across the room at her friend. "No, I'm going to panic and call the Red Cross before noon."

"Smartass." Felicia grinned, and sipped the last of her coffee. It was a peaceful Sunday morning, and Tygue was almost nine days old. Felicia had gone back to San Francisco and had returned to the country for the weekend. Now she watched as Kate nursed the baby. "Doesn't that hurt?"

Kate shook her head with a slow smile, and then looked down at her son, pink and white and shiny after his first week of life. "No, it doesn't hurt. It sounds corny, but it almost feels like this was what I was made for. And I didn't really think I'd like it."

"I never thought I would either. But you know, you're beginning to make me wonder about a lot of things. I always thought having a baby had to be the ultimate horror. Until Pipsqueak here came along." Felicia smiled at him again; she still hadn't gotten over the beauty of the experience. "I'm going to miss you two something awful."

"It'll do you good. I haven't been to Europe in so long, I forget what it looks like." Felicia was going over for a month, for the store.

"Want to come along on my next trip?"

"With Tygue?" Kate looked surprised, and Felicia smiled.

"Either way. It would be fun."

"Maybe so." But she looked away and her face was very closed.

"Kate, you're not really serious about staying down here, are you?" It was beginning to worry her.

"Very much so. I just signed another lease on the house."

"For how long?"

"Five years."

Felicia looked appalled. "Can you get out of it?"

"I have no idea, love. I'm not planning to. Licia, I know you don't understand it, but this is my home now. I don't think I'd ever have wanted to go back, no matter what. But with Tygue, I'm ready to start a new life. I'd have had to do it somewhere, and this is where I want to be. It's a good place for a child. He'll have a simple, healthy life. I can get up to see Tom. And in a town like this, Tygue never really needs to know what happened to Tom. Harper is a perfectly ordinary name. No one will ask questions. If we go back to San Francisco, one day—it'll all come out." She sighed deeply and looked Felicia square in the face. "I'd be crazy to go back." Just thinking of the reporters still made her cringe.

"All right. Then what about Los Angeles? Someplace civilized for God's sake." Kate grinned at Felicia's fervor, but she knew that she meant well. There was an even stronger bond between them now, ever since Tygue's birth. They had shared one of life's most precious moments.

"Why Los Angeles, Licia? I have nothing there. It's just a city. Look, love, I have no family, no place to

85

be, nothing I have to do. I have a little boy who will thrive here, and it's a good place for me to write. I'm happy here."

"But you are planning to come up to the city from time to time, aren't you?" There was a long pause, and Felicia was finally seeing it all. *"Aren't* you?" Her voice was soft and sad. She was sad for Kate, who was gone for good. This was no place for her, but by the time she realized it, it would be too late. Maybe not until the boy was grown and gone. "You will come up to the city, won't you?" She was pressing the point, but Kate's face was set when she looked up from Tygue's sleeping face at her breast. She buttoned her blouse.

"We'll see, Licia. I don't know."

"But you don't plan to, is that it?" Dammit. How could she do that to herself?

"All right. I don't plan to. Does it make you feel better knowing that?"

"No, you ass, it makes me feel like shit. Kate, you can't do that to yourself, shut away down here in the weeds and the fields. That's nuts. You're beautiful, you're young. Don't do this!"

"I have nothing back there, Licia. Not anymore. No family, no memories I want to keep, nothing. Except you, and I'll see you here, when you can get away."

"What about life and people? Theater, opera, ballet, modeling, parties? Jesus, Kate, look what you're throwing away!"

"I'm not throwing it away. I've walked out on it. It'll all be there if I ever change my mind."

"But you're twenty-three now. This is when you should be out there enjoying it all, taking advantage of everything life tosses at your feet."

Kate smiled at the words and looked down at her son again, and then with a purposeful look she brought her eyes back to Felicia's. There was nothing left to be said. Felicia had lost.

Felicia closed her eyes for a moment and then stood up. "I don't know what to say."

"Just tell me you'll come to see us when you have time, and that you'll have a good time in Europe." Kate wore a firm little smile that didn't invite argument or discussion.

"And what'll you do?"

"I am going to start work on a book."

"A book?" Christ, it was like adolescence. Kate was throwing her whole damn life away, all because her husband had gone bananas and wound up in a sanatarium. But it wasn't *her* doing. Why did she have to bury herself alive because he was? The bracelets on Felicia's arm clanked as she nervously put her coffee cup in the sink. She wished she could talk sense into the girl, but she'd just have to give it another try when she got back from Europe. Something told her, though, that she would never win. Kate had changed a lot just in the few days since the baby was born. She seemed much surer of everything. And stubborn as hell.

"Why does it surprise you so much that I want to write a book?"

"That just seems like such a funny thing to do. And awfully lonely, frankly."

"We'll see. And I've got Tygue to keep me company now."

"After a fashion." Felicia looked bleak. "What'll you do with him when you go to see Tom?"

"I don't know yet. One of the nurses at the hospital thought she might know of a reliable sitter, an older woman who is wonderful with babies. Or I might take him with me. But it's really too long a trip, and . . . well, I'm not sure." Tom wouldn't understand. It would be better leaving him home with a sitter.

"The sitter sounds like a good idea."

"Yes, mother."

"Up yours, Mrs. Harper. You know, you're going to give me more gray hairs than the store does."

"On you, it'll look marvelous."

"Such remorse!" But Felicia was smiling again. "Just remember me in one of your books." Kate laughed at the thought, and put the baby in the elaborate blue and white basket Felicia had brought down. And in another month she would start to use the antique cradle his father had bought, but it was still a little too big. He would have been lost in it. Felicia walked over, and stood looking at him for a long time. "Is it neat, Kate?" There was infinite softness in her eyes.

"It's better than I ever dreamed it would be. It's perfect. Until the four A.M. feeding." She grinned at Felicia. "Then, I begin to wonder."

"Don't. Just enjoy it." Felicia couldn't shake off the mood of seriousness that had fallen over her. She felt as though she were saying good-bye to Kate for good. But Kate had already seen that in her face.

"Don't take it so hard, love."

"I still think you're a fool to stay down here. But I'll be down the first weekend after I get back. And whenever I can after that." But they both knew it wouldn't be every weekend anymore. They had their lives to get on with. Things wouldn't be the same. There were tears swamping Felicia's eyes as she picked up her bag, and Kate looked sobered as she opened the door. They walked slowly to Felicia's little red car, and then silently Kate hugged her tight.

"I'm sorry, Licia." There were tears in her eyes now too. "I just can't go back."

"I know. It's okay." She laughed through her tears

and gave Kate another fierce squeeze. "Take good care of my godchild, kiddo."

"You take good care of you."

And with that, Felicia saluted, tossed her bag into the car, and slid behind the wheel with a smile. She stopped for a moment and looked at Kate. Both women smiled a long quiet smile full of love and understanding. Their ships had set sail. And they waved to each other as Felicia faded from sight.

Kate looked at her watch as she walked back inside the house. She had another two and a half hours before Tygue woke up for his next feeding. That would give her plenty of time to work on the book. She had already written thirty pages, but she hadn't wanted to admit it to Felicia. The book was her secret. And one day—she smiled to herself at the thought—one day . . . she already knew.

PART
TWO

CHAPTER 6

"Kate? Kate!"

Kate jumped in surprise at the sound of her name, as she sat barefoot at her desk in an old shirt and a worn pair of jeans.

"Hey, lady, is your hearing going too?"

"Licia!" She was standing in the doorway, looking as trim and fashionable as ever in a wine-colored suede suit. "You didn't tell me you were coming down!"

"I wanted to take a look at the Santa Barbara store, so I thought I'd surprise you. That's some outfit. Things getting as bad as that?" Kate flushed in embarrassment and zipped up her fly.

"Sorry. I was doing some work. I wasn't expecting guests."

"How's it coming?" Felicia hugged her and cast an eye at the typewriter.

"Okay, I guess. It's hard to tell." She shrugged and followed Felicia into the living room. She hadn't seen her since Christmas, two months before, when Felicia had spent a week with them, spoiling Tygue rotten.

"Don't be so hard on yourself. If you sold one, you can sell another one."

"Tell my publisher that, Licia."

"I'd be happy to. Care for a martini?" Kate grinned but shook her head. Felicia never changed. Her outfits followed the fashion of the moment, the men in her life came and went, and once every few years she rented a slightly larger, more expensive apartment, but essentially she hadn't changed in years. It was reassuring. The martinis, the husky voice, the style, the loyalty, the solidity, the good legs, none of them changed a bit.

"I don't know, Licia. I'm serious. The first book stank, even if it did get published. And they wouldn't even take the last one. I'm getting nervous."

"Don't be. Three's a charm. And besides, your first one did not 'stink.' It sold very nicely, as I recall."

"Bullshit." Kate looked glum.

"Don't be so insecure. How many women your age have even written two books?"

"Hundreds probably." But Kate liked the reassurance; she had no one else to give it to her, no one to talk to, in fact. She was careful to avoid getting past the "Hi, how are you?" stage with anyone in town. She had Tygue, and Felicia, and her work, and her visits to Tom. And no room for anything else. "I'm just beginning to wonder if I have what it takes to write a successful novel."

"Maybe you don't want to." Felicia looked over her shoulder as she expertly poured her martini into a glass from the pitcher she kept in Kate's cupboard. Whenever Felicia arrived, it seemed to them both that she had just been there the day before. Kate loved that about their relationship. "Maybe you just don't want the hassle of success. Wouldn't that force you into a lot of choices you don't want?" It was a question Felicia had long wondered about.

"What choices? Whether or not Tygue goes to college?"

"That's a benefit, love, not a choice. I'm talking about what would happen to *you* if your book was a smash. Could you go on living here? Would you expose yourself to publicity? Would you condescend to 'visit the big city' for interviews? Those, my love, are choices."

"I'll deal with them when I have to."

"May it be soon." Felicia toasted her with the martini, and Kate laughed.

"You never give up."

"Of course not." It had been three and a half years, and she still wanted Kate to come back. She admitted Tygue was thriving and happy, a beautiful child with healthy pink cheeks and his father's huge cornflower-blue eyes. He hadn't suffered yet from the cultural deprivation of the life his mother had chosen, but in time he would. That had been Felicia's latest tack, but it hadn't worked any better than the others. "You are the stubbornest woman I know."

"Thank you." Kate looked pleased.

"Where's my godchild, by the way? I brought him a present."

"If it weren't for you, Licia, the child wouldn't have a thing to play with. But thanks to you"—Kate grinned at her friend—"he has more than all the kids in town. The train got here last week."

"Oh did it?" Felicia tried to look innocent. Maybe he was a little young, but she'd felt he ought to have one. "After all, living in this wasteland, the poor child needs something to amuse himself with. So where is he?"

"At nursery school."

"Already? He's too young!"

"He started right after Christmas, and he loves it."

"He'll get germs from the other kids." But Kate just laughed at Felicia as she finished her drink. It was a sunny Friday afternoon in late February, and in Kate's part of the world, it already felt like spring.

"He should be home in half an hour. He goes from

95

two to five, after his nap. Want to take a look at the new manuscript while you wait?" Felicia nodded acquiescence with a slow happy smile. "What are you staring at?"

"I was trying to remember if I looked that good at twenty-six. But I just remembered. I didn't."

"That's because I live here, and not in some wretched city."

"Bullshit." But maybe it was true. And in any case, Kate did look well. Even the visits to Tom didn't seem to weigh her down as they used to. Nothing had changed there, she had just adjusted.

Tom was still at Mead, and Mr. Erhard was still taking extraordinary care of him. Tom was still playing the same games, reading the same books, working out the same puzzles—it was like an eternity of first grade. Now that Kate had Tygue to compare him with, Tom's stagnation was more noticeable, but he remained gentle and lovable. She still saw him twice a week. Tygue thought she went away to work. It was just something his mother did.

Kate looked at her watch as she handed Felicia the manuscript. She still had a little time before Tygue came home, and she was anxious to know what Felicia thought of the new book. Licia made some surprisingly perceptive comments about her work. It was almost twenty minutes later when Felicia lifted her head with a look of surprise.

"How did you manage the sex scene?"

"What do you mean, how did I manage it?"

"You been having more fun down here than I credit you with?" Felicia looked over with a sly smile, and Kate was annoyed.

"Don't be ridiculous. I just wrote it, that's all. It's fiction."

"Amazing." Felicia looked impressed, but there was mischief in her eyes.

"Why? Is it lousy?" She was worried.

"No. Surprisingly good. I'm just surprised you can remember that far back. You know, with the wonderful, normal, healthy life you lead down here, all the men you see . . ."

"Felicia Norman, up yours." But she grinned as Felicia went back to the book. For a minute, she'd had her worried. Felicia was always bugging her about her sex life, or lack of it. Felicia might never have had a mad passion in her life, but there was always someone at hand to keep the juices flowing properly. Kate hadn't made love with a man in four years. She didn't even let herself think about it anymore. That wasn't part of her life. She put all her energies into Tygue, and the books. Maybe it even made the books better. Sometimes she wondered about that. The books were her lovers. And Tom and Tygue were her kids. It was an hour later when Felicia put down the manuscript with a serious look on her face. Kate trembled looking at her.

"You hated it."

For a moment, Felicia only shook her head. "No. I loved it. But kiddo, you're walking right into something you're refusing to look at."

"What?" A plot problem obviously. Dammit, and she'd been so careful.

"Exactly what I warned you about—success." Felicia's face remained grave, and Kate grinned.

"You mean it?"

"I do. But do *you* mean it?"

"Oh, stop being such a worrier. I'll face it when I get there."

"I hope so."

And then the conversation ended abruptly as the school bus arrived with Tygue. He came bounding into the house in blue jeans and a red flannel shirt, little cowhide cowboy boots, and a bright yellow parka. "Aunt Licia! Aunt Licia!" He bounced into her lap, cowboy boots and all, and Kate cringed at what would happen to the suede suit, but Felicia seemed to mind not at all.

"Wait till you see what I brought you!"

"Another twain?" His face lit up like a spotlight, and both women laughed.

"Nope. Take a look. There's a big box in the car. Can you get it yourself?"

"Sure, Aunt Licia." He went thundering outside again, and Kate watched him go. He was growing so fast . . . and then she caught a funny look on her friend's face.

"Okay, you, warn me now—what did you bring him? A live cobra? White mice? Tell me the truth."

"Nothing like that, Kate. Really." But she could already hear the squeals from outside the house. Felicia had been nervous about it since she'd arrived. She'd even sneaked out to the car once with a saucer of water. But he had been asleep. He wasn't asleep now though, he was being passionately squeezed by Master Tygue.

"It's weall!"

"Of course it's weall!" Felicia grinned at the look on the boy's face, and for a minute Kate rolled her eyes, but she was smiling too. "Is he yours, Aunt Licia?" It was the droopiest sad-eyed basset hound puppy Kate had ever seen, and just looking at him made her want to laugh. Tygue put him on the floor, and the dog's legs seemed to slide out from under him. His ears fanned out and he looked mournfully up at the little boy and wagged his tail.

"Do you like him, Tygue?"

Tygue nodded ferociously and then sat down next to the little black and white dog. "You're so lucky. I wish we had one too. I want one, Mommy."

"You've got one, Tygue." Aunt Licia was on her knees next to her godchild, holding both the boy and the dog.

"I got one too?" Tygue looked confused.

"This one's yours. Just for you." She kissed him softly on the top of his blond head.

"For me?"

"For you."

"Oh! Oh!" It was all he could say for minutes, and then he threw himself on the dog with delight. "What's his name?"

"That's up to you!"

"I'll have to ask Willie." Willie, the treasured teddy bear, had become his best friend. Tom still had his too, and it was hard to decide which one looked more loved and weather-beaten, Tygue's or his father's. Tygue bounded out of the room a minute later and Kate stooped down to pet the little dog.

"Are you furious, Kate?" Felicia looked only slightly remorseful.

"How could I be, you nut? Just don't bring the kid a car next time you visit. Save that till he's six." The dog was irresistible though, and she lifted him happily into her lap. Tygue was back in a minute with Willie.

"Willie says his name is Bert."

"Then Bert it is."

Tygue squeezed him again, and Bert wagged his tail. The family was complete. And Felicia had even liked the beginning of her new book. Kate felt as though good things were in store. And Licia was crazy with that bullshit about success. Hell, if the publisher just accepted the book, that would be enough. It didn't have to be a best seller. That only happened one time in a million, and she knew it wasn't for her. She could feel it. This was her life.

CHAPTER 7

"Going to teach today, Mom?" Kate nodded and handed Tygue another piece of toast. "I thought so. I can always tell." He looked pleased with himself, and Kate watched her son with a warm glow. Graceful and sturdy and thoughtful and bright, and so pretty, but in an appropriately boyish way. He looked a little less like Tom now. And he was nearly six.

"How can you always tell when I'm going to teach?" They had long since established a chatty rapport over breakfast, and on this beautiful spring day she was feeling playful. Tygue was the person she spoke to most. Now and then it made her respond to him on his own childlike level, but most of the time they found a mutually acceptable middle ground.

"I can tell 'cause you wear gooder clothes."

"I do, huh?" She was grinning at him, and there was a fierce sparkle of mischief in his eyes, not so very different from her own. "And the word is 'better,' by the way."

"Yeah. And you wear that goopy stuff on your face."

"What goopy stuff?" She was laughing with a mouthful of toast.

"You know—the green stuff."

"It's not green, it's blue. And it's called eye makeup.

Aunt Licia wears it too." As though that would make it okay.

"Yeah, but she wears it all the time, and hers is brown." He grinned broadly at her. "And you only wear yours to teach. How come you only wear it then?"

"Because you're not old enough to appreciate it, hot stuff." But neither was Tom. Anymore. She just wore the eye makeup and the "gooder" clothes, as Tygue called them, because she felt she ought to, for visiting Tom at Mead. It seemed suitable. There she was "Mrs. Harper." Here she was only "Mom." And occasionally "ma'am" at the supermarket.

She had long ago explained to Tygue that she taught writing at a school in Carmel for disturbed children. It allowed her to talk about Tom sometimes, or some of the others she saw. She had often told him stories of Tom, of his drawings, of Mr. Erhard—the stories were dusted off just enough so that she could tell Tygue and feel some relief. Or sometimes when Tom had had a moment of great victory, done a wonderful drawing, learned a game, or completed a puzzle that had seemed so much beyond him—sometimes then, she could share the triumphant feeling with Tygue, even if she shouldn't have. And by telling him that she taught at a school for disturbed children, she could also provide an excuse for going to her room and closing the door after a rough day. Tygue understood that. He felt sorry for the children she told him about. And he thought she was a good person for going there. Sometimes she wondered if that was why she had told him that story . . . poor Mommy . . . good Mommy . . . she drives all that way to work with retarded children. She shrugged off such thoughts. It was crazy to need strokes from a six-year-old child.

"How come they don't ever get vacation?" He was

slurping through his cereal now, and Kate's thoughts had already drifted ahead to Tom.

"Hm?"

"How come they don't get vacation?"

"They just don't. Want to bring Joey home from school today? Tillie will be here when you get back." But she didn't need to tell him. He knew that. "She could drive you guys over to see the new horses down at the Adams ranch, if you want."

"Nah."

"No?" Kate looked at him with astonishment, as he plowed on through the cereal with a blasé look on his face, but that same bright little flame in his eyes. He was up to something. "What's with you? Other plans?"

He looked up with a quick smile and a faint blush, but a vehement shake of his head. "No."

"Listen, you, be a good boy for Tillie today. Promise?" Tillie had the phone number at Mead, but Kate was on the road so much of the time that she still worried a little, even after all these years. "Don't do anything wild or crazy while I'm gone. I mean it, Tygue." The voice was suddenly stern, and his eyes met hers with a promise.

"It's okay, Mom." As though he were a thousand years old. And then suddenly the staccato honking of his car pool, and she could see the big yellow Jeep in the driveway.

"They're here!"

"Gotta go. See ya!" The spoon flew, a last grab at the toast, his favorite cowboy hat, a stray book on the table, a wave as she blew him a kiss, and he was gone. As she took another swallow of coffee, she couldn't help wondering what he was up to, but whatever it was, Tillie could handle it. She was a large, grandmotherly, affectionate woman, but she had been a widow for too many years herself to take any nonsense from Tygue. She had brought up five boys and a daughter, managed a ranch by herself for years before finally turning it over to her eldest son, and she had been baby-sitting for Tygue since he was born. She was rough and ingenious, and they had a marvelous time together. She was a real country woman, not an immigrant like Kate. There was a difference, and probably always would be. Besides, Kate was a writer, not a woman of the kitchen and garden. She enjoyed the country around her but she still knew little about it.

She looked around the kitchen for a minute before grabbing her jacket and handbag, wondering what she'd forgotten. She felt a strange tug this morning, as though she shouldn't be going. But she was used to that too. She no longer listened to those feelings. She just steeled herself and went. Tillie was unquestionably reliable. She shrugged into the jacket and looked down at her slacks. They still fitted her as they had eight years before when she'd bought them after modeling them. They had been beautiful then and were still beautiful, a soft caramel-colored gabardine, and the jacket was a tweed she had worn riding years before. The only thing new was the pale blue sweater she'd bought in town. She smiled again as she thought of what Tygue had said about what she wore. She liked looking pretty for Tom. She almost wondered if she should make more of an effort for Tygue too. But at six? That was crazy. What did he know? Or did he? The thought of dressing up for a six-year-old boy made her laugh as she walked out to the car.

She put her mind into automatic pilot all the way up to Carmel, and it turned out to be one of those days when she stayed on automatic throughout the day. The road had been tedious and all too familiar, Tom was dull and listless, the day turned foggy. Even the lunch was one she'd had hundreds of times before. Some days with Tom stood out like rare gems, their facets gleaming and brightly hued, casting rainbows of dancing light. Other days were dark and cold and had the taste of ash. And some days she felt nothing at all. Today she felt nothing. except fatigue as she left. She was anxious to hit the freeway as soon as she could, and drive back to the little house in the hills, and Tygue, and the silly sad-eyed basset hound who had become a member of the family. She had missed them all day. Maybe she should have stayed home after all. The speedometer hit well over ninety as she drove home. It often did, but she seldom got caught. Only twice in six years. The trip was so boring, only shortening it by speeding made it bearable. Now and then a pang of conscience toward Tygue would make her slow down, but not often. Fifty-five was intolerable. She cruised at eighty-five most of the time.

It was almost five as she drove, still too fast, over the back roads that led to the house. Why had she had this damn uneasiness all day? She ground across the gravel on the driveway, keeping an eye out for the dog, but anxiously combing the area around the house for Tygue. And then she saw him, and smiled as she stepped on the brakes and slid into park. He was filthy and smiling and beautiful and she had been crazy to worry. What the hell was wrong with her? She made the trip all the time. What had made her think that anything would be wrong today, or that anything would come up that Tillie couldn't handle? Tillie, in fact, was looking as filthy as Tygue, and even Bert looked as though he needed a bath. The three of them were covered with mud. Tillie even had a great smudge of it on one cheek, and there was lots of it matted in

Tygue's hair, but they looked delighted with themselves.

Tygue was waving frantically now and shouting something. It was time to move. To get out of the car. To be Mom again. And Tillie was peeling a pair of overalls down from her shoulders. The outfit she was wearing underneath was scarcely more elegant, and as always when returning from Carmel, Kate instantly felt overdressed. She grabbed her handbag and stepped out of the car. Her day as Tom's Kate had ended. It was Tygue's turn now. She took a deep breath of the fresh country air, and then sighed as she reached down to pat Bert, snuffling happily at the cuffs of her slacks.

"Hi, guys. What've you been up to?"

"Wait till you see, Mom! It's terrific! I did it! I did it! Tillie didn't do nothing!" Anything. To hell with it. "Nothing" was good enough. She was too tired to correct him, and too happy at seeing him safe and sound.

"She didn't, huh? Well, guess what?" She had already scooped him into her arms, mud and all, and he was squirming to be free.

"Come on, Mom, you gotta come look."

"Can I have a kiss first?" But she had already given him one, and was holding him close, as he looked up at her with that heart-melting smile of a boy of six.

"Then will you come look?"

"Then I'll come look." He bestowed a perfunctory kiss and pulled ferociously at her arm. "Wait a minute, what am I going to look at? Not snakes again . . . right, Tillie?" She cast a rapid eye in the older woman's direction. Tillie had said nothing yet. She was a woman of few words, particularly with other women; she had more to say to Tygue than to Kate.

But there was a certain warmth and respect between them. Tillie didn't really understand what Kate did at the typewriter, but the one published book she could tell her friends about had impressed her. It hadn't been much of a book, sort of a nonsense novel about fancy people in San Francisco, but it had been published, and that was something. And she said she had another one coming out in a month. Maybe she'd be famous one day. And anyway, she was a good mother. And a widow too. They had that in common. There was something different about her, though, that kept a distance between them. She wasn't a snob, and she didn't put on airs, and she didn't have anything anyone else didn't have. There was just a feeling one got about her. It was hard to explain. Refined. Maybe that was it. It was a word Tillie's mother had used. She had said Kate was refined. And smart. And pretty maybe, but too thin. And there was always that sad, hidden look in her eyes. But Tillie knew that one, she had seen it in the mirror for years after her own man had died. Not for as long as she'd seen it in Kate's eyes though. The look was still as fresh in her eyes as it had been when she'd first met her, after Tygue was born. Sometimes Tillie wondered if the writing kept her pain alive. Maybe that was what she wrote about. She didn't really know.

Tillie watched now as Kate rounded the corner of the house, impatiently pulled along by her son, and then they both stopped and Tygue grinned broadly and held tightly to his mother's hand. He was still such a little boy, yet now and then he seemed very grown up, probably because his mother often talked to him as though he were already a man. But that wouldn't do him any harm. Tillie had done that to her own boys, after their father died. It brought back memories, watching the boy look up at his mother in front of the patch of garden they'd worked on all day while she was gone.

"We made it for you. Half of it's flowers and half of it's vegetables. Tillie said we should do vegetables so you could make salads. You know, peppers and stuff. And next week we're gonna do herbs. You like herbs?" He looked suddenly dubious. Herbs sounded like girl stuff to him. "I want to plant pumpkins. And coconuts." Kate grinned, and bent to kiss him again.

"It's beautiful, Tygue."

"No, it isn't. But it will be. We planted all kinds of flowers. We bought all the seeds last week. And I hid them." That was what that look of mystery had been about this morning. It was his first garden.

"He did all the hard work too." Tillie walked up to him and patted his shoulder. "He's going to be mighty proud when he sees what a fine garden he planted too. Won't be long."

"Tomatoes too."

For a moment, Kate felt herself fighting tears, and then suddenly she wanted to laugh. She had worried about him all day, and he had been planting her a garden. What a beautiful world it was. No matter how fast she drove on the freeway.

"You know something, Tygue? This is the most beautiful present anyone's ever given me."

"For real? How come?"

"Because you worked so hard at it, and because it's alive. And because we'll watch it grow, and get good things to eat from it, and pretty flowers. That's quite a present, sweetheart."

"Yeah." He looked around, doubly impressed with himself, and then shook hands soberly with Tillie, as the two women tried not to laugh. It was a beautiful

108

moment, and then Tillie looked up, as though she had just remembered something.

"You got a call." Felicia obviously. Kate nodded, pleased but not overly interested. "From New York."

"New York?" For a moment, there was a tiny catch somewhere in her heart. New York? It couldn't be. Probably something stupid like the main office of her insurance company. Something like that. She'd gotten wound up over nothing before. She knew better now. After six years, she knew.

"They want you to call back."

"Too late now." It was already five-thirty in the West, three hours later in the East. Kate didn't look particularly upset.

Tillie nodded in her easygoing, never-hurried country way. "Yeah. He said it might be too late. Left a number you could call in L.A."

The something in her heart caught again. Harder this time. This was ridiculous. She was playing games with herself. Why was she so damn jumpy today?

"I wrote it all down inside."

"I'd better go take a look." And then she looked down at Tygue with a tender smile, and her voice softened again.

"Thank you for my beautiful garden, sweetheart. I love it—and I love you." She stooped for a moment and held him tight, and then hand in hand they walked toward the house, with Bert loping along beside them as best his stumpy legs would allow. "Want a cup of coffee, Tillie?" But the older woman shook her head.

"I've got to get home. Jake's kids are coming by tonight for supper, and I've got some things to do." The usual understatement. Jake had nine kids. There would be dinner for twelve. More, if assorted boy friends and girl friends came too, which they often did. Tillie was always prepared.

She got into her truck with a wave, and then hung out the window. "You going up to teach again this week, Kate?" It was funny she should ask, and Kate looked at her with a barely perceptible frown. She always went twice, but she had wondered the same thing herself on the way home today. She just didn't feel like going the second time this week.

"Can I let you know tomorrow?" It wouldn't alter what she paid Tillie—a set amount, once a month, to baby-sit twice a week. It was easier just writing one check a month, and the arrangement suited them both. If she decided to go to a movie in the evening, she just dropped Tygue off at Tillie's place on the way, and picked him up on her way home. Tillie didn't charge her for that, he was just like one of the "grand-kids." But Kate hardly ever did that. She spent her evenings at the typewriter. And going out at night still made her long for Tom. It was easier to stay home.

"Sure, call me tomorrow, or the day after if you want, Kate. The day's yours, one way or the other."

"Thanks." Kate smiled and waved, as she gently pushed Tygue ahead of her into the house. Maybe she would take a day off, and skip seeing Tom later in the week. Maybe she could plant some more things in the garden with Tygue. What a super idea Tillie had had. Why didn't she think of things like that?

"What's for dinner?" He threw himself on the kitchen floor with Bert, spewing mud around him on the clean floor as his mother grimaced.

"I'm going to make you eat mud pies, kiddo, if you don't get into the bathroom and get clean in about fourteen seconds. And take Bert with you."

"Come on, Mom . . . I wanna watch . . ."

"You'd better watch some soap and water, mister,

and I mean it!" She pointed determinedly toward the bathroom and then Tillie's message caught her eye and she remembered the call from New York. It turned out to be from the New York office of the agency she used in Los Angeles to sell her books. All the publishers were in New York, so her agent just shipped her manuscripts there, and let the eastern office handle it. Her Los Angeles agent did hold her hand a lot, and would get into the act if she ever sold a film, but the very thought of selling a film made her laugh. That was the stuff of writers' fantasies. Only novices believed they really had a chance. She knew better now, and she was just damn grateful to sell a book now and then, even if it was only for a lousy two thousand bucks every three years. It helped pad out the small income she still got from Tom's investments.

So she wrote her book, and sent it to the agent in L.A., who would then mail it on to New York. And then New York would take two months even to tell her they knew she was alive, and after that—with any luck at all—they sold the book. Then she got a check from them, and twice a year she got royalty statements from the publishers. It was no more exciting than that. The first time it had taken them almost a year to sell her book, the second time it had taken them that long to tell her the new book stank and they couldn't sell it. This last time they had told her they were "hopeful." But they had taken almost two years to sell it. That had been a year ago. And it finally would be out in another month. All of which was reasonable by publishing standards. She knew that publishers sometimes sat on a book for two or three years before publishing it. She had been given an advance of three thousand dollars, and that would be that. It didn't even disappoint her anymore. Just a nice polite print run of five thousand books, and eventually she would see it in her local bookstore if she took the trouble to go down there to look for it. And a year later it would be out of print. It would go as quietly as it had come. But at least she'd have written it. And she was pleased about this one. It was a little unnerving to think this book might actually sell. Its subject was a little too close to home. She had almost hoped it wouldn't sell, in case someone remembered her. But how could they? Publishers didn't advertise the work of relatively unknown authors. And who was Kaitlin Harper? No one. She was safe. The book was a novel, but there was a lot in it about professional football, and the kind of pressure that was put on the players and their wives. Writing it had done her good. It had freed her of some of the old ghosts. There was a lot in it about Tom, the Tom she had loved, not the Tom who had snapped.

"Mom, did you start dinner yet?" His voice woke her out of her reverie. She had been standing by the phone for almost five minutes, thinking about the book, and wondering what the agency had wanted. Maybe something was wrong. A delay. They wouldn't bring it out in a month after all. They'd make her wait another year. So what? She'd gotten her advance. And she had been playing with an idea for another novel anyway. Besides, her real life was car pools for Tygue and mud on the kitchen floor. What difference did it make that she was a writer? Except to her.

"No, I haven't started dinner yet."

"But I'm hungry." He was suddenly whining and dirty—a tired little kid. He had worked hard all day, and it was starting to show. But she was tired too.

"Tygue"—the word was a sigh on her lips—"will you please take your bath, and then I'll get dinner. I have a phone call to make first."

"Why?" From child to beast in one quick minute.

But he was only six. She had to remind herself of that at times.

"It's for business. Now come on, sweetheart. Be a sport."

"Oh . . . all right . . ." He left, grumbling, with Bert sliding along behind him, nibbling at his heels. "But I'm *hungry!*"

"I know. So am I!" Damn. She didn't want to snap at him. It was twenty to six. She dialed the agency's number in Los Angeles, wondering if anyone would even be there. If not, she'd call New York in the morning. But the phone was answered quickly, and the receptionist put her through to the man she normally dealt with: Stuart Weinberg. She had never met him. But after speaking for years on the phone, they felt like old pals.

"Stu? Kate Harper. How've you been?"

"Fine." She always imagined what he looked like, young, short, thin, nervous, and probably good-looking, with very dark hair and expensive Los Angeles clothes. Tonight he sounded as though he were in a good mood. "How've you been, out there in the boonies?"

"We're not that far from L.A. The boonies, what a thing to say!" But they were both laughing. It was a game they played whenever they spoke.

"Listen," she went on. "I got a call from Bill Parsons in New York. The message is a little garbled, but it says to call him, or call you if I got back too late to call him, which I did. I didn't even think you'd be in this late."

"See how hard we work for you, madam? Burning the midnight oil, working our fingers to stumps . . ."

"Stop. You're making me sick."

"Sorry. I just thought I deserved a little sympathy."

"Mom! I'm hungry!" The voice warbled out from

113

the bathroom with suddenly loud splashing sounds, and Bert started to bark. Jesus.

"Cool it in there!"

"What?" Weinberg sounded momentarily confused, and Kate laughed.

"Crazy hour around here, I'm afraid. I think my kid is drowning the dog."

"Fine idea." He chuckled and Kate fumbled for a cigarette. She didn't know why, but he was making her nervous.

'Stu?"

"Yes, ma'am?" There was something funny in his voice. The way Tygue had sounded at breakfast, before planting his surprise garden.

"Do you know why Parsons wanted me to call you?"

"I do."

"Well?" Why was he doing this? It was killing her.

"Are you sitting down?"

"They're not going to publish the book?" Her heart sank. She could already feel tears well up in her eyes. Another bomb. She'd blown it again. She'd never publish another one. And this one had been so good.

"Kate—" There was an interminable pause as she squeezed her eyes closed and tried to force herself to listen to him. "Today has been a fairly incredible day, love. Parsons closed a deal in New York. And I closed one out here. Your publisher sold your paperback rights, and I sold your movie." Her mouth opened, her eyes filled, and no sound emerged. And then suddenly everything happened at once. Tears, words, confusion, chaos. Her heart was pounding and so was her head.

"Oh my God." And then she laughed in the midst of it all. "Oh my God!"

"Kate, you won't remember a thing I tell you, but we'll talk again tomorrow. In fact, we're going to be

114

doing a whole lot of talking in the next weeks and months. Contracts, plans, publicity. Lots of talking. And I think that you should come to Los Angeles so we can celebrate."

"Can't we do it over the phone?" Panic had crept through the elation. What was happening?

"We'll discuss everything later. Anyway, the paperback rights sold for four hundred and fifty thousand dollars. And"—there was another endless pause—"I sold the movie for one twenty-five. You have to split the paperback money with your publisher fifty-fifty, but that's still one hell of a figure."

"Good lord, Stu, that still makes—two twenty-five?" She was dumbstruck. What did it all mean?

"All told, you stand to make three hundred and fifty thousand dollars. Not to mention royalties, the exposure, and what this could mean for the future of your career. Baby, this could be a quick ride to success. In fact, I'd say you're already there. Parsons spoke to the hardcover publisher today, and they're upping the second print order to twenty-five thousand copies. For hardcover, that's beautiful."

"They are? It is?"

"Mom, I need a towel!"

"Shut up!"

"Take it easy, Kate."

"Yeah I don't know what to say. I never thought this would happen."

"This is just the beginning."

Oh God, and then what if someone remembered about Tom? What if someone made the connection between her and what had happened six and a half years ago? What if . . .

"Kate?"

"I'm sorry, Stu. I'm just sitting here, trying to absorb it."

"You won't be able to. Just sit there and relax, and we'll talk tomorrow. Okay?"

"Okay. And Stu . . . I don't know what to say. I . . . it just knocks me out . . . it's . . . you . . ."

"Congratulations, Kate."

She blew out a long sigh and grinned at the phone. "Thanks." It took another minute to get to her feet after she hung up, and even begin to gather her thoughts. Three hundred and fifty thousand dollars? Jesus. And what about the rest of it? What did he mean, this was only the beginning? What . . .

"Mom!" Oh Lord.

"I'm coming!"

And there, in the bathroom, was the reality of her life. Tygue Harper was sitting in the bathtub with his dog, wearing a cowboy hat, and splashing three inches of water into the hall.

"What the hell are you doing?" She could hardly stand up on the wave of soap and water swishing under her feet on the bathroom tile. "For chrissake, Tygue!" Anger exploded in her eyes and the boy looked suddenly hurt.

"But I made you a garden!"

"And I sold a movie! I . . . oh Tygue . . ." She sat down in the river on the bathroom floor, grinning at her son, with tears spilling from her eyes. "I sold a movie!"

"You did?" He looked at her somberly for a moment, as she grinned through her tears and nodded. "Why?"

CHAPTER 8

"What do you mean it makes sense to you?" It had been three days since the news, and she was on the phone to Felicia for at least the seventeenth time.

"Kate, for chrissake, you're talking about making a fortune. He's not just going to mail those contracts to you. He wants to explain them to you." Felicia was trying to sound soothing, but she was failing dismally. She was too excited to sound anything but elated, and pushy.

"But why here? All these years we've dealt perfectly happily at this distance. And . . . oh shit, Licia. I should never have written the damn book." She sounded agonized.

"Are you crazy?"

"What if someone finds out? What if there's more of that bullshit that almost drove me nuts six years ago? Do you have any idea what it was like to be constantly hunted by reporters? They lived outside the house, they squeezed into my car with me, Jesus, they practically knocked me down the stairs. Why the hell do you think I came down here?"

"I know all that, Kate. But that was a long time ago. It's not news anymore."

"How do you know that? How does anyone? Maybe those maniacs would revive it. What if they found out where Tom was? What would that do to Tygue? Just

117

think of it, Licia!" She paled at the thought, but in her office in San Francisco Felicia was unsympathetically shaking her head.

"You should have thought of that when you wrote the book. The fact is, it's a damn good book, and it's a *novel*, Kate. No one is going to know it's true. Will you please relax for chrissake? You're driving yourself into a frenzy for nothing."

"I won't see Weinberg."

"You're being impossible, dammit." But Kate had already hung up, and was frantically dialing the agency in L.A. He might not have left yet. He said he'd arrive around three. It wasn't quite noon. But his secretary told her he had left an hour before.

"Damn."

"Sorry?"

"Nothing."

She dialed Felicia back in San Francisco, and her friend sounded grim. "You'd better get a hold of yourself, Kate. You're getting out of hand. I told you this would happen when I read the book."

"I thought you were just saying it. And who gets known with a book, dammit? Who sells paperback *and* film? Jesus, I know writers who sell on the back shelves of the dime store forever."

"And you're crying that that's not you?" Felicia was exasperated and Kate sighed again.

"No, I'm not crying that that's not me. I just don't know what to do, Licia. I've hardly seen anybody in six years, and this guy is coming up here from L.A. to discuss hundreds of thousands of dollars with me. I'm so damn scared I can't see straight."

"Come on, baby, you can deal with this." Her voice softened as she thought of Kate. "You're a pro. You're a hell of a writer, a beautiful girl, you're twenty-nine years old, and you're on the threshold of success.

Christ, you could meet this guy wearing burlap and a mudpack and you'd do fine."

"That's about all I've got to wear."

"That's your own goddamn fault. You haven't let me send you anything in years."

"I don't wear anything. Anyway, what to wear is not the problem. What to say . . . what to do . . . he wants to talk publicity. Jesus, Licia, I can't deal with it." She was near tears and chain-smoking nervously.

"What exactly did he say about publicity?" Felicia sounded intrigued.

"Nothing exactly. He just mentioned the possibility of it. But he didn't explain."

"You're damn right he didn't." The deep, husky laugh rang in Kate's ears. "Has it ever occurred to you that he doesn't know if you have three heads or two, or if you wear curlers and pink suede sneakers to church?"

"Which means that I have about two and a half hours to come up with curlers and pink sneakers. Wait, I have an idea." Now Kate was laughing too. "I'll get Tillie to stand in for me." Felicia laughed.

"Nope. You face the music. You meet the guy. He is your agent, after all. He isn't going to throw you to the lions, and he can't make you do anything."

"What'll I say to him?" It had been six and a half years since she'd been alone with a man.

"He's not going to rape you, Kate. Not unless you get very lucky."

"You're terrific. Dammit, how did I get myself into this?"

"Your big mouth, your fine mind, and your typewriter. But it's a hell of a good combo." Kate sighed again in answer, and Felicia shook her head with a grin. The earthquake was just beginning. And the aftershocks might be felt for months. Even years.

"Anyway, I'd better get off the phone and find something to wear."

"Yeah. And Kate?"

"What?"

"Zip up your fly."

"Oh shut up." She was smiling when she hung up, but the palms of her hands were drenched. What if he did put the make on her? What if he was a pushy jerk? What if . . . She sat outside in the sunshine for half an hour, trying to calm down, thinking. Of the book, of Tom, of Felicia, of Tygue. Why had she written it? Because she had had to. Because the story had been tearing her up inside and she had needed to get it out, and she had. It was a beautiful book and she knew it. But she hadn't expected this. She had wanted the book to sell, but she hadn't expected it to affect her life. And now what? Once she opened the door to publicity, her secluded life would be over, all her efforts to protect Tygue futile. But it was too late now and she knew it. She had just finished dressing when Stu Weinberg rang the bell. She took a deep breath, stubbed out her cigarette, looked around the living room, and walked to the door. She was wearing black slacks and a black sweater, and a pair of expensive Italian suede loafers that had survived the years. She looked very tall and very thin, and very serious as she opened the door.

"Kate Harper?" He looked a little uncertain, and not at all the way she'd pictured him. He was about her height, and had bright red hair. He was wearing Levis and a beige cashmere sweater. But the shoes were Gucci, the briefcase Vuitton, the watch Cartier, the jacket slung over one arm was the classic Bill Blass. All the status accouterments of Los Angeles. But he had the face of a kid, and ten thousand freckles. It made her smile and she had to laugh at the idea that this was the guy she had entrusted her career to for six years. Maybe if she had seen him, she wouldn't have. He looked about twenty-two. But he was forty-one, the same age as Felicia.

"Stu?" She smiled at him from the doorway.

"I know, I know. You want to see my driver's license and you want to tear up your contract immediately. Right?"

"Hardly. Come in." She waved him inside, wondering if the house looked shabby or merely comfortable. She watched him summing her up, and then casting a quick eye around the room. He looked intrigued. "Coffee?"

He nodded, and put his jacket and briefcase on a chair as he looked out the window. "It's a beautiful view here." She stood very quietly for a minute, and was surprised at how peaceful she felt. He wasn't the enemy. He was a harmless man who wanted to help her make money. And he looked like a nice guy.

"It is pretty. And I'm glad you came all this way to see me."

"So am I."

She poured him a cup of coffee and they both sat down.

"Kate, can I ask you a crazy question?" The way he smiled made her like him more. He looked like one of Tygue's friends, not like an agent.

"Sure, what's the crazy question?"

"What the hell are you doing here?"

"You said it when you looked out the window. It's pretty. It's peaceful. It's a good place to bring up kids."

"Bullshit."

She laughed at his bluntness and took a sip of coffee. "Not at all."

"Tell me something else? Would you have come to L.A. if I hadn't come here?" With a small smile, she shook her head. "That's what I thought. Why?"

"Because I'm a hermit, and I like it. When I lost my husband, I just . . . I stopped going places."

"Why?"

"I'm busy here." He was coming too close. Suddenly she was scared again.

"What do you do?" The eyes were quick, busy, probing, but not unkind.

"I write, I mother. I teach. I'm busy, that's all."

And scared. Oh Jesus, was she scared. But of what? He couldn't figure it out. Men maybe? People? Life? Something. He couldn't put his finger on it. But it was in her eyes.

"You don't look the part. Did you ever model or act?" Bingo.

"No." She shook her head nervously, smiling as she lit another cigarette. Dammit, there was something about her. And he knew she was lying. The way she sat, moved, walked, all of it spoke of something else. Breeding. Training. Modeling? Or maybe she'd been a stewardess. But she hadn't sat in this nowhere town all her life. And he had noticed her shoes. Eighty-dollar shoes. In Shit Town, U.S.A. But whoever she was, she was going to thrill the publishers, if he could pry her out of her shell. That was why he had come up to see her, to find out just how marketable a property she was. And now he had his answer. Very. If she'd cooperate. He smiled gently at her, and sipped his coffee, thinking she'd look great on TV.

"How many kids do you have?"

"Nine." She laughed at him nervously again. "No, seriously. One. He just acts like nine."

"What's his name?"

"Tygue."

"How does he feel about his mom being a huge success?"

"I don't think he's figured all that out yet. As a matter of fact," she sighed and let her shoulders relax for a minute, "neither have I."

"You don't need to worry about it for a while, Kate. In fact, you don't need to worry about it at all. We'll handle it for you. All you need to do now is look over the contracts, and then spend the next month enjoying yourself. You know, buy new curtains, a new ball for the kid, a bone for the dog . . ." He glanced around innocently and she laughed. He had gotten the message: she liked the simple life. But she also knew that he was refusing to take that seriously.

"What happens when the book comes out?"

"Nothing for a couple of weeks." He was stalling her.

"And then?"

"Then you make a few appearances for the book, do a couple of interviews. No more than you can handle."

"And if I don't?"

"The book suffers. It's as simple as that. It's statistically proven." He looked serious as he said it.

"Is it in my contract that I have to?"

Regretfully he shook his head. "No. Nobody can force you to do any of it. But it would be a big mistake for you not to, Kate. If you had buck teeth, a big nose, and crossed eyes, well, then I'd say that maybe you ought to consider skipping any appearances, but under the circumstances"—he looked at her with a rueful smile—"you could do a hell of a good job, Kate." And he didn't give a damn what she said, when he watched her walk across the room again, he knew she'd been a model. What intrigued him most, though, was the impenetrable shield around her. He had never sensed that on the phone. Now he wondered why he had never been curious about meeting her. He had to confess, though, that he had never expected her to be a biggie, not until the last book. *A Final Season.* He hadn't thought she'd been capable of a book like that. "We can talk about the publicity stuff later. Why don't we check out some of the points they'll want in the contract first?"

"Okay. More coffee?"

"Thanks." He devoured five cups of coffee in the two hours it took to sort out the contracts. And now she knew more than ever why she liked him as her agent. He was suddenly the same man he had been on the phone for all these years. He explained every possible inference, statement, danger, benefit, every line, every word, every nuance. He did one hell of a good job.

"Jesus, you should have been a lawyer."

"I was. For a year." The kid? Howdy Doody with the freckles a lawyer? When? She grinned at the thought. "I hated it. This is a lot more my speed."

"Mine too." She thought of the three hundred and fifty thousand dollars again.

"You've got that look, Kate. Just don't let it go to your head."

"Not a chance, Stu. Not a chance." She said it with a rocklike certainty and a faintly bitter smile. "This is strictly for new curtains and a bone for the dog."

"Glad to hear it. But just in case you pull up outside my office in a new Rolls, say in three months—what do I get for being right?"

"A kick in the pants?"

"We'll see." He grinned broadly.

She heard the car pool roll up outside then. It was already five-fifteen. They had worked hard. "Would you like to stay for dinner?" Dinner. Meat loaf, macaroni and cheese, carrots and Jello. The idea made her want to laugh, but he was shaking his head and looking at the flat-faced Roman-numeraled watch that looked like a Dali painting draped over his wrist.

"I'd love to, Kate. But I have a dinner date at eight in L.A."

"Beverly Hills, I hope."

"Is there anywhere else?" They laughed together, and Kate walked to the door to greet Tygue. Stu Weinberg watched the boy come in, throw a quick hug around his mother, and then come to a sudden halt when he saw him.

"Hi, Tygue. My name's Stu." He reached out a hand but the boy didn't move.

"Who's he?" Tygue looked almost stricken.

"This is my agent from Los Angeles, sweetheart. Don't you have a better hello than that?" Tygue looked as frightened as his mother, and Stu instantly felt for the boy. He looked as though he were as unaccustomed to strangers as Kate.

Tygue grudgingly approached and held out a hand. "'Lo." His mother glowered, and Stu slowly put the contracts back in the briefcase.

"Well, Kate, nothing left for you to do but relax." She had signed everything.

"What about the other matter?"

"What?" But he knew. Let her say it. Let her try it out.

"The publicity."

"Don't worry about it."

"Stu . . . I can't do it."

"Can't or won't?" His eyes were very hard on hers.

"Won't."

"Okay." He sounded very calm. Too calm. And all the while, Tygue watched silently.

"You mean it?"

"Sure. I told you. No one can make you do it. You're

foolish if you don't. But it's your book, your decision, your royalty check, your career. It's your trip, baby. I just work for you." He made her feel small somehow, stupid and cowardly. If he had known, he'd have been pleased.

"I'm sorry."

"Then think about it. And I'll keep the publicity directors of both the publishing houses off your back until you decide. Okay?"

"Okay." He let her feel that she had won something, but she wasn't sure what. They shook hands at the door, and she watched as he backed a long plum-colored Jaguar out of her driveway.

She waved from the doorway, and Tygue watched her as Stu smiled at them both from the car. All three of them suddenly knew that everything was about to change.

CHAPTER 9

"You survived it?" Felicia called after Tygue had gone to bed.

"Yes. I survived it. Actually, he's a very nice guy. I suspect that underneath the veneer, he's a pushy sonofabitch, but I like him."

"Damn right he's pushy. How do you think he got you that fortune you just made?"

Kate laughed at the thought. "Good point. If I'd looked at it that way, I'd really have gotten nervous. You know what's amazing though, Licia?"

"Yeah. You."

"No. Seriously. After all these years. I wasn't that scared talking to him. We sat here like regular people, drinking coffee, looking at the contracts. It was really very civilized."

"You're in love?" Felicia sounded amused.

"Christ, no. He looks like Alice in Wonderland's kid brother, with carrot-red hair yet. But he's a good agent. And I didn't have a heart attack from talking to a man." Felicia was pleased for her.

"Okay. So now what?"

"What do you mean, now what?"

"I mean what happens next?"

"Nothing. I put the money in the bank, I send Tygue to college. Stu suggested we buy Bert a new bone"—she grinned—"and I might just buy those pink suede sneakers we discussed this morning."

"You're leaving something out, dear one." Felicia sounded sarcastic and determined again. Kate knew that voice only too well. "What about publicity for the book?"

"He says I don't have to."

"I don't believe you."

"That's what he said."

"Didn't he ask you to?" Felicia was floored.

"Yes."

"So?"

"I said I wouldn't do it."

"You know, you're an ingrate and a bitch, Kate Harper, and if I were your agent, I'd kick your ass from one side of the room to the other."

"That's why you're not my agent, and he is."

"He let you off the hook that easy?"

"Yup." Kate sounded like her son as she grinned.

"Then he's crazy." Either that, or very very smart. She suddenly wondered.

"Maybe so. Anyway, I signed the contracts and I'm all through. Finished. Until the next book."

"What a drag." Felicia was smiling to herself.

"What do you mean 'what a drag'?"

"I mean just that. You crank them out, stay up late, smoke a lot, drink a lot of coffee, and you don't even get to do any of the fun stuff. You don't even get to spend the money."

"Why the hell not?"

"On what? Groceries? What a drag. The least you could do for yourself is go on a spree somewhere civilized. L. A., here, Santa Barbara. Hell, you could even go shopping in Carmel."

"I don't need anything new to wear."

"Obviously. You don't go anywhere." And why did that make her a failure? Why did she have to go, dress, do, be in order to not "be a drag"? Why wasn't just writing the book enough, dammit? Besides, maybe she would do some shopping in Carmel the next time she saw Tom. And that was another thing. She had to go tomorrow.

"Listen, Licia, I'm not going to get into a hassle with you about this. Anyway, I've got to get off the phone."

"Anything wrong?"

"No. I have to call Tillie."

"Okay, love." Felicia sounded cool and distant when they hung up, and she wondered if she'd gotten through at all. But maybe . . .

At her end, Kate made plans with Tillie for the next day, and then took a hot bath and went to bed. It had been a nerve-racking day, and she had none of the feelings she wanted to have. She wanted to feel proud of herself, and instead she just felt annoyed, as though she had failed at something. At last she fell asleep. Until the alarm woke her at six.

"You teaching again, Mom?" Tygue looked at her over breakfast, only this morning he whined the question, and it annoyed her.

"Yes, love. Tillie'll be here for you."

"I don't want Tillie."

"You can work on the garden. You'll have a good time. Eat your cereal."

"It's not crunchy enough."

"Come on, Tygue."

"Yerghk! There's a bug on my toast!" He pushed it away and Bert grabbed it off the edge of the table with a contented smacking of his lips.

"Goddammit, Tygue!" And then suddenly there

were tears in his eyes, and she felt awful. It was a hell of a way to start the morning. She sat down again and held out her arms. He came to them slowly, but he came. "What's up, love? Something bothering you?"

"I hate him."

"Who?"

"Him."

Now what? "Who, for heaven's sake?" She was too tired to play games.

"The man . . . the one in that chair."

"You mean yesterday?"

He nodded.

"But he's my agent, sweetheart. He sells my books."

"I don't like him."

"That's silly." Tygue shrugged and the car pool honked. "Never mind about him. Okay?" He shrugged again, and she grabbed at him and held him fast. "I love you and only you. You got that, mister?" A small smile crept back to his face. "So relax and have a good day."

"Okay." He grabbed his jacket, patted Bert, and headed for the door. " 'Bye, Mom."

" 'Bye, love." But when he left, she realized that she was angry at him. What was his problem? Jealous of Stu Weinberg? But it was hardly surprising. He had never seen a man in their house before. And it was time he got used to at least an occasional stranger. But still his recalcitrance made her feel pushed. He was pulling her one way, they were pulling the other. Everyone wanted something from her. And what did she want? She wasn't sure. And she didn't even have time to ask herself. She had to get going if she wanted to see Tom . . . wanted to see Tom . . . wanted . . . what an amazing idea. It suddenly made her stop dead in the middle of the kitchen. *Did* she want to see Tom? She hadn't thought of it that way in years. She *went to* see Tom. But did she *want* to see him? Probably. Of course. She picked up her bag, patted Bert, and left, without answering the phone.

CHAPTER 10

Kate stood up and stretched. She had only been with him for two hours and she was already tired. Tom was in a tiresome mood. Even Mr. Erhard looked worn out.

"Come on, love. Why don't we take a walk to the boat pond?" There was silver threaded into his hair now, but he still had the clear, happy face of a child. Happy most of the time anyway. But sometimes he had the fretful nervousness of a child in distress.

"I don't want to go to the boat pond. I want Willie."

"Then let's go get Willie."

"I don't want Willie."

Kate tightened her jaw and closed her eyes for a minute. Then she opened them again with a bright smile. "Want to lie in your hammock?" He shook his head in answer, and looked as though he was going to cry. In fact he looked just the way Tygue had that morning. But Tygue had been jealous of her agent. What was Tom's problem? And dammit, he was so easy sometimes, so lovable. Why did he have to be like this today? She had enough on her mind.

"I'm sorry, Katie." He looked up at her and held out his arms. It was as though he suddenly understood, and she felt guilty as she took him in her arms, leaning down to reach him in his chair.

"It's all right, sweetheart. I guess you just need some new games." It had been months since she'd brought him any. And then she had brought him the ones Tygue had just outgrown. Cast-off games and puzzles from his son. But she didn't see it that way. It was just cheaper buying one set than two. She held him close as she leaned over him and she felt him tighten his grip on her. For the strangest moment, she had an urge to kiss him. Like a man, not like a little boy.

"All I need is you, Katie. You don't have to bring games."

Just hearing him say that gave her the oddest feeling. She pulled away suddenly and looked into his eyes. But there was no one there. No one but Tom, the child. Not the man.

"I love you too." She sat down on the grass next to him, holding his hand, and the irritation of the first half of the day started to fade. For a moment she wanted to tell him what was happening. The book, the movie, what it all meant . . .

"Want to play Bingo?" He looked down at her sunnily, and she smiled a small tired smile, with her head tilted to one side. She had worn an old lavender wool skirt and soft matching cashmere sweater. He had bought them for her shortly after they were married. He had loved them. Once. Now he didn't notice or remember. He wanted to play Bingo. "Want to?"

"You know what, love? I'm kind of tired. In fact . . ." She took a deep breath and stood up. She had played enough games for one day. With Tygue, with Tom, with herself. "In fact, I think it's time for me to go home."

"No, it's not!" He looked heartbroken. Oh Jesus. No! She didn't want him pulling at her too. "It's not time to go!"

"Yes it is, my love. But I'll be back in a couple of days."

"No, you won't."

"Yes, I will." She smoothed the soft lilac skirt and looked up at him as Mr. Erhard approached. He had Willie and some books under one arm. "Oh, look what Mr. Erhard has for you." But Tom looked like a sad, angry little boy. "Be a good boy, darling. I'll be back soon." He held her close for a minute, and for the first time in a long time it tore at her soul again. She needed him now. And he wasn't there. "I love you." She said it softly and then backed away with a wave and a too bright smile in her eyes. But Tom was already holding Willie and reaching out for his books.

Kate walked back to the car with her head bowed and her arms tightly crossed, as though giving herself the hug she suddenly felt she needed so badly. And then as she slid into the car, she sighed and looked up at the trees. It was crazy. She had so much. She had Tygue, in a way she still had Tom, and she had just sold a book and a movie. She had just made three hundred and fifty thousand dollars, and she felt like a kid with a busted balloon.

"This is crazy!" She said it out loud and then laughed and lit a cigarette as she started the car. And then she had a better idea. She sat back for a minute with a mischievous smile, forgetting where she was and why she was there. Or rather, remembering where she was in a way she hadn't in years. Carmel. For six and a half years she had come to see Tom, and she had never driven the last twelve miles into town. Never gone to see the shops. Never had lunch there. Never walked along the main street. Never sat on the beach for an hour to unwind. Six and a half years and she had traveled the same well-worn path back and forth. And suddenly, she had a wild urge to drive into town. Just to see it. To wander along a little bit . . . the shops . . . the people . . . she looked at her watch. She was early. She had cut the visit short by almost two hours today. Two hours. With a grin she released the brake and turned left when she reached the road. Left. The road to town.

It was a pretty road bordered with palm trees, and eventually little pastel cottages dotted the road. She was coming closer to Carmel. Nothing looked familiar yet, but her heart was pounding horribly. God, what was she doing? Why now? In two days she was venturing farther out into the world than she had in almost seven years. She had let Stu Weinberg come up to see her from L.A., and now she was going into Carmel. Such tiny acts, but they were a chink in the wall she had built. And then what? What would come next? A torrent? A flood? Or a slow trickle of the outside world over a long period of time? What if it got out of hand? What if . . . she couldn't go on. She pulled the car off the road, and stopped. She was almost out of breath, and the road suddenly looked menacing instead of inviting.

"I can't." Her voice trembled as she said it, and there were tears backed up in her throat. "I can't . . ." But she wanted to. Dammit, she wanted to. For the first time in years, she wanted to see what the place looked like, what they were wearing, how their hair was done. It was crazy to care about nonsense like that. But in the town where she had made her home they were still wearing teased beehives and mini-skirts ten years past their prime on bodies thirty years past theirs. She wanted to see people who looked like people she had known. But what about all the decisions she had made, everything she had chosen? It was threatened now. She had written a book that told more than it should have, of Tom, of herself, of her life. And the damn thing was going to be splashed all over the country. Hundreds of thousands of copies, and a movie . . . and . . .

"Bullshit." She opened her eyes wide and looked around as she eased the car back on the road. She *had* sold a book and a movie, she had a right to an hour in Carmel. Her face set into a mask of determination and she stepped on the gas. And suddenly things started looking familiar. Nothing had changed very much in all the years since she'd last been there. The pastel-colored cottages looked the same, the bends in the road, the quaint little hotels, and then suddenly the main tree-lined street leading right to the beach two blocks away. And along those two blocks, dozens of tiny boutiques. A few tourist traps, but for the most part they were elegant stores. A world she hadn't seen in six years. Gucci, Hermes, Jourdan, Dior, Norrell, Galanos, Givenchy . . . names, labels, scarves, perfume, shoes, she saw it all as she drove slowly down the street and slid into a parking place. It felt good now. She was glad she had come. She was even smiling broadly to herself as she hopped out of the car.

The first thing that caught her eye was an exquisite cream-colored silk suit in a shop window. They were showing it with a peach-colored blouse, and cream-colored shoes with a tiny gold chain that looped around a naked heel. She felt like a little girl again. She wanted the bride doll and the teddy bear and the doll with the stockings and the bra and . . . she practically giggled as she walked into the shop. She was suddenly glad she had worn the old cashmere sweater and skirt. They had weathered well. And she had worn her long hair in a loose ladylike knot at the nape of her neck. Today, she hadn't even let it down for Tom.

"Madame?" The woman who ran the shop was obviously French, and she looked at Kate with a measuring glance in her eyes. She was a small, trim woman with graying blond hair, and she was wearing a gray silk dress and a rather staggering triple strand of pearls. But Kate still remembered that side of Carmel. People dressed. Shopkeepers, restaurateurs, visitors, natives. Only the handful of "artists" in the area looked artsy craftsy. Everyone else looked as though they were going to Maxim's for lunch. "May I help you?"

"May I just look?"

"But of course." The woman was gracious, and turned her attention to the latest copy of *L'Officiel* on her desk. Kate remembered modeling for them once. A thousand years ago. And then the suit in the window caught her eye. The woman in the gray silk dress looked up with a smile. She hadn't wanted to suggest it, but she had thought of it immediately. And then their eyes met and Kate laughed. There was laughter dancing in the other woman's eyes as well.

"May I?"

"I'd love to see it on you. We just got it in."

"From Paris?"

"New York. Halston." Halston. How long had it been since she'd felt those kinds of fabrics? Seen the clothes? And what the hell did it matter, dammit, except somehow . . . it did. Now it did. She needed to celebrate her success.

She grabbed three dresses and a skirt as the owner of the boutique got the suit off the mannequin with the help of an assistant. Kate was loving every minute of it, and when she tried on the suit, she loved it even more. It was made for her. The peach blouse turned her pale, delicate skin to a warm rosy blush, and her green eyes danced as she looked at the suit. It flowed over her body. The skirt was mid-calf and draped itself around her like a caress, the jacket was long and feminine and graceful. She tried the shoes on too, and she felt like a princess, or maybe even a queen. The suit was two hundred and eighty-five dollars. The shoes were eighty-six. Shameful. Sinful. And where in God's name would she wear it all? It was what she had been telling Felicia for years. Where would she use stuff like that? At the supermarket? In the car pool, taking Tygue and his little buddies to school? Bathing Bert?

"I'll take it." And in a hasty gesture she added the red wool skirt and print blouse and the high-necked, long-sleeved black dress she had tried on first. It looked terribly grown up and almost too serious, but it was so damn elegant. And subtly sexy. Sexy? That was crazy too. Whom did she need to look sexy for? Willie the Bear? What in hell was she doing? She was spending just slightly over five hundred dollars on clothes she would probably never wear. Maybe she could get away with the cream silk suit at Tygue's college graduation. But even then, only if he went to Princeton or Yale. The idea made her grin as she wrote out the check. She was going nuts. It was all that money those lunatics in Hollywood and New York were going to be paying her. It was a delicious kind of craziness though, and she reveled in it. She even added a tiny bottle of perfume, the kind she had worn years before. And it was only as she walked back to the car with her arms full of bundles that she noticed where she had parked. The hotel where she and Tom had stayed on their last visit to Carmel . . . their hotel . . .

"Not anymore." She said it softly and looked away as she put the packages in the trunk. Maybe she'd leave them there. Maybe she'd sell them with the car. She didn't need them after all. But as she thought of them again, she couldn't wait to try on the suit again when she got home. And the black dress. Tygue would think she was crazy. She'd wait until he went to bed.

She drove home faster than she ever had before. This time, she didn't even feel guilty. And the funniest part was that no one knew she had done anything different; no one had to know. Maybe she could even do it again. The idea made her laugh as she turned into the driveway. Right on time. She had used the extra two hours well. She waved at Tillie as she parked the car behind the house. They were busy in the garden again, and Tygue looked a lot happier than he had that morning. He waved at her frantically as he burrowed into his planting.

"Hi, love!" She left the packages in the car and went to kiss him, but he was too busy. Even Bert had a new bone and was off by himself. Kate wandered happily into the house. Everything was just fine. And there was a message from Felicia, saying she'd be down for the weekend.

And she was. She came down with three bottles of champagne, and an armload of presents. Silly presents, fun presents, things for Kate's desk, for her house, for her room, and then from the bottom of the bag of goodies she handed Kate a small silver-wrapped box.

"Not another one!" Kate was still laughing, but Felicia's face had grown quiet and serious and there was a look of tenderness in her eyes. "Oh Jesus, something tells me this one's for real."

"Maybe so."

There was a small neat card stuck into the ribbon of the silver box. Kate opened the card carefully, and read it as tears filled her eyes. "To the lady with the golden heart, all you need is courage. The Cowardly Lion discovered that he had the courage all along. All he needed was a medal to remind him of it. You are hereby reminded that you are not only brave, but able and good and wise and much loved." And it was signed "The Good Witch of the North." Kate smiled through her tears.

"From *The Wizard of Oz*?"

"More or less."

Kate opened the package, and inside, on a blue velvet lining in a red satin box, was a gold watch with a watch chain. It was like a man's, except that the watch was in the shape of a heart, and as Kate turned it over, she saw that on the back was inscribed "For courage, for valor, with love." Kate held the watch tightly clasped in one hand and threw her arms around Licia in a tight, crushing hug. And Licia hugged back. It was a hug Kate had longed for so badly, from someone who would tell her that everything was all right.

"What can I say?" The tears trickled down her face.

"Just say you'll be a good kid and give yourself a chance. That's all I want for you." For a minute, Kate almost wanted to tell her about the shopping spree in Carmel. But she couldn't. Not yet.

"I'll try. Hell, with a watch like that, I almost feel like I have to. Licia, I'd be lost without you."

"No, you wouldn't. You'd relax, and nobody would bug you anymore. It would be heavenly."

"Horseshit."

They both grinned at each other and talked about the book and the contracts and the store. For Kate the romance of success was just beginning. They finished the bottle of champagne just after 4 A.M., sleepily said good night, and went to their beds.

It was a cozy wonderful weekend. Kate wore the new watch pinned to her favorite tee-shirt the next day. They had a picnic, and then took Tygue to the

Adams ranch, where all three of them took out horses and rode over the hills. On Sunday, Licia slept late, while Kate took Tygue to church, and they had a leisurely lunch on the grass after they got back. It was five o'clock before Licia even started to think of leaving. She was lying on the warm grass, looking up at the sky, holding Tygue's hand, and trying to fend off Bert.

"You know, once in a while, Kate, I can understand why you love it here."

"Mmhm." Kate's mind had been a thousand miles away, but she smiled at her friend.

"It's so goddamned peaceful."

Kate laughed at the look on her face. "Is that a complaint or a compliment?"

"Right now a compliment. I really hate to go back. And it'll probably be several months before I can come down again." Kate was looking straight at her as she said it, and there was a strange look in Kate's eyes. "Something wrong?" Felicia had never seen that look before.

"Just thinking."

"What about?"

"Some stuff I've got in the car."

"So?" She wasn't making any sense.

"What are you doing tomorrow, Licia?"

"Oh Jesus. Don't ask. I've got three meetings before lunch, we're coordinating all the fall shows, and the whole winter look."

"And then?"

"What do you mean 'and then'?" Kate was making her nervous. What the hell was she getting at?

"Are you busy for lunch?"

"No. Why? Can I do something for you?"

"Yeah." Kate was grinning now. She just sat there

141

and laughed at Felicia. To hell with it. "As a matter of fact, Miss Norman, there is something you can do for me."

"What?"

"Take me to lunch."

"But I have to go back, you dummy." Felicia sat up now too. And she was smiling, but confused. It was just a silly Sunday.

"I know you have to go back. I'll go with you."

"To San Francisco?" Felicia was grinning broadly now too, with a look of astonishment on her face as Kate nodded.

"Yeah. What the hell."

Felicia threw her arms around her friend and the two women exchanged a ferocious hug of joy, as Tygue watched wide-eyed, with a look of dismay.

"Who'll stay with me?"

Kate looked over at him in surprise, and drew him into the hug. "Tillie, sweetheart. And maybe one of these days I'll take you to San Francsico too."

"Oh." But he didn't look impressed, and in a moment Kate left him with Licia. She had things to do. Tillie to call . . . things to get out of the car and pack . . . things to do. San Francisco. It had been six and a half years.

"Hallelujah!" She could hear Felicia shouting as she walked into the house with a wide grin and her arms full of the clothes she'd bought in Carmel. Kate was going to town.

CHAPTER 11

They had driven along in silence for almost an hour, after the initial excitement and bursts of conversation. They were already more than halfway there, and Kate had just noticed her turnoff in Carmel. Felicia had noticed it too.

"Kate?"

"Hm?"

It was dark in the car, but Felicia could see her profile as she glanced over. She looked no different than she had six and a half years before when Felicia had driven her down to her "retreat." If she had known then how long Kate would hide there, she would never have agreed to find her the house.

"What's bugging you, Licia?" Kate turned to her with a quiet smile.

"What made you change your mind?"

"I don't know that I have, on the whole. I just . . . oh damn. I don't know, Licia. Maybe this crazy thing with the book has thrown me off. I was so damn happy with my life down there, in the hills. The kid, the dog, all of it."

"Bullshit."

Kate glanced over at her sharply. "You don't believe me?"

"No. I think you've been bored for a long time. You wouldn't admit it to me, but I think you knew it. You can't bury yourself alive like that. You have a whole fantasy life in your books, but that's not real and you know it. You're young, Kate. You need people, places to go, trips, men, clothes, success. All of it. You gave up too soon. Tom had his big time. He lived, it, he enjoyed it while it lasted. I think that if he . . . if he were still the same, it would kill him to see you locked up like some old woman. You're not Tillie for chrissake. Anyway, you've heard all that from me before. I'm sorry. I didn't mean to make a speech."

Kate was still smiling in the darkness. "I'd think you didn't love me anymore if you stopped doing that. Anyway, in answer to your question, maybe you're right. Maybe I did know I was bored. Bored isn't really the right word, though. I like my life. I just . . . all of a sudden I just got hungry for more. I wanted to see people. *Real* people. Friday, when I went to see Tom, it was kind of a lousy day and I left early. And for no reason at all, I just got the itchies and drove into Carmel."

"You did?" Kate nodded with guilty pleasure. "You little wretch. You didn't say a thing. What did you do?"

"Spent a fortune." Kate's cackle made Felicia grin.

"On what? I'm dying to know."

"Ridiculous stuff. Clothes. Nothing I need. Jesus, I don't even know where I'll wear them. Or rather, I didn't know where I'd wear them till tonight. Maybe that's why I decided to come up to the city with you. To wear my new clothes." She was only half teasing. She still wasn't entirely sure herself why she'd come. Except that there was this new little demon in her that was beginning to shout "Go! Move! Live! Dream! Spend! Be!" And then she had a sobering thought. "Do you think it's an awful thing to do to

Tygue?" Her eyes loomed large in the darkness as Felicia glanced over at her.

"What, go away for a couple of days? Don't be ridiculous. Most parents do it all the time. It'll do him good."

"Maybe I should have taken more time to prepare him."

"You'd just have backed out." Kate nodded silent agreement and lit a cigarette.

It seemed only moments later when Felicia looked over at her with a smile. "Are you ready?"

"For what?" Kate looked vague and then suddenly she realized what Felicia meant. She had been so engrossed in her own thoughts that she had missed the first landmarks. They were nearing it now.

They were already past the airport. Yes. She was ready. Another two miles, and the freeway rounded the last obscure bend and there it was. Kate sat in silence, smiling slowly, as tears filled her eyes. It was home. No matter how long she stayed away. It was home. The skyline was a little taller, a little more jagged, but in essence it was the same. San Francisco was a city that never changed that much. It always kept the integral part of its personality intact. And its beauty. The TransAmerica spire pointed sharply into the air from downtown. And suddenly Kate allowed herself to think of places she had blotted from her mind for years. The tree-lined streets of Pacific Heights, the little Victorian houses, the yacht club on a summer's night, the Marina on a Sunday morning, the majesty of the Presidio, the sweep of the Golden Gate Bridge, and all the tiny hiding places she had shared with Tom. Just seeing the skyline, as Felicia raced toward the city, brought back a thousand memories she had long since put away in musty old trunks. Now she held them in her hands and they smelled faintly of old familiar perfume. She rolled down the window and let the night air whip her face.

"It's chilly. The fog must be in." Felicia smiled at her and said nothing. Kate really didn't want to talk. She wanted to watch and listen and feel. They were already on the off ramp into the city.

They were on Franklin Street heading north toward the Bay. As the car crested the hills, you could see the lights twinkling on the other side of the Bay. Even the traffic looked sophisticated. Jaguars and Mercedes and Porsches hobnobbing with vans and VWs and an occasional motorcycle zooming by. Everything seemed to be moving very quickly, and everything looked bright and alive. It was ten o'clock on a Sunday night.

Felicia turned right on California Street, and a block later they found themselves following a cable car up the hill as Kate started to laugh.

"Oh God, Licia, I'd forgotten. I love this town. It's all so pretty." Felicia wanted to stand up and shout. Victory! She was back. Maybe she'd even come back for good.

Felicia swooped carefully around the cable car at the top of Nob Hill, and Kate fell silent again as she took in the sober splendors of the cathedral, the Pacific Union Club, the Fairmont and the Mark, and then they were speeding down the other side of the hill into the financial district, with the Ferry Building straight ahead. And Kate was laughing again.

"Okay, Licia. Confess. You did this on purpose, didn't you?"

"What?"

"The guided tour. You know what I mean, you bitch."

"Me?"

"You. But I love it. Don't stop."

"Anything else you want to see?"

"I don't know." So many feelings were being awakened at once that she couldn't decide what she wanted to see next.

"Are you hungry?"

"Sort of."

"Want to stop for something to eat at Vanessi's?"

"Like this?" Kate looked down in horror at the blue jeans, red shirt, and fading espadrilles.

"On a Sunday, who notices? And it's late."

"I don't know, Licia." She looked nervous again, and Felicia waved a hand as she sped up Kearny toward where it met Broadway. And then suddenly they were catapulted into the uproarious vulgarity of Broadway. "Teen Age Co-ed Wrestlers Topless Here," and the usual promises delivered by barkers—"Virgins, all virgins"—side by side with Finocchio's and its female impersonators. In the midst of the madness, the traffic and the trucks coming off the Bay Bridge, Enrico's sat with artsy courage, offering one of the city's first *al fresco* sidewalk cafes. Somehow, with the roses on the pink marble-topped tables, the friendly noise, the colorful passers-by, it all felt very Via Veneto, and not quite so Broadway. And to maintain the illusion, across the street, sat Vanessi's, catering to the beautiful and the nearly beautiful, the important and the soon-to-be and the never-was-but-thought-they-were. Governors and ghouls, matriarchs and madams, portly men in blue suits, women in black with great chunks of gold bracelets, and then at the next table jeans and wildly frizzy hair. It was a place to get lost in, a place to be found in. It was, simply, Vanessi's. Kate and Tom had loved it. At first they had found it too noisy for their romantic evenings alone, but after a while it had

147

grown on them. And Tom was always left in peace there. A few autographs, a couple of handshakes, a wave, but no hassles. No kisses and grabs. Vanessi's.

"You up to it?" Felicia had come to a screeching halt in the parking lot next door. She hated to give Kate a choice, but it seemed only fair. There was a long pause as Kate looked around, and then absently, her hand went to the heart-shaped watch pinned to her shirt. For valor, for courage.

"Okay." She stepped out of the car, stretched her legs, and almost cringed from the noise and the bustle. But even she knew that what she now considered "bustle" was still half-dead for San Francisco.

Felicia got her stub for the car, and arm in arm they strolled toward the restaurant. "Scared?"

"Terrified."

"So are most people about ninety percent of the time. Don't forget that."

"They don't have anything to hide." It was out then. That was it. That was always it. Damn.

Felicia stopped walking and faced her, still holding her arm. "You don't have anything to hide either, Kate. You have a lot of pain in your past. But that's it. It's the past. And it's someone else's past. It's his past, not yours. You have a child, a book, a nice clean life in the country. That's all." Kate closed her eyes with a smile and took a deep breath.

"I wish that's what I felt, Licia."

"Then make it what you feel."

"Yes, sir."

"Oh shut up." The moment of seriousness had already passed and Kate giggled as she sprinted along on her long coltlike legs.

"I'll race you!" They ran the last few steps, laughing and choking, and the headwaiter opened the door for them, and even at ten o'clock they were instantly swallowed up in the noise and bustle and avalanche of smells that was Vanessi's. Waiters shouting at the grill, people laughing in the bar, political battles being waged, romances being begun, all of it. It was fabulous. Kate just stood there and smiled. To her the noises sounded like an orchestra playing "Welcome Home."

"Table for two, Miss Norman?" Felicia nodded with a smile, and the headwaiter looked blankly at Kate. He was new there. He didn't know her. He didn't know Tom. He only knew Felicia. And Kate wasn't anyone anyway. Just a girl in jeans and a red shirt.

They were seated in the back, and the pinkish lighting made everyone look rosy and young. The waiter handed them menus. Kate handed hers back. "Cannelloni, house salad, zabaglione for dessert." The zabaglione was a warm runny feast of rum and egg whites.

Felicia ordered steak, salad, and a martini, as Kate looked at her watch. "Already have a date?"

"No. I was wondering if I should call Tillie."

"She's probably asleep."

Kate nodded, as a wave of guilt tried to creep into the evening, but she wouldn't let it in. She was having too good a time. And dinner was just as good as it had always been. Afterward they walked for a few minutes through the narrow colorful streets of North Beach. Hippie boutiques, artists' hangouts, coffee houses, and the smell of marijuana heavy in the air. Nothing had changed there either. After a few blocks they wandered back to Felicia's car. It was just midnight, and Kate was beginning to yawn.

"Just call me Cinderella."

"You can sleep late tomorrow."

"What time do you leave for work?"

"Don't ask. You know how I feel about mornings."

Kate yawned all the way home, suddenly overwhelmed by the feelings her return to San Francisco had brought back. She could hardly keep her eyes open as Felicia pressed a button in the car as they reached the top of Telegraph Hill, and a garage door half a block away swung open.

"Good Lord, Licia, how fancy."

"Just safe."

Kate was looking at the building with amusement. It was even more elegant than the one Felicia had lived in when Kate had left town. It was the typical older bachelors' building. Expensive, well-run, quiet, one- or two-bedroom apartments with extraordinary views of the port and the Bay. Not a place for children, and really not much warmth or charm. Just expensive.

"You disapprove?" Felicia looked amused as they slid into the garage.

"Of course not! What made you say that?"

"The look on your face. Remember me, I'm the city mouse. You're the country mouse."

"All right, all right, I'm too tired to fight you." Kate grinned again through a yawn, and then they were in the elevator and rapidly upstairs. Felicia unlocked her apartment door right from the elevator, and they were immediately let into a hall with delicate French wallpaper in a rich dusty rose and thick creamy beige rugs. There were watercolors on the walls, two large palm trees and an antique English mirror. It was all done in exquisite taste. And perfectly Felicia.

"Should I take off my espadrilles?" Kate was only half teasing.

"Only if you plan to shove them up your ass. I'm not prissy for chrissake, Kate. You can roll on the floor if you want to."

"I'd love to." The foyer alone would have made a beautiful bedroom.

But Felicia was already turning on the lights in the living room, which was done in off-white silks and creamy damasks, with dark oriental inlaid tables. There was a breathtaking view and the room's decor was wonderfully stark. The dining room beyond it was much the same with a black and white marble floor, numerous crystal sconces, and a small chandelier. Kate was sure Felicia's life-style hadn't actually been as grandiose six years before. Elegant, but not as spectacular. And there was a terrace that wrapped itself around the apartment and was covered with lush flowers and plants. Kate knew it for the work of a gardener, not her friend.

"You like it?"

"Are you kidding? I'm overwhelmed. When did life get like this?"

"With the last big promotion." She smiled and then sighed softly. "I have to do something with the money. And you won't let me buy Tygue a car for a while. So this is it."

"It sure is."

"Thanks, love. I'll show you your room." She was pleased that Kate liked it, though actually she was getting a little bored with it herself. It had been two and a half years now. She was almost ready for something else. Something even more elaborate, another step up.

The guest room was in keeping with the rest of the apartment—a blue and white room in another delicate French print. There was a tiny fireplace with a white marble mantel, more plants, a door onto the terrace, a little French desk, and a Victorian love seat.

"I just want you to know that I may never leave." And then she laughed as she had a horrifying thought.

"What's so funny?"

"The thought of Tygue here. Can you imagine our

old peanut-butter pal plonked down on that love seat?"

"I'd love to imagine just that." Felicia looked almost annoyed and then shrugged. "Well, maybe . . ." And then they were both laughing again like kids. Talking about Tygue made Kate miss him a little though. This was the first night since he'd been born that she had been away from him. What if he needed her? If he had a nightmare? If he couldn't find Willie? If . . .

"Kate!"

"Huh?"

"I can see what you're thinking. Stop it. You'll talk to him tomorrow."

"I'll go home tomorrow. But in the meantime . . ." She tossed herself onto the bed with a happy smile. "This is sheer heaven."

"Welcome home." Felicia strolled out of the room and across the hall to her own room as Kate called after her, "Can I see it?"

It was white and stark and very cold, much like the living room. Kate was disappointed.

"You expected mirrors on the ceiling perhaps?"

"At least."

"Want a drink, by the way?"

But Kate only smiled and shook her head. She knew exactly what she wanted, and after they had said good night and she had heard Felicia's door close, she got it. She stood barefoot on the terrace, in her nightgown, watching the fog hang low over the Bay, looking at the ships below, the Bay Bridge and the cars whizzing across it. She stood there for half an hour, until she was trembling so hard from the cold that she had to go inside. But when she went inside, she was still smiling.

CHAPTER 12

When Kate got up, she found a plate of croissants and a leftover pot of coffee from Felicia, with a note. "Meet me at the office at noon. Shopping with discount before or after if you want. Love, F." Shopping with discount. It was not her most pressing wish. She wanted to see the city again. Only the city. Places, memories, moments. Squealing with delight as she raced over the top of Divisadero with Tom, with the bay breeze whipping their hair into their faces as they swooped down again toward the tiny lip of beach, or headed out on the freeway across the Bay Bridge. Walks down narrow brick-paved streets in the upper part of town, browsing along Union Street, wandering down around the piers, or nibbling shrimp among the tourists at Fisherman's Wharf.

She stretched lazily as she stood barefoot in the kitchen, her brown hair showing soft red highlights in the sun as it hung long and loose down her back. Felicia even had a view from the kitchen. Kate stared at it happily as she nibbled at a peach, waiting for the coffee to warm. The phone rang just as she finished the peach. Probably Licia for her.

" 'Lo."

"Well, hello. You're back." For a moment her heart stopped. Who was he?

"Uh . . . yes." She stood very still, waiting to hear his voice again.

"And enjoying a lazy morning, I see. Is it a shock to be back?"

It was now. "No, it's very pleasant." Jesus, who was this guy? He seemed to know her, but she had no idea who he was. His voice was deep and interesting. It rang no familiar bells though. Still, something inside her was shaking. It was like being seen without being able to see.

"I tried you for dinner last night, but you weren't home yet. How was your friend?"

And then Kate let out a long sigh. So that was it. But he couldn't know Felicia very well, if he had mistaken Kate's voice for hers. "I'm sorry, I think there's been an awful mistake."

"There has?" Now he sounded confused, and Kate laughed.

"I'm the friend. I mean, I'm not Felicia. I'm sorry. I don't know why on earth I thought you knew who I was, but you seemed to."

"I just assumed." He sounded amused too, and his laughter was as pleasing as his voice. "I'm sorry. You're the friend from the country?"

"The country mouse. At your service." Well, not exactly, but it was fun talking to him, now that she knew that she wasn't on the spot. This had to be one of Licia's current men, if he knew about the trips to the country. "I'm really very sorry. I didn't mean to mislead you. Can I give Felicia a message? I'll be seeing her at lunch."

"Just tell her, if you would, that I've confirmed this evening. I'll pick her up at eight. The ballet's at eight-thirty, and we have a table at Trader Vic's for dinner afterward. That ought to meet with Miss Norman's approval."

"Hell, yes." Kate laughed again, and then was embarrassed. Maybe he was more formal than that.

"I'll tell her you approved."

"I'll tell her you called."

"Thanks very much." They hung up, and then Kate realized with horror that she had never gotten his name. How awful. But it had been so strange to talk to a man again. That made two in one week. But she assumed that Felicia would know who he was. If not, she was being taken to the ballet by a total stranger. The idea amused Kate, and she laughed to herself as she poured a cup of coffee. Men. She still liked her celibate life, but it was fun playing with them again. Fun hiding in a telephone, or just talking business with Stu. For some reason, she felt like playing again. Not "doing," just playing. She was still grinning to herself when she went to get dressed.

She pulled the new dresses out of her suitcase with a look of mischief and excitement. The black was out, it was too dressy. The red skirt would be about right. She had also brought a pair of gray flannel slacks from the year one, with a white shirt and a big soft gray shetland sweater. But she didn't want to wear something like that. She wanted to wear the suit. The creamy silk suit with the peach blouse, and the delicate little shoes with the gold chain at the heel. She almost wanted to jump up and down with excitement. And half an hour later, she was delighted with herself as she stood in front of the mirror. Bathed, made up, perfumed, and draped in the divine suit she had bought in Carmel. Her hair was loosely swept up in a Gibson Girl knot that looked wonderfully ladylike, and she had brought little pearl earrings, "just in case." As she looked in the mirror, she felt like a model again. But a much older one. She was almost thirty, and she was ready for the high-fashion look. She had never owned anything quite like the cream suit. She grinned at herself again and twirled on one heel. Who was this person? Was she a celebrated writer stopping in San Francisco for a day to have lunch? Was she a quiet young matron, up from the country for a visit? Was she the mother of a small boy, a teddy bear, and a basset hound named Bert? The heartbroken wife of . . . no, that she was not. Not now. But she was all the others, and none of them. Was the woman she saw in the delicate peach silk blouse really Tygue's mother? Did he even exist? Where? What country? She was in San Francisco now. This was real. How could anything else be?

She picked up the flat little beige suede bag she had brought up to go with the suit, and tucked it under her arm. It had a coral clasp and had been her mother's, long ago. In another life. Now it was just a bag. And it was a beautiful day in a beautiful town, and she had things she wanted to do. She walked down Telegraph Hill from Felicia's apartment and found a cab in Washington Square. From there she reached a car-rental place and then she was on her own. Up Broadway into Pacific Heights, past all the great houses, and into the Presidio. Then back. Divisadero and over the hill, with a broad grin and an irresistible squeal. And then back into the Presidio until she reached the cliffs that looked out to sea, with the Golden Gate Bridge stretching out, seeming to be only inches away, in all its rust-colored splendor, and with the majesty of the cliffs on either side. It was a view that had always taken her breath away and still did. And it was a place she suddenly knew she had to bring Tygue. He had to know the town where they had lived. He had a right to this. To the excitement, the beauty, the cable cars, the bridge, the people, all of it. Just thinking about him confirmed in her mind the decision she had really made when she'd left him the day before. She was going back that night. She had answered her own questions. She *could* do it. She *had* faced it. No photographers were lurking in corners. No one knew or cared who she was. This was a new era, filled with new people, in all the most beloved old places. She wanted to share it with Tygue. She would tell him all about it that night.

Feeling at peace, she slid into the rented car and headed downtown. Even that was fun now. She could remember a time when, just before she left for good, it filled her with dread. Terror. She would get claustrophobia everywhere she went. Pregnant, frightened, alone, with her whole life having fallen apart, just the simple act of going downtown had been a nightmare. Now it was funny. All those busy little people in gem-colored dresses running in and out of buildings, dodging cars, hopping cable cars, as the dowager queen, the St. Francis Hotel, looked benevolently out upon Union Square. For a moment Kate stopped and smiled. Nothing had changed here. It had barely changed since she was a child, and certainly not in six years. The green of the square was as pretty, the pomp of the big stores just as apparent, the pigeons were as plentiful, the drunks equally so: all was well with the world. She rounded the bend into Geary, and slowed the car in front of the store. For a moment she thought maybe that had changed, but no—the doorman rushed out to help her.

"Leave the car, miss?"

"Thank you."

"Be long?"

"I'm seeing Miss Norman."

157

"That's fine." He smiled pleasantly as she handed him the keys and a dollar. It was simpler and cheaper than a garage. He'd do something with it. God knows what. The store probably had an arrangement with the garage across the street, or the police department, but one always got one's car back.

With a feeling of trepidation, Kate pushed open the heavy glass door, and walked inside the pale cocoa marble halls. Hallowed halls. Sacred halls. Bags to the right, jewelry to the left, men's department to the extreme right only bigger now, and cosmetics and perfume in the alcove at the far left. The same, all the same. Gloves had vanished now. Stockings seemed to have moved, but nothing essential had been displaced. And God, it was pretty. Incredibly so. A riot of wares that no woman could resist. Red suede shoulder bags, black lizard clutches, marvelous great chunks of gold and silver, purple threaded with gold to weave around one's waist in the evening, thick rich capes in wonderful pastel colors, Lanvin scarves, and the smell of perfume heavy in the air . . . silk flowers . . . suedes . . . satins . . . an endlessly abundant palette of colors. It made you feel you could never be beautiful without all of it. She smiled to herself as she watched the women devouring whatever they could touch. She wanted to do it herself, but she wasn't even sure she knew how to play the game anymore and she didn't want to keep Felicia waiting and besides, she felt extravagant enough in the suit she was wearing.

As the elevator carried her upstairs, it stopped for a moment on the second floor, then the third. She had lived on those floors, worn the dresses, shown the minks, been the brides. She saw new faces now in the moments the elevator door was open. Fresh faces. No one left from her time. She was grown up now.

The others were gone too. Twenty-nine. Was that really old?

The elevator stopped on the eighth floor, and she stepped out. She was no longer sure exactly where Felicia's office was, but she was quickly informed by a guard. A corner office naturally. The fashion director for all the company's stores in California would have to have a corner office. At least. Kate smiled to herself again as she walked into a small anteroom and was instantly stopped by two very stylish-looking young women, and a man wearing pale blue suede pants.

"Yes?" He hissed it through perfect teeth and delicate lips.

"I'm Mrs. Harper. Miss Norman is expecting me." The young man checked her out, then rapidly disappeared. In a moment, Felicia came stalking out of a huge white room behind her. Everything was white, glass, or chrome. It was cold, but exquisite. And white definitely seemed to be Felicia's color these days.

"Good God! You're for real!" Felicia stopped dead in the doorway, and looked at her friend. If she had ordered a model's setup for their biggest show, she would have done nothing differently. And suddenly, looking at her, she was proud of Kate. And pleased that the new watch was carefully adjusted on the delicate suit.

"Do I pass?"

Felicia rolled her eyes and practically dragged her inside. Kate was even walking differently, with a kind of sway of the hips and swagger all at the same time, as though she felt as beautiful as she looked. It made Felicia want to sing. "Is that what you bought in Carmel?"

"Yup."

"It's divine. Did you get stopped by every man in the store?"

"No." Kate grinned at her. "But you're going to the ballet tonight with a nameless stranger who is picking you up at eight, and then taking you to dinner at Trader Vic's."

"My, my. Peter."

"Then you know him."

"More or less." Which meant physically more and mentally less, but so what. That was Felicia's business. She looked pleased with the announcement about dinner. "Want to join us?"

"I'm sure he'd be thrilled. Anyway, love, I'm going home."

"You are? Why?" Had something happened? Felicia looked horrified. "Already?"

"No, this afternoon. And I've already done a lot. A lot more than you know." But Felicia did know. When she looked into Kate's eyes, she knew. Kate looked confident again, in a way she hadn't in years.

"Will you come back again?" Felicia held her breath.

She nodded quietly, and then smiled. "With Tygue. I think he ought to get to know the place a bit. He's old enough to enjoy it." And then there was a pause as her smile broadened. "And so am I. Maybe."

"Maybe my ass. Come on, let's go to lunch."

She took Kate to a new restaurant tucked in between the piers, and again they had champagne to celebrate. Every day seemed like a celebration now. The restaurant served a lavish lunch, and catered to the cream of the downtown clientele. It was kept locked, and considered itself more or less a club. "By reservation only," and they were extremely careful about who got reservations. Felicia always did. She brought the right people, looked marvelous, gave them good publicity. "Miss Norman" was a venerated figure at Le Port, as they had called themselves. But

Kate was beginning to realize that Felicia had become something of a personality around town.

"Does everyone know you?" It seemed as though everyone at this place did, and all the best-looking men.

"Only the right people, darling."

Kate shook her head and laughed. "You're impossible." But Felicia had also grown. In Kate's years of hiding out, Felicia had been busy. She was important now, whatever that was. There was a certain aura around everything she touched. Success. Money. And style. Felicia had vast quantities of the latter, and had been quietly earning and amassing the former for years. Watching her in her own milieu, Kate had a new respect for her.

"Did you talk to Tillie, by the way?" Felicia asked the question nonchalantly, but Kate's heart almost stopped.

"Did she call?"

"Of course not. I just thought you might have called." Felicia was sorry she'd brought it up.

"No. I was going to, but Tygue had already gone to school when I got up. I'll talk to him tonight. I'm going to try and get home in time to see him."

"It'll do him a lot of good to see you like that, Kate. He needs to know more than torn blue jeans, kiddo." She looked momentarily stern.

"That's why I thought I'd bring him up here. So you could teach him the facts of life. Right, Aunt Licia?"

"You bet, sweetheart." They toasted each other with the last of the champagne, and Felicia regretfully looked at her watch. "Dammit, I hate to go. When are you coming back?" She was going to pin her down. Now. Before she changed her mind.

"I thought I'd bring him up next month, when his

school closes for the summer." Then she meant it.
Felicia beamed.

"Oh God, Kate, I can hardly wait till you tell him!"

"Neither can I."

CHAPTER 13

Kate had made it home in just under five hours, and without a single speeding ticket. That in itself was a miracle. Ninety-five. Ninety-eight. But she wanted to see Tygue before he went to bed. She wanted to tell him about San Francisco. About taking him up there. About cable cars and the bridge. She had brought him chocolate from Ghirardelli Square, and she would tell him about that too. She had so much to tell him. Just the thought of it made her jumpy as she turned into the gravel drive. She had worn the red skirt and bright print blouse to come home in. Maybe Licia was right. Maybe it would do him good to see her looking pretty. She wanted to share the newness with him. The excitement.

The house looked cheerful and well lit as she pulled the car slowly into the parking space. There were no calls of hello, no barking, but she knew they were all cozily tucked inside. She unlocked the door with her key, and there he was, at the kitchen table, doing a puzzle with Tillie. He was wearing soft blue flannel pajamas and the little yellow robe Licia had sent God knew when. He looked cozy, and comfortable, and warm, and all hers. She stood there for a moment, watching him, while Tillie smiled at her, and Tygue stayed intent on his puzzle.

"Hi, guys." Silence. Tillie raised her eyebrows but

said nothing. She knew what Kate wanted to hear, and it had nothing to do with her. But it didn't come. No "Hi, Mom." Only Bert sleepily wagging his tail at her feet. "Hey, tough guy. Aren't you going to say hello?" She walked quickly over to him and folded him into a hug, but he ignored her.

"Yeah. Hi." And then Kate's eyes found Tillie's. So that was it. He was pissed. Kate slowly sat down in one of the kitchen chairs and watched him. He still hadn't looked at her. And Tillie got up and went to find her things. One thing about Kate, she always came back when she said she would. No fooling around. She had said she'd be home Monday night and she was. Tillie liked that about her. She also knew that Kate was going to have some serious fence mending to do. Tygue hadn't been himself since she had left. "Overnight, Tillie! She went overnight!" The boy had been shocked.

"Where'd you get the new puzzle?"

"Tillie. We bought it today."

"That's nice. Aunt Licia sends you her love." Silence again. Jesus. It was going to be a long thawing out, at this rate. She almost wondered if it was worth it. But as she thought back over the last twenty-four hours, she knew it was. He was just going to have to understand. "Hey, guess what." She snuggled up to him and tried to kiss his neck, but he made himself stiff and hard to reach. "I have a surprise for you."

"Yeah?" It was the least curiosity he had ever shown about a surprise. "What is it?"

"A trip." He looked at her with horror. But she went on. "How would you like to come up to San Francisco with me sometime, to see Aunt Licia?" She waited for the intake of breath, the widened eyes, but it didn't happen that way. Instead he shrank from her and his eyes filled with tears.

"I won't go! I won't!" He ran away from the table, and a moment later she heard the door to his room slam shut. Tillie watched her as she slipped into her coat, and Kate let out a long tired breath.

"I knew he'd be mad at me for going, but I didn't expect this."

"He'll get over it. It's a big adjustment for him." Tillie sounded sorry for them both, but it irritated Kate.

"A big adjustment that I leave him for one night?" Hell, she had a right to that much, didn't she? Well, didn't she, dammit? She knew she did. He was only a kid. He couldn't expect all her time. But he had always had it before. That was the bitch of it.

"How often have you left him overnight before, Kate?" Tillie already knew the answer to that of course.

"Never."

"Then that's a big change for him. He'll get used to it, if you plan to go on doing it. I think he senses a change. Maybe he's confused by it."

"Oh damn, Tillie. So am I. I made a very big deal on one of my books last week. It means a lot of nice things for us, but it also means some things I don't understand yet. I've kind of been experimenting with how I feel about it all."

"He doesn't understand that. He feels it, but he doesn't understand. All he knows is what he's always known. He hasn't gone very far from here, you know. And now you're off for the night, and you're telling him that you're taking him to San Francisco. You and I know it's exciting. He just thinks it's scary. And to tell you the truth, it would scare a lot of older folks from around here."

"I know. It scared me for a lot of years too." For

whatever the reasons. "I guess I'm expecting too much of him."

"He'll come around. Give him time. You know"— she looked at Kate apologetically—"probably even see-ing you dressed like that scares him a little. Maybe it tells him he's losing you, or that you're changing. You never know with kids. They think the craziest damn things. When my husband died, my youngest son thought that meant we'd put him up for adoption. Don't ask me why, but he thought we were sending him away too. He cried for three weeks until he finally came out and said it. Maybe Tygue is afraid you'll leave him, all dressed up like that. You look awfully nice though."

"Thanks, Tillie."

"Take it easy. Oh, and are you going up to teach tomorrow?"

"I think I'd better wait a couple of days before I tackle that."

"Nice that they can be that flexible."

"Yeah." Oh Christ, Tillie. Don't challenge me on that too. Please. But she didn't. She just waved and quietly shut the door.

Kate suddenly felt alone in the house. Only Bert made his presence known, wanting to play with the shiny gold chain on her new shoes.

"Not for eighty-six bucks you don't, Bert, m'boy." She swatted him away with her hand, and noticed how empty the house sounded with only her voice in it. She sat very still for a moment, and then stood up and slipped off the skirt. She unzipped the valise she had taken to the city with her, and fished out the jeans and red shirt as she tossed the new skirt and blouse over the back of a chair. "So long for now." She care-fully put the shoes in the suitcase, or Bert would have eaten them for dinner. And then, on stockinged feet, she walked softly toward Tygue's room and knocked. "Can I come in?" There was a silence and then finally his voice.

"Yeah." He was sitting in the dark, and the bright moon of his little face looked tiny in the dark room.

"Don't you want a light on?"

"Nope."

"Okay. Have you got Willie?"

"Yeah."

"I'll bet that feels good."

"What?" His voice was so little and wary.

"I'll bet having Willie feels good. You know you've got him. He's all yours forever."

"Yeah." The voice was softer now in the dark, as she lay across his bed and tried to watch what she could see of his face.

"Do you know you've got me, just like you've got Willie? Only more so. Forever and ever. Do you know that?"

"Sort of."

"What do you mean, 'sort of'?" It wasn't an accusation. It was a question.

"I mean, sort of."

"Okay. What happens if you tie a red ribbon on Willie? Does it make him different?"

"Yeah. It makes him look silly."

"But do you love him less?" Vehement shaking of the head as he held the bear closer. "Okay, so no matter how funny-looking I may seem to you, or what I wear, I'm still old Mom, right?" A nod. "And I love you just the same no matter what I'm doing, or what I look like, or where I am."

"Willie doesn't leave me."

"Neither do I. I never leave you either. Sometimes I may go away. But I don't leave you, darling. And I never will. Not ever."

"But you go-ed away." The voice was trembling and full now.

"Only for one night, and I came back. Just like I said I would. Didn't I?" Reluctantly, he nodded.

"Why did you do it?"

"Because I needed to. Because I wanted to. Sometimes grown-ups need to go places, without kids."

"You never needed to before."

"No. But I did this time."

"Did that man send you away?" She knew instantly who he meant.

"Stu Weinberg?" He nodded. "Of course not. I sent myself away. And was it really that bad, for just one night?" He shrugged noncommittally and then suddenly he was crying and holding out his arms. She was stunned.

"I missed you! And I thought you didn't love me anymore!"

"Oh darling, oh baby . . . how could you think a thing like that? I love you so much. And I missed you too. But . . . I just . . . I had to. But I'll always, always, always come back. And next time I go, you'll go with me." She wanted to promise him that she wouldn't do it again. But she knew that she would. How could she give that up, now that she'd just found it again?

He cried for almost half an hour, and then slowly it stopped. And he looked up at her with the tiniest smile.

"If I squeezed my shirt, we could give Willie a bath just with your tears. Did you know that?"

He chuckled hoarsely and she gave him a kiss as she smoothed the blond hair falling over his forehead. "Can I interest you in some chocolate?"

"Now?"

"Sure." She had bought a huge bar of it wrapped

in gold. It was the size of a hardcover book. And she had also brought him a box of chocolate lollipops and a chocolate pistol. Better than Easter or Halloween. When he saw the gold foil-wrapped chocolate gun, his jaw dropped and his eyes grew as he held out his hands.

"Wow!"

"Not bad, huh, hotshot?"

"Wow, Mom, it's terrific!"

"So are you." She pulled him back onto her lap as he gobbled the chocolate from the large bar. But he was saving the pistol to show his friends in school.

"What if somebody breaks it?"

"Then we'll buy some more when we go up to San Francisco together." Something deep inside trembled for a moment, but he looked at her with a big grin and a look of greedy glee.

"Yeah. That must be some place."

"It is." She held him close that evening for a very long time.

CHAPTER 14

"Okay, now close your eyes, sweetheart." Tygue sat very still in the seat next to her, with his eyes closed. She had recognized the last bend in the road before the skyline would come into view. She wondered what he would think of it. He had never seen anything like it. She took the bend smoothly, and smiled to herself at the zigzag of buildings that lay ahead. "Okay. You can open your eyes now." He was very quiet as he did. He took it all in, but said nothing. Kate was surprised. "Well? What do you think?"

"What is it?"

"San Francisco, silly. Those are all the big buildings downtown." Tygue had never seen anything taller than four stories. It was amazing to realize that. At his age she had already been to New York, and gone to the top of the Empire State Building.

"I thought it had hills." He sounded disappointed. And a little scared.

"It does. You can't see them from here."

"Oh."

She didn't know what to say to him, as he sat there looking straight ahead. He wanted to go home. And she wanted him to love San Francisco. She and Felicia had planned everything. They would be there for a week. A whole week! Fisherman's Wharf, Sausalito, cable cars, the beach, the zoo, a ferry ride, bike riding on Angel Island, they had thought of everything. Felicia had even gotten the location schedules of the local TV shows, so he could watch them filming chase scenes on the hills. Inevitably, there was one scheduled on Divisadero.

"Want to see the crookedest street in the world?"

"Sure." He held Willie tightly on his lap and Kate was about to snap at him. He was in San Francisco. It was exciting. It was the first trip he had ever taken. Why wasn't he happy? Why didn't he feel what she did? And then she felt mean for what she was thinking, and she turned right off Franklin Street, so that she could pull over. "This is it? Aunt Licia's house?" He looked up at the ramshackle hotel with unconcealed horror, and Kate laughed. It had been a long drive, and she realized suddenly how tense she had been about what he was feeling.

"No. And I love you, you silly kid. C'mere and give me a hug."

His little freckled face melted into a smile and he reached out to her. She wound up hugging both her son and his bear. Tillie was keeping Bert for them until they got back. "Tygue Harper, I promise you that you're going to have a good time here. Okay? Will you trust me a little?" He nodded as she looked down at him and kissed the top of his head.

"It's so big." There was real awe in his voice. "And so . . ." He looked around the dreary neighborhood she had temporarily parked in and the disappointment was clear on his face.

"Yeah, it's big. Bigger than we're used to now. But you know E Street, in town?" He nodded somberly. E Street was horrible. Way past the old railroad tracks, near the dump. There were drunks and old deserted cars there. It smelled bad, and it was the kind of place you never wanted to go to. He knew E. Street. Every-

171

body did. He looked up at his mother with big eyes. "Well, where we are right now is just like E. Street. But there are beautiful places here. And we're going to see all of them. Okay? Deal?" She held out a hand with a smile and he took it in a hard businesslike little shake. "Ready to roll?"

"Ready to roll!" He sat looking ahead, but he was holding Willie less ferociously now, and Kate smiled to herself as she started the car again.

"Hungry?" She knew they weren't far from the Hippo on Van Ness, but he shook his head. "Ice cream?" The head turned, and there was a smile in his eyes. A small nod. "Then ice cream it is." That was perfect. She'd stop at Swensen's on Hyde Street on the way to Licia's. Licia was waiting for them at the apartment. And she was as anxious as Kate.

Kate parked the car outside Swensen's on Union and Hyde, and as they got out and stretched, two cable cars came clanking down Hyde. "Look!" Tygue jumped up and down waving his bear. "Look, Mom! It's a . . . a . . ." He could hardly stand it, and his mother grinned. Everything would be all right after all. And the ice cream was terrific. A double scoop of rocky road and banana, sugar cone, and chocolate dip. Tygue was already wearing most of it on his nose and chin when they left the store, and another cable car came down the hill. She could hardly get him back in the car.

"We'll go for a ride later." But first, she had another idea. Two of them. The steepest hill. The crookedest street. They were near both.

The steepest hill did not impress him, but he loved the crookedest street as they inched their way down the narrow, winding brick road banked with flowers and bordered with pastel-hued Victorian houses. Tygue loved it so much he almost forgot the ice cream

172

dripping on his bear. He happily licked a gob of chocolate off Willie's ear.

"Tygue, yerghk!"

"Uh uh, yummy!" He was happy again. "What's that?" He settled back in his seat and pointed ahead to Coit Tower on Telegraph Hill.

"That's a memorial to the fire department. It's called Coit Tower, and it's right near Aunt Licia."

"Can we go see it?"

"Sure. But first let's see what Aunt Licia has planned."

"This is fun."

And so was the rest of the trip. They did everything. Hippo dinners, picnics at Stinson Beach, the wax museum, Fisherman's Wharf, ten or fifteen rides on the cable car, the aquarium, the planetarium, Chinatown, and the Japanese Garden in the park. It was sheer heaven, and by the following Saturday, Tygue knew San Francisco better than most children who had lived there for years.

"Well, champ? What do you think? Gonna ditch your Mom and come live with me here?" They were all sprawled out on Felicia's impeccable, white, living-room rug eating popcorn. For the first time all week, they had been too tired to go out. Felicia had agreed to order pizza. It had been totally Tygue's week, and both women were exhausted. They smiled at each other over his head.

"You know, Aunt Licia." Tygue was looking thoughtfully out at the Bay Bridge just beyond the terrace. "When I grow up, I might come up here and work on the cable car."

"Great idea, champ."

"And if you buy him his own real one for Christmas, Licia, I'll kill you." Kate laughed at the thought, as she shoved a handful of popcorn into her mouth.

"When do you think you guys'll be back?"

Kate shrugged, looking down at Tygue. "I don't know. We'll see." She had been neglecting Tom lately, and she had some ideas for a new book. "I really ought to do some work. And I've got Tygue set up with a group that's going to ride every day at the Adams ranch until school starts in the fall."

"And the book?" Leave it to Felicia to bring that up. She had been trying not to think of it. Publication date was only a few days away.

"That's their problem now. I wrote it. Now they can sell it."

"That simple, eh?" Felicia raised an eyebrow and looked pointedly at Kate. "You wrote it, and that's it. Did it ever occur to you that they're going to want your help selling it?"

"How about door to door?" Kate lay on the floor with a giggle.

"You know what they want." Felicia was not going to be pushed off the track. Not that easily. She had waited weeks to bring it up.

"How do I know what they want? And that's not the point."

"Oh really? Then what is the point? What *you* want?"

"Maybe. I don't see why I should do anything that makes me uncomfortable."

"Don't be an ass, Kate." Tygue got up and snapped on the TV. He was bored. He removed the bowl of popcorn and took it with him, and there was nothing left for Kate to hide in. She looked up at Felicia, and then out at the view. "You heard me. And you're crazy if you don't do promotion work on the book. This is your big chance. You've made it. This time. If you capitalize on that now, your next book will be even bigger. And then you'll be a permanent fixture in the realm of literary successes. But this is your tryout, kiddo. Blow this one, and you'll never have the chance again. You can't afford to ignore it."

"How do you know that's what they want? The book can sell itself."

"You're crazy. You're throwing your career away. And you know as well as I do that that's what you want. And you can do it, dammit. You've got everything it takes to make it. Everything. Looks, brains, and talent."

"But no balls."

"Bullshit. You're just so busy hiding them from yourself, you've forgotten you have them. And you know that's true. Besides, look what you've done in the last month. You've been up here twice. You're not a hermit anymore, Kate, and you know it. You don't even want to be."

"This is different though, Licia. This isn't public. I'm not sticking my face out there on television, asking for someone to throw a pie in it. Or worse, put a knife through my heart. Or Tygue's." She said it softly, so the boy couldn't hear. But he was wrapped up in the program he was watching on the huge color TV. "I'm just not going to take that chance, Licia."

"You're a tough woman to argue with, damn you. Because if you did do it, and something went wrong, I'd feel like shit."

"So would I. That's why I won't do it."

"But think how much fun it would be."

"Would it? I'm not so sure. It wasn't really fun for Tom."

"Yes it was."

"Not really."

"Maybe not for you. But it was for him. It's got to be. It's got to be the biggest high in the world."

"I'm happier without it."

"And lonelier too."

"Licia, my love, success is no antidote for loneliness."

"Maybe not. But doesn't it turn you on to see all the ads for your book? Christ, lady, it'll be out in three days. Doesn't that knock you on your ass?"

Kate grinned up at her friend sheepishly. "It sort of does."

"See what I mean. And think what would happen if you did some publicity appearances!" Felicia was at it again, and Kate held up a hand with a grin and a shake of the head.

"Enough. *Basta!* No more!" But Felicia would never stop and they both knew it.

"Maybe Weinberg will change your mind."

But this time Kate shook her head with a look of assurance. "Not a chance. And he's too smart to try."

Kate and Tygue left San Francisco early Sunday afternoon. Felicia had taken the week off to be with them, but she was going back to work the next day, and Tygue was scheduled to start his riding group the following morning. And there was Tom. Poor Tom. He hadn't had a visit in almost two weeks. She had been so busy before she left. She would go up to see him first thing the next morning. It was a little crazy driving all this way down on Sunday, and then halfway back up on Monday. But there was no other way to do it. She couldn't take Tygue with her to Mead.

"Mom?"

"What, sweetheart?" They were just easing into the Sunday-afternoon traffic leaving the city.

"Can we come back?"

"I told you we could."

"Soon?" She smiled over at him and nodded.

"Soon."

176

And then he giggled to himself and she looked over at him again.

"What's up?"

"I can't wait to see Bert."

She laughed at the thought too. "Neither can I." It would be good to get home. All these expeditions were exhausting. For a minute, she was reminded of the traveling she had once done with Tom. That had been exhausting too. She wondered how she had done it. Constantly packing, flying, driving, staying in hotels. But he had always made it fun. An adventure. A honeymoon.

"What were you thinking?"

"How much fun I used to have taking trips with your dad." She was surprised at herself for saying it. She rarely spoke of Tom to Tygue. The subject was better left alone. And he knew she didn't like to talk about it. All he knew was that his father had died. In an accident. Before he was born. He had never even asked what Tom did for a living. But one day he would. She'd cross that bridge when she came to it. She'd come up with some lie like all the others. She'd have to.

"Did you take a lot of trips?"

"Some." She was closing up again.

"Like to where?" Now he was all boy, settling down in his seat with Willie, wanting to hear about her adventures. The way he looked made her laugh.

"Lots of places. We went to Cleveland once." Their first weekend together. Why had she told him that? Why had she thought of it? She felt a wave of pain turn over slowly in her heart.

"Was it neat?"

"Yes, very neat. It's not a very pretty place, but your father made it pretty." Tygue looked bored. Pretty was for girls.

"Did you ever go to New York?" Felicia was going there soon, and he had heard them talk about it.

"Yes, with my mom and dad. Never with your dad."

"Mom?"

"What, sweetheart?" She prayed it wouldn't be a tough one to answer. Not today. Not now. She felt so good, she wanted the mood to last.

"How come all your people are dead? Your mom and dad, and my dad? How come?" And the strangest part of it was that none of them really were—but they might as well have been.

"I don't know. It just happens that way sometimes. But I have you." She smiled over at him.

"And Willie and Bert, and Aunt Licia. And we're never gonna die. Maybe Aunt Licia will. But we won't. Right, Willie?" He looked down at the bear seriously, and then up at his mother. "He says right." She smiled at them both, and reached over a hand to rumple his hair.

"I love you a lot, hotstuff."

"I love you too." But he said it in a low, little voice, as though afraid someone might hear. It made her laugh, and feel good about life as she brought her eyes back to the road. They rode on in silence for a while, and the next time she looked at him, he was asleep. They had just passed Carmel, and three hours later they were home. They picked up Bert on the way, at Tillie's place, and had a comfortable dinner at their own kitchen table.

Right after dinner Tygue was ready for bed, and less than an hour later, so was she. She didn't even bother to unpack or open her mail. She just took off her clothes and piled into bed. And it felt like only an hour later when the phone rang, but the sun was already shining brightly, and she could hear Tygue clattering around somewhere in the house. It took her four rings to get to the phone. It was Stu Weinberg.

"I thought you said you didn't go anywhere."

"I don't." She tried to force herself awake and at the same time sound pleasant.

"I've called. I've written. I thought maybe you died. I would have committed hara-kiri on my desk."

"Bad as that, huh? Anything wrong?" Jesus. What if they were canceling those contracts? Suddenly she was wide awake.

"Of course not. Nothing's wrong. Everything's right. The book is coming out in two days. Or had you forgotten?" No. But she was trying to.

"I hadn't forgotten." But she sounded wary now.

"We have something to talk about, Kate." Oh God. And first thing in the morning yet. Before coffee.

"Oh?"

"You've had a wonderful offer."

"Another one?" Her eyes opened wide. Good Lord. What now? The movie rights in Japan? She grinned.

"Yup. Another one. We got a call from the 'Case Show.' "

"Jasper Case?"

"You bet. And they'd like you on it. It's a marvelous opportunity for the book. We're all very excited."

"Who's 'we're all'?" She sounded distant and suspicious.

"The people who care about the book, Kate." He rattled off the names of her editors, and the publishers. "Not to mention the movie guys. This could do beautiful things for the book." Silence. "Kate?"

"Yeah."

"What are you thinking?"

"About what I told you."

"I think you'd be wrong not to do it. I kind of think

179

this is one of those things you have to grit your teeth and do. For the sake of God and country, lady. And the book." The book, the book, damn the book. "Case is a hell of a nice guy. He's a good place to start. Easygoing, mellow, very correct. He's English."

"I know. I watch the show." It was the best late-night show on, and the whole country watched it. And Jasper Case was a gentleman. She had never seen him make anyone uncomfortable. But what about the people who watched it? What if someone saw her and remembered? Oh Christ. Who the hell was going to remember a tall skinny brown-haired kid who'd dragged around behind Tom Harper? Who knew? Who cared? "I'll do it."

"I'm so glad, Kate." He rolled his eyes and wiped a thin veil of sweat off his forehead. "They've made some terrific arrangements. They've scheduled you for a week from today. And they thought you might like to come down and stay at the Beverly Hills Hotel. They booked it for that Monday night. You can come down in the morning and relax a little bit. Someone from the show will join us for lunch, and give you an idea of who's on the show that night, what to expect. They'll get a feel for what you want to talk about and what you don't. You call the shots. And then you sit around the swimming pool all afternoon or get your hair done or do whatever you want to do. The show is taped at seven, and shown later. But after the taping, at nine, your time is your own. We'll have dinner or something, to celebrate. And that's it. You spend the night, you go home the next day. Painless."

"Sounds like a damn pleasant way to lose my virginity." She was smiling at her end of the phone. Weinberg had done it. And they both knew it. He'd had her pegged from the start, had known just how to handle her. Damn.

"Kate, trust me. You're going to love it." Now they were both laughing.

"If I don't, do I get my money back?"

"Sure, baby. Sure. Don't forget. A week from Monday. Oh, and by the way, the L.A. *Times* wanted an interview. How do you feel about that?" She hesitated for a long moment.

"No."

"*Vogue?*"

"Jesus. What the hell is happening, Stu?"

"A lot more than you realize, m'dear." Or want to. "All right, what about this one?" He mentioned an inane women's magazine. "No photographs, just a nice quiet interview over lunch on Tuesday."

"Okay, okay. You drive a hard bargain. How many more of those do you have to throw at me? Tell the truth now!" She sounded as though she were talking to Tygue.

"Nine magazines, five newspapers, and three other talk shows. And one radio show in Chicago. They'll tape it by phone. If you'd read your mail, love, you'd know all about it."

"I've been away." She said it sheepishly.

"Any place fun?"

"San Francisco."

"Terrific. We have an interview up there, if you want it. You can go back whenever you want."

"Christ, Stu. I'm not ready for this."

"That's what I'm here for. You let me be the buffer. Right now all you have to deal with is one thing— 'The Jasper Case Show.' The rest can wait. Try your wings out with Case. And then we'll see. Sound reasonable?"

"Very. Oh God." She was panicking again. "What'll I wear?"

Stu Weinberg started to laugh. They had it made.

If she was worrying about what to wear, they were home free. "Sweetheart, go naked if you want to. Just enjoy it."

Five minutes later, Kate was on the phone to Felicia, who sat at her desk with her mouth open and her eyes wide. "You're going to be what?"

"On 'The Jasper Case Show.' " Kate almost sounded proud. What the hell had that man done to talk her into it? Mentally, Felicia took her hat off to him. "What the hell should I wear?"

But Felicia only smiled at the phone. "Kate, baby, I love you."

CHAPTER 15

The car slowed to a halt in front of the covered entranceway to the hotel. Instantly, a doorman and three porters approached the car. Three? For a station wagon? Kate glanced around nervously. She had brought only one very small bag. She smiled uneasily at one of the porters, but he remained expressionless as she got out. He slid behind the wheel of the car as the other porter grabbed her bag. The third disappeared, and the doorman stood there looking impressive as a bright red Rolls Royce and a black Jaguar sedan pulled up behind her. A veritable fleet of porters appeared for them. And at the same time there was a constant hum of activity. Suitcases, golf clubs, armsful of mink whizzing by, anonymous cars arriving and departing, and a constant touching of hands with the doorman. As Kate fumbled in her handbag, she looked up quickly to see what the man nearest her was giving the porter, and she gasped as she thought she saw ten dollars changing hands. Ten dollars? Oh God, she prayed she hadn't said it aloud. Another glance to her left and she caught a glimpse of a five. It was insane. It had been ten years since she'd handled this sort of thing when she traveled with Tom. But five and ten bucks to the porter? Things couldn't have changed that much in seven years. But this was Hollywood. The outfits alone told her that.

The people disembarking from their cars were wearing blue jeans that seemed to be soldered to their souls, equally tight shirts left open to the waist, vast quantities of gold jewelry, and a fair amount of bright, flashy silk, which clung and dripped and draped over starlet bodies and middle-aged men. And here and there, a dark suit hurrying into the hotel, presumably to launch into metamorphosis and emerge again in jeans.

"Reservation, ma'am?"

"Hm?" She was startled from her staring by the porter. She realized that she looked out of place. She had worn a simple white cotton dress from the batch of "possibilities" Felicia had sent her from the store. It had a careful V at the neck, which she had thought too low, but down here didn't even count, delicate little white sandals, and her hair was looped into an easy knot on top of her head. She looked deeply tanned and relaxed, and as though she were going to have lunch next to the tennis courts in Palm Springs, not compete with the sex symbols of Hollywood. The thought made her smile. And then she remembered the porter again. "Sorry. Oh yes. I have a reservation." He walked quickly inside and she followed him along the open but protected breezeway flanked by pillars on either side. Between the pillars frothed tiny jungles of exotica, strewn there in the thirties, when the women slithered into the hotel in ermines and diamonds instead of blue jeans and mink.

She found herself almost instantly crossing miles of green carpet, in sharp contrast to the washed-flamingo façade that had assaulted her outside. Here again people were bustling past, going to meet or discover or be discovered, discuss or disdain, destroy a career, their own or someone else's. One sensed that the business of Hollywood was being conducted nearby. One could almost feel the pulse; the building throbbed with the power inside it.

"Yes?" The man at the desk looked up at her with a smile. There were seven men at the desk.

"I'm Mrs. Harper. I believe—"

"But of course." He smiled again as he cut her off mid-sentence, and disappeared somewhere behind the desk. But of course? How did he know who she was? He reappeared only to wave vaguely at the porter and hand him a key. "We hope to see you here often." You do? Kate felt like a kid in a dream. Who were they? Who was she? And where was the Mad Hatter in all this? Surely he belonged here. But she was already following the porter down a wide hallway bordered with shops. Jades, emeralds, diamonds, maribou-trimmed bed jackets, satin nightgowns, a little white mink bolero, Vuitton luggage, suede handbags, a lizard briefcase. She wanted to stop and stare at it all, but she felt obliged to look unimpressed, to be grownup. And beneath it all, there was a wild urge to tug at someone's arm and whisper, as they raced along the hall, "Look . . . over there! . . . and there! . . ." As she thought of it, she noticed three familiar faces from the movies. Even she knew who they were. Her head snapped around as she watched them laughing together, and she almost bumped into someone else, a face from television. It was fantastic! She was smiling to herself as she walked along, wondering suddenly if this was what it had been like for Tom, living in a world of celebrities. No, it couldn't have been. This was fabulous! And unique.

They were passing a pool now, surrounded by tables and white-jacketed waiters. Women in bikinis strolled by wearing perfectly browned skins and hairdos that had not been affected by the water. Kate watched them in fascination as they too disappeared, and she suddenly found herself standing in front of a small, manicured-looking cottage. For the tiniest moment, it reminded her of Mead, and she had a wild urge to giggle, but she didn't, she couldn't, not with the porter standing there, waiting for what? A fifty-dollar bill? Surely if that other porter could make ten dollars just by opening a car door, this one would expect fifty or a hundred for walking her down all these halls, and past all these exotic sights. He opened the door to the bungalow, as he referred to it, and she handed him a five-dollar bill as she stepped inside, feeling ridiculous for having given him so much money. The door closed softly behind her, and she looked around. It was indeed very pretty. Flowery prints, chaise lounges that seemed to invite one to recline on them in one of the satin nightgowns she had seen in the shops. With a long cigarette holder undoubtedly. There was an entirely mirrored dressing room and a vanity table worthy of two hours of makeup. A pink marble bathroom and a separately lit tub set into an alcove. She was grinning to herself again. And then the phone rang, startling her. She found it on a bedstand next to the huge double bed. She noticed then that there was another phone, in a little sitting room beyond. And there was yet another entrance to the cottage. Two entrances? Why? To make a fast getaway? She laughed as she picked up the phone.

"Hello?"

"Welcome to Hollywood, Kate. How's it going?" It was Stu, sounding as even and unruffled as ever, with the smile built in to his voice.

"I just got here. This place is amazing."

"Isn't it though?" He laughed too. He was relieved that she hadn't panicked and already left. When they had booked her into the Beverly Hills Hotel he had worried a little. For a neophyte, this was a stiff dose. "How's your bungalow?"

"I feel as though I should dress up as Jean Harlow. At least." This time his laugh was less restrained. Katharine Hepburn maybe. But Harlow? He chuckled again.

"You'd sure surprise the hell out of the people on the 'Case Show.' They're expecting something else."

"They are? What?" She sounded nervous again.

"You. Just as you are."

"That's good, Stu. 'Cause that's all I got. God, I'd love to have a swim before lunch, but I take it nobody swims here."

"Sure they do. What makes you say that?"

"Their hair." She said it like a mischievous kid, as she remembered what the women at the pool had looked like. But Stu was already laughing again.

"Sweetheart, I wish I'd been there when you arrived."

"So do I. Do you realize what people tip around here?" They were both laughing now. "Why do they do it?"

"To be remembered."

"Are they?" She was fascinated.

"Not for that reason. If they are remembered, it's because they're already somebody. If they're not, no one'll remember them anyway, no matter how much they tip. Do you realize, by the way, that your preferences and foibles will all be marked down on a little file card at the desk, and the next time you arrive you'll have everything your little heart needs and desires, without your even asking for it?"

"What the hell do you mean?" She suddenly felt uncomfortable, as though people were watching her through the walls.

"I mean, like if you'd brought that ridiculous hound of yours with you and he only ate pink grasshoppers and lemonade, next time you showed up, they'd have a full plate of pink grasshoppers and lemonade for him. Or special towels for you, or martinis very dry, or satin sheets, or nine pillows on the bed, or only French gin and English scotch, or . . . name it, love, and you got it."

"Good God. Do people really get away with that here?"

"They don't get away with it. They expect it. It's all part of being a star."

"Which I'm not." She said it with relief, and he smiled again.

"Which you are."

"Does that mean I have to order pink grasshoppers and lemonade?"

"Whatever you like, Princess. The palace is yours." But a stiletto of pain pierced her heart. Princess. Tom had always called her that. There was something in her eyes that Stu couldn't see when she spoke again.

"It feels more like 'Queen for a Day'."

"Just enjoy it. By the way, we're meeting Nick Waterman in the Polo Lounge at twelve-thirty. That's at your hotel."

"Who's Nick Waterman?"

"The producer of the 'Case Show.' Himself, my dear. No assistants, no feeling around. He's coming to meet you and brief you about the show."

"Will it be scary?" She sounded like a kid dreading a trip to the dentist, and he smiled. He wished she'd sit back and enjoy it. But in time she would.

"No, it won't be scary. And there's a party tonight after the show. They want you to go to it."

"Do I have to?"

"Why don't you just see how you feel after the show?"

"Okay. What am I supposed to wear to the Polo Lounge, by the way? Everyone around here seems to be wearing denim and mink."

"In the morning?"

"Well, they're wearing denim, but they're carrying mink."

"Is that what you wore?" He sounded amused.

"I wore a cotton dress."

"Sounds refreshing. Lunch might be a little dressier than that. But it's up to you. Be comfortable, be yourself. Waterman is a very nice, easygoing guy."

"You know him?"

"We've played tennis together a few times. Very pleasant. Just relax and trust me." He could hear her starting to get nervous.

"All right. I guess I'll go order my pink grasshoppers and lemonade and relax by the pool."

"You do that." A moment later they hung up. He was relieved that she sounded relatively calm. The "Case Show" was important, a lot more so than Kate realized. She was about to be catapulted into the eye of the American public, and she was either going to be loved or hated—or they'd decide they didn't give a damn. But if they decided that she was someone they cared about, someone who made them laugh and cry and know she was human, then every book she wrote would sell. She had talent, but it took more than that. They had to love *her*. And Stu Weinberg knew that if she let herself go, they would. The big If. He had taken a big chance leveling with Waterman. Maybe he was crazy to trust the guy. But he had a gut feeling about him, and he hoped he wasn't wrong. He rarely was. They had played tennis the evening before, and had had a long round of drinks after the game. He had told Waterman that Kate had been something of a recluse, a beautiful one, but a recluse nonetheless. And he suspected that she had been that way since the death of her husband. It was important that no one hurt her now, or frighten her back into her cave. Stu didn't want Jasper Case playing with her on the show, or setting her up side by side with some Hollywood bitch. This had to be done gently or not at all. Her career depended on it. And Waterman said he'd take care of it himself. He had even agreed to come to lunch himself, instead of sending the woman who usually went. And there had been a quick shuffling in the seating for the show. The cancelation of the big female star this morning would be a break for Kate too. Stu was just praying that all would go well. And he was counting on Waterman. It was going to be an interesting lunch, watching Kate slowly step out into the world.

CHAPTER 16

She waited in the bungalow until twelve twenty-five, tapping her foot nervously on the thick beige carpet in the little sitting room. Should she be on time? Or was she supposed to be late? Should she leave her room now? Or in five minutes, at exactly twelve-thirty? And what if what she was wearing was totally wrong? She had tried on three of the outfits she'd brought, and she still wasn't sure. She was wearing a white linen pantsuit Felicia had insisted was "very L.A.," white sandals, and no jewelry other than her wedding band and the watch Licia had given her "For courage, For valor." She pressed her hand to it for a moment as she sat there and closed her eyes. She could still smell the flowers that had arrived for her. A huge arrangement of spring flowers, with big bright red and yellow tulips, and all the flowers she loved. The arrangement was from the "Case Show." And the hotel had delivered a bottle of Bordeaux, Chateau Margaux '59, and an exquisite bowl of fresh fruit. "With our compliments." She liked the idea of wine rather than champagne, it seemed simpler. The thought made her smile. There was nothing simple about Margaux '59.

"Well, this is it." She said it aloud as she got to her feet with a sigh and took a look around the room. She was terrified. But it was time to go. It was exactly twelve-thirty. But what if he was a jerk? What if he hated her and didn't want her on the show? Or what if he did, and they were awful to her on the air? "Oh shit." She said it aloud again and then grinned as she left the room.

The walk back to the main building of the hotel seemed endless, and she caught a glimpse of the pool and the tennis courts again, and wished she were there. The suit felt cool on her back as the breeze played with her hair softly framing her face, and she wondered again if she should have worn a dress, or maybe something more glamorous-looking. Felicia had sent her a navy-blue chiffon halter dress too, but she'd never dare wear it on the show. She felt so naked in it. She just couldn't. Maybe tonight, if she went to the party. The party . . . she felt as though she were running along a railroad track, with an express train rushing up behind her.

"Madam?" She was already there, staring into a black pit. The Polo Lounge was a well of darkness she couldn't see into. A glimpse of pink tablecloths, a tiny bar, a series of red banquettes. After the bright sunlight she could only guess at who was there and what she saw. She could hear them though. It sounded like hundreds of people, eating and talking and laughing and asking for phones. Just outside the room there was a bank of unoccupied pay phones. Obviously they were never used. No one would dream of going outside, when you could ask for a phone at the table and impress passers-by. . . . "Four hundred thousand? You're crazy. . . ." The phones at the table were more fun. "Madam?" He said it again, looking her over. She looked pretty but not glamorous. He was used to dazzling women, like the actresses and subtly noticeable call girls she thought she glimpsed threaded into the group at the bar.

"I'm meeting Mr. Weinberg, Stuart Weinberg.

And . . ." But the headwaiter was already smiling. "Miss Harper?" She nodded, incredulous. "The gentlemen are waiting for you outside on the terrace. Mr. Waterman is already with Mr. Weinberg." He carefully led the way, as Kate followed him, still barely able to see. But she didn't need to see the faces. Even their voices sounded important. And there seemed to be a lot of long, blond hair, a lot of clanking of bracelets, and a lot of men with clinging, open shirts and clusters of gold around their necks. But she barely had time to look more closely in the gloom, as the headwaiter sped toward the back and led her out to the terrace with a look of enormous decorum. It was nice to be out in the sunshine again, and it was good to see someone familiar, as she caught sight of Stu.

"Well, well, you made it. And don't you look pretty!" She blushed beneath her tan as Stu stood up and hugged her in a warm brotherly way. He looked into her face approvingly and they exchanged an easy smile.

"I'm sorry I'm late." She glanced around the table, not really allowing herself to see the other man, and looking at the chair which a waiter quickly pulled out for her. And then she was seated, and Stu swept an easy hand in the direction of the man to his right.

"You're not late. And Kate, I'd like you to meet Nick Waterman. Nick, Kate." Kate smiled nervously and let her eyes stray to Nick's face as she shook his hand. It was a large, very firm hand, and the eyes were a fierce tropical blue as they held hers.

"Hello, Kate. I've been anxious to meet you. Stu gave me a copy of the book. It's terrific. Even better than your last." He showered her with what felt like a torrent of sunshine from his eyes, and she felt herself start to relax.

"You read my first one?" He nodded and she looked

193

at him, stunned. "You *did*?" He nodded again and laughed as he sat back in his chair.

"Didn't you think anyone read them?" He sounded vastly amused.

"Not really, I guess." How do you explain to someone that you haven't been anywhere to find out if anyone was really reading them? Tillie had read her book, and Mr. Erhard, but she always figured they did it because she gave them free copies. It was incredible to meet a stranger who had read her too.

"Just don't say that on the show." Stu looked at her with a grin and signaled to the waiter. "What'll you have?"

"Pink grasshoppers." She said it in a careful whisper and grinned, Stu started to laugh again, and Nick looked bewildered as the waiter rapidly made a note.

"A grasshopper for the lady?"

"No, no!" And then she was laughing too. "I don't know. Iced tea, I guess."

"Iced tea?" Stu looked surprised. "You don't drink?"

"Not when I'm nervous. I'll pass out over lunch."

Stu glanced over at Waterman with a smile and patted Kate's hand.

"I promise I won't let him attack you till after dessert." And then they were all laughing again.

"Actually, I think I'm drunk already. Oh, and by the way, the flowers were beautiful." She turned to Nick Waterman and felt herself blush again. She wasn't sure why, but he made her faintly uncomfortable. There was something magnetic about him, that made you want to seek out his eyes, made you want to reach out to him, but it frightened her. It was terrifying to be drawn to a man after all these years, even if only in conversation. And he was so big, so *there*. It was impossible to avoid him. And she didn't really want to. That was what frightened her.

"What do you think of Hollywood, Kate?" Standard, ordinary question, but she felt herself start to blush again under his gaze and hated herself for it.

"After two hours, I'm already overwhelmed. Is this really it? Or is the hotel some sort of mad oasis in the midst of a saner world?"

"Not at all. If anything, this is the mainstay. It becomes crazier and crazier the further away you get." The two men exchanged a sympathetic glance and Kate smiled.

"How do you stand it?"

"I was born here," Stu said proudly. "It's in the genes."

"How terrible, can they operate?" Kate gave him a serious look. Nick laughed and she bravely turned to look at him too. "What about you?"

"I'm clean. I'm from Cleveland."

"Gawd," Weinberg said derisively as the waiter set the iced tea down in front of Kate. She smiled softly.

"I went to Cleveland once. It's very pretty." She was lost in her iced tea.

"Lady, I hate to tell you this." The voice at her side was a deep, baritone caress. "But you didn't go to Cleveland."

"Oh yes, I did." She looked up at him with a told-you-so smile, and his blue eyes flashed at her.

"Not if it was pretty you didn't."

"All right, let's just say I had a good time."

"That's better. Now I believe you."

They ordered huge bowls of shrimp on ice, and asparagus vinaigrette, and there was delicious hot French bread.

"Well, Kate, shall we talk about the show tonight?" Nick looked over at her with a gentle smile.

"I'm trying very hard not to."

"That's what I thought." The smile broadened.

"You don't have anything to worry about. Not a thing. All you have to do is what you just did."

"Stuff my face?" She grinned at him and he wanted to reach out and ruffle the carefully done hair. But he wouldn't do anything to surprise her, or she would run like a frightened doe back into the forest. He had listened carefully to what Weinberg had said. When she spoke, there was no trace of skittishness about her. In fact, she was kind of ballsy, and he liked it. But there was something different in her eyes. Something frightened, something sad, something older than her body or her face. Wherever she had been hiding, it had not been a happy place. It made him want to reach out to her and take her in his arms. That would have blown it for sure. Weinberg would have killed him. He grinned at the thought and brought his mind back to what she was saying about the show.

"No, Kate, I'm serious. All you have to do is chat, laugh a little, say what comes to mind—but no four-letter words, please!" He rolled his eyes. They had had to bleep two "shits" and a "fuck" the night before with that goddamn comic Jasper had been so hot to have on. He had enough problems without a night full of language. "But all you have to do is be you. Relax. Listen. Jasper is a master at the art. You'll feel like you're at home in your own living room."

"I can't imagine feeling that way, between worrying about whether I'm going to pass out or throw up."

"You won't. You'll love it. You'll never want to get off."

"Bullshit."

"Say that, and I'll get you off myself!"

"Is it live?" She looked horrified but he shook his head.

196

"Nope. So all you have to do is look pretty and have fun. Is there anything you particularly want to talk about?" He looked serious now and she liked him better than ever.

She thought about it for a minute, and then shook her head.

"Think about it, Kate. Any particular aspect of the book that means a great deal to you? Something that would make it more real, bring it closer to our viewers? Something that will make them want to run out and buy it? Maybe something that happened to you while you wrote it? In fact, why did you write it?"

"Because I wanted to tell that story. I guess it was just something I cared about, so I wanted to write about it for other people. But that's not very remarkable. The decay of a marriage and a love affair is hardly hot stuff."

"Bleep that!" Weinberg rolled his eyes. "Whatever you do, love, don't talk them *out* of buying the book!"

"Seriously, Kate." Nick was watching her again as he talked. The eyes, the eyes, there was something in her eyes. What the hell was it? Fear? No, something else. Something deeper. He wanted desperately to know what it was, to reach out to her. The feelings were wildly inappropriate at this lunch, and she was looking away from him now, down at her hands, as though she sensed that he saw too much. "All right then, why did you write about football?"

She didn't look up. "I thought it would provide background. And that men might relate to the book too. Good commercial value." He didn't know why, but he didn't believe her, and when she looked up at him, he knew he didn't. Almost as if something had clicked.

"You put some beautiful insights into that, Kate.

197

I almost got more excited about that than about the rest. You know the game. Not just football, the sport, but the *game*. I loved that."

"Did you play in college?" She felt as though they were alone now. Stu Weinberg knew he was forgotten, but he didn't mind.

Nick was nodding in answer to Kate's question. "All through college, and one year of pro. I tore up both knees in my first season, and had to call it quits."

"You're lucky. It's a shitful sport."

"Do you really think that? That's not what I heard in the book."

"I don't know. It's a crazy savage way to kill people."

"How do you know all that, Kate?"

Her answer was quick and very smooth, and delivered with a Hollywood smile. "Careful research for the book."

"That must have been fun." He was smiling too, but still searching, still watching. She wanted to hide from him again, but she couldn't. And the bitch of it was that she wished she didn't have to hide. But she couldn't afford to get to know this man. He knew football. He was dangerous. She couldn't afford him even as a friend. "Would you talk about the research on the show?"

She shook her head and then shrugged. "It wouldn't be very interesting. Some games, some listening, some interviews, some reading. That really isn't the main point of the book."

"Maybe you're right." He wasn't going to push. "Well then, what about you? Married?" He looked at the thin gold band still on her left hand, and remembered what Weinberg had said about her being a widow. But he didn't want it to look as though he knew too much. As far as he could tell, he didn't know enough.

"No. Widowed. But for God's sake, don't say that on the show. It'll sound so melodramatic."

"Good point. Kids?"

Her face lit up at the question and she nodded, but hesitantly. "Yes. One. But I don't really want to talk about him either."

"Why not?" Nick looked surprised. "Hell, if I had a kid I'd talk about nothing but." Maybe there was a bitchy side to her after all, but he didn't think so.

"I take it you don't have kids."

"Brilliant deduction, madam." He toasted her with the last of his bloody mary. "I am totally pure and untouched. No kids, no wife, no nothing."

"Never?" She was surprised. What was a man like that doing wandering around on the loose? Gay? He couldn't be. Maybe he had a heavy starlet habit. That seemed the only answer. "I guess that makes sense around here," she said. "There's so much to choose from." She looked around the terrace with a mischievous grin and he threw back his head and laughed.

"Ya got me."

Weinberg smiled at them both, and then sat back with pleasure. She was doing just fine. He didn't need to say a word.

"So why won't you talk about your kid? Boy or girl, by the way?"

"A boy. He's six. And terrific. A real little cowboy." She looked as though she were sharing her best secret and Nick smiled again as he watched her, and then her face grew serious. "I just don't want to expose him to what I do. He leads a nice, simple life in the country. I want to keep it that way. Just in case . . . in case . . ."

"In case Mom becomes a celebrity, huh?" Nick looked amused. "What does he think of all this?"

"Not much. He was barely speaking to me when I left. He's . . . he's not used to my being away. I . . . he was pissed." She looked up with a broad smile.

"You'll have to take him back something he wants."

"Yeah. Me."

"And you spoil him rotten, don't you?"

"No. A friend of mine does that." A friend. So that was it. There *was* somebody. Dammit. But nothing showed in his face.

"So, let's see, where does that leave poor Jasper tonight? You won't talk about football or your research, and you won't talk about your kid. How about a dog?" He was grinning at her and Stu rolled his eyes and got back into the conversation.

"You shouldn't have said that. You just blew it."

"She has a dog?"

"I have a Bert." Kate looked prim as she said it. "Bert is not a dog, he's a person. He's black and white with long ears. And a fabulous face."

"What does that make him? A cocker spaniel?"

"Of course not!" She looked offended. "A basset hound."

"Great. I'll be sure to tell Jasper. Okay, lady, be serious, what'll you talk about? Marriage? How about marriage? Any views on marriage?"

"I love it. It's very nice." So why didn't she marry the "friend" who spoiled her kid? Or was she still carrying the torch for her dead husband? He hadn't figured that one out yet. But he would.

"Living together? Any feelings about that?"

"That's nice too." She grinned and finished her iced tea.

"Politics?"

"I'm not political. And, Mr. Waterman"—she looked

up mischievously again—"I must tell you that I am very boring. I write. I love my kid."

"And your dog. Don't forget your dog."

"And my dog. And that's about it."

"What about your teaching?" Stu stepped into it again with a serious look on his face. "Don't you teach retarded kids or something?" He had gotten Tillie on the phone a few times when she was visiting Tom.

"I promised the school I wouldn't mention it." That was a lie she was still good at, and Nick Waterman sat back with a smile.

"I've got it! Weather! You can talk to Jasper about the weather!" He was teasing but Kate looked suddenly crestfallen.

"Is it really that bad? Jesus. I'm sorry."

But instantly his hand covered hers and his face softened from laughter to something that almost looked like love. It startled her, it happened so quickly. "I'm only teasing you. It's going to be just fine. We never know what's going to come up. Subjects may come up that you never knew you cared about. You may end up carrying the whole show. But no matter what, you're bright enough and pretty enough and amusing enough to carry the ball for as long as you have it. Just relax. And I'll be out there waving at you, and grinning, and making terrible faces to keep you amused."

"I'll never make it." She practically groaned as she thought of it.

"You'd better, sweetheart. Or I'll kick your ass." It was Weinberg again and they all laughed. But she had to admit that she felt better now. At least she knew she had a friend on the show. Nick Waterman was already a friend.

"What are you doing this afternoon?" Nick was looking at his watch as he asked. It was already ten after three, and he had things to do back at the studio.

"I thought I'd take a swim and relax for a while. I have to be there at a quarter to seven?"

"Better make it six-fifteen or six-thirty. We tape at seven. You can check your makeup, chat with the other guests in the Red Room, and just kind of settle in. Oh, and before I forget, you can't wear white. It'll glare on us."

"I can't?" She looked horrified. "What about off-white?"

He shook his head.

"Oh my God."

"That's all you brought?" He said it the way a husband would looking over his wife's shoulder as she dressed, and she felt awkward at the intimacy.

"I was going to wear a cream-colored suit with a peach-colored blouse."

"Sounds gorgeous. I'll have to take you to dinner sometime just to see it. But not on the show, Kate. I'm sorry." He looked sorry, too, and she looked sick. She should have listened to Licia, and gotten a bunch of things from the store, but she had been so sure about the suit. And the only other thing she had to wear was that half-naked, navy-blue, chiffon halter dress. And she didn't want to be that bare on national television. Christ, they'd think she was a hooker. "Do you have anything else? You can always go shopping, you know."

"I guess I'd better. I brought something else, but it's too naked." Weinberg perked up his ears, and Waterman glanced at him. They had both been afraid she'd wear something too serious.

"Whatcha got?" Waterman asked.

"A navy-blue halter dress. But I'll look like a tart." Weinberg whooped and Waterman grinned.

"Believe me, Kate, you wouldn't know how to look like a tart."

"Is that a compliment?" She had a feeling it wasn't, but Nick looked around with an air of acute boredom at the overdecorated women at the surrounding tables.

"In this town, Kate, that's a compliment. Is the dress sexy?"

"Sort of. It's more just dressy."

"Glamorous?" She nodded again, almost apologetically, and he beamed.

"Wear it."

"You mean it?"

"I mean it." The two men exchanged a smile, and Nick Waterman signed the check.

CHAPTER 17

Kate took a last look in the mirror as she got ready to leave the bungalow. She had been planning to order a cab, so she wouldn't get lost driving herself around L.A. But Nick's secretary had called an hour before to tell her he was sending a car for her. At six. And the desk had just called to tell her it was there. She had already phoned Felicia twice, in a panic. Talked to Tygue. Gone for a swim, washed her hair, done her nails, and changed earrings and shoes three times. She was finally set. She still felt like a tart in that dress. But a very high-priced one.

The dress bared her narrow, elegant shoulders and showed off her long, delicate neck. It had a high-necked halter, and there was very little fabric at her back, but no one would see that on the air—she'd have her back against the chair. The dress nipped in carefully at the waist and then flowed gracefully away again. She had decided finally on the navy silk sandals Licia had suggested she wear with it, pearl earrings, and her hair swept up in a carefully done knot. It was the same hairdo her mother had been wearing, years ago, the last time she'd seen her, but Kate didn't remember that anymore. The hairdo just looked right to her. And other than the pearl earrings, the only jewelry she wore was her wedding band. She looked striking and understated and the mirror told her that everything worked. She hoped Nick thought so too, and then she blushed again at the thought. Not Nick as a man, just Nick as the producer of the show. But there was an overlap in her mind between Nick's functions as mentor, advisor, friend, man. It was a confusing rush of feelings for a man she'd known only since noon. But she was anxious to see him and know that she looked all right for the show. And if she didn't, she was up shit creek. She hadn't gone shopping that afternoon. She had decided to take a chance on the one suitable dress she had. If they hated it for the show, she was stuck. But Felicia said they'd love it. And she was usually right.

Kate wrapped a midnight-blue shawl of web-thin crochet around her shoulders, picked up her bag, and opened the door. This is it: She couldn't get the words out of her head. This Is It. She wouldn't let herself listen to that feeling as she walked quickly to the main lobby and then down the breezeway under the awning until she stood next to the doorman at the curb.

"Miss Harper?" How the hell did he know? There were armies of people passing by. It was amazing. She noticed a floor-length chinchilla coat on a very old, very ugly woman, followed by three middle-aged fags, and she forced her attention back to the doorman.

"Yes. I'm Miss Harper."

"The car is waiting." He signaled to a limousine parked to one side, and an endlessly long chocolate-brown Mercedes sped to her feet. For me? Talk about Cinderella! She wanted to laugh but she didn't dare.

"Thank you." The driver held open the door for her, having leapt out almost before the doorman could reach it, and the two uniformed men stood there as she slipped inside. Once again, she had the wild urge to poke somebody, to collapse, giggling, in the back seat. But there was no one to giggle with. She was suddenly dying to see Nick and say something to him. And then she realized that she couldn't. To him this was everyday. To her, it was once in a lifetime.

The car sped through unknown neighborhoods, past mansions and palm trees, and into uncharted areas of freeway she knew she would have been lost on forever, and then they reached a long, unpretentious, sand-colored building. The studio. The car stopped, the driver opened her door, and she stepped out. It was difficult not to make An Exit. Difficult not to look imperious just for the hell of it. But she reminded herself that Cinderella had lost the glass slipper and almost broken her ass on the stairs.

"Thank you." She smiled at the driver, and was pleased that the voice still sounded like Kate's, not "Miss Harper's." But she was getting to like the "Miss Harper" stuff. It was a riot. Kaitlin Harper. The Author.

Two security guards stood just inside the door, and asked for her identification when she got inside. But before she could give it to them, a young woman with sheaves of blond hair appeared and smiled at the guards.

"I'll take you up now, Miss Harper." The two guards smiled now too, one of them looking apprecia-tively at the blond girl's ass. She was wearing the standard pair of jeans, with Gucci shoes, and a little see-through white top. Kate felt like her mother. The girl was probably only twenty-two, but she had an air about her that Kate hadn't had for years, if ever. Maybe, way back when, a thousand years ago . . . it was hard to remember.

"Everything's all set in the Red Room." The girl continued to chat amiably as they took an elevator to the second floor. They could have walked just as easily, but Kate sensed immediately that would not have been the thing to do. This was a town where everything one did reflected one's status.

They emerged into an anonymous corridor, and Kate tried to glance at the photographs mounted on the walls. They were faces she had seen in major movies, in newspapers, in news reports on television, even some faces from the backs of book jackets. She wondered if one day they'd have her face up there too, and for one mad heavenly moment she wanted her face up there. Kaitlin Harper . . . Ha! That's me! See! Me! I'm Kate! But the girl was already holding open a door. The inner sanctum. A ring of guards protected it outside and in, and the door opened only by key. A long white-carpeted hall now. White? How impractical. But obviously nobody gave a damn. It was beautiful. More photographs. These were more personal, and in all of them there was Jasper Case. He was an attractive man in the photographs, silver-haired and very tall. He had a certain elegance about him. And she knew from watching the show that his English accent added to the distinguished image. And he got the best interviews on television, because he was never pretentious, never vicious, always warm, thorough, interested, and he somehow managed to draw the viewer into the conversation. The man sitting at home drinking Ovaltine and watching Jasper before he went to bed felt as if all Jasper's guests were sitting in his own living room and including him in the party.

Kate was still engrossed in the photographs when she heard another door open with one of the girl's magical keys, and she found herself looking into what appeared to be a guest room. It was done in dusty rose and looked very glamorous. There was a couch, several easy chairs, the now standard chaise longue, a vanity, a jungle of orchid plants, and other leafy wonders hanging from the ceiling. It was the kind of room Kate would have dreamed of as an office, instead of the grubby hole where she, and most writers, did their work.

"This is your dressing room, Miss Harper. If you want to change or lie down. Whatever. When you're ready, just press the buzzer and I'll take you down to the Red Room." You will? You promise? But do I gotta? Kate liked the pink room. Who needed the Red Room?

"Thank you." They were the only two words she could think of. She was too busy being overwhelmed. And when she stepped inside and the door closed, she noticed a delicate bouquet of pink roses and baby's breath, with a little card. She walked over to it, wondering if the flowers were for someone else. Surely someone more important. But her name was on the envelope. She opened it with curiosity and trembling fingers. Stu maybe?

But they weren't from Stu. They were from Nick. "Don't forget the dog and the weather. Nick." She laughed at the card, and sat down and looked around the room. She had nothing to do there, except gape. She felt the shawl fall away from her shoulders as she sat in one of the large comfortable chairs and let it swallow her. And then, nervously, she jumped up and looked in the full-length mirror. Did she look all right? Was the dress awful? Was she . . . did she . . . should she . . . there was a soft knock which interrupted her glaring at herself in sheer panic.

"Kate?" It was a man's voice, a deep one, and she suddenly smiled. She wasn't alone after all. She pulled open the door, and there he was, tall and smiling. Nicholas Waterman. He was even taller than she had remembered from lunch, but his eyes were just as she had left them, warm and kind, the eyes of a friend. "How're you doing?"

"I'm a wreck." She beckoned him inside and shut the door like a fellow conspirator, and then she remembered the roses. "Thank you for the flowers. How do I look?" Everything was coming out staccato and bumpy and she wanted to lie facedown on the floor and hide. "Oh, I can't stand it." She sank onto the couch and almost groaned. Nick laughed.

"You look beautiful. And you're fine. Just remember. The dog and the weather. Right?"

"Oh shut up." But then she noticed him looking at her and squinting. "What is it?"

"Take your hair down."

"Now? I'll never get it back up." She looked horrified.

"That's the whole point, silly. Come on. That dress needs long hair." He sat back on the couch next to her and waited, as she looked at him with an astonished grin.

"Do you do this with everybody who comes on the show?" What a disappointing thought. She hoped he didn't.

"Of course not. But not everybody comes on this show on the strength of her dog and the weather."

"Will you stop that!" She was grinning broadly now. And she had just decided again that she loved his eyes.

"Take your hair down." He looked like a big brother trying to teach her a new sport. She was going to resist, but she decided to let herself be persuaded.

"Okay. But I'll look a mess."

"You wouldn't know how to."

"You're crazy."

It was bathroom patter. He shaves while she dries. She combs her hair while he does his tie. She looked at him with a smile as her hair cascaded past her shoulders in soft, loose, gentle waves. He grinned. He had been right.

"Some mess, gorgeous one. Take a look in the mirror."

She did, and frowned uncertainly. "I look like I just woke up." There was something he wanted to say to her, but he didn't say it. He just smiled.

"You look perfect. And you have just sold your book to half the men in America. The other half are either too old or too young. But if they're awake for the show, Kate—you've sold 'em."

"You like it like this?"

"I love it." And he loved the dress. She looked exquisite. Tall and delicate, elegant and sexy. There was a kind of naïve glamour about her. She didn't know it, but she was the kind of woman men were going to crawl over each other to get to. It was the subtlety, the hint of shyness behind the humor, the reserve mixed in with the mischief. Without thinking, he took her by the hand. "Ready?" She had to pee, but she couldn't tell him. She just nodded, with a smile.

"Ready." She was so breathless she could hardly say it.

"Then on to the Red Room."

There was champagne there, and coffee. There were sandwiches, and a plate of *pâté de foie gras*. There were magazines, aspirins, and assorted other remedies for minor ills, including several rather ferocious hangover remedies. And there were faces Kate had never expected to be in the same room with. A journalist from New York, a comedian she had heard of all her life, who had just flown in from Las Vegas to do the show, a major singing star, an actress, and a man who had spent four years in Africa writing a book about

210

zebras. She had heard of them all, seen them all. There were no unknowns there. And then she grinned to herself. She was the unknown.

Nick introduced her to everyone and handed her the ginger ale she had asked for. At exactly a quarter to seven he left the room. The zebra man was sitting across from her, making inane conversation in his almost unintelligible Etonian accent, and the female singing star was looking Kate over.

"Looks like the producer's got the hots for you, darling. Old flame or new one? Is that how you got on the show?" She filed a clawlike crimson nail and then grinned over at the actress, who was her friend. There was a new face in town and they didn't like it. Kate smiled at them, wishing she were dead. What the hell did you say? Fuck off? May I have your autograph? She continued to smile inanely and crossed her legs, wondering if they could see her knees shake. And then the comedian and the journalist saved her, as though they had been dropped from the sky just for that purpose. The journalist insisted that he needed her help with the *pâté,* and the comedian immediately pelted her with funny remarks, and the three of them wound up together for the duration, on the other side of the room, while the other two women seethed. But Kate didn't notice. She was too nervous, and too busy chatting. Nick had been right; every man in the room would have given his right arm to go home with her. But Kate was too worried about the show to notice the effect she was having on them.

"What's it like?"

"Like falling into a bed of marshmallows." The comedian looked at her with a smile. "Want to try that sometime?" She laughed at him and sipped her ginger ale. Oh Jesus, what if it made her burp? She put it down, and squeezed the paper napkin with her damp hands. "Don't worry, baby. You're gonna love it." The comedian whispered it to her gently with a warm smile. He was old enough to be her father but she could feel his hand on her knee. She wasn't sure if she was going to love it or not. And then suddenly, it was air time. A sudden current of electricity seemed to pass around the room, and everyone fell silent.

The singing star went on first. She did two songs, and left after five minutes of chatting with Jasper, who was "enormously grateful that she could stop by, and knew she had a special to tape." Kate was enormously grateful when she left five minutes later. The journalist was next, and was surprisingly amusing. He was almost a regular on the show. Then the actress. The comedian. And then . . . oh my God . . . no! Only she and the zebra man were left, and the man at the door with the earphones on his head was beckoning to Kate. Me? Now? But I can't. But she had to.

It felt like walking into a jet stream, or off a cliff. She was numb. She couldn't hear what he was saying. And worse yet, she couldn't hear herself. She wanted to scream as she sat there, but she didn't. She heard herself laughing, chatting, admitting to the appalling outfits she wore when she wrote, talking about her feelings about living in the country. Jasper's boyhood had been spent in a place that he said was much like the place she described. They talked about writing, and the discipline of the profession, and even about how funny it was to come to L.A. She found herself cracking jokes about the women she'd seen around the pool, and the droopy-assed old men squashed into their jeans and body shirts with their dangling doodads of gold around their necks. She almost made an outrageous allusion and then backed off, which made it even funnier, because the audience caught the allu-

212

sion without her having to say it. She was fabulous
and she was Kate. And somewhere out there, in the
lights and electric lines and confusion and cameras,
was Nick, making victory signs and grinning at her
with pride. She had done it! And then there was the
zebra man, and by then Kate was right at home, laughing and loving it, part of the jokes and the conversation. The journalist and the comedian kept aiming
good lines at her, and she and Jasper looked as though
they'd been dancing together for years. It was one of
those shows that jelled from beginning to end, and
Kate was the diamond in the night's tiara. She was
still flying high when they went off the air, and Jasper
kissed her on both cheeks.

"You were marvelous, my dear. I hope we see you
again."

"Thank you! Oh it was wonderful! And it was so
easy!" She was blushing and breathless and loving it
and then suddenly she found herself in the comedian's
arms.

"Want to try that bed of marshmallows now, baby?"
But she even laughed at him too. She loved them all.
And then, there was Nick, smiling down at her, and
she felt her insides turn to mush.

"You made it. You were terrific." His voice was very
soft in the wild confusion of the studio.

"I forgot to talk about the dog and the weather."
They exchanged a slow smile. She felt shy with him
now. She was Kate again, not the mythical Miss
Harper.

"We'll have to have you back then."

"Thank you for un-scaring me." He laughed and
put an arm around her shoulders. He liked the feel
of her skin on his arm.

"Anytime, Kate, anytime. We have about ten minutes until we ship out for that party, by the way. All set to go?" She had almost forgotten it. And what about Stu? Wasn't she supposed to see him?

"I don't know. I . . . I think Stu . . ."

"He called before you got here. He'll meet us there. It's Jasper's birthday, you know. Everyone will be there." Cinderella at the ball. But why not? She was dying to celebrate.

"Sounds wonderful."

"Do you want to go in one of the brown bananas, or shall we escape the crowds?" He looked away to sign a paper on someone's clipboard and then glanced at his watch.

"The brown bananas?" She looked at him in confusion.

"That's what I sent to pick you up. The brown limo. We have two of them. Everyone is going to the party in the two limos. All the guests from the show, and Jasper. But we could avoid the rush and go in my car." It sounded simpler, but also a little unnerving. She would lose the safety of the group. On the other hand, Kate had a feeling the comedian would find some way back to her knee. It would be easier to go with Nick.

"May I bring my flowers?" He smiled at her question. She had remembered. No one ever did. They left them in the dressing rooms and the maids took them home. But Kate had remembered. She was that kind.

"Sure you can. What's a little water all over the car?" They both laughed as he led her back to the dressing room. There was a slowing of the pace around them, a feeling of winding down, in direct contrast to the mounting tension Kate had sensed before the show. What a way to live. Getting jacked up like that

214

every day. But what a high too. She had never felt as good in her life. Or not in a long time at least. A very long time.

She carefully picked up the vase with the little pink roses and the baby's breath. She had long since slipped the card into her bag. A souvenir of her Cinderella evening. "Thank you for these too, Nick." She wanted to ask him if he was always this thoughtful, but she couldn't. It would have been rude.

It was over now. The performance was finished. They were both real people again. He was no longer The Producer, and she was no longer The Star. She felt a little awkward as they walked quietly out to his car, and then she stood back and whistled. The sound was incongruous with the way she looked.

"Is that yours?" It was a long, low, dark-blue Ferrari with a creamy leather interior.

"I confess. I gave up eating when I bought that."

"I hope it was worth it."

But judging by the way he looked at the car, she knew it had been. In his own way, he was a big kid too. He held the door open for her and she slid inside. The car even smelled expensive, a rich mixture of good leather and expensive men's cologne. She was glad it didn't reek of perfume. That would have upset her.

It was comfortable there in the dark, as he pulled into the constant flow of traffic, and she sat back and started to unwind.

"Why so quiet all of a sudden?" He had noticed.

"Just unwinding, I guess."

"Don't do that yet. Wait till you see the party."

"Will it be a madhouse?"

"Without a doubt. Think you can stand it?"

"This is some debut for a country girl, Mr. Water-

215

man." But she was loving it, and he could see that.

"Something tells me, Kate, that you were not always a country girl. None of this is new to you, is it?"

"On the contrary, it's all new. Or at least, I've never had the limelight on me before."

"But on people near you?" She jumped in her seat, and he looked at her, startled. What had he said? But she looked away and shook her head.

"No. I led a very different sort of life from all this." But he had almost lost her and he knew it. She had hidden again. And then unexpectedly, she looked at him with a warm smile and a sparkle in her eyes. "I certainly never rode around in Ferraris."

"Where did you live before the country?"

"San Francisco." She had hesitated only for a fraction of a second.

"Did you like it?"

"I loved it. I hadn't been back in . . . in years, until about a month ago and then I took my little boy up a week ago, and he fell in love with it too. It's a neat town."

"Any chance you'll move back there?" He looked interested.

She shrugged. "I can't see it really."

"That's too bad. We're thinking about moving the show up there." She looked surprised.

"And away from the mecca of Hollywood? Why?"

"Jasper doesn't like it here. He wants to live someplace more 'civilized.' We suggested New York. But he's tired of that. He was there for ten years. He wants San Francisco. And I suspect"—he looked at her with a rueful grin—"that if he wants it badly enough he'll get it."

"How do you feel about that?"

"Okay, I guess. I've had my kicks here. But it gets old very quickly."

"Quick, bring in the Vestal Virgins!" She laughed at him, and he ran a hand through her hair playfully.

"Vestal Virgins, eh? You must think I use 'em up a dozen a day."

"Don't you?"

"Hell, no. Not anymore! Try as I might, I can't get past eight or nine ladies a day. Must be old age."

"Must be."

They were playing, feeling each other out. Who are you? What do you want? What do you need? Where are you going? But what did it matter? She realized with a little sinking feeling that she'd probably never see him again after tonight. Maybe in another five years, if she had a book that was a big success, if he was still with the show, if there still was a show . . . if.

"Scared?"

"Hm?"

"You looked so serious. I wondered if you were nervous about the party."

"A little, I guess. It doesn't really matter. I'm an unknown. I can be invisible."

"Hardly, love. I don't think you could ever manage that."

"Bullshit."

They laughed again and he pulled into a palm-lined driveway in Beverly Hills. They had been passing mammoth palaces for the past ten minutes.

"Good lord. Is this Jasper's house?" It looked as big as Buckingham Palace. Nick shook his head.

"Hilly Winters."

"The movie producer?"

"Yes, ma'am. Shall we?" Three attendants in crisp white jumpsuits were waiting to take the cars, and the door to the house was being opened by a butler and a maid. One could just glimpse a brilliantly lit hallway before the door closed again. Kate couldn't decide whether to look inside or out at the nonstop stream of Rolls Royces and Bentleys rounding the bend into the drive. It was easy to see why Nick had bought the Ferrari. He moved in a world that resembled no other.

The door opened again, and they were instantly sucked into the eye of a glittering storm. There were easily three hundred people, and Kate had a blurred impression of chandeliers, candles, sequins, diamonds, rubies, furs, and silk. She saw stars from every film she had ever seen, read of, or heard about.

"Do people really live like this?" Kate whispered to him as they stood at the edge of the crowd in the ballroom. The house had a fully mirrored, magnificent ballroom, which had been brought over piece by piece from a chateau on the Loire. How could this be real?

"Some people live like this, Kate. Some of them do it for a while, some forever. Most don't do it for very long. They make a fortune in the movies, spend it, blow it, give it away." He eyed a pack of rock stars at the other side of the room. They stood in skin-tight satin, and the wife of the lead singer was wearing a very bare skin-colored dress and floor-length sables with a hood. A little warm for the ballroom, but she looked happy. "That kind comes and goes quickly. People like Hilly will be here forever."

"It must be fun." She looked like a little girl peeking through the banisters at a Mardi gras ball.

"Is that what you want?" But he already knew it wasn't.

"No. I suppose I don't really want anything different from what I have." Yeah. The friend who spoils your kid. He remembered that, and suddenly felt bitter. She had more than anyone in that room. And much more than he had. Lucky bitch. But she wasn't a bitch. That was what bothered him. He liked her. Too damn much. And she was so naïve. He wondered what would happen if he just grabbed her and kissed her. She'd probably slap him. Marvelous old-fashioned gesture. The thought of it made him laugh as he put an empty glass of champagne back on a tray. And then he noticed that she was gone. She had drifted off in the throng, and he could see her twenty feet away, being harangued by some guy in a maroon velvet dinner jacket. He was one of the local hangers-on. Somebody's hairdresser, somebody's boy friend, somebody's son. There were a lot of guys like him around Hollywood. Nick started to move slowly through the crowd to get back to her. He couldn't hear the conversation, but she didn't look happy.

"Harper? Oh yeah. The writer on Jasper's show tonight. We saw you."

"That's nice." She was trying to be polite, but it wasn't easy. The guy was drunk, for a start. She still couldn't understand how she could have gotten pushed this far away from Nick, but there were so many people, and the ballroom was becoming the big attraction. The band was beginning to play some hot rock.

"How come a broad like you wrote a book about football?"

"Why not?" She looked at Nick. It was hopeless to try to get to him. But he was slowly making his way toward her. Another two minutes maybe.

"You know, there was a football player years ago with the same name as yours. Harper. Bill Harper. Joe Harper. Something like that. Went nuts. Tried to kill somebody and shot himself instead. Nuts. They're all nuts. Killers. You related to him?" He looked up sloppily at Kate and burped. It would have been funny except that suddenly she knew the clock had struck twelve. It was over now. It had happened. Someone had remembered. Someone. That was all it took.

From where he stood, Nick could see panic break out on her face. "You related to him?" The guy was persistent, and smiling ghoulishly.

"I . . . what? No. Of course not!"

"I didn't think so." But Kate didn't hear his last words. She pushed herself in the direction of Nick who forded the last clump of bodies between them, and finally reached her. There was terror stamped all over her face.

"Are you all right? Did that guy say something out of line to you?"

"I . . . no . . . no, no, nothing like that." But there were tears swimming in her eyes, and she looked away. "I'm sorry, Nick. I'm not feeling well. It must be all the excitement. The champagne. I . . . I'll call a cab." She was squeezing her handbag and looking around nervously as she spoke.

"The hell you will. Are you sure that guy didn't say something?" He'd kill him if he had. What the hell had he done to her?

"No, really." He knew she wouldn't tell him the truth, and that made him madder still. "I just want to go home." She said it like a child, and without another word, he put his arm tightly around her and led her out into the main foyer, and then quietly out of the house, after collecting her shawl.

"Kate"—he looked down at her as they waited for the car—"please tell me what happened."

"Nothing, Nick. Nothing. Really." He tilted her face up to his without saying a word, and in spite of herself, two tears spilled out of her eyes and onto her cheeks. "I just got frightened, that's all. I haven't been around . . . around people for a very long time."

"I'm sorry, baby." He folded her into his arms and held her there until the car came. She stood there, feeling his jacket, and breathing the scent of him in the night air. He smelled of spice and lemons and he was warm and solid next to her. When the car came, she pulled away slowly, took a deep breath, and smiled.

"I'm sorry to be such a fool."

"You're not. I'm sorry that happened. This should have been your big night."

"It was." She looked at him as she said it, and then slipped into the car. She had done it at least. Done the show. Gone to the party. It wasn't anyone's fault that someone had remembered Tom. But it was heartbreaking to know that some people still did. Why couldn't they remember the good years? The happy times? Why did they remember only the end? She looked up and realized that Nick was watching her. He hadn't started the car yet. He wanted to take her home, to his place. But he couldn't, and he knew it.

"Want to stop off someplace for a night cap?" But she shook her head. He'd known she would refuse. He didn't want one either. And he didn't know what else to suggest. A walk? A swim? He was at a loss. He wanted to do something simple with her, not something Hollywood. There were times when he hated this town, and tonight was one of them. "Back to the hotel then?" She nodded regretfully, but with a small, grateful smile.

"You've been wonderful, Nick." A dismissal. He wanted to kick something. And she didn't understand his silence all the way back to the hotel. She was afraid he was angry. But he didn't look it, he looked sad. Or maybe hurt. He was feeling helpless.

"Sure I can't talk you into something glamorous, like an ice-cream cone?"

"Do people indulge in simple pleasures like that here?"

"No, but I'd find you one."

"I'll bet you would." She said it warmly, and she

221

wanted to touch his face as they drove up in front of the hotel. "I'm afraid Cinderella has had her big night at the ball. And if I were you, I'd beat it before this jet plane of yours turns into a pumpkin." They both laughed at the thought, and she picked up her bouquet of roses from the floor. "See, they didn't even spill." He was watching her, and she found his eyes again. "Thank you, Nick. For everything." He didn't move, and for a moment neither did she. She hesitated. She wanted to touch him. His hand. His face. To hold out her arms again and let him hold her. But this was different. She knew she couldn't do that. And she knew, too, that she wouldn't see him again.

"Thank *you*, Kate." He said it very carefully. As though he meant it, but she wasn't sure why.

"Good night." Gently, like a quiet whisper of air, she touched his hand and then opened the car door and was gone. The doorman closed the Ferrari door behind her, and Nick watched her go. He didn't get out, or call her back, or even move. He just sat there, for a very long time. And when he called her the next morning, she had already checked out. It took all his connections through the show to find out from the manager that she had checked out a little after 1 A.M. That was when he'd brought her home. It didn't make any difference, but he had wanted to know. It was that sonofabitch at the party. Damn. And he didn't even know where she lived. He wondered if Weinberg would tell him.

CHAPTER 18

"Tygue, I said no!"

"You always say no. Besides, I don't care what you say!"

"Go to your room!" There was a moment of fierce glaring between them and Tygue gave in first. It was fortunate for him because his mother was in no mood to fool around. She had gotten in just after four in the morning. Tillie had left at six-thirty. And it was now only seven. Kate had had two and a half hours of sleep. This was not the day for Tygue to decide to give Bert a bath before school, with her best soap from Licia. Any other day, Kate would have laughed. Today, she wasn't laughing. And her head was still full of what had happened in L.A. She called Tygue back when breakfast was ready. "Are you going to be reasonable now?" But he said not a word as he sat down to his cereal. She drank her coffee in silence, and then suddenly she remembered something. It was in her suitcase. "I'll be right back." It wasn't really the right time to give it to him, but maybe it was what they both needed. A silly moment. Of her spoiling him and his feeling loved. She had felt so lonely driving home last night. As though she had lost. But she had forced herself out. No one had sent her away. The whole thing was stupid. So what if the guy remembered a football player named Harper? Why did she

223

have to leave like that? And she knew Stu would be angry at her. She had arranged for the hotel to deliver a message to him first thing in the morning: "Was called home unexpectedly, please cancel magazine interview. Terribly sorry. Thank you for everything. Love, Kate." But he'd be mad anyway. She knew it. And she was angry at herself as well. And then with a soft whisper of pleasure she remembered the feel of Nick's hand when she'd said good-bye to him in the car.

"What are you thinking about? You look silly." Tygue had wandered into her room and was watching her from the doorway, his bowl of cereal in his hand, tilting at a precarious angle.

"Don't walk around with your breakfast. And what do you mean, I look silly? That's not a nice thing to say." She sounded hurt, and he looked down into his bowl.

"I'm sorry." He was still mad at her for leaving.

"Go put that in the sink and come back here." He looked up at her and then vanished, clomping loudly along the floor. He was back in seconds with an expectant look on his freckled face. "Wait till you see what I brought you." It was totally outrageous. She had found it in the children's shop at the hotel, and she had had to have it. She had bought it at a scandalous price, but why not? He was the only son she had, and he was never going to have another outfit like this.

"What is it?" He looked suspiciously at the fancy dress box, and the pale blue curlicues of ribbon put him off.

"Go ahead. It won't bite you." She grinned to herself, thinking of the dusty blue velvet suit they'd had too. The idea of her son in that getup had made her laugh right there in the shop, much to the salesperson's horror. But blue velvet on a boy of six was pushing it. Tygue wouldn't have worn it at two. She watched him as, gingerly, he pulled off the ribbons, and then stared at the box for one brief moment before yanking off the lid, pushing aside the tissue paper, and then gasping as he saw it.

"Oh, Mom! Oh! . . . Mom! . . ." There were no words to describe what he felt, and tears burned her eyes as she watched him. They were still tears of fatigue and excitement, but they were tears of joy too. He pulled it out of the box and held it up. A miniature cowboy suit in leather and suede. There was a fringed vest, and chaps. A cowboy shirt, a belt, and a jacket. And when he tore off his clothes and tried it on, it fit him perfectly.

"Well, hotshot? You look gorgeous." She beamed at him from her seat on the bed.

"Oh, Mommy!" She hadn't heard "Mommy" in a while. Only "Mom." Now "Mommy" was saved for special occasions, when no one else was around to hear. He ran up to her in the little cowboy suit and threw his arms around her with a huge mushy kiss.

"Am I forgiven?" She hugged him close with a smile.

"For what?"

"Going away." She cringed at the precedent she was setting, but her son was smarter than she was.

"No," he said matter-of-factly, with a big smile. "But I love the suit. And I love you best of all."

"I love you best of all too." She sat down on the bed, and he piled into her lap. "You should take that off. It's a little fancy for school, darling, isn't it?"

"Awww, Mommm . . . please . . ."

"Okay, okay." She was too tired to argue. And then, unexpectedly, he looked up at her.

"Did you have a good time?"

"Yes, I did. I was on TV, and I stayed in a big hotel, and I had lunch with some people, and went to a party with some other people."

"It sounds terrible." She laughed and looked at him. Maybe he was right. Maybe it had been terrible. But she couldn't really make herself believe that. "When are we going back to San Francisco?"

"Soon. We'll see. Do you want Tillie to take you down to the Adams place today, so you can ride in your new suit?" He nodded vehemently, looking down at the vest with delight. "I'll leave Tillie a note."

But the boy looked up in terror. "Are you going away again?"

"Oh Tygue . . ." She held him tight. "No, sweetheart. I'm just going to see . . . to teach." Jesus. She had almost said it. To see Tom. She was exhausted. She was really too tired to drive up there too. But she felt that she had to. It had been days. "I'll even try to come back early today, and we'll have a nice quiet dinner. Just us. Okay?" He nodded warily, but the terror had left his eyes. "I told you, silly. I'm not going to run off and leave you. Just because I'm gone for a day, or even a couple of days, doesn't mean I'm leaving you. Got that?" He nodded, silent, his eyes huge. "Good." And then the honking of his car pool threw them both into chaos. Lunch pail, books, hat, big kiss, squeeze, good-bye, gone. Kate sat in the kitchen for a moment, trying to summon enough energy to get her jacket and go. She was crazy to make the trip on two hours' sleep. But it was never the right time to go to Carmel anymore. There was always something else she wanted to do. She picked up her bag and her jacket, wrote a note for Tillie, and left as it started to rain.

The soft rain continued as she drove up to Carmel, and it pattered gently on the roof of the cottage as she visited with Tom. It was the kind of gentle summer rain that made her want to turn her face to the sky and run barefoot through the long summer grass, feeling twigs tickle her toes. She didn't do that though. She was too tired to do more than walk to the cottage and sit down. She had nothing much to tell him. She couldn't tell him about L.A., he wouldn't understand. But he was in a peaceful mood. The rain seemed to soothe him, and they sat hand in hand, side by side, he in his wheelchair, she in a cozy rocker, and she told him stories. They were the stories she had known as a child, the same ones she had told Tygue for years. Tom loved them too. And shortly after lunch, he fell asleep. The rhythm of the rain soothed them both and she had to jolt herself a few times to keep from falling asleep too. But once Tom had drifted off, she sat for a moment, watching his peaceful face, letting the rush of memory drift over her . . . the thousand times she had seen that face asleep before, in other places, other days. It made her think of Cleveland, so long ago, and then unexpectedly of Nick Waterman. She didn't want to think of him here. This wasn't his place, it was Tom's. She kissed him gently on the forehead, ran a hand softly over his hair, put a finger to her lips as she looked up at Mr. Erhard, and tiptoed carefully from the room.

It was a long drive home. The roads were fairly deserted and she was anxious to get back, but she didn't dare drive as fast as she normally did. And eventually she had to open the windows and turn on the radio to keep awake. Twice she had to pull over to the side of the road to shake the cobwebs out of her head. She was pushing it and she knew it. She was tempted just to stay there and sleep for a while, but she knew Tillie would want to get home. It was Friday and there was always some member of her family coming for dinner, or the weekend. She only had another fifty miles to go, and she decided to make a run for it, as the thunder clapped and the lightning flashed, and the rain splashed in over the top of the window and washed her face. It made her smile as she felt it. It felt good just being back in her part of the world again. She didn't belong in L.A., but it had been fun for a visit, for a moment. And never again. What totally mad people. She let her mind drift back to the pink dressing room, the tension of the Red Room, and then the opulence of the party in Beverly Hills . . . and then the feeling of Nick Waterman holding her as they waited for his car. She pushed that from her mind with the rest of it, and turned up the radio. L.A. was their world. Not hers.

She turned off at the familiar exit and followed the back road until she reached her driveway. There was a rainbow over the hills. And there was a car in her driveway. As she saw it her foot hit the brakes, hard, and she jolted forward. How . . . but how did . . . where . . . it was a dark-blue Ferrari, and Nick Waterman was standing in the driveway next to Tygue. Tillie waved sheepishly from the door. And with her heart pounding, Kate pulled slowly into the drive. The sound of the gravel startled them both and they turned to look at her. Tygue ran toward the car, waving, with a big grin of excitement, and Nick simply stood there and watched her, with that endless smile of his. She stopped the car and stared back. What could she say? And how had he found her? Weinberg, of course. That was easy. She should have been angry at Stu, and normally she would have been. But she wasn't. Suddenly all she wanted to do was laugh. She was so goddamn tired, all she *could* do was laugh. And Tygue was reaching into the car window and talking as fast as he could.

"Hey, you, wait a minute, slow down. Wait till I get out of the car." But the child certainly looked happy.

"Did you know Nick was a football hero? And he worked in a rodeo?"

"Oh really?" What had happened to him? When Weinberg had been there for only an hour, Tygue had instantly detested him. But Nick was a football hero and a rodeo star. Apparently, he had the touch. She stooped to kiss Tygue and looked across at Nick. He hadn't moved. He just stood there. She walked slowly toward him with a careful smile on her face. Her eyes looked tired, but there was still laughter in them, and the smile was turning into the mischievous one he remembered from lunch.

"How was teaching?"

"Fine. Should I ask what you're doing here?"

"If you like. I came to see you. And Tygue."

She was standing in front of him now, and he looked down at her as though he wanted to kiss her, but Tygue and Bert were already underfoot.

"You make a terrific detective."

"You're not hard to find. Are you angry?" For a moment, he looked worried.

"I suppose I should be. At Stu, not at you. But"— she shrugged—"I'm so damn tired, I couldn't get mad at anybody if my life depended on it." He put an arm around her shoulders and pulled her closer.

"You couldn't have gotten much sleep, Mrs. Harper. What time did you get home?"

"About four." She liked the feel of his arm around her. It was heavenly as they walked slowly back to the house. For a moment she worried about Tygue, but he didn't seem to notice. She couldn't understand how Nick had put the boy so quickly at ease.

"Why did you leave like that?"

"I wanted to come home."

"That badly?" He still didn't believe her.

"The party was over. Cinderella had been to the ball. And what was the point of spending the night in a strange hotel, when I could have been here?"

He looked around and nodded. "I see your point. But I didn't feel that way about it this morning when I called. I got this sinking feeling that . . . that I'd never see you again." His face sobered as he remembered it, and they walked into the house. "Weinberg was damn close-mouthed about it too."

"What changed his mind?" Kate peeled off her damp raincoat. She was wearing jeans and a blue gingham shirt. It was a far cry from the lady in the navy halter dress of the night before. Cinderella was just Cinderella again.

"He changed his mind because I threatened never to play tennis with him again."

"Now I know where his allegiance lies, not to mention his priorities." Kate looked at him and laughed. This was crazy. She had met him yesterday at lunch and now he was here? In her house? With Tygue leaping at his feet? Suddenly it all seemed ridiculous. She sat down in a chair and started to laugh, and she couldn't stop till tears ran down her face.

"What's so funny?" Nick looked blank.

"Everything. You, Weinberg, me, that damn crazy party you took me to last night. I can't even begin to sort out what's real and what isn't." And then Nick started to laugh too, but now there was mischief in his face and he went to his briefcase. He hoped he had guessed right.

"What are you up to over there, Waterman?"

"Well, Kate"—he had his back to her, but there was humor in his voice and Tillie was smiling broadly as she watched the proceedings—"I know what you mean about not being able to sift what's real from what isn't, so . . . to figure things out"—Kate was already grinning as she listened—"I thought I'd come up here once and for all and find out if you were really Cinderella, or just one of the ugly stepsisters." And with that he wheeled around, and produced a glass slipper, reposing on a gold-bordered red velvet cushion. It was a life-sized shoe, the best plastic made, and it had taken his secretary three hours to locate it through the prop department at Paramount. And now she was sitting there, in her blue jeans, laughing again.

"Well, Cinderella, shall we give it a go?" He walked over to where she sat, and she saw that the slipper was a high-heeled, pointed-toe number with a glass rosette. He kneeled at her feet while she broke into fresh whoops of laughter, as she stuck out the "dainty" red rubber boot she had worn in the rain.

"Nick Waterman, you're crazy!" But the entourage was loving it. Tillie couldn't stop laughing, Tygue was hopping around like a flea, and even Bert was chasing and barking as though he knew what was going on. But the boot came off, the shoe slid on, and Nick sat back on his heels with a grin.

"Cinderella, I presume." He couldn't help feeling victorious, and looking it. He had guessed exactly the right size.

She stood up on it gingerly and broke into laughter again. "How the hell did you guess my size?" Practice, obviously. But whatever else he did, he certainly didn't do *this* every day. "And how did you find it?" She sat back down in the chair with a thud and a grin and looked into those magical blue eyes of his.

"God bless Hollywood, Kate. But it did take us a while."

"What time did you get here?"

"About three. Why? Was I late?" He laughed again,

and sat down hard on the floor, narrowly missing Bert, who then crawled onto his lap, leaving two muddy footprints on his clean beige linen trousers. But Nick didn't seem to care. He was more interested in Kate, who was looking at him in astonishment.

"You got here at three? What have you done all this time?" It was already past five.

"Tygue took me down to look at the horses. With Tillie of course." He smiled in her direction, and she blushed, not unlike Kate. There was something about him, so open, so direct; there was no avoiding him, no shying away. "Then we went for a walk down by the river. We played cards for a while. And then you came home."

"Just call me Cinderella." She glanced down at her foot again, and wondered if she could keep the shoe. "You came up here just for this?" She couldn't get over it, but he averted his gaze.

"I was coming up this way anyway, as a matter of fact. I rent a house in Santa Barbara from time to time. I have it this weekend." Something made her doubt him, but she wasn't quite sure what. Why would he lie to her? "May I invite you two over to visit tomorrow?" He looked hopeful, but Tygue immediately jumped in with a fierce shake of his head.

"No!"

"Tygue!" Now what? The man had come all the way up from L.A. with a glass slipper, and Tygue was going to keep her from seeing him? But she wanted to see him! To hell with Tygue.

"But Joey's mom invited me for the weekend! And they have two new goats and his dad said he might get a pony tomorrow!" It was the best news Kate had had all day.

"Hey, podner, that's dynamite!" Nick looked enormously impressed, and Tygue looked at him as though they were the only two people in the room who made any sense.

"Can I go?" He looked imploringly at his mother.

"Why not? Okay. And tell Joey he can come here next weekend. I may regret that, but I'll take my chances."

"Can I call Joey and tell him?"

"Go ahead."

Tillie took her leave as Tygue dashed into the kitchen to use the phone, and Kate held out a hand to Nick. He took it in his, as he sat down more comfortably near her chair.

"I'd like to know what you did to win him over. It must have cost you a fortune."

"Nope. Not yet anyway."

"What does that mean? Nicholas Waterman, what have you been up to? Any man who can show up here with a glass slipper, and in the right size, is a man to be reckoned with."

"I'll accept that as a compliment. No, honest, I didn't do a thing. I just promised to take both of you to Disneyland."

"You did?" She was stunned. He carefully took off the glass shoe, and she wiggled her toes.

"Yes, I did. And your son accepted. He thinks Disneyland is a terrific idea. And he invited me to San Francisco to meet his Aunt Licia. I hope you don't mind."

"Not at all. 'Aunt Licia' would love you. Which reminds me, would you like a martini?"

"That's it? The whole shot? A martini?" He laughed again. "All or nothing, huh?"

"You can have coffee. But the only booze I have right now is the stuff Licia leaves here to make her martinis."

"Your sister?" He was only slightly confused, but

he liked the chaotic family scene he was seeing. And he loved the boy.

"Felicia is my best friend, my conscience, and my alter ego. And she spoils Tygue rotten." That rang a familiar bell with Nick but he wasn't sure why. "Anyway, a martini?"

"I think I'll opt for the coffee. By the way, am I totally disrupting your life?"

"Yes."

"Good." And then his face grew serious and he stopped teasing for a moment. "I mean it though. I asked Weinberg if he thought I'd get punched in the mouth by some six-foot-nine sumo wrestler when I got here, and he said he didn't think so, but he didn't really know. He suggested I take my chances, and proceed at my own risk. Which I did. But all kidding aside, am I going to make trouble for you by being here?" He seemed upset at the thought. She had looked so unhappy at the end of the party the night before. He didn't want to see her that way again. But he had had to see her, even if only once more.

"Of course you're not going to make trouble. Who would you make trouble with? Tygue seems to approve of you. He's the only sumo wrestler around here." She knew what he meant, and she liked him for asking. As she got up to make him coffee, she was wearing one red boot and one stockinged foot and her hair was tangled and loose, the way he liked it. He thought she looked even more beautiful than she had on the show.

"Let me just get this straight. Tygue is the only one around here to object?" He said it slowly and carefully, as though she might not understand.

"That's right."

"Seems to me you said something about a friend." She looked at him quizzically and then shrugged.

"Someone who spoils the boy. You said it at lunch yesterday." And then they both grinned and they said it together, as Nick suddenly understood.

"Aunt Licia."

He smiled broadly and followed her out to the kitchen, where Tygue hung up the phone.

"Okay, Mom. All set. His dad'll pick me up tomorrow morning. And he'll even bring me home Sunday afternoon." He looked up at both of them matter-of-factly, as though he'd known Nick forever. "What's for dinner? Did you know Nick is going to take us to Disneyland? Right, Bert?" Bert wagged his tail, and Tygue left the room in search of Willie, without waiting to hear what was for dinner.

"He's a riot."

"Sometimes." Kate smiled at his retreating back as he left, and then looked up at Nick. "He's a nice kid and I love him a lot."

"You're a good mother. What is for dinner, by the way?"

"Does that mean you'd like to stay for dinner?"

"If it's not too much trouble."

It was amazing. She hardly knew him, and here he was, hanging out in the kitchen, and asking to stay for dinner. But it felt good. Her defenses were not what they should have been; she was just too tired.

"It's not too much trouble. And you made it here just in time for Tygue's favorite gourmet treat."

"What?"

"Tacos."

"That's my favorite too."

She handed him a mug of coffee and sat down at the kitchen table. It was a long way from Carmel right now. A long way from Tom.

"What were you thinking just then?"

"When?"

235

"Just now."

"Nothing."

"You're lying." He was suddenly very intense as he reached out again for her hand. "Are you happy here, Kate?" She looked up at him honestly and nodded.

"Yes. Very." Then what was the shadow? Why the fleeting lightning bolts of pain?

"Are there good people in your life?" he wanted to know. Suddenly it mattered to him.

"Yes. Very. You've met them all now. All except one. Licia."

"That's it?" He looked shocked. "Just the boy?"

"And Tillie, the woman who was here with Tygue when you got here. And Bert, of course." She smiled, remembering her threat to talk about him on the show.

"Of course. But you're serious? This is it?"

"I told you. I'm a hermit." No wonder she had freaked at the party. "I like it this way."

"Was it like this when you were married?" She shook her head, but her eyes gave nothing away.

"No, it was different."

"Does Tygue remember his dad?" His voice was very soft as they sipped their coffee in the quiet kitchen, and she shook her head again.

"He couldn't. His dad died before he was born."

"Oh God, how awful for you, Kate." He looked at her as though he understood what it must have been like. It was the first time in a long time that she had thought of it.

"It was a very long time ago."

"And you were alone?"

"Nope. I had Felicia, she was here with me." Maybe that was it. All that incredible aloneness. Maybe that was the pain he saw.

"No family, Kate?"

236

"Only what you see. This is it. It's a lot more than most people have." And more than he had. She had hit close to home, without even meaning to. All those chicks with the big tits that he'd been taking out for the last twenty years, and where was that? He was thirty-seven years old and he had nothing.

"You're right. Kate."

"What?"

"Will you come to Santa Barbara tomorrow, for the day?" She was the sort of woman he felt he had to say that to. For the day. If he even hinted at more, she wouldn't come. But she nodded slowly, watching him, as though weighing something, considering.

"Okay."

CHAPTER 19

She found the house easily with the map he had drawn her. She hadn't let him come to pick her up. She wanted to drive there on her own. It was only half an hour away, but the drive gave her time to think. She wasn't sure why she was going, except that she liked Nick. And he was easy to talk to. He had stayed until almost eleven the night before, when she had started to fall asleep on the couch. She was exhausted, and he just kissed her chastely on the cheek when he left. But it had been a lovely evening. They had built a fire, and he had popped corn for Tygue, and the boy had shown him the new cowboy suit. Nick was in awe of it.

"Where did you ever find that?"

"At the hotel." Other people bought jade and maribou bed jackets, she bought her son the kind of outfit every little boy dreamed of.

"I wish I'd been your kid."

"No you don't. I'm a monster. Ask Tygue." But Tygue had only chuckled and shoved another handful of buttery popcorn into his mouth.

"Some monster." He had wanted to kiss her then. But not in front of the boy. He knew she wouldn't like that. And he didn't want to do it that way either. He wanted a lot from this woman. Her love as well as her body, and even more than that. He wanted her time, her life, her children, her wisdom, her gentleness, her compassion. He saw all that was there. But she saw what was in him too. She had begun to see it that first day. He had cared enough to come looking for her, to find her, to bring her a silly plastic slipper. But he cared enough to be good to Tygue too, to see what was in her eyes, to hear what she didn't say. She had to be careful of that, she reminded herself, as she pulled into the driveway of the address he had given her in Santa Barbara. Nick Waterman saw too much.

It was a white house, with well-tended black trim and beautiful large bronze fixtures. There was a carriage light, and an enormous bronze sea gull hovered on the door as the knocker. She flapped its wings to knock, and then stepped back. The house was on a little hill overlooking the water, and three willow trees stood nearby. It was in sharp contrast to her own simpler house. But this one had less warmth, only beauty.

He opened the door barefoot and wearing cut-off jeans, and his shirt was an old faded tee-shirt that matched his eyes.

"Cinderella!" His face lit up when he saw her, in spite of the teasing words.

"Should I have worn the slipper just to be sure you'd recognize me?"

"I'll take your word for it. Come on in. I was outside painting the deck."

"Sounds like you work hard for your rental." She followed him into the house, and noticed the stern Early American decor. It was as she had thought, all beauty and no warmth. It was a pity, because the house was filled with beautiful things.

"I enjoy puttering around here. The guy who owns it never gets out of L.A. So I dabble around when I have time." He was painting the deck a breezy sky blue, and he had painted two gulls in flight in a corner.

"You need clouds." She said it in a businesslike way, as she looked at the deck.

"Huh?"

"Clouds. You need clouds. Do you have any white paint?"

"Yeah. Over there." He grinned at her, and she smiled back as she rolled up the sleeves of her shirt, and then the cuffs of her jeans. "Want some of my old clothes to wear, Kate? I'd hate to have you wreck your stuff." He was serious but she only laughed at him. She had worn comfortable old clothes to lie on the beach. And underneath it all was a little orange bikini. But that was for later. Maybe. She wasn't sure yet.

"How's Tygue?"

"Fine. He said to say hi. He left at the crack of dawn to go see those goats. Now he wants one too."

"He should have his own horse." Nick was painting another gull in the far corner.

"That's what he tells me. Maybe you'd like to buy him one." She was teasing, but she got worried when she saw his face.

"Nick, I'm only kidding. Now, seriously, don't you dare. I've been fighting Felicia off on that one for two years."

"Sounds like a sensible lady. I'll have to meet this Felicia of yours. How long have you known her?"

"Oh, for years. I met her when I was modeling for—" And then she looked up as though she had said something she shouldn't have.

"You think I didn't know?" He smiled at her from his corner. "Come on, love. I'm a producer. I can tell when people have modeled, or done ballet, or lifted weights."

"I lifted weights." She looked over at him with a

broad grin and flexed an arm as he laughed at her.

"Great clouds you're painting, Cinderella."

"You like 'em?" She looked pleased.

"Sure do. Especially the one on the tip of your nose."

"Creep. I lied to Weinberg, you know. I told him I'd never modeled. I thought if I admitted it, he'd sell my body to the highest bidder and make me do a lot of publicity stuff."

"That's my girl. Chicken Little." He made rude clucking noises and she threatened to splash paint in his direction.

"Can you blame me for not wanting to do all that crap? I'm happy here, away from all that crazy stuff. Nick, I don't belong there."

"Nobody does." He sat down on the railing and looked at her. "But I'll tell you something else, babe, you don't belong here either. You're wasting yourself. One of these days you're going to have to get ballsy and get back out there, at least part of the time." She nodded somberly.

"I know. I've been trying. But it's rough."

"Not as rough as you thought though, is it?"

She shook her head, wondering how he knew. He seemed to understand so much. She had the feeling he really knew her.

"And there are compensations in getting out in the world," he said. She laughed at that one.

"There certainly are."

"Hungry?"

"Not really. You? I can go out to the kitchen and make you some lunch if you like." They had finished the deck, and agreed it was a work of art. "I hope the guy who owns this place appreciates your improvements. He ought to pay you to stay here."

"I'll tell him you said so." He put a casual arm

around her shoulders, and they wandered out to the kitchen together, barefoot and brown. Nick had bought prosciutto and melon and a roast chicken that morning. And another package yielded peaches, strawberries, and watermelon. There was a long baguette of French bread and a beautiful slice of ripe Brie.

"That's not lunch. It's a feast."

"Well, Cinderella, for you, only the best." He swept her a low bow, and then straightened to stand very close to her. He held out his arms. She felt a pull like nothing she had ever felt before, and slowly she melted toward him. She couldn't have resisted if she'd wanted to, but she didn't want to. She just wanted to be there, next to him, feeling the warmth of his skin and the strength of his arms, and smelling the scent of lemon and spices that was already so familiar to her. Nick.

And then gently he put a hand under her chin and lifted her face to his and kissed her, softly at first, and then harder, his arms holding her close, his mouth holding tightly to hers.

"I love you, Kate," he said as he stood there, breathless, wanting her, watching her. But he had spoken the truth. She said nothing, not knowing what to say. He couldn't love her. He didn't know her. It was too soon. He said that to everyone. She couldn't do this. She couldn't let this happen to her.

"I love you. That's all. No questions, no demands. I just love you." And this time she reached out to him, and when she let go of him she said it, with a soft smile and a mist over her eyes.

"I love you too. It's crazy. I hardly know you. But I think I love you, Nick Waterman." She looked down at her feet. Seven years. Seven years. And now she had said it to a stranger. I love you. But he wasn't a stranger. He was Nick. There had been something infinitely

242

special about him from the first moment she'd met him. As though he'd been waiting for her. As though they both knew he was there to stay. Or was she crazy? Did she only *want* to think that? She looked up at him searchingly and he smiled gently and made light of the moment to make it easier for her.

"You 'think,' huh? Boy, that's a gyp. You 'think' you love me." But the look in his eyes was teasing and he gently swatted her behind as he put their lunch into a basket. "Let's go eat on the beach." She nodded and they went off together, hand in hand, as he carried the basket with one powerful arm. He had the same kind of shape as Tom had had years ago. Tom had none of that left anymore. He had diminished over the years of sitting in his chair. But this man had never been diminished by anything. He was throbbing with life. "Want to go for a swim, Cinderella?" She grinned to herself. That name was going to stick.

"I'd love it." She had decided to trust him.

"So would I." He was leering unabashedly at the tiny orange bikini that had suddenly appeared, with a great deal of skin, as she peeled off her shirt and jeans. But his leering was so open and friendly that it only made her smile. "You expect me to go swimming with you looking like that? I'll drown for chrissake."

"Shut up. I'll race you." And she was off in a flash of orange and brown, long graceful legs dashing toward the water, as he followed appreciatively and then streaked out ahead, flashing past her and diving into the first wave. But she was close behind him, and they surfaced together a good distance out. The water was brisk and delicious on their sun-baked skin. "Beats the hell out of the pool at the hotel, doesn't it?" He laughed at her remark and tried to dunk her, but she was too quick. She slipped quickly under water and

243

darted between his legs. An attempt to catch her almost removed the top of her bathing suit, and she surfaced spluttering and laughing.

"See, smartass. You're going to lose that little Band-Aid you're wearing if you don't watch out." It was barely decent and she knew it. But all her bathing suits were like that. Felicia sent them to her, and the only one who ever saw her was Tygue. "Show-off," he accused.

"You're impossible."

"No. But I will be if I have to look at you like that much longer." She laughed again as, side by side, they set out for shore. It had been a long time since anyone had talked to her like that. And Nicholas did it in a way that amused her.

"I'm starving." She collapsed on her towel on the beach and looked hungrily at the basket.

"Go ahead, silly, dig in. Don't be so polite." He sat down next to her, and gave her a salty kiss. "Your family must have been very strait-laced. You're a very well-behaved young lady."

"Not anymore."

"Kate, are your folks dead too?"

She looked at him for a minute before answering, and then decided to tell him the truth. About that at least.

"They disowned me."

He stopped unwrapping the lunch to look at her.

"Are you serious?" He looked so shocked that it made her want to laugh. It didn't matter to her anymore. It was too long ago.

"Yes, very serious. I disappointed them, so they crossed me off their list. Or I suppose it would be more honest to say that they felt I had betrayed them."

"Do you have brothers and sisters?"

"Nope. Just me."

"And they did that to you? What kind of people are they? You were an only child and they threw you out? What the hell did you do?"

"Marry someone they didn't like."

"That's it?"

"That's it. I dropped out of college after my freshman year and went to live with him. And then we got married. They never came to the wedding. We never spoke again. They crossed me off the family tree when we started living together. They didn't think he was good enough."

"That's a hell of a price to pay for a man."

"He was worth it." She said it very softly and without regret.

"That's a nice thing to say about somebody. He must have been a very special guy."

She smiled again then. "He was." They didn't talk for a few minutes, and she helped him unpack the lunch. And then she saw something in Nick's face. Something a little bit hurt, or left out. "Nick?"

"Yeah?" He looked up, surprised. He had been lost in his own thoughts.

She reached out and took his hand in hers. "All of that was a long time ago. Some of it hurts, some of it doesn't. It all mattered then. A lot. But it's gone now. All of it. And . . ." She couldn't say it, but she had to. She knew she had to. No matter how much it hurt. ". . . so is he. He's gone too." Her eyes shone too brightly for a moment and Nick pulled her into his arms.

"I'm sorry, Kate."

"Don't be. There've been such good times too. Tygue. The books. Licia. You . . ." She said it in a tiny voice and he sat back from her for a minute with a tender smile.

"Lady, one day . . ." But he didn't dare say it. He just sat there smiling at her.

"What?"

"Just—one day . . ."

"Nicholas, tell me." She propped herself up on one elbow and smiled at him.

"One day, Cinderella, I'd like to make you Mrs. Charming."

"As in Prince Charming and Mrs. Charming?" She looked at him wide-eyed and he nodded. "But you're crazy, Nick. You don't even know me." Who was this man? Why was he saying all this?

"Yes, I do, Cinderella. I know you to the tip of your soul, and I'm going to know you better. With your permission, of course." He handed her the bread and kissed her softly on the lips. But she was looking more serious than he liked. "Does that upset you?"

"No, not the thought behind it. But Nick—I'm never getting married again. I'm serious about that."

"Famous last words." He tried to make light of it. He was sorry he'd brought up the subject. It was much too soon.

"I mean it. I couldn't."

"Why not?" Because my husband's not dead. Jesus.

"I just couldn't. Once, but not again. Up until two days ago, I could never even imagine loving a man again, and now I can imagine that, but not getting married." Then there was hope after all.

"Then let's just take one step at a time." She could tell that he wasn't taking her seriously, but she didn't know what else to say to him. "Prosciutto, melon?"

"You're not listening to me." She looked unhappy but he ignored her.

"You're absolutely right. Besides which, I'm an optimist, and I love you. I refuse to take no for an answer."

"You're a lunatic."

"Absolutely." He sat back happily with a hunk of bread and Brie and smiled at her. "And you are a fairy princess. Care for some Brie? It's terrific."

"I give up."

"Good." And then even he had to smile, when he thought of all the women over the years who would have given anything to hear him propose marriage, and the third time he'd seen them yet.

They polished off most of the lunch and then lay side by side in the sun for a time before going back to the water. And by then it was after four. "Had enough of the beach, Kate?"

"Mmm . . ." She was lying in the sunshine again, and tired from swimming. The salt water was running in little rivers from her temples to her neck and he leaned over and kissed them off with his tongue as she opened her eyes.

"Let's go home. We can get rid of all this sand. And oil, and salt, and bread crumbs, and watermelon seeds."

She laughed as she stood up and looked at the mess they'd left on the blankets.

"Looks like it was quite a party." She wrapped up the towels, he picked up the basket, and they walked slowly back to the house.

"We'd better go in the back way. He'll have a nervous breakdown if we get sand all over the house." It seemed a crazy way to live at the beach, but no crazier than anything else people from L.A. did.

"Yes, sir." She followed him in the back way, to a brightly decorated little yellow room. It had a striped circus awning, and three separate shower stalls, a half-dozen director's chairs, and a marvelous old-fashioned wicker chaise longue with a huge striped parasol overhead.

"The dressing rooms, Miss Harper. They're usually not co-ed, but if you trust me—"

"I don't."

He grinned at her. "You're right. Tell you what. Leave your bathing suit on." And laughing along with him, she complied and climbed into the shower with him. She was still laughing as he told her funny stories about the show while he washed the sand off her back, and then suddenly the chattering stopped, and he turned her slowly around to him. And slowly, hauntingly, under the spray of warm water, they kissed. She felt his arms go around her, and his body press against hers, and suddenly she was as hungry for him as he very plainly was for her, and they couldn't get enough of each other as the water rained down on them.

"Wait, I'm drowning!" She giggled as he moved and the shower ran full in her face. And laughing down at her, he turned off the water.

"Better?"

She nodded. It was very still without the purring of the shower in their ears. And the shower stall was filled with steam. Their hair hung loose in dripping strands, and there were beads of water on her eyelashes, which he gently kissed as he slowly peeled down the top of the bikini. He whispered gently in her ear as she ran her hands over his chest. "You just lost your Band-Aid, Cinderella." She smiled but her eyes were still closed when she kissed him, and then he stooped to kiss her breasts. He did it so gently that her whole body cried out for him.

"I love you, Prince Charming."

"Are you sure?" His voice was very serious as he stood up again, and she opened her eyes. "Are you sure, Kate?"

"Yes, I'm sure. I love you."

"It's been a long time, hasn't it?" He had to know, though in his heart he already did. She nodded. He had sensed that about her from the first, once he had realized the extent to which she had been cloistered for years. In an odd way, it pleased him. It made him feel special, and made him know just how special she was. "Very long, darling?"

She nodded again, and he loved her all the more for it. "Since before Tygue."

"Oh, sweetheart . . ." And then he pulled her close and held her very tight for a long time. He wanted to make up to her for years without loving, without a man. But he couldn't give her those years back. He could just give her now. And ever so gently he wrapped her in an enormous pink terry-cloth towel and carried her upstairs to the room where he slept. It was a lovely airy room that seemed to sail out over the sea. There were big picture windows, and fine old Early American pieces, and there was a somber-looking brass bed. It was not the room he would have chosen for her, but it was the room where he first loved her, and he loved her gently and well, caressing and stroking and entering her again and again, and at last she slept in his arms as he watched her. When she awoke it was dark.

"Nick?" She remembered what had happened but not where they were.

"I'm right here, darling. And you can't even begin to know how much I love you." It was a beautiful way to wake up, and she smiled as she cuddled back into his arms. And then suddenly she stiffened.

"Oh my God."

"What's wrong?" Had she remembered something painful? He was suddenly frightened.

"What if I get pregnant?"

He smiled and kissed the end of her nose. "Then Tygue has a baby brother. Or sister, as the case may be."

"Be serious."

"I am serious. I'd like nothing better."

"Good lord, Nick. I've never even thought of having another child." She sounded so subdued in the darkness, and he held her closer.

"There are a lot of things you haven't thought of for much too long. We'll do something about all that next week. But this weekend, we can take our chances. And if something happens . . . we'll live with it." And then he had a thought. "Or would you hate that very much?" Maybe she didn't want his child. He'd never even thought of that, and he looked down at her in the darkness. He could see her face clearly, and her eyes.

"No, I wouldn't hate it at all. I love you, Nick." He was all that mattered in the world as she kissed him again, and he slipped the covers away from her body and let his hands roam across her skin, as she smiled a long, slow, womanly smile.

CHAPTER 20

It felt as though they'd been together forever. They had gotten up at seven and puttered around the house together. Gone into town for the paper, taken a walk down the beach, and had a huge breakfast which they concocted as a team. Even that went smoothly, as though someone had catalogued their abilities and figured out how each could complement the other. And there was such ease and comfort between them—it was that that astounded Kate. After years of celibacy, she did not even feel uncomfortable wandering around naked under his tee-shirt, and now the two of them were lying naked on a towel behind the dune nearest the house, concealed from any eyes but theirs. She marveled again at his beautiful body, as she propped herself up on one elbow and looked at him.

"Do you have any idea how extraordinary all this is? Or do you do this all the time?" The words embarrassed her as soon as she had said them. It was none of her business what he did "all the time." But perversely, she wanted to know. The unexpectedly hurt look on his face as he sat up told her a great deal.

"What do you mean by that, Kate?"

"I'm sorry. I . . . it's just . . . you live in a different world, Nick. That's all. Things are very different for you than they are for me." She said it softly and regretfully. Maybe she didn't want to know after all. He reached out and gently took her shoulders in his hands, and looked at her until she looked back at him.

"You're right. Things are different, Kate. Or they have been. In some ways, anyway. When I was much younger, I ran my ass off. I chased every woman who turned me on, and a few who didn't. I ran and ran and ran, and you know what? I ran myself out. I finally realized that there was nothing left to run after. Things got a lot quieter after that, and a lot saner, but a lot lonelier too. There aren't many women worth the trouble out there. Hollywood seems to be a mecca for stupidity, selfishness, and vacuousness. Women who'll sleep with you to further their careers, to get closer to Jasper Case, to be seen at the Polo Lounge at the right hour of the day, to get to the best parties, or maybe just to get a free meal and get laid. You know what I got out of all that? Zero. So why bother? Most of the time I don't. In a lot of ways, Kate, I've been as lonely as you have. And you know what I've wound up with? A slick apartment, a few rooms full of expensive furniture, a couple of good paintings, a fancy car. And all added up, my love, it's not worth shit. And then, once in a lifetime, one moment, one face, one tiny speck of time, and you know you've seen every dream you've ever had. It's like that feeling of waking up in the morning, dazed and bleary-eyed but you don't quite know why, and suddenly in the middle of your coffee, you remember a dream. A flash of it and then a corner of it, and then a whole chunk of it. And suddenly you know the story and the place and the people you dreamed about. You know the whole thing, and all you want to do is get back there. But you can't. No matter how hard you try you can never get it all back. But it haunts you. Maybe for a day. Maybe for a lifetime. I could have let that happen to me, Kate. I could have let you haunt me for a lifetime.

But I didn't want to do that. I decided to run like hell and get back to the dream before it was too late, for both of us. That was why I came up to see you. I couldn't lose you, not after all these years of waiting. I didn't even know I was waiting for you, but by Thursday night, I did. And so did you." He was right too. She had. She had tried to avoid seeing it. She had told herself she'd never see him again. But she had known something, that strange feeling deep in her soul . . . a whisper . . . a promise. . . . "I love you, Kate. I can't explain it. I know it's only been a few days. But I just know this is right. I'd marry you today, if you'd let me." She smiled at him and let her head rest on his shoulders, as she gently kissed his neck.

"I know. It's incredible though, isn't it?" She lay back on the blanket and looked up at him as he watched her with those rich morning-blue eyes. The sky behind him was exactly the same color. "It's all moving so quickly. I don't know what to make of it. I keep thinking I can't be feeling like this. I keep thinking—I *kept* thinking," she corrected herself with an apologetic look and a smile, "that maybe you did this all the time. But that didn't explain how *I* feel. How can I feel this way about you so quickly? After all these years . . . I don't understand myself." But she did not look unhappy. In fact, it was the first time he had seen her without the shadows haunting her eyes. That darting look of pain had been gone when they'd woken up that morning. She looked like a new person. And she felt reborn.

"Maybe that's how it happens though. Over the years, I've heard stories about people who've lived together for five or ten years, and then suddenly—zap— one of them meets someone else and gets married in two weeks. Maybe if you had to wait all that time to check it out, you knew it wasn't right all along. Maybe when it really happens, when it's right, when it's the person you were meant for, maybe then it just happens, bang, and you know it. That's what happened to me."

He lay down next to her on his stomach and kissed her on the mouth. "Kate?"

"What, love?"

"Were you really serious about never remarrying?"

She nodded and looked hard at him before answering. "Yes." He could hardly hear the word, but he was sorry when he did.

"Why?"

"I can't explain it. I just know I can't."

"That's not fair. And it doesn't make sense." Or maybe it was just too soon to push. He searched her face and saw something pained come into her eyes again. He was sorry he'd brought it up. "Maybe you don't owe me any explanations."

"There are none to give." She ran a hand softly down his back and looked at him in a way that made his insides tie into a satiny knot. "All I can tell you is that I'll do anything you want, but not marriage." She said it intensely, and he gave her a lecherous smile.

"Given what I'm thinking at this very moment, Cinderella, that suits me just fine." And he did not mention marriage again. He made love to her on the towel, in the sand, and then bobbing in the waves in front of the house.

"Nick, you're indecent!" She ran laughing and breathless back to the towel and lay down, smiling up at him, as he fell carefully on top of her, catching himself on his arms.

"Look who's talking. I didn't do it by myself, you know."

"Nicholas . . . Nick . . . N . . ." Her voice faded

away as he kissed her again and spread her legs softly with his in the warm sand. It was well into the afternoon before they went back to the house, tired and brown and happy, and as though they'd been lovers for years. And then with shock, Kate looked at a clock on the wall in the kitchen. "Oh my God!"

"What's wrong?" He looked over his shoulder with a mouth full of grapes.

"Tygue. He'll be home at four. I totally forgot!" It was the first time in six years she had done that. She had even forgotten Bert, but at least she had fed him before leaving the house the day before. He only ate once a day, and he could get in and out through his own special door.

"Relax, darling. It's only three."

"But . . ." He shut her up with a kiss, and shared one of his grapes passed delicately and uncrushed through his lips. "Will you stop that? I have to . . ." But she was laughing now. "I'm serious."

"So am I. I packed this morning. All I have to do is shower, and strip the bed, and we'll get back in plenty of time. Do you want to call Joey's parents?"

"Maybe I should. Christ, I probably should have done that last night. What if something happened to him, or . . ." He kissed her again while picking up the phone, which he handed her with a smile.

"It's not a sin to have a good time yourself for a change." He kissed her again. "Call. I'll start the shower." She joined him in it five minutes later. "Everything okay?"

"Fine." She looked sheepish. "He doesn't even sound like he missed me."

"Of course not. Not with two new goats to distract him. Did Joey's dad get the pony?" He lathered himself and handed her the soap. It smelled of carnations.

"Two of them. One for Joey's sister."

"Sounds like a good man."

"So are you." They kissed again under the spray, with the smell of carnations all around them.

"No funny stuff, young lady. We have to get home."

"Well, listen to you." But she was amused. He seemed to be good at all things. Being a lover, being a father, being a friend. He was right to want to get married. He would have made a marvelous husband ... would have made ... she thought the words with regret as she handed back the soap, and let the spray of hot water rinse her clean.

They were dressed and the house was closed twenty minutes later. She had packed up the kitchen while he finished dressing, and she stood next to him with a sorrowful look as he locked the front door. He turned and saw her, and then pulled her into his arms with a smile.

"Aw, sweetheart, come on. It's not over. This is just the beginning." It was crazy but there were tears in her eyes. The weekend had been so lovely, she didn't want it to end. She wanted it to go on forever. And now she had to go back to being Tygue's mother, and driving up to see Tom. She wanted to stay in Santa Barbara with Nick forever. But he had to get back to reality too.

"But what happens now?" She sagged against the railing for a moment, and looked into his eyes. But there was nothing frightening there at all, only oceans of love.

"Why don't we just see what happens? I can have this house every weekend for as long as I like. The guy who owns it never uses it. It's not flashy enough for him so he just lets it sit here and rents it out. So it's all ours if we want it. And I can drive up from L.A. every night if you want me to. After the show. I could be there by midnight, and gone by the time Tygue gets up."

"Nick, that's crazy. You'll be a wreck." But she had to admit she loved the idea.

"We could give it a try, and you can come down to L.A. and try it on for size. Ease into it, if you want. There's a whole lot we can do, Cinderella. I told you, this is just the beginning. The glass slipper fit, didn't it?" He leaned over and kissed her, brushing the soft, flying hair from her eyes. "I love you. That's all." That's all. So simple. And everything he said sounded wonderful . . . except that she had her own decisions to make. She had to move at her own pace, in her own time. And there was Tygue to think of too.

"What do we do about Tygue?"

"Let him grow into things too. Trust me. I think I can manage that."

"I think you can too."

"So, is it settled then? Are you satisfied?" She nodded happily as she slid a hand into his arm and walked down the steps to their cars. Nothing was settled, but it all sounded damn good.

"Do you want to follow me back?" It seemed obvious that he'd come home with her, but he shook his head and unlocked his car as she stood next to hers with a look of surprise.

"No. I think you need some time with Tygue. How about if I come by around six? I have some things I could do in Santa Barbara."

"For two hours?" He nodded, and she felt a sudden wild stab of jealousy. What if he had a woman in town? What if that was why he usually came to this house? What if . . . but he saw the look in her eyes and started laughing.

"Darling, you are perfect and I adore you." He walked over to her and took her tightly into his arms.

257

"You looked like you were about to kill somebody."

"I was." She looked over his shoulder with an embarrassed smile.

"Not me, I hope."

"No. The woman I imagined you were seeing."

"Kate, my love, I can honestly tell you that I don't have a single woman friend in this town. I usually come up here to get away from it all. And as for the rest of them, I will happily hold a public burning of my little black book in front of city hall at high noon on Monday."

"Why wait that long? I'm sure I've got a match." She fumbled with the pockets of her shirt and he tweaked her nose.

"I'm sure you do. We'll use it later. Now get your ass back to your kid, you jealous bitch, before I rape you right here on the front steps."

"In front of my *station wagon*?"

"Anytime." He held the door to her car open and she slipped inside. He shut the door carefully and leaned inside for a last kiss. "Drive carefully, please."

"Yes, sir. See you at six."

"On the dot."

He waited until she had pulled away, and then got into his own car and turned toward town.

CHAPTER 21

"Hey, Mom! It's Nick!" His shouts of glee echoed precisely what she felt, and the two of them raced outside with Bert as the long blue Ferrari came to a gravelly stop. The two exchanged a quick look over the child's head, and then Nick's attention was entirely Tygue's. He hopped out of the car and swept the boy into his arms with ease.

"How were the goats?"

"Great! And Joey got two ponies. Well, one is supposed to be for his sister. But it isn't. She's a creep, and she's scared of it. What a dumb girl, it's a great pony."

"I'll bet it is." He put the boy down and turned to reach into his car. "Tygue, when you visit a lady, when you grow up, it is always a good idea to bring her flowers and candy. So . . ." He pulled out an armful of lilac and tulips, and handed Tygue a huge box wrapped in gold. "Your mom gets the flowers, you get the candy." Tygue looked immensely pleased with the arrangement, and his mother looked equally so.

"You're spoiling us, Nicholas."

"Anytime, Cinderella." He put an easy arm around her shoulders, and held out a hand to the boy, and together they walked inside. It was a warm summer night, with only a slight breeze to bring a chill to the air. Tonight it was too warm for a fire. Instead, they sat on the floor and sang songs and ate hot dogs and potato salad until Tygue went to bed. He was already half asleep when he got there, deposited by Nick, and tucked in by his mother, He was sound asleep when they left the room. And Nick took her into his arms as soon as she closed the door. "Okay, sexy one, which way to yours?" And then he stunned her by picking her up off her feet. "Next." She was laughing softly as she gave him directions, and he deposited her on her bed. It was a cheery room done in bright flowered prints. Licia had given her the matching bedspread and curtains and beautifully covered chairs as a house-warming present six years ago, but they looked as pretty and cheerful as ever.

"It looks like a garden." He looked surprised and pleased. There were flowers and plants all over the room, and lots of white Victorian wicker.

"What did you expect? Black satin?"

"Jesus. I'd have dropped you on your ass in the door-way."

"Is that so?" She was smiling broadly as she un-buttoned his shirt. "And what did you do in Santa Barbara, monsieur?"

"Shopped a little, walked a little, and missed you a lot." And with that, he sat down carefully on the bed and took her in his arms. She forgot all about what he had done in Santa Barbara.

Until the next day, when a message arrived. He had called her three times that morning after going back to L.A. He had left at six-thirty, half an hour before she got Tygue up. And so far so good, the system worked, but she wondered how long he would be able to stand it. It was a hell of a commute to L.A., three hours each way. But he had sounded chipper on the phone, and he hadn't said anything to prepare her for the arrival of a message shortly after three. It came just after Tygue got in from school. The message said that there was a package for Tygue Harper at the post office in Santa Barbara. It gave the address of a branch Kate didn't know, and said he had to pick it up in person. Kate suspected Licia was at it again. Now what? Maybe a car. She had jokingly promised to wait till he was six. Kate grinned to herself as she started the car. He had insisted on setting out at once, and he'd have been impossible to live with if she hadn't.

It took them half an hour to reach the address, but when they did, she knew there must be some mistake. It wasn't a post office, it was a house, with a tidy-looking white barn out back, and a few small corrals. Kate was about to drive away when she saw a man wave with a cowboy hat and a grin. Tygue waved back, and then the man hurried toward them, as Kate sighed. She wanted to get on with it. They still had to find the post office before it closed. But the man was already abreast of the car and looking in at them purposefully with the same big smile.

"Tygue Harper?"

"Yes!" He practically shouted it.

"We have a package for you." He winked at Kate, who was totally at a loss.

"Is this the post office?" Tygue looked excitedly from his mother to the man.

"No. But we do have the package for you." And then suddenly Kate knew. She would have groaned, but she didn't dare. He had done it. She put her face in her hands and started to laugh as Tygue jumped out of the car and ran off excitedly with the man. Kate got out of the car more sedately and followed them to one of the corrals. She saw the man in the cowboy hat open the gate, and still holding tightly to Tygue's hand, lead him over to a beautifully groomed brown and blond Shetland pony. "See that, son?" Tygue nodded in awe-struck silence as his mother and the man in the hat looked on. "That's your package, Tygue. He's all yours."

"Oh . . . Oh! . . . OH! MOM!" And then he ran toward the pony and threw his arms around its neck. It was wearing a bright red bridle and a spanking new saddle. Kate watched his face, wishing Nick could see it too. Then the man in the cowboy hat reached into his pocket and fished out two letters, one for Tygue and one for his mother.

"Want me to read it to you, sweetheart?" She knew he was too excited to be able to read his own name. He was cooing and stroking the little pony, who seemed enchanted with the attention.

"What does it say?"

"It says . . ." She opened the letter carefully and smiled at the message. "It says, 'Thought this would look nice with the new cowboy suit your mom got you in L.A. He's all yours. Give him a good name, and I'll be seeing you in the rodeo real soon. Nick.'"

"Wow! Can I keep it?" He looked at her imploringly and she nodded.

"I guess so. Nick said he's all yours, didn't he?"

Tygue nodded ferociously.

"Then you can keep him. What are you going to call him?" But in the pit of her stomach there was suddenly a squeamish twinge. This was an enormous gift. Just what did it mean?

"His name is Brownie." This time he didn't need to ask Willie. He knew instantly.

And then she had a minute to open her own letter from Nick. "Fifteen minutes to buy flowers. Ten minutes to buy chocolates. Five minutes looking in the phone book for name of stables. Twenty minutes getting here. Sixty-five minutes to choose pony and make arrangements. Five minutes to dream of you. Two hours, all accounted for. I love you, darling. See you later. Love, Nick." And then he had added a P.S. explaining that he'd made all the necessary arrangements to leave the horse there, unless she wanted him taken over to the Adams ranch, but they could discuss that later—"among other things."

The "other things" took priority when he reached the house at midnight. When he arrived, they went straight to the bedroom and Nick unraveled his tired body on the bed with a sigh and a smile.

"Long night?" Kate smiled over at him, still a little startled at the newness of seeing a man on her bed.

"Not really. I was just anxious to get back here all day. And it felt like it took forever to tape the show tonight and drive up here."

"That's quite a commute, Mr. Waterman."

"I think you're worth it, Mrs. Harper." He sat up on the bed and held out his arms as she stood for a moment and watched him. And then slowly she walked toward him and sat down next to him as he pulled her closer. "Feeling shy tonight, Kate?"

"Maybe a little." They smiled again, and he pressed his lips down softly on hers. She didn't feel shy a moment later when he slid his hand into her shirt and ran it over her breast until her nipple was hard in his fingers. She felt an urgency begin to build in her loins as his mouth pressed harder on hers, and his hand found her other breast. The years of celibacy seemed to melt from her body once again, as his hands searched the silk of her flesh, and then finally moved downward until he found what he wanted.

It was hours before they had had enough of each other, and they lay side by side amid the rumpled sheets. He was smoking a cigarette and she was drawing circles on his chest with a lazy finger. He turned to her then and for the first time in hours, he remembered Tygue.

"What about the pony? Did he like it?"

"Are you kidding? He almost died on the spot." But there was a moment of silence before she said anything further, and Nick glanced over at her with a smile.

"And? . . . There's more in your voice, Kate. Angry at me?"

"Angry? How could I be? No . . ." But he was right. There was something more. She looked at him squarely and her brow furrowed for a moment. "I don't know how to say this, Nick, it sounds so ungrateful. He was thrilled with the pony, and it's an unbelievable present for a little boy. It's like a dream come true. You're like a dream come true. Maybe that's what's bothering me though. What I'm trying to say . . . I don't want all of this to be just a dream. I don't want *you* to be a dream. I want all of this to be real. And maybe . . . maybe if . . ."

"Maybe if I just vanish, then where will you both be? Is that it, Kate?" He looked as though he understood all that she felt, and she was relieved that he didn't look angry.

"I guess that is it, Nick. What would happen if suddenly you weren't here anymore? One minute ponies and presents and promises of Disneyland, and the next . . ." She didn't want to finish the sentence, but she looked truly worried. And the business of spoiling Tygue worried her too. It was too much like Tom's grandiose generosity . . . near the end.

"I'm going to be here, Kate. For a long, long time. As long as you'll let me be here. I'm not going anywhere." That was what Tom had said. But life wasn't like that. She knew better now.

"You don't know that. You have no control over that. You may want to be here, but you never know what fate has in store for you."

"Darling"—he leaned carefully toward her and took her worried face in his hands—"what I love most about you is your optimism." She grinned sheepishly up at him and shrugged.

"I guess it'll just take me time to adjust to all the good things that are happening to me."

"It may take Tygue a little while to adjust too. Don't kid yourself, even the bearers of ponies and promises of Disneyland can be viewed with suspicion."

"I think you've gotten off lucky though. I was all set for him to resent you like crazy, but he doesn't." She was still amazed.

"He probably will, when he figures out that I'm here to stay." He kept saying that—"here to stay." How did he know? How could he be so sure? What if it didn't work out? In a way, it frightened her that he was so sure of himself.

"Come on, Kate, you look tired. Enough of all this worry-wart shit. I love you, and I think Tygue is terrific, and I'm not going to run out on either of you. And I also won't spoil him rotten if you don't want me to. No more ponies." He grinned at her and tugged at a lock of her hair. "Not for at least a week anyway."

"You sound just like Licia."

"Christ, I hope I don't look like her."

"Not in the least, my love." And with a slow happy smile, Kate forgot about her son and stretched out her arms to her lover again. It was almost four o'clock in the morning when they stopped making love, and Kate lit a cigarette with a contented sigh. She glanced over at her alarm clock and winced.

"You're going to be so tired tomorrow."

"What about you? Can you go back to bed after Tygue goes to school?" He looked worried about her. She did a lot in a day too. He could always sleep when he got back to L.A.; except on rare occasions, he didn't have to be at the studio until three. Most of the show's procedures were pretty well set, so he rarely left his house before two, except when he had a date for lunch.

Kate sighed in answer to his question about going back to bed. "No. I'm going up to Carmel tomorrow."

"To teach?"

She nodded. But she hated lying to him.

"Could I go with you sometime? I'd like to see what you do."

But she looked away and stubbed out the last of the cigarette before answering. He couldn't see her face, and when he could, he wasn't sure what he saw. Distance more than anything else. It surprised him. And he saw something hidden in her eyes, which bothered him more.

"They don't let me bring anyone with me. It's kind of a difficult place."

"Do you like it?" He was searching for something as he looked at her, but he wasn't sure what.

She closed her eyes. "As those places go, yes." Oh God, she wanted to get off this subject, but she had to sound convincing. She had to make it sound like a *job*. She couldn't tell him about Tom. Not yet. Not even Nick.

"Can't you do something like that closer to home?" She shook her head. He almost hated to ask any more questions, and besides, they were both tired. He had other things on his mind, too. He ran a hand softly up her leg, and she looked at him in surprise. She was glad he wasn't pushing the subject of what she did in Carmel. The hand on the inside of her thigh traveled up and she smiled and reached out for him.

"Again?"

"Is that a complaint?" He was smiling softly too. Something happened between their bodies that had never happened to him with anybody else, not quite like that. It was a kind of ecstasy neither of them had ever known. And when the alarm rang at six neither of them regretted their night without sleep.

CHAPTER 22

"Did you teach today?" He looked at her carefully as he sat down in a chair by the fire. He had just come in, and with a smile at Kate he loosened his tie. She looked almost as tired as he did.

"Yeah, I taught." There was a moment's pause. "How was the show?" It had been a hard day with Tom too. He had a cold and sore throat and twice he had cried.

"The show was a killer." He named three of Hollywood's top stars, two of them female and known to be at war with each other. But he didn't want to talk about the show. He wanted to talk about the one thing she wasn't telling him. And he wanted to know why. Something had continued to bother him for weeks. Discrepancies, little threads. Something. It had gnawed at him on the drive back to L.A. that morning. It had been gnawing at him ever since he met her. Just tiny, tiny pieces of the puzzle that were always left out. Things she didn't say, years she didn't talk about. And some of the things she did talk about had bothered him too. The way her parents had abandoned her, her distrust of "fate," her years alone with Tygue, and the "teaching job" where she couldn't bring anyone along. As he sat over his third cup of coffee on his terrace in L.A., he had felt a sudden urgency about knowing the answers, and he had plenty of sources for the answers he wanted. Maybe yet another night without sleep was giving him crazy ideas, but what the hell, he had nothing to lose by looking for an explanation, and she didn't have to know. He wasn't even sure what he was looking for, but he knew there was something. And his first question had to do with her name, and the book. That was the first coincidence that didn't sit right. She knew too much about football, about . . . the answers had come back over a period of days and had finally tied into one solid story one afternoon, just before five o'clock as he sat in his office at the studio. The answer didn't surprise him at all. The man at the studio research office was his friend, and Nick had already told him that the inquiry was highly confidential and entirely personal. He wasn't worried about a leak. But he hated what he heard. For her sake.

"I found out just about all I can on the girl you had me check out. But first, let me tell you what else I found.

"Funnily enough, I didn't even remember the guy until we came across the clips from the show. I called the papers and the newsroom archives at the network after that. Tom Harper, he was a big football star about ten years back. We had him on the show three or four times, when Jasper still worked out of New York. Before your time, Nick. Anyway, he was a nice guy, I think. America's number one hero. I don't know why the name didn't click when you asked me this morning. He was a pro hero for eight or nine years until his career started to slide. I don't remember the details but he started getting into trouble, his career was on the rocks, he was getting too old for pro ball. Did some crazy thing like try to shoot the team owner, or manager or something, and wiped himself out instead."

"Killed himself?" But now Nick was remembering the story too. He had even met Harper once or twice when he himself was starting out in pro football. How quickly they had all forgotten. Six, seven, maybe eight years before, it had been big news, and now it took a research office to jolt the name back into mind. Kate would have been pleased to know that.

"I don't think he died, not right off anyway. I couldn't get you all the details on that, but originally he was only critically wounded, paralyzed, something like that. Eventually they moved him down to some fancy sanatarium in Carmel, and I guess everyone forgot him after that. No one seems to know if he's still alive or not, and I couldn't find out the name of the sanatarium or I'd have called. But that's about all we got on him. One of the newsroom guys had a story that explained that Harper was paralyzed from the waist down, and permanently impaired mentally when they moved him to Carmel, but that's about it on Harper. As for the girl, she was his wife. There's not much on her. Some footage of her coming and going from the hospital. They sent it over here and it made me sick to watch it. She has that godawful look of people living in a nightmare, and there was another clip of when they were loading him into the ambulance for the trip to Carmel. He looks like he doesn't know what's happening, kind of childlike and dumb. There's absolutely nothing on either of them after that. I got a little background on her, but damn little. She went to Stanford for a few months, went to live with Harper after her first year there, traveled everywhere with him, but stayed pretty much out of the limelight. She was a model or something for a while. Kind of a pretty girl, then at least, but that was quite a while ago. And the only bit of scandal about her was that apparently her parents disowned her or something for marrying him. They were your basic staunch upper-middle-class snobs, who couldn't stand the idea of their princess marrying a jock or something. Anyway they cut her off.

"That's all I know, Nick. What happened to him, if he's still alive, or what happened to her, I couldn't tell you. There's just no press record on any of that. If you can find the name of that sanatarium in Carmel they'll probably be able to tell you if he died, but the name of the place may have been kept out of the press. I don't know. Want me to work on that?"

"No, I can do that myself. And listen, thanks a million. You got me everything I wanted to know." And more. He knew everything now. The rest he could figure out for himself. Obviously, Tom was alive, and still in Carmel. That was the mysterious "school" she went to. It had happened seven years before. And Tygue . . . Tygue was six. Kate must have been pregnant when Tom Harper shot himself. What an incredibly long time for Kate to live the way she had. He felt subdued for the rest of the evening as he mused over what he'd heard, and thought about her. He wanted to talk to her about it, to air it out, to hold her in his arms and let her cry if she still needed to after all these years. But he knew he couldn't say a word. Not until she did. He wondered how long it would take.

He looked at her now as she sat across from him, watching him, and he looked at the circles under her eyes. She was paying a price, too, for their happiness and her double life.

"How did it go in Carmel, Kate? Difficult today?" He hated that look of pain in her eyes. It told him the rest of the story, the part the research office didn't know. He wondered just how bad off Tom Harper still was. He had gathered from the research material that the mental damage had been irreparable. That had to be an incredible strain. But he still couldn't imagine what it was really like, dealing with someone like that on a regular basis. Someone you had loved.

"Yeah, it was difficult today." She smiled and tried to shrug it off, but he wasn't letting her. Not just yet.

"Are they very demanding?" He was asking her about Tom, not about "them," but he hoped she'd tell him the truth anyway. Some kind of truth at least.

"Sometimes. People like that can be very sweet, and very childlike, or very difficult, like children too in that respect. Anyway, never mind that, tell me about the show." The subject was definitely closed. He saw it in her face.

"The people on the show can be 'very sweet and very childlike' too, or total shits and equally child-like. Maybe most actors and celebrities are retarded too." He smiled at her and sighed.

"Did you get the house for this weekend, by the way?" She was happily unbuttoning his shirt and he nodded.

"Yes. And you know, I was thinking. How about if all three of us stayed there this time?"

She thought about it for a long moment and then looked up at him. "Why not here?"

He shook his head carefully. "Not yet. This is Tygue's turf. I don't want to crowd him." He thought of everything, and he cared about everything. Just as she cared about him. Enough to worry about the way he looked. Exhausted.

"Nick?"

"What, love?" He lay back against the couch, his eyes closed, holding her hand. He was trying not to feel hurt that she wouldn't tell him about Tom. But he knew he'd just have to wait until she was ready.

"What are we going to do?"

"About what?" But he knew. He was wondering the same thing. Neither of them had had a full night of sleep in three weeks.

"You can't go on running around like this forever."

"Are you telling me I'm over the hill?" He opened an eye and she grinned.

"No. I'm telling you I am. And if it's killing me, I can imagine what it's doing to you. I'm not driving to Los Angeles every day."

"Never mind. Why don't we just ride out the summer? And then we'll see."

"But then what?" She had worried about it all the way back from Carmel. The drive gave her an idea of what Nick was doing every morning and every night. The distance was the same. "What the hell are we going to do after the summer?"

"I could buy a plane. A helicopter maybe." He was only half teasing and she kissed him softly on the cheek. It was all her fault too. But there was Tygue, and she couldn't just . . . "Hang in there, darling. And then we'll see. I'm waiting to find out what Jasper wants to do about the show. That might change everything. And he has to make up his mind in the next two weeks."

"What do you mean, it'll change everything?" She looked even more worried.

"Never mind. Now stop worrying about it, Kate. And that's an order."

"But . . ."

"Shh!" He pressed his mouth against hers, and met every objection with a kiss until at last she was laughing, and they fell into bed. But tonight they didn't even make love. They just slept, wrapped around each other, exhausted. And Nick was already gone when Kate woke up the next morning.

"Where'd you get this?" Tygue picked up a huge

white tee-shirt and held it in the air with a look of suspicion, as his mother covered herself with the sheet. This was the first time Tygue had appeared in her bedroom before she'd wakened to put on a night-gown, and she felt oddly defensive. And they had been so tired that Nick had forgotten his undershirt under the bed.

"I used that yesterday to do some gardening in."

"It smells like Nick." He eyed her fiercely. Jealousy was beginning to set in. Nick had been right. The initial glow had been too good to be true, or to last.

"Nick gave it to me. What do you want for break-fast, cereal or eggs?" And why was she making ex-planations to him, dammit? She had a right to have anyone's undershirt under her bed. Jesus.

"I want French toast or pancakes." He said it in a tone of argumentative accusation.

"That's not on the menu." She looked at him stern-ly.

"Oh all right. Eggs. When's Nick coming up to see Brownie again?" The funny thing was that he sounded anxious to see Nick, and yet angry too, and as though he was looking for a fight with his mother.

"He said he'd be up this weekend. In fact"—she held her breath—"he invited us both to stay at his house in Santa Barbara. How does that sound?"

"Okay. Maybe. You coming too?"

"Sure. Any objection?"

"Nick doesn't like to talk about horses when you're around. When we're alone he talks about better stuff."

"Well, maybe you two could go off to the stables alone, or for a walk on the beach or something. How about that?"

"Okay." There was the first glimmer of a smile. "Can I bring Joey?" She hadn't even thought of it, but it wasn't a bad idea. It would keep him busy, and give her and Nick more time alone.

"I'll ask, but I suspect Nick will say yes." Nick said yes to everything Tgyue wanted. Sometimes that bugged her. He had kept his promise about not spoiling Tygue too much, but still he indulged the boy, and it irritated her. It made it harder for her to control Tygue. It made Nick look like the good guy, and made her look like a louse when she disciplined him. Besides, it was new to her to have someone else become the source of special treats for Tygue. Tygue had looked to her for everything for so long that it was a little hard to share the glory. She didn't like to admit it, but she knew it was true. There had been Felicia of course, but Felicia's trips were a rare event, Nick was becoming part of every day, and with familiarity came a certain assumption of authority that was also a little hard to take. Tygue wasn't the only one with some adjusting to do. Kate had some new things in her life to accept too, but the lessons were worth learning, for Nick.

"Don't forget to ask Nick about Joey." Tygue muttered the reminder over his shoulder as he left the room.

"I won't. Now go get dressed for school." He vanished into his room and she scooped the large white undershirt into a drawer, but she sniffed it first. It smelled just like him, lemons and spice. Just holding the shirt made her want him.

But that morning, he didn't call. Stu Weinberg did.

"I have a surprise for you, Kate." He sounded immensely pleased with himself.

"Good or bad?"

"I only have good surprises." He tried to sound insulted but couldn't.

"Okay, tell me."

"Well, m'dear, we have just been asked to invite you to spend eight days at the Regency Hotel in New York, three days in Washington, two days in Boston, and a day in Chicago on the way back. It's a tour for your book, and you're on the best possible shows in all four cities. You're being offered first-class accommodations everywhere, and strictly four-star treatment. Miss Harper, you've made it."

"Oh God." Another mountain to climb. And she was so happy at the plateau she had just reached. Why did she have to move up now? "Do I have to?"

"Are you kidding?" He sounded horrified. "Look, Kate, to put it bluntly, do you want a best seller or a bomb? Baby, if you like your royalties, you have to do some of this too."

"In other words, sing for my supper." She didn't sound pleased. "How many days does that make altogether?"

"Exactly two weeks. Now that's not so bad, is it?"

She sighed deeply. "I guess not. Can I let you know though? I have to see if I can get someone to stay with Tygue."

"Sure, love. That's fine. I'll call you back later."

"How soon would I have to go?"

"Monday." He didn't even apologize.

"In four days?" It was already Thursday.

"He didn't give me much notice for chrissake." And then he stopped. Dammit.

"Who didn't?"

"The guy in the publicity department at your publisher."

"Oh. Well, I'll call you later." She wanted to call Nick, and at his end, Stu let out his breath softly. Jesus. He'd almost blown it. And he had promised

Nick he wouldn't. It must have been going great guns for Nick to call and make a request like that. Why couldn't he just ask her himself? But Stu knew why. If Nick had asked her, she wouldn't have gone. This just might get her going.

She got Nick at his apartment, and he sounded sleepy. "Did I wake you up?"

"No, just daydreaming. What's up, love?" She could hear him yawn, and imagined him stretching.

"You forgot your undershirt."

"No place outrageous, I hope." He smiled to himself as he remembered how she had looked that morning sound asleep when he left.

"It was under the bed. Tygue found it."

"Oops. Any problem?"

"Not with Tygue."

And then he noticed that she sounded worried. He sat up in bed with a frown.

"Stu just called me." The frown deepened. And he waited.

"He has a two-week tour for me. New York, Boston, D.C., and Chicago. Eight days of it in New York. Oh Jesus, Nick, I don't know what to do. I'm scared to death." She sounded near tears, and he wondered if he'd done the right thing. Maybe he had no right to meddle.

"Don't get excited, darling. We'll talk about it. What's he booked you on?"

"I don't know. I forgot to ask. And it's for Monday. And . . . oh Nick, what'll I do?"

"I have an idea." He forced his voice to sound cheery as he closed his eyes, feeling as if he were pushing her off a cliff.

"What?"

"Why don't you go on the show with Jasper again?"

"I can't for chrissake. I just told you. Stu wants me to go to New York." She sounded nervous and exasperated.

"That's where Jasper is doing the show for the next two weeks." And then he opened his eyes wide and waited for a moment. There was no sound. "Would you go to New York with me, Kate? I know it's hard for you, darling, but I'll be there. I promise. I'll be right there with you."

"Did you tell Stu to do this?" She sounded incredulous.

"I . . ." Crap. He had blown it. But there was no point lying to her. He would swear never to meddle again. "I did. I'm sorry, I shouldn't have, I . . ." But suddenly she was laughing. "Kate?"

"You jerk. You did that? I thought it was for real. I thought my publisher had a tour for me that I had to do, or *else*. I thought . . ."

"He does. Only they didn't line it up until I told Stu I thought you'd do it. You can fly in and out of Boston and D.C., and keep on staying with me in New York."

"What about Chicago?" She was still laughing. Thank God.

"Did they do that too?" Nick sounded amazed.

"Oh yes."

"Zealous, aren't they?"

"You know something? You're crazy, that's what you are. Totally crazy. Did you know about all this when you got home last night?" Her house was home now to both of them.

"Okay, I confess."

"How long have you known?"

"Since Monday. Jasper sprang it on us."

"Terrific."

"So what are you going to do now?" He was more

than a little curious. "I mean, other than give me a black eye when I come home tonight."

"Are you sure you want me to tell you over the phone?" The voice was pure Mata Hari, and he started laughing too.

"Never mind that. Will you go with me?"

"Do I have a choice?"

He waited for a long moment, wondering what he should say, but he decided to take a chance. "No. You don't have a choice. I need you too much. Get Tillie to stay with Tygue, and we'll buy out F.A.O. Schwarz for him."

"He accepted your invitation for the weekend, by the way, and he wants to bring Joey."

"Wonderful. I don't care if he brings King Kong. I want to know if you're coming to New York with me."

"Yes, dammit, yes! Okay? Are you happy?"

"Very!" They were both smiling.

"Do I still have to do all that publicity bullshit?"

"Of course." Nick sounded shocked. "And I meant what I said. I'll put you back on the show with Jasper."

"Do I gotta?" She was lying in bed grinning at the phone.

"Yes. You gotta."

"Hey, Nick?"

"What, sweetheart?" The voice was suddenly soft in answer to hers.

"Any chance you could come home?"

"You mean now?"

"Uh huh."

He had a mountain of work to do, a thousand things to arrange . . . and a woman he adored.

"I'll be there."

And he was.

CHAPTER 23

"Kate?"

"Mm?" She was asleep next to him on the plane. It had been a hectic few days. She had insisted on "teaching" on Friday, but the trip to Carmel had given her a chance to shop. They had all spent the weekend at the house in Santa Barbara, Joey included, and on Sunday night Nick had driven her down to L.A. with him, so that they could leave together Monday morning. This was the first time he hadn't flown with Jasper. He wanted to be alone with her. A glance at his watch told him they would land in New York in an hour. He kissed her softly on the top of her head and folded her hand into his.

"Miss Harper, I love you." He said it more to himself than to her but she surprised him by opening one eye, and looking up with a yawn that crept into a smile.

"I love you too. What time is it?"

"Two o'clock our time. It's five o'clock there. We'll get in at six."

"And then what?" She hadn't even thought to ask him. She stretched her long legs out ahead of her and looked down at the now familiar cream-colored suit. She was getting more wear out of it than she'd ever expected to when she'd bought it. "Oh my God."

"What?"

She was looking up at him with horror in the big green eyes he loved.

"Is it Tygue? Did you forget something?"

"No. Licia. I forgot to tell her I was going. If she calls and Tillie tells her I've gone to New York, she'll have a stroke."

"Will she disapprove?" He was curious to meet this character who was the only important person in Kate's life besides Tygue. Maybe she'd hate him, be jealous of his role in Kate's life. He looked at Kate curiously.

"Licia? Disapprove?" Kate snuggled in next to him with a soft laugh. "She'd give you the Legion of Honor for dragging me out of my cave."

"Have you told her about me yet?"

Kate shook her head slowly. She hadn't. And she wasn't sure why. Maybe because she was afraid the magic would all fade away and telling Licia would make it that much harder to live with the loss when he was gone. "No. Not yet."

"I'd like to meet her. She sounds like a character. Would I like her?"

"I think so." And what if he didn't? She loved Felicia, always would. But she already felt herself slipping into Nick's world. Nick had a special place in her life now.

He looked down and saw the serious look in her eyes, and he held her close. "You look so pensive sometimes, love. One day you won't look like that anymore." When she looked like that, he knew she was thinking about Tom.

"Like what?"

"Like your only friend in the world is about to walk out."

"Are you sure he won't?"

"Positive."

She could feel it in his arms, and she felt peaceful

as she closed her eyes. She was so happy with him. But it couldn't last forever. Nothing did. No matter what he said. Tom had made those promises too. But she hadn't had the same worries then. She hadn't realized how quickly things come to an end.

"Scared about New York?" He forced her mind back to the present, as he tilted her face up to his. He was smiling at her again, and she smiled back.

"Sometimes. Once in a while I panic and want to hide in the ladies' room, and then I forget all about it and get curious. It's been so long, I hardly remember it."

"Good. I want to give it to you brand new." He looked pleased. They were going to stay at the Regency, only three blocks from Jasper's hotel. Jasper was addicted to the Pierre. But Nick wanted to stay somewhere else, so Kate wouldn't feel awkward. "I ordered separate rooms for us, by the way."

"You did?" She looked disappointed, and he laughed.

"Don't look like that, you dummy. They're adjoining, and we can use one of them as an office. I just thought it would look better in case some nosy reporter gets wind that you're staying with me. This way, you're just staying at the same hotel. A cozy coincidence." She looked pleased again.

"How do you manage to think of all that? Glass slippers, separate rooms to protect my lily-pure reputation—is there anything you don't think of?"

"That's why I've managed to stay the producer of Jasper's show all these years, my love. It's all part of the job." But she knew it was part of the man. They exchanged another smile and looked out over the city. It was still bright daylight outside, and would be for several hours, but already there was the softened hue of late afternoon. "It's going to be hotter than hell, by the way. Did you bring lots of naked clothes?" She laughed as she accepted the glass of champagne he was handing her from a passing tray. First class was delightful. Champagne coast to coast.

"I did what I could. I didn't have a lot of time to shop." And Carmel was not San Francisco. But she hadn't done badly. And when they got off the plane in New York she understood what Nick meant about the heat. She had never been to the city in mid-summer, and it was blistering, even at six o'clock.

Nick had arranged for them to be met by the airline's special customer service cart, and they were whisked right to the door of the terminal. Their bags would be separated from the others and brought out to the car. And the little golf cart whizzed through the terminal, plowing through countless bodies. Everyone looked hot and tired and gray, not brown and healthy the way they did in California. It had been a long time since Kate had seen people looking like this, and so many of them. She felt breathless as they launched through the crowds in the ice-cold terminal. The air conditioning was blasting full force on the hot, tired, sweaty crowds.

"It's a wonder they don't all die of pneumonia." She held tightly to his hand as she watched them from the cart. It was all so busy and so loud. It was terrifying and fascinating at the same time. Like visiting another planet.

"It's a wonder they don't all die from lack of air, you mean. Have you ever seen so many people?"

She shook her head as he watched her. He had made all the arrangements very carefully, so she wouldn't be overwhelmed right from the first. They were already at the terminal door, and the driver was waiting for them at the curb.

They were shoved through the revolving door by

the force of the crowds, and Kate found herself pushed outside, into what felt like a vacuum. It was white-hot and humid, without so much as a breath of air.

"My God." It was like being punched in the stomach by an elephant.

"Lovely, isn't it?" He grinned as she rolled her eyes, but the driver was already holding open the door of the air-conditioned car, and Nick was urging her gently inside. It was all wonderfully quick and efficient. And five minutes later, the driver had their bags, and they were on their way to the city. She looked back over her shoulder through the smoky glass of the limousine and she could still see the people in line for cabs. There was a short fat cab driver waving a cigar in another man's face, and as they sped away she started to laugh.

"Isn't it crazy?"

"It's like the circus." She didn't remember the city as quite so intense. Everything had seemed more sedate when she had been there on Easter vacation with her parents when she was seventeen. They had stayed at the Plaza and had tea in the Palm Court and at a place called Rose-Marie. That all seemed a thousand years ago. And Tom had never let her go to New York with him. He hated it, and usually stayed outside the city with friends. Now she could see why. This wasn't Tom's scene. And it wasn't really Nick's. But he handled it perfectly. He had shielded her from everything unpleasant, even the heat.

She watched the constant fury of the traffic on their way to the hotel. Even on Park Avenue, the cars moved along as though they were angry. Jerk, bump, stop, screech, honk, shout, and jerk on again. The noise was deafening even in the carefully sealed car.

"How do they stand it?"

"I don't know. Either they don't notice it, or they love it."

But the crazy thing was that she loved it too. She loved the aliveness of it. The frenzy and the sparkle, the crackle of electricity as everything moved at breakneck speed. She suddenly wanted to get out of the womblike car and walk. But she was afraid that if she told Nick, he would think she was crazy. And ungrateful. He had gone to such lengths to protect her from her fears. And yet, there she sat, dying to push and shove along with the rest of them.

They had arrived at the Regency, and the driver helped her into the doorman's hands, from whose protective grasp Nick took her and led her quickly inside. They knew him there. He signed the registration card and they were instantly led to their rooms. Hers was a suite, his a large double room with a door that adjoined her living room. They decided to use his as the office, and hers as their "house." The bags were stacked on elaborate little gold and white stands, and Kate looked around as her feet sank into the thick carpet, and then with a sigh she settled onto the rose-colored silk couch. Everything was very subtle and very lovely. It looked like an English watercolor painting. And they had a beautiful view of the city facing south. She looked around the room again and then at Nick with a smile and a sigh. She felt like the poor little rich girl, shielded from everything that was fun, like dirt and noise and all the crazy people she was dying to gape at, and run along on the sidewalk with. Nick meant well by shielding her from it all, but she felt as if he were keeping her from the fun. Maybe it was nuts to feel that way. But she did. Suddenly she wanted to break loose from her shell, and even from Nick . . . from the past . . . from Tom . . . from Tygue . . . from all of them. She wanted to be free.

"Want a drink?" He loosened his tie, and smiled down at her. He had already made reservations for them at Caravelle. He had had his secretary do that from Los Angeles that morning. The reservations were for nine. He didn't think they'd be hungry until then. That would give them time to have a drink and relax, maybe have another drink in the bar of the hotel, and go off to a quiet dinner. But Kate only shook her head at the offer for the drink. "What's up, Cinderella? You look like those wheels are turning a mile a minute. Want to call Licia now?"

"No." And she didn't really want to call Tygue either. Not yet.

"Then what would you like to do?" He sat down next to her on the delicate couch and put his arms around her as she started to laugh. And he loved the fire he saw in her eyes. New York was doing good things to her. Already. It was as though she were coming to life in a way he had never seen before. "Name your pleasure, milady, and it's yours."

"You mean it?"

"Of course I mean it."

"Okay. I want to go for a walk."

"Now?" He looked stunned. At seven o'clock, it was still ninety-five, and the humidity was close to the same figure. "In this heat?" She nodded excitedly and he threw back his head and laughed. He understood. Kate, who had hidden for years, almost since she was a girl, was suddenly young again and hungry for life. "Okay, Cinderella, you're on. Do you want to change first?" She shook her head with a grin and looked just like her son. "In that case"—he held out an arm and she slipped a hand through it as they both stood up— "we're off."

And it was just what she wanted. They wandered

up Madison Avenue as she looked into all the shops, and then over to Central Park, where people were still playing games on the grass. Balls were being thrown, radios were blaring, buses zoomed by, and hansom cabs clopped along behind tired, flower-bedecked horses. It was as though someone had assembled every possible moving part, every face, every car, every smell, every color, and jammed them all into one town and called it New York. "God, I love it." She took a deep breath of the polluted air and sighed with delight as Nick laughed.

"I think I've created a monster." But he loved seeing her like that. She was so alive. It was what she should have had for years. Fire, and excitement and success. He was glad he could share them with her now. He looked at his watch. It was already after eight, and they were nearing Sixty-first Street and Fifth. It was only two blocks to the hotel. But they had walked at least twenty, drinking everything in—Kate watching the city with passion, and he watching her with delight. "Ready to go back and get dressed?"

"Where are we going?"

"To the best restaurant in town. All for you, Cinderella." He swept a wide arm toward the skyline, and she beamed. She smiled all the way back to the hotel, and when he closed the door to their room, she advanced on him with a purposeful gleam in her eye.

"Does this mean what I think it means?" He was grinning at her from the bathroom door, and she suddenly reached over and unzipped his pants.

"It certainly does."

"Lady, I don't know what this town does to you, but I love it."

They didn't even make it to the bedroom, but made love on the richly carpeted floor of their room, as her tongue and delicate hands brought soft moans from Nick. This time it was Kate who took the lead, and Nick who lay back spent when they had both come. Kate lay on the floor, in the twilight, smiling victoriously at her life.

CHAPTER 24

"Miss Harper?" The woman in the expensive black dress and the Cinandre-sculptured hair walked into the room and extended a hand. Kate shook it nervously, and smoothed her dress. "You'll be on in a minute." It was her first television appearance in New York, and she was terrified. But prepared. She had gone over what she would say with Nick that morning. And the dress was a new one she'd bought in Carmel. It was a warm coral linen that set off her deep tan. She wore it with some of the coral jewelry Felicia had brought her from Europe the year before, despite her protests. Now she was glad Felicia had insisted she keep it. "You never know." Kate remembered the words with a smile. Her hair was pulled back. She hoped she looked like a writer. At least she felt like one.

"I've been admiring the view." It was breathtaking. They were in the southwest corner of the thirty-something floor of the General Motors Building, with a sweeping view of Central Park if you looked uptown and an unbroken panorama of Wall Street downtown. "It must be fabulous living in this town."

The woman in the black dress laughed, shaking the well-coifed hair and flashing a large emerald ring. "I'd give my right arm to live on the Coast. But Audrey does the show here, so . . ." She threw up her hands.

289

This woman was the biggest female producer in daytime television, and her job was not unlike Nick's. Now Kate better understood what it entailed.

"Ready?"

"I think so."

She held open a door and Kate walked through it. The door to the studio showed a brightly lit sign: "On the Air."

She was on for almost an hour, with three other prominent women, a representative from the United Nations, a nationally known lawyer, and a woman who had won the Nobel Prize in biochemistry the year before. Good God. She felt breathless as she looked at them. What was she doing there? But as they looked at her, she realized they were wondering the same thing. She was an unknown.

"How does it feel to write your first best seller?" Audrey Bradford, the host of the show, smiled at Kate, and the other women looked interested but hardly overwhelmed.

"It hasn't quite gotten there yet, but I must admit so far it feels awfully good." She laughed and Audrey smiled with her. This was the biggest high in the world. The ego trip of the century. Success. Public success. On national television. But still she could feel an undercurrent from the other guests. Envy? Suspicion?

"Our research shows that you're in your third printing and have sold fifty thousand copies in five weeks. I'd say that's a best seller, wouldn't you? In fact, it's starting to show up on the national charts." It is? It had? . . . It was? Why hadn't anyone told her? Jesus. Fifty thousand copies? She almost gasped, but instead she smiled.

"In that case, I concede." After a few minutes of nervousness, Kate was surprised at how easy the show became. The other women were fascinating, and Audrey was good at what she did. She turned a potentially chilly situation into a cordial one. And Kate was still riding high when she met Nick at Lutèce for lunch, and swooped down on him at his table in the little garden.

"Hi, darling. God, it was scary." And then, all in one breath, she heard herself telling him how tense she had been, how terrifyingly successful the other women had been, how impressive Audrey Bradford was, how well put together the woman producer was, how . . .

"Hey, hey, wait a minute. Slow down there, lady, or you'll pop your girdle. Relax." He was amused at her excitement. She was suddenly as hyper as everyone else in New York.

She sat down with a sheepish grin and took a breath. "I don't wear a girdle, by the way."

"Thank God. Now, did you make sense on the show?"

"Didn't you watch me?" She looked stunned.

"My darling, you are about to discover what my life is like in New York. I sat down peacefully in Jasper's suite to watch you there, and all three phones started to ring at once. He's had two extra lines put into the suite for his stay. The secretary he brought with him ran in with a major crisis on her hands. Our big name for the first show here is in the hospital with a stroke, it'll be front page by tonight. The additional secretary he hired here walked in and quit. Jasper's oldest boy called from London, had run over some kid with his car and was in jail. And meanwhile, I had calls in to nine different people to try and make a substitution for tonight's show. No, my love, I did not see your show. But I'm sure you were splendid." He looked at her with a grin and she tried to hide her disappointment. Sometimes she forgot how much he had to do. "By the way, Jasper was thinking that you might like to come back on the show. Maybe at the end of the week?"

"Already? He just had me on."

"That's all right. You're getting to be a hot property these days, with the book doing as well as it is, and with the daytime exposure you're getting, the women in his audience will like seeing you on our show." For a moment, he wasn't even Nick. He was a producer, a stranger, a nervous man with the nation's most important talk show to run. He hadn't even had time to watch her on her first New York show. "I'll have Stu talk to your publisher about putting you on. Jasper definitely wants you." He pulled out a little book, jotted something down, and then looked up, surprised, as the headwaiter brought him a phone.

"Call for you, Mr. Waterman." What followed were ten minutes of unintelligible conversation with someone on his production staff as Kate looked around at the other tables nearby. She was having lunch at one of the most expensive restaurants in New York, surrounded by the illustrious and the powerful. Nick signaled to the waiter and pointed at his watch midway through the conversation. The waiter nodded and hurried back with a menu for Kate. It was another five minutes before he was off the phone.

"I'm sorry, love. Some days are just like this, I'm afraid." More than he let on to her in fact. She never realized just how busy he was. But she was getting a ringside view of it in New York. He looked at his watch again. "Damn."

"Something wrong?"

"No. Except that I'm going to have to leave you in about twenty minutes. I've got about thirty-seven things to discuss with Jasper before tonight."

"Lucky man, sounds like he's going to be seeing more of you than I am." She was almost miffed, but not quite. She didn't have a right to be too demanding; they were both here to work not just play.

"I'm sorry I missed your show, Kate. I really am. Next time I'll watch, no matter what. I promise. If I have to bolt all the doors and take the phones off the hook."

"Okay, then I forgive you." They kissed just as the Louis Roederer arrived. It was an exquisite champagne, 1955.

They had caviar on paper-thin slices of white toast, quenelles Nantua, endive salad, fresh raspberries and whipped cream, and knocked off the whole bottle of champagne in less than half an hour. The result was that Kate sat back against the banquette, looking slightly drunk.

"You know . . ." She looked at Nick philosophically and he smiled as he signed for the check. Thank God for expense accounts. "You know," she started again, "sometimes it's hard to remember that all of this fun can lead to disaster."

"Now what's that supposed to mean?" He looked at her and was about to laugh, and then suddenly he remembered Tom. "Only if you let it go to your head, Kate. There are ways of having the success without the insanity."

"Are you sure?" She looked worried. She hadn't forgotten what all of this had done to Tom—and to her.

"I've seen people handle it well. You just can't lose your perspective. You can't let yourself forget what *you* really care about. And maybe you have to know too that it's nice while it lasts, but it's not everything. You're lucky, Kate. You have something real to go home to. You have Tygue, the house . . ."

"You forgot something." She was looking very subdued.

"What did I forget?"

293

"You forgot that I have you to come home to, Mr. Waterman. There's that too."

"Yes, there is. And don't *you* forget it either, Mrs. Harper."

And she didn't. She thought about it at great length as she walked back to the hotel, still feeling the effects of the champagne. It was so easy to be intoxicated by one's own self-importance, by expensive meals in lavish restaurants, by adulation and attention and acclaim. She had to admit she was enjoying it, but it frightened her too. Suddenly, for the first time, she understood all that had tempted Tom. And especially Tom, because his life had been so simple before all that. It was impossible for him to resist all the glitter that came along. But was she much different now? Was she making more sense? She wasn't sure.

She went back to the hotel to sleep off the wine, and was awakened by the hotel operator at four. She had left a wake-up message just in case she overslept. She had to be at a radio station on the West Side at six. And this time, the taping was horrendous. The interviewer asked her all the wrong questions, and prodded interminably about how a woman knew so much about football; he was a pushy, aggressive sexist, and she hated every minute of the interview, but she told herself that the exposure would be good for the book. Her publisher had also promised her a car and driver to take her back to the hotel, but they never arrived after the show, and she found herself walking down some of the more dangerous streets of Manhattan, praying for a cab. It was nine by the time she got to the studio to meet Nick. He had had a hectic evening, and problems for the next day's show had already begun to crop up. It was ten-thirty before they got out for something to eat, and then, hot and bedraggled, they wound up at La Grenouille, where even the elegant fare no longer appealed to her. She was hot and tired and she wanted to go to bed. Instead, a photographer from *Women's Wear Daily* snapped her photograph on the way out, and she found herself almost snarling as the flash bulb went off in her face.

"Now, now, take it easy, Kate. It's all in a day's work." She sighed briefly and then smiled at him.

"I don't know. I'm beginning to think that running after Tygue and Bert wasn't so bad."

"I told you so, madam."

They strolled up Fifth Avenue arm in arm, and Kate was exhausted when they fell into bed at one o'clock. She was almost as tired when she woke up the next day, and when he handed her a copy of *Women's Wear* her face puckered into an immediate frown. There was a photograph of them leaving the restaurant the night before, mention of who they were, mention of the book, and a catty remark about her dress.

"Christ, it was a hundred and four degrees and I'd been running my ass off all night. What do they want from me anyway?"

Nick laughed and shrugged as he sipped his coffee. "This is the big time, baby. In New York, they don't pull any punches."

"Well, they can go to hell. And I don't like being in the papers." She looked decidedly nervous as she lit a cigarette. It was a lousy way to start the day.

"How do you know? Have you ever tried it?" She only stared at him, saying nothing. "What's the matter, baby?" He sat down quietly on the bed and took her hand. "It's just a little blurb in the paper. It's no big deal."

"I just hate that kind of thing. It's none of their goddamn business."

"But they're interested in you. You're new, you're intelligent, you're beautiful. Your book is a smash. This is all part of it."

"I hate it." She looked at Nick again and her eyes filled with tears. It was all going to start again. They were going to spoil everything. She wanted to go home.

"Hey . . . come on, love . . . it's nothing." He folded her into his arms, and then looked down at her. "And if it bothers you that much to be in the papers, we'll be more careful. We'll go someplace quiet for lunch." He wrote down the name of a French restaurant on Fifty-third Street, where they wouldn't be noticed, gave her a last kiss, and left for a meeting with Jasper. But when they met for lunch, there was still a thread of fear woven into the tapestry of excitement. She found herself looking around warily, and Nick watched her closely.

"What's up?"

"Nothing."

"Worrying about the *paparazzi* again?"

"Yeah. Sort of."

"Well, don't. None of them would be seen dead here. And as far as *Women's Wear* is concerned, anyone who eats here isn't worth mentioning."

"Good." She looked relieved and took his hand. "I just hate that stuff."

"Why?" Why wouldn't she tell him? Didn't she trust him yet? Even now?

"It's such a violation. It's like rape. They tear your clothes off, stare at your body, and take what they want." She looked mournful, and he laughed and leaned closer.

"Can I be first?"

"Oh shut up."

"Well, stop worrying about it. It's all part of the

296

package. We all get used to it. I've been called everything from a male nymphomaniac to a faggot. So what?" She grinned up at him.

"They called you that?"

"Yup. Especially the former." But he didn't say it with pride. Anyway, that was over now. He hadn't looked at another woman since he'd met Kate. Six weeks exactly, to the day. "Hey, today is our anniversary."

"I know. Our sixth." She beamed up at him and forgot the papers. To hell with them. This was all that mattered now.

They dined that night at "21" with Jasper and a well-known New York theatrical producer. And Kate watched them tape the show. It was nice getting to know Jasper better, and she didn't mind his knowing what was happening with Nick. He seemed to approve wholeheartedly and treated her like someone very special.

The next day they all met for lunch in his suite at the Pierre, and that afternoon she and Nick went shopping for Tygue at F.A.O. Schwarz.

"Want to try out the boat?"

"Now?" She laughed at him as they left the store. It was the only thing they had carried. The rest they had sent back to the hotel. All kinds of cowboy equipment, a fabulous little bike, and Kate had had to fight Nick not to buy him a boy-sized log cabin. Nick wanted to buy it all. But she didn't want him doing that and he knew it. She had wanted to buy something for Tom too, but didn't know how to do it without Nick knowing. Now he was looking down at her, holding tightly to the elaborate remote-controlled boat. Tygue was going to use it on the lake.

"Listen, there is the most fabulous model-boat pond

here in Central Park. All these old guys hang around there with models of windjammers and schooners. We'll be outclassed. But it's terrific."

And it was. They spent two hours there, chatting with old men, watching the boats, smiling at the nannies passing by with large lace-laden English prams. New York gave one the impression that everyone was either terribly rich or terribly poor, and the people in between were banished somewhere else. To New Jersey perhaps. Or the Bronx.

They walked slowly out of the park past the zoo, and Kate stopped for a moment at the pony rides. "I wish Tygue were here. He'd love it."

"Maybe next time." He pulled her hand more tightly through his arm and thought of the boy, and then looked down at Kate again. "Want a pony ride, Cinderella?"

"Are you kidding?" She burst into laughter. "I'd break the cart. Or kill the horse." It was designed for very small children.

"Answer the question."

"Just what do you have in mind?"

"You'll see." He strolled her out of the park and right to the hansom cabs lined up at Fifty-ninth Street. There, he paused for a moment, spoke to one of the top-hatted drivers, and then turned to hand her inside. "This is a little more our speed." It was still blazingly hot, but she was almost used to the temperature now. And it was five o'clock as they strolled lazily through the park in the musty old carriage. People looked up and smiled, children waved. It was like living a fairy tale. Nick bought them both ice creams at a red light farther into the park. It was an hour later when he had the driver deposit them at the hotel.

"I smell like the horse." She whispered it to him

with a giggle as they walked sedately past the marble desk.

"I love it." He grinned at the smudge of ice cream on her chin. "You're a mess." But he could hardly wait to close the door behind them. They spent an hour in bed, and then they both had to run. He had to do Jasper's show, and she was scheduled on a rival talk show on another network.

It went very well, as did one of the two radio shows she did the next day. The second one was a bomb where no one seemed to know who she was or why she was there. And there had been nothing more in the papers. She was enjoying the trip, despite the frantic pace, and she was amazed at how quickly one adjusted to the interviews and the cameras. She was much less nervous this time when she did Jasper's show. And she let Nick help her pick out a dress, a clinging pearl-gray Halston. It was the sexiest dress she had ever seen, yet it was ladylike too. It was perfect for her. Even Jasper was a little startled when she appeared. She was a very striking-looking girl. And her appearance on the show was the climax of her trip.

"So, Mr. Waterman, what's on the agenda for today?"

"I don't know. Want to go to the beach? It might be nice to see some sand again." It was Saturday.

"Is there any around here? I thought they didn't approve of that sort of thing."

"Southhampton." He lay on his side and looked at the woman he loved, just as the phone rang. "You get it. This is your room. Remember?" He thought of everything.

"Hello?" She expected it to be Licia, or maybe Jasper for Nick. Who else would call? But it wasn't. It was Tillie. "He is? He did? What . . . oh my God. Is he all right?" She sat up very straight, and Nick's face puckered into a worried frown. "Now? Why did they keep him there? Can't he come home?" The one-sided conversation was driving Nick nuts and he started asking questions, but she waved him back to silence. "This afternoon? All right. I'll see what I can do." She hung up with a frown, looked at Nick, and then at her lap with a sigh. "Damn."

"What happened, for chrissake?"

"Tygue fell off the gate at the Adams ranch and broke his arm. Tillie said he was just swinging on it with Joey, but he fell over backward. They thought he might have a concussion, so they kept him in the hospital overnight. She said she tried to call us last night, but we weren't home, and she was afraid to leave a message and scare me half to death. Godamnit." She got off the bed and stalked across the room.

"Poor little thing. Are they sure there's no concussion? And what kind of a hospital did Tillie take him to?" Nick looked suddenly very worried and Kate smiled.

"He's in Santa Barbara and he's fine. He can go home this afternoon. All he has is a cast on his arm."

Nick looked at his watch. "If I put you on a plane in an hour, you could be there at noon California time, catch a plane to Santa Barbara . . . hell, Kate, you could be there by two." He smiled helpfully and she sank into a chair.

"Yeah. I know."

"What's with you?" Nick stared at her in confusion. "You're going back, aren't you?"

"I don't suppose I have much choice." But she looked as if she wanted one.

"What's that supposed to mean?" It was the first time she had ever seen him look disagreeable. In fact, he looked shocked.

"It means that I know I should go, but I don't want

to. I was having such a good time. And Tillie says he's fine, but I know that if I don't go back, I'll feel awful and he'll hate me, and . . . oh, Nick. I haven't done anything with my life in seven years and this has been so much fun."

"It's not his fault you locked yourself in a closet for all those years, for chrissake. You're his mother!" He was actually shouting. It stunned her.

"Okay. I know that. But I'm me too. I'm Kate, not just Mom. I'm almost thirty years old, and I've been Mom nonstop for six years. Don't I have a right to more than that?"

"Yes, but not at his expense, lady. Never at his expense." He was stalking the room now, furious. "Let me tell you something, Kate. I've seen a lot of assholes come and go from where I sit. They screw up their lives, they fuck over their children, they cheat on their husbands, they break up their marriages, and you know why? Because they're so goddamn in love with themselves they can't see straight. They love the noise and the lights, the introductions and the applause, the cameras and the microphones, and you know what else? I can see you falling for that bullshit too. Well do yourself and Tygue and me a big favor, kiddo—don't. There's nothing there. Fame is a nice place to visit, but that's it. And now, your kid broke his arm, and you're going home, and that's it." He leaned past her, grabbed the phone, and asked the hotel operator for TWA, but before he could finish his sentence, Kate's finger was on the button, disconnecting his call. He looked at her in astonishment. Her eyes were blazing, but when she spoke, her voice was soft.

"Don't ever do that again. When I want to call the airline, I'll do it. When I decide to go home, I'll let you know. And when I need your advice about my

301

maternal responsibilities, I'll ask for it. In the meantime, mister, keep your ideas and your threats and your righteous indignation to yourself." She stood up and walked across the room with her back to him. When she reached the window, she turned to look at him, and he had never seen such fury in a woman's face. "I have given everything to that child for years. Everything I have, everything I am, everything I know how to give has been his. But it's my turn now. And I know better than anyone the price to be paid. I watched someone I loved grow cancerous with that bullshit fame trip. I know all about it, thank you. And I'm scared to death of it. But that doesn't mean I want to be buried alive either. I've done that to myself for years and I've had enough of it. I have a right to this. I have a right to my time with you, my career, my own life, and if I'm disappointed because I have to go back to reality now, then I have a right to that too. But don't you ever try to guilt-trip me out, and tell me what I owe that child. I know what I owe Tygue, and believe me, I've paid my dues. And don't you ever tell me what to do again. I've been there. I've tried that. I've relied on a man until there was no me left. I let him make all my decisions, and I loved it and I loved him, but it almost killed me when he wasn't there to do the telling anymore. So I grew up. I make my own decisions. And I like it that way. I love you, Nick, but you will never tell me when to go home. I'll make that decision. Is that perfectly clear?" He nodded silently and she walked back across the room with her head bowed. She stopped when she stood right in front of him.

"I'm sorry if I said too much, Nick, but it's been a long hard road from there to here, and I've paid a hell of a price for everything I have. I don't know how to deal with anyone messing with that. I'm not even sure I know how to deal with someone helping me. And there's an awful lot happening to me right now. I need time to absorb it . . . maybe going home isn't such a bad idea after all." Her voice was deep and gruff as she ended the words and reached for the phone. She asked for the same airline Nick had asked for only a moment before. He said nothing now. He only listened as she made a reservation on the next flight. He stood up when she was through on the phone, and they both remained still for a moment, neither of them speaking, neither of them sure what to say, both of them shaken by what they had felt and said. It was Kate who spoke first. "I'm sorry, Nick."

"Don't be. I had no right . . ." He pulled her gently into his arms and sighed. He wanted to do everything for her, because he knew that no one had for so long, but he knew she had to grow into this new life herself. He wanted to spare her the pain and the price, but he couldn't. He held her tight for a long moment and then swatted her behind and pulled away. "You'd better go get ready, or you'll miss your flight."

"No, I won't." She was smiling now. A small, womanly smile, and it evoked a real smile from him. "Listen, you . . ."

"Oh shut up." She led him gently by the hand into the bedroom they had shared during their stay in New York and she pulled him onto the bed and began to laugh. "Don't be so serious, Nick. The world hasn't come to an end." As a matter of fact, she felt as though it was just beginning. And as he carefully pulled off her shirt, she reached out to him with a longing and hunger she could barely control. She pulled him down to her, her mouth and her body aching for his.

CHAPTER 25

"Tillie, can you stay with Tygue for a few hours?"

"Sure. I'll be over right away."

Kate smiled as she hung up. Nick was coming back from New York. It had only been a week, but it felt more like years. Tygue's cast made his arm itch and he was constantly restless. She had been up to see Tom twice and he seemed in poor form too. He looked tired and gaunt, and she could see that he was losing weight. And he cried the second time when she left. Everyone was pulling at her. But it was no different than it had been before. Only she was different. The past week had been like a living reminder of what her life had been like before Nick. But now he was coming home. And she had two chapters of a new book to show him.

"Where are you going?" Tygue looked worried as she pulled out the coral dress she had worn in New York.

"To meet Nick. I'm going to surprise him." And then she knew she shouldn't have said it, because he'd want to come too. The boy's face lit up like a fire-cracker on the Fourth of July.

"He's coming home?" She nodded, with a smile. She felt the same way.

"Can I come?" She paused for a long moment, and then sighed.

"Okay, tough guy. You win." Motherhood, Inc. And

suddenly she wanted so much to be alone. But she knew Nick would be happy to see him. She called Tillie back and told Tygue to change his clothes. He could manage pretty well with the cast now.

They were in the car half an hour later. Tygue had on his new cowboy boots and his favorite hat, and she felt pretty again in the coral dress. It felt nice to wear good clothes. She was sick of blue jeans and old shirts.

They had three and a half hours to get to the airport, and they made it just in time. They ran to the gate just as Nick walked off the plane. Tygue shouted his name, and Kate stood there, breathless. It had been a mad dash through the building.

"Hey, Tiger!" Nick looked at the boy in astonishment and then at his mother. It had been years since anyone had met him at a plane. He just stood there and beamed, with the child in his arms. But the hug he gave Kate told him what her surprise meant.

"We brought you a present!" The boy was ecstatic too. All three of them were, as they stood there blocking traffic.

"You did?"

"Yup. A picture of Brownie with me on it. Mom had it framed for your desk."

"That's terrific." He put an arm around Kate's shoulders and they walked slowly along. "Hi, darling." He said it just for her and she reached up and kissed him again.

"I missed you something awful."

He rolled his eyes in answer, pulled her closer, and turned his attention back to Tygue.

"I missed you too, Nick. And I can ride Brownie, even with my arm."

"Is that a good idea?" He looked at Kate with a frown.

"The doctor says it won't hurt him, as long as he doesn't go galloping around. They just walk."

"Okay."

They collected his bags as the three of them charged in and out of the conversation, and then went to get the car. They chatted all the way home, where even Bert seemed happy to see Nick.

"Now the whole family is together again!" Tygue said it with a fervor that tore at Kate's heart. He was getting so attached to Nick. But he wasn't alone in his affection. Nick could hardly wait to get his hands on the boy. They tried out all his new toys before dinner.

"And wait till you see the boat go! Your mom and I tried it out in New York." They exchanged a smile at the memory.

"They have a lake there?"

"A boat pond. And a zoo. And pony rides. We'll take you there sometime. As a matter of fact, young man, I have another trip in mind for you now."

"You do?" Tygue's eyes opened wide. Nick was always full of surprises, and Kate stood by waiting to hear about a weekend in Santa Barbara. But this time she was surprised too.

"Do you know what we're all doing tomorrow?"

Tygue shook his head wordlessly.

"We're going to Disneyland!"

"We are?" His eyes couldn't open wide enough, and Kate and Nick laughed.

"We are. All three of us."

"How on earth did you manage that?" Kate walked over and put an arm around him.

"Jasper went to the South of France for a week. So I'm all yours. If you can stand me." And after a week in New York, busting his ass for the show, now he was taking them all to Disneyland. Kate looked at him in amazement.

"Mr. Waterman, I must be the luckiest woman alive."

"Nope. I'm the luckiest man."

The trip to Disneyland was perfect. They came home three days later, exhausted and happy, spent a day at Kate's place, and then went to Santa Barbara for the weekend. Kate hadn't been up to Carmel all week, but she didn't even care. She was happy where she was. And Tom had Mr. Erhard. For once, that would have to be enough. She had her own life to lead now.

Tygue looked miserable when the weekend came to an end.

"I'll see you next weekend, Tiger."

"But I want to see you sooner than that." Nick would be there every night, but Tygue didn't know that.

"Maybe you will."

Nick didn't know how honest the promise was, until the next day. He started the drive back to Kate's at four o'clock, and got there at seven. She was surprised to see him at first, and then worried. There was something brutally unhappy in his face, but he insisted that they'd talk when Tygue went to bed.

"Okay, tell me. I can't stand it." They had just closed Tygue's door.

"I talked to Jasper today, Kate. And . . . he's made up his mind." Had he been fired? God, he looked awful. Kate reached for his hand.

"What about?"

"The show moves to San Francisco."

"When?"

307

"In six weeks."

"Is that awful?" She didn't quite understand.

"I think so. Don't you? That's a five-hour drive, at best. Sometimes six. I can't drive that every morning and every night. Not even for you." Now what would they have? Weekends? But she was smiling at him and took him into her arms.

"Is that why you're upset? God, I thought you'd been fired."

"I might as well have been." He had been thinking all day about quitting. Hell, any one of a dozen shows in L.A. would love to have him. But she was looking at him in astonishment.

"Are you crazy? What's the big deal?"

"I'll never see you, for chrissake. Doesn't that matter to you?" He looked as if he were going to cry, but Kate was smiling.

"So I'll move to San Francisco. So what?" She looked at him as though he were being ridiculous, and he closed his eyes and then opened them with a tired smile.

"You'd do that for me, Kate?"

"Sure. Or would that only make problems for you?" Maybe it wasn't what he wanted after all. Maybe he still wanted some freedom. But so did she. They could still have freedom and each other.

"Problems? Lady, you are amazing." And then he had a thought. "But what'll you do with the house?"

"We can use it on weekends. And the timing is perfect for school. We'll just enroll Tygue someplace up there, and he can start the school year next month, along with everyone else." She had thought it all out the last time he'd mentioned the possibility of the move. But she hadn't said anything to him, and he had been worried sick.

"Are you serious about all this, Kate?" He still

couldn't believe it. But she looked serious. He didn't know whether to laugh, or cry, or dance.

"Of course I'm serious, Mr. Charming."

"Oh Kate . . ." He held her in his arms for hours. The weeks of worry had been for nothing. It was going to be a whole new life. Together.

CHAPTER 26

Her heels clattered through the empty room, leaving an echo behind her. It was a large open room with an endless span of picture window looking out on the Bay. The floors were a beautiful dark inlaid wood and there were bronze sconces on the wall. To the left, they could see the Golden Gate Bridge, to the right Alcatraz, and Angel Island sat straight ahead.

"It's really a remarkable view." Kate nodded pleasantly, but said nothing. It was a beautiful view . . . a splendid view . . . but it reminded her a little of the house she had shared with Tom. But that was silly. That had only been an apartment. This was a whole house. And a lovely one. Nick said he wanted a house.

She stood in the dining room with the same view of the Bay, her back to the fireplace. It was a warm room with beam ceilings and bay windows instead of the flat picture window of the living room. She squinted, seeing white organdie curtains and plants, inviting cushions in the window seats, a soft white rug, and a rich, dark wood table. . . . She squinted again, seeing it all, and started to smile.

"I'm going to take a look at the upstairs again." The realtor nodded silently this time. She was tired. They had been doing this for three days, and there was nothing left to show. Kate had seen everything.

Sunken living rooms, sweeping views, seven bedrooms, and only three, wood paneling, marble floors, crooked Victorians in need of work. She had seen everything from the decrepit to the divine in Pacific Heights and Presidio Heights, along the Presidio Wall and on Lake Street, and even on Russian Hill. But she seemed to know exactly what she wanted, and she apparently hadn't seen it yet. Her kind was the worst. She wasn't going to settle for anything less than the house she had laid out in her head. The realtor sat down heavily in the window seat, and flipped through her book for the thirtieth time in three days. This was it. It was the last suitable rental she had. She could hear Kate wandering around the uncarpeted rooms above, and then she noticed her footsteps stop.

Upstairs, Kate was looking out at the view from the master bedroom. The Bay again, and the same cozy window seats that she had seen downstairs in the dining room, a tiny fireplace with a marble mantelpiece, and a dressing room just big enough for a flea to change shoes in. But there was a friendliness to the place. She could imagine Nick passing her in the hall, squeezing past her in the dressing room and pinching her behind as he reached into his closet. She could imagine sitting in the window seat with Tygue looking out over the Bay at twilight, talking about something important, like baseball or snakes. She could even see Bert here, clattering between the rooms. There were two other bedrooms on the second floor. A large one, which faced the garden at the front of the house, with lots of sunshine and tall French windows. That room could be Tygue's. And another equally pretty bedroom. A guest room perhaps. They didn't really need one, but it was always good to have a spare room. And there was a tiny maid's room be-

311

hind the kitchen which she could use as an office. It wasn't pretty, but at least it would give her a room in which she could write.

The kitchen she'd seen downstairs was open and warm, a room to have dinner in when they didn't have guests. It had two brick walls and a built-in barbecue, and the rest of it was painted yellow with a bright yellow ceramic floor. The tiles had been brought over from Portugal by the last tenants. It was perfect . . . all it needed was copper pots, and a wrought-iron hook with salamis and peppers . . . glass jars filled with spices . . . curtains, and the butcher-block table Nick had in his kitchen now. She was bringing very little up from her place in the country. Only a few treasured things, the pretty pieces she had acquired over the years. The ordinary, functional things Nick said they could buy. It would be a little strange setting up housekeeping with him, without being married. What would belong to whom? And who decided what they bought? But Nick seemed to be comfortable with the arrangement, and was giving her carte blanche.

She looked around the bedroom that could be Tygue's again, and down at the well-tended little garden. It was surrounded by a high hedge which would give them privacy, and there was a gate, so Bert couldn't get lost. In fact, the house seemed to have everything they needed. The view and fireplaces and high ceilings Nick had said were a must, an elegant sweeping staircase that led upstairs, and three bedrooms, which even gave them a spare. And a small, dark room near the kitchen in which she could work. She didn't love the workroom, but the rest seemed to be just what they wanted. She sat on the top stair and looked up. Directly over her head there was a skylight, and to her right a slightly open door. More closets maybe. She leaned backward to take a look. It looked like a stairway. She frowned and got up, calling down to the realtor still waiting downstairs.

"Is there more upstairs?"

There was the sound of shuffling through the now familiar book, and then a vague "I'm not sure." And then as Kate walked toward the door, the realtor came to the foot of the stairs. "Maybe some kind of an attic. But it doesn't say in the book. It just says here 'three bedrooms, den, and maid's.'"

"Den?" She hadn't seen a den. There was a den?

The stairway was narrow but carpeted, and the walls were still tapestried with a new-looking beige silk. It hardly looked like the kind of thing you'd put on the way to the attic, and as Kate reached the top of the stairs, she saw why. This was no attic, it wasn't even a den, it was an oasis, a dream. A small, well-proportioned wood-paneled room with a fireplace and a 360-degree view of San Francisco. The Bay, the Presidio, downtown, and the hills leading south. The room was well carpeted, boasted the now familiar bay windows, and there was even a little extension to it, a kind of solarium, which would be heavenly when it was filled with plants. And there would still be room for a desk and her file cabinets. The extension had two discreet glass French doors, which did not impair the view, but still allowed one to shut oneself off . . . the perfect office. And a wonderful room to sit quietly in with Nick, after he did the show. They could light the fire and look out at the city. Their special hideaway, a room to fill with beauty and children and love. The whole house was that way. It was exactly what she had wanted. Better than that. It was exactly what she had dreamed, and known they would never find. Beauty, elegance, simplicity, warmth, privacy, and convenience. The realtor had thought she was crazy when she'd ticked them off. But she'd found them all in one house. And it didn't look a bit like the house she'd had with Tom.

"We'll take it." She said it in a decisive voice as she turned to the realtor, who had followed her upstairs.

"It's a remarkable place," the woman agreed.

Kate nodded victoriously. "It's perfect." She was beaming. She could hardly wait to show Nick. "How soon can we have it?"

"Tomorrow." The realtor grinned. They had done it after all. She couldn't get over it. She had been sure this one was hopeless. The woman wanted everything and wouldn't settle for less. But that upstairs room did make the house an incredible find. Why the hell hadn't someone else snatched it up? Maybe no one else had noticed the upstairs room before. It wasn't on the listing. "It says here that it's available immediately. We can draw up the lease and it's yours."

"I really ought to show it to . . . to my husband. But I'm absolutely sure. This is it. In fact, just to be sure of it . . . how much do they require as a deposit?" The realtor checked her book again and came up with a most unexceptionable figure. Kate wanted to shriek "That's all?" but she kept quiet. This one was too good to blow. She hastily wrote out a check and handed it to the woman. "I'll bring him back tonight."

She did, and he fell in love with it too. "Isn't it super?" With him she could be exuberant. "Oh Nick, I love it!" She plonked herself down in one of the window seats with a grin.

"I love you." He walked over to her with a peaceful smile, and then looked out at the bay. "But I love the house too. It's going to look terrific with you and Tygue running around in it."

"And Bert." She corrected him with a serious look.

314

"Excuse me. And Bert. But not Brownie, if you please. I've already called the stable in the park. They'll give Brownie a very comfortable stall. At about the same price we'll be paying to rent this house."

"God, how awful. Maybe we should leave him in Santa Barbara."

"Hell no. You can't do that to Tygue. Besides, I think I can still manage it." He was looking around what Kate was already calling "the Ivory Tower," the wood-paneled room on the top floor. He could already imagine nights in front of the fire, Kate in his arms, the lights across the Bay twinkling just past Angel Island, and Tygue sound asleep downstairs. Or he could see Kate busy at her desk on the other side of the glass doors, oblivious to anything but her work, concocting a new book on the typewriter with three pencils and a pen stuck haphazardly into her hair. He loved what he saw, in his mind and around him.

"Do you think we should take it?" She was smiling at him like a child, anxious and excited and proud.

He laughed. "You're asking my advice? I thought that was already settled, Cinderella. I owe you for that deposit, by the way."

"The hell you do. That was my share."

"What share?" He looked at her in surprise.

"You don't expect to support me, do you? We go fifty-fifty on this. Don't we?" She suddenly looked embarrassed. They had not yet discussed the financial aspect of the move.

"Are you serious?" Nick looked offended. "Of course I expect to support you."

"But you're not marrying me, for chrissake. We're just living together."

"That's your decision, not mine. Tygue is your responsibility, if you like, but you're mine. I'm not going to have you paying rent to live here."

"That doesn't seem fair."

"Then mind your own business. And I'd happily support Tygue too, if you'd agree." He looked at her seriously, but she shook her head.

"Nick . . ." She looked across at him with a tender look in her eyes. It had been only two months, and he was offering her everything. He was offering to support her, entertain her, take care of her, take on her son. It was all very much like a dream. "Why are you always so good to me."

"Because you deserve it, and I love you." He sat down next to her in the window seat. "I'd do more, if you'd let me."

"What more is there?" She looked around with a twinkle in her eye, but he was looking unusually serious.

"Marriage." He said it very softly, and she looked away. "You still won't even consider it, will you?" But hell, it had been only two months. And she still hadn't told him about Tom. In time . . . he knew that in time . . . at least that was what he hoped. And he liked the idea of the spare bedroom next to Tygue's. He had an excellent idea of how to fill it, and not with friends from L.A. or New York. But Nick was looking at her very carefully in the twilight and she finally lifted her eyes to his. And then very carefully she put her arms around him and held him very tight.

"I'm sorry, Nick. But I can't think of marriage . . . I can't." She sounded as though something were breaking inside of her.

"Are you still hung up on your husband?" He didn't want to push, but he couldn't let this go.

"No. Not in the way you mean. I accept what happened. I told you. He's gone. Part of another life, another century. And the funny thing is that you already know me better than he ever did." And then she felt like a traitor for saying that. Tom had known her perfectly, but she had been a girl, a child, not yet a woman, not until the end. She hadn't even known herself then. But she did now, and Nick knew her too. It was a very different relationship.

"But you still hang on to him, don't you?"

She started to say no, but then nodded. "In some ways."

"Why?"

"Maybe out of loyalty. Out of what we once had." It was a strange double-edged conversation. She was answering his questions with more truth than she thought he understood.

"You can't live like that forever, Kate."

"I know. I just always knew I'd never remarry."

"That's ridiculous." He stood up with a sigh then. "We can talk about it later. In the meantime, Cinderella"—he looked down at her with the smile that never failed to melt her—"welcome home." He took her face in his hands and kissed her very gently.

Three weeks later, they moved in, amidst chaos and laughter and loving. Tygue ensconced himself in his room, Bert took over the entire house, the kitchen became everyone's favorite meeting place, and the maid's room became an instant depository for ice skates, bicycles, and skis. Nick was teaching Tygue to skate, and he was going to take them both skiing as soon as the first snows came. The dining room looked just as she had envisioned it, with a table they found at an auction, with eight rustic old ladder-back chairs, and white organdie curtains. The living room was a little grand for everyday, in brown velvets and beige silks, but it would be perfect for entertaining Nick's friends, or people from the show. And the room upstairs became just what they had dreamed. A love nest. When they were not tucked into their cluttered Victorian blue and white bedroom, they were to be found hiding out in the wood-paneled room upstairs. Kate filled it with plants and books, some old paintings she loved, the leather chairs Nick liked best from his apartment, and his most treasured private things—trophies of his boyhood, favorite photographs, and the stuffed head of a lion smoking a hysterically oversized cigar, one eye sewn into a wink. There was also a tuba hanging from the wall, in memory of a past even more distant than that commemorated by the trophies or the lion, and there were endless baby pictures of Tygue. Her past seemed to go no further back than that. But before Tygue had come her parents, and Tom, and both of those eras were now closed. This was a new life. And she made it that when she moved up from the country. Just as she had when she'd moved down there. She closed a door behind her with each move.

Tygue loved his new school, and the show was going well. Even Kate's new book was progressing nicely. She was sure she would finish it before Christmas. And *A Final Season* was already in its fifth printing.

"You know, I can't get over this place." Felicia was their first dinner guest. She sat down in the living room after dinner and looked around. "Some of us just happen to hit it lucky on the first try." Or the second, but she didn't say that. She looked warmly at Nick. "You've managed to accomplish in a couple of months what I couldn't push the kid into in almost seven years. Mr. Waterman, hats off." She smiled at Nick and he executed a neat bow. Their affection was mutual. He liked what she did for Kate, the way she had stood by her for so long.

Nick grew serious for a minute. "I think she was just ready to come out of her shell."

"*Come* out? I was *blasted* out."

Felicia concealed a grin with another sip of her coffee. Even their belongings had combined well to make a home. Felicia looked around, and shared another smile with Nick, and then he glanced at his watch.

"Ladies, with deepest regrets, I'm afraid I'll have to leave you." They had eaten dinner early so he could get to the taping on time. The "girls" were going to stay home and chat. "I'll be back after nine. Stick around, Licia. We can play poker or something when I get home. Or I'll take you two out for a drink."

"I'll take a raincheck, love. I've got half a dozen early meetings tomorrow. It'll really be a bitch of a day. I don't hang around in bed till noon the way you two do."

"The hell I do. I spend half my life car-pooling Tygue and his pals around here."

"Oh you do." Nick arched an eyebrow and she laughed guiltily.

"All right, all right. I'll do it next week, I swear."

"Kate Harper, you are spoiled." Felicia looked at her in amazement. "Nick even car-pools for you?" Kate nodded guiltily, but with a grin. "Jesus. You don't deserve the gold mine you got." She looked at her friend in mock horror, but Kate's happiness was exactly what she had longed to see for years. And this new living situation obviously suited Kate perfectly. Just enough domesticity and just enough sparkle.

Nick hugged Felicia and kissed Kate, and they heard the Ferrari pull out a moment later after he had gone upstairs to say good night to Tygue, who was playing with Felicia's train in the spare room.

"Is there anything that man doesn't do for you, Kate?" Felicia looked over at her, sitting peacefully at the other end of the brown velvet couch.

"Nothing I can think of." She looked totally content. "I know. I'm spoiled rotten." But he wasn't all teddy bear either. They had their moments and their fights, but she liked that about him too.

"You deserve it, love. He's really an extraordinary man." And then after a pause, she looked up with a question in her eyes, and Kate looked away. "He still doesn't know, does he? I mean about Tom." But Kate had known what she meant. She looked up at her and shook her head, with a look of pain and sorrow. "Have you stopped going?" She hoped . . . she hoped . . . but she didn't get her wish. Kate shook her head again and sighed.

"Of course not. I can't stop going. How could I stop? What could I say? 'I'm leaving you now. I've found someone else.' You don't say that to a seven-year-old boy. You don't walk out on him. You don't stop, Licia. You can't. I'll never stop as long as he's alive."

"Will you tell Nick?"

"I don't know." She closed her eyes for a moment and then looked at the fire. "I don't know. I guess I should. But I don't know how. Maybe in time."

"You'll have to, if this goes on for a long time. Where does he think you go?"

"To teach."

"Doesn't he get sick of that? I mean, all the way to Carmel to teach is pushing it a little, isn't it?"

Kate nodded again. "I just don't have any choice."

"You don't want to have a choice. I think he'd understand."

"But what if he didn't, Felicia? He wants to get married, to have children, to have a normal life. How can you have a normal life living with a married woman? A woman who's married to a seven-year-old physical and emotional cripple? What if I tell him and he decides it's too much for him?" She closed her eyes for a moment at the thought.

"And you think not telling him would change that, Kate? What if he finds out eventually? What if he presses you about getting married? What if you tell him in five years, or two years, or ten years? What do you think he'll say then? He has a right to know the truth." And so did Tygue. She had thought so on and off for years. Now and then she had been wooed by Kate's insistence that not telling Tygue had been the right decision, but in her gut she had always thought that the boy might be better off if he knew. But she wasn't going to tackle that one with Kate again. And if only Nick knew, he could help Kate deal with the issue of telling Tygue. "I think you're playing with dynamite by not telling him. You're also not showing a lot of faith in him, and you're not being very ballsy."

"My, my, that's quite a speech, Licia."

"I'm sorry, Kate. But I think it needs to be said, before you make a big mistake."

"All right. I'll see."

"Doesn't he ask you about Carmel?"

"Sometimes. But I cut him off."

"You can't cut him off forever, Kate. And why should you? It's not fair. Look what he's doing for you, what he's giving you, how much he loves you. You owe him the truth."

"All right, Licia, all right. Just let me work it out for myself." She stood up and walked to the fire with her back to her friend. She didn't want to hear it. She knew that Licia was right. She did have to tell him. Eventually. But not yet. And Licia was also right that she couldn't stall him forever. She was already getting nervous about the days she went away. She had tiptoed downstairs three days before, hoping he wouldn't be up. But he had been. And she had hated the act she had put on as she left.

"How often do you go?" Felicia, as usual, wouldn't let up.

"Same as always. Twice a week." And with a sigh she realized that she was going again the next day. Maybe Nick would sleep late.

CHAPTER 27

She closed the door as the car pool rounded the corner. A last wave just before the little blond head in the back seat disappeared from sight, and Tygue was off to his day. And she to hers. She walked softly into the kitchen for a last sip of her coffee. She didn't want to wake Nick.

"You look awfully done up for a foggy Tuesday morning." He looked at her from the large kitchen table and she jumped.

"Hi, darling. I didn't know you were up." She tried to sound light as she bent to kiss him. "Want some coffee?" He nodded. "Eggs?"

"No, thanks. I'll make my own when I can open my eyes. You teaching again?"

She nodded, looking into the coffee she was pouring.

"Your schedule seems to vary a lot." There was something strange in his voice. An accusation. A suspicion. Something she didn't like. She looked up at him, but she couldn't quite tell what it was. "Last week you went Monday and Thursday. Didn't you?"

"I guess so. I don't know." She poured in the two sugars he liked and busied herself at the sink.

"Come here a minute."

Her heart was pounding, but she tried to think empty thoughts as she turned toward him. She didn't want him to see anything, know anything . . . know she was lying. She stood looking at him, but there was no smile in his eyes.

"Why won't you tell me what you really do down there?"

"Are you serious?"

"Very." And he looked it. Her heart only beat faster and seemed to fill her ears.

"I told you. I teach retarded children and adults."

"Can't you find something comparable in the city? Surely San Francisco has lots of retarded kids who'd love you. Why Carmel?" And why not the truth, dammit? Why?

"I've been going there for years." That much he knew.

"While you were married?"

"No." And then there was a strange silence and she looked hard at him again. "What difference does that make?"

"I don't know, Kate. Maybe I should ask you that."

"What the hell difference does it make, dammit? I don't bother you. I leave at eight, I'm back at five. Sometimes four-thirty. It doesn't take anything away from you." She was angry now, and frightened. She had never seen him look like that before.

"It does take something away from me, Kate." He looked at her in a way that shriveled her soul. It was a cold, angry look. "It takes you away."

"For a few lousy hours?" Christ, she owed Tom that much. He had no right to . . .

"Have you ever looked in the mirror when you get back?" She stared at him silently. "You look like a ghost. You look haunted and hurt and tired and sad. Why do you do that to yourself?" He found himself staring at her even harder, but found no answers. "Never mind. It's none of my business." She said nothing, but walked out of the kitchen. She should have gone to him, hugged him, kissed him. She knew it. It would have been smarter. But she didn't want to be smart. And she didn't want to be pushed. She wasn't going to tell him until she was ready to, if ever. And she would never let him stop her from going. Those two days a week were sacred. They were Tom's.

"I'll see you at five." She said it from the front door, with her eyes closed, wanting to go to him, but afraid he'd do something to stop her from going, or worse, force the truth out of her. Why the hell did he have to wake up? It was so easy when he was asleep. She hesitated a moment and then spoke again. "I love you." She heard him walk softly out of the kitchen and into the dining room. He stood there with the Bay at his back and looked at her for what felt like an eon.

"Do you, Kate?"

"You know I do." She walked slowly toward him and took him into her arms. "Darling, I love you so much."

There was a long pause as his arms held her too, and then he pulled away.

"Then tell me about Carmel." He almost prayed that she would. God, how long could he go on pretending not to know. But Kate only looked at him, with wide sorrowful eyes.

"We've already talked about Carmel, Nick." Her eyes never left his.

"Have we? Then why don't I feel more comfortable about your going there?" What else could he say, dammit? Jesus, if she'd only give him an opening.

"There's nothing for you to worry about."

"Isn't there, Kate? Wouldn't it worry you if I went somewhere every week without telling you more about it than you tell me?"

She was silent for a moment and then she looked away. "But I tell you about it, Nick. You know why I go." She tried desperately to sound soothing.

His eyes held a penetrating quality she didn't understand. He wanted to tell her that he *did* know. He felt almost compelled to tell her, but he couldn't. He had to hear it from her. She had to want to tell him. "Never mind, forget it. Have a nice day." He wheeled around then and walked back toward the kitchen, as she stood there wondering if she should run after him. But she couldn't. He wanted answers that she was not yet ready to give him.

She walked out the door and to the car, but she felt as though she were dragging chains around her feet. Should she go? Should she stay? Did she owe him an explanation? Should she tell him the truth? What if he left her? What if . . . and then, as she started the car, she forced him from her mind. She owed the trip to Tom, she owed him these visits, these days . . . but did she owe it to him to lose Nick? The thought made her step on the brakes and think for a minute. Was she really playing for those kinds of stakes? Could Felicia be right? Could she lose Nick if she didn't tell him and he eventually found out?

"Shit." She muttered the word to herself as she let herself gently into the traffic outside their house. She just couldn't tell him yet. Not yet . . . but maybe soon.

CHAPTER 28

It was pouring as she drove back to San Francisco from Carmel. Where was all this gorgeous October weather Felicia always talked about? Christ, it had been raining for days. It had rained the last three times she had gone there. It was even raining in Carmel. And the rain was so hard on Tom. He looked so pale now, and he wasn't eating well. There was a lost quality about him lately, like a tired sick child hatching some terrible illness. He would hold her hand for hours and beg her for stories, looking at her with those eyes that seemed to see her, really see her, but never did. Those eyes still remembered nothing. And the arms still reached out for her as he called out "Katie," the way Tygue shouted "Mom." He seemed so helpless now though. He had been this way for so long, and something about him seemed to be slipping away. The teasing was gone. The laughter had dimmed. Mr. Erhard looked concerned too. But the director of Mead said it was "normal." Normal . . . what the hell was normal about a man who thought like a child? A man who had once been so alive and had now lived in a wheelchair playing with paper airplanes for seven years? But the doctor insisted that people in Tom's condition did "fade" from time to time, and eventually, one day . . . but that could be years away. In the meantime, he could have these "spells" and still rally, as long as one kept his interest up and "challenged him." Although, the director admitted, that didn't always change things. He admitted, too, that Tom might have these spells more and more frequently over the next years, until the end. It was neurological, and inevitable, but it wasn't acute. And she didn't understand it any better than anything else that had happened in the past seven years. Whatever it was, Tom hadn't been right for almost a month. And she could sense that Nick wanted her to stop going to Carmel. Christ. She sighed as she drove off the freeway onto Franklin Street. It was going to be good to get home. She was so tired. And thank God Nick hadn't been up when she left that morning. She had been getting up earlier for the past two weeks, in order to avoid him. And she was making special efforts to keep his mind off her trips to Carmel.

She turned left on Green Street and followed it west until she almost reached the Presidio, then unexpectedly she swooped up a narrow, curved, brick-paved street, and there, hidden amidst the sculptured landscape, concealed by the hedges, trees, and bushes, nestled their house. After little more than a month in it, she already loved it more than any house she had ever lived in, maybe because she was so happy there.

She let herself into the house with a sigh of relief. It was only four-twenty. Tygue was at his special art class, and would be delivered by the car pool at four forty-five. She had just made it. And the Ferrari had been nowhere in sight. Safe. No explanations, no excuses, no little bits of chatter to cover up the worry and the pain. It was always so hard confronting Nick after all that. He hated it too. And he always saw too much. She slipped off her wet shoes and left them on a mat in the front hall. She hung up her umbrella in the kitchen, and then with another sigh she sat down at the kitchen table, and rested her head on her arms.

"Hi, Kate." The voice was only inches away from her and she leapt from her seat at the table with a look of terror in her eyes. "Oh darling, I'm sorry." His arms went instantly around her as she sat there and trembled. She was speechless, and not at all prepared for the usual games. She had thought he wasn't home. But he had been sitting there, watching her, from the corner, and she hadn't even noticed.

"You scared the hell out of me." She smiled shakily. It had been a long day. "I didn't know you were home. How was your day?" The efforts at chitchat were futile, Nick refused to be diverted. He looked strangely serious and walked to the stove without even bothering to answer her question.

"Tea?"

"That would be nice. Anything wrong?" She hated the way he looked. He reminded her of the way her father looked when her report card arrived. She could feel her heart pounding as it had during their last confrontation over Carmel. Only this time was worse. She wasn't sure why, but she could sense that it was. "Something wrong?" He still hadn't answered her.

"No, nothing's wrong." The words were carefully measured. "I missed you today." He turned to look at her and there was already a cup of tea in his hand. He had even had the water boiling and she hadn't noticed the steam. When she had walked into the kitchen, she had been exhausted. Now she was terrified. And she still wasn't sure why.

"I missed you too."

He nodded and picked up a second cup. "Let's go upstairs."

"Okay." Her smile went unanswered as she took her cup and followed him meekly to the den on the third floor, where he settled slowly into his favorite chair.

It was a big red leather one that was satiny smooth and wonderfully soft with the rich smell of good leather. It had a matching ottoman, but he pushed it aside with one foot. He wasn't planning to relax. And then he did the unexpected and set down his tea and held out both arms to her. She came to them willingly, kneeling next to his chair. "I love you, Nick."

"I know. I love you too. More than I've ever loved anyone." He looked down at her, smiled tiredly, and then sighed. "And we need to have a talk. I have a lot to say. I don't know where to start, but maybe the best place is where we just did. I love you. And I've waited a hell of a long time for you to level with me, but you haven't. So it's time we just sat down and let it all out. What bothers me most in all this is that you don't trust me." She felt her blood turn to ice.

"That's not true." She sounded hurt, but her heart was pounding with terror. What did he mean? Did he know? How? Who had told him?

"It *is* true. If you trusted me, you'd have told me about Carmel. About Tom." An interminable silence filled the room as her eyes flew to his.

"What about Tom?" She was stalling and they both knew it, as she put down her cup of tea with a trembling hand.

"I don't know much, Kate. I had some vague suspicions in the beginning. What you knew about football in your book, the behind-the-scenes stuff, things you said. I did a little research, very little in fact. Just enough to find out that you'd been married to Tom Harper, *the* Tom Harper, and that he had shot himself and become paralyzed and mentally, well . . . I don't know the right words. I know he was moved to a sanatarium in Carmel after a lengthy hospital stay, but I wasn't able to find the name of the home. I knew

330

then that he hadn't died, and I think he's probably still alive now. I think that's what you do in Carmel. Visit him, not teach retarded children. I could understand that, Kate, I could even accept it, I could understand a lot of things. What I don't understand is why you won't share it with me. Why you wouldn't tell me the truth in all these months. That's what hurts." There were tears in her eyes and his when he stopped speaking, and Kate let out a long, rattling sigh.

"Why didn't you tell me you knew? I've made an ass of myself all these months, haven't I?"

"Is that what bothers you now? Making an ass of yourself?" He looked suddenly angry and she shook her head and looked away.

"No. I . . . I just don't know what to say."

"Tell me the truth, Kate. Tell me what it's like. What kind of shape he's in, whether you love him, is it any kind of a life for you, where does it leave us . . . I don't know what hope there is for our future, or for his. I have a right to know those things—I had a right to know them from the first. But I didn't tell you I knew because you had to trust me enough to tell me yourself. You never did. I had to confront you."

"I think I was trying to protect both of you."

"And maybe yourself." He turned away from her and looked out at the Bay.

"Yes." Her voice was very quiet in the room. "And maybe myself. I love you, Nick. I didn't want to lose you. We have something with each other that I've never had before, with anyone. Tom knew me as a girl. I was a child with him, until . . . until the accident. And now he's the child. He's like a little boy, Nick. He plays games, he draws, he's a little less grown up than Tygue. He cries . . . he needs me. And he gets about as much from me as he wants. I can't take that away from him. I can't leave him." Her voice caught on the words.

"No one is asking you to, Kate. I never would have asked you that. But I just wanted to know. I wanted to hear it from you. Will he go on that way for a very long time?"

"Until the end, whenever that comes. It could be days, or months, or years. No one can know. And in the meantime . . . I visit."

"How do you stand it?" He turned to look at her again and there was pain and compassion in his eyes.

She smiled a small wintry smile. "I owe it to him, Nick. Once he was everything to me. He was all I had, after my parents closed the door on me. He gave me everything. Now all I can give him are a few hours a week. I can spare those hours. I have to." She said it defiantly as she watched him.

"I understand that." He went to her and put his arms around her with a sigh. "It's something you have to do. I respect that. I wish I could make it easier for you though."

"It's not that hard anymore. I got used to it a long, long time ago. If you ever really get used to that sort of thing. At least it doesn't shock me anymore—or break my heart the way it once did."

"Was Felicia around then, darling?" He cuddled her close and she looked up at him with a small smile. It was a relief to tell him, and she hated herself for not doing it sooner.

"Yes. She was around through the whole thing. She was marvelous. She was even in the delivery room with me when Tygue was born."

"I wish I'd been there then."

She smiled tiredly. She had a peaceful feeling she hadn't had in years. He knew everything now. There were no more secrets. No more dreading he'd find out. "I was so afraid of what you'd think if you knew."

"Why?"

"Because I'm married. Because I'm not free. That's not really fair to you."

"It doesn't make any difference. One day you won't be married anymore. There's time for us, Kate. We have a lifetime ahead of us."

"You're an incredible man, Nicholas Waterman."

"Bullshit. You'd feel the same. . . . Kate?"

"Mm?"

"Your parents never contacted you after he . . . after the accident?" He had understood that that was the euphemism she used for the shooting.

"Never once. They made up their minds when I went to live with Tom, and that was it. What he did just confirmed everything they'd thought about him, I guess, and as far as they were concerned I was no better than he was. I'd gotten what I deserved. They were just very black and white in their thinking. There were acceptable people and unacceptable people . . . I was no longer acceptable because of Tom, so they felt justified in cutting me out of their lives."

"I don't know how they could live with themselves."

"Neither do I, but that's not my problem anymore. It hasn't been for a long, long time. It's all very remote. And I'm glad. It's really all over. The only thing that isn't, that never will be, is my obligation to Tom."

"Tygue doesn't know, does he?" He was sure that he didn't, but there was always a chance that the boy had been hiding it from him too.

"No. Felicia says I'll have to tell him one day, but I haven't figured that out yet. It's too soon now anyway."

Nick nodded and then looked at her strangely. "Can I ask you an odd question?"

"Of course."

"Do you . . . do you still love Tom?" He made himself say it. He had to know.

Her voice was full of astonishment when she answered him. "Do you think I could love you as I do, live with you like this, be yours, if I did? Yes, I love him. As I love a child, as I love Tygue. He's not a man, Nick. He's my past . . . and only a ghost . . . the ghost of a child."

"I'm sorry I asked."

"Don't be. You have a right to all the answers now. And I suppose it's hard to understand. There's no man there to love. Oh, before you came along, once in a while, I'd pretend to myself that there was a glimmer of something. But there wasn't. There hasn't been in seven years. I go to see him because that's what I do. Because once he was good to me, because a long time ago I loved him more than anyone I'd ever known or loved before, and because Tygue is his son." Suddenly she was crying again, and the tears were streaming down her face. "But I love you, Nick, I love you . . . as . . . I never loved him. I've waited such a long time for you." He reached for her then and pulled her into his arms so hard that they were both stunned by the force of his grip on her. He needed her just as desperately. He had needed her for years.

"Oh darling, I'm so sorry."

She pulled away with a sigh. "I've been so afraid, ever since the book's been a success, that someone would find me out. That someone would dig up all that shit and spread it all over my face." He cringed again at the thought of what she must have been going through. It was a wonder she had gone to Los Angeles at all. "And when you said you'd played football, I almost died." She laughed as she looked up at him, but his face was still almost gray.

"The funny thing is that I knew him. Not well. I was in and out of football too fast, and he was already on top when I came into it. But he seemed like a nice guy."

"He was." She looked sad at the words. He was.

"What made him do it? What broke him?" The papers he'd read hadn't really given him any insight. It was as though the reporters didn't care why.

"Pressure. Fear. He was being shoved out and it drove him crazy. He had nothing else in his life, only football. He didn't know what else to do. And he had also invested his money pretty badly and he wanted everything for Tygue. That was all he could think of. 'His son.' He wanted one more season so he could sock away a fortune for Tygue. And they canned him. You read the papers. You know the rest."

He nodded somberly. "Does he know about Tygue?"

"He wouldn't understand. I visited him the whole time I was pregnant. He had no more interest or understanding than any kid that age. I think he just thought I was fat."

"Has there been any change over the years?" He was embarrassed to ask.

But she only shook her head. "No. Except in the past few weeks. He's not himself. But the doctor says it's nothing unusual."

"Is it a decent place?"

"Yes, very." She reached out to him then and he came to sit next to her on the floor. "I love you, Mr. Waterman, even if you did scare the hell out of me. I thought you were going to tell me we were through."

"What do you mean, you crazy woman? Did you think I'd really let you go?"

"I'm a married woman, Nick." She said it with a

tone of despair. She knew how badly he wanted to get married. And there was no chance. Not as long as Tom was alive.

"So what? Does it bother you that you're married, Kate?"

She shook her head very simply. "I thought it out very carefully before I drove to Santa Barbara to see you this summer. In my heart, I'm not married to him anymore."

"That's all that matters. The rest is nobody's business but ours. Is that the only reason why you didn't tell me, Kate?"

"No . . . I . . . well, that's part of it. The other part was just cowardice, I suppose. I had kept everyone outside the sacred walls for so long that I couldn't imagine telling anyone the truth. And by the time I *could* imagine telling you, it seemed impossible to start from the beginning and admit I had lied. How do you say to someone, 'Oh, remember when I told you I was a widow, well, actually, I was lying. My husband is in a sanatarium in Carmel and I go to see him a couple of times a week.' I don't know, Nick, it sounded nuts, and admitting it, talking about it— it's like reliving it. It's like feeling it all over again."

"I'm sorry about that." He held her closer.

"Maybe I'm not. Maybe it's time the whole thing was aired. But you know what else I was afraid of? I was afraid that once you knew, you'd make me stop seeing Tom. I couldn't do that, Nick. He means too much to me. I owe him a debt until he dies."

"Is that the only reason why you do it? Because you 'owe' him?" She shook her head.

"No. For a lot of reasons. Because I loved him, because of the strength he gave me at times, because of what we shared . . . because of Tygue. . . . I could

336

never stop going, and I didn't think anyone could understand that. Not even you. Does that make any sense?"

"A great deal of sense, Kate. But I have no right to take that away from you. No one does."

"But can you live with it?"

"Now that it's out in the open between us, I can. I respect what you're doing, Kate. My God, if something like that ever happened to me . . . What an incredible thing to realize that someone cared enough to keep on visiting like that, for years and years and years."

She sighed. "It's not as noble as you make it sound. Sometimes it's damn hard. Sometimes it's exhausting, and I hate it."

"But you do it anyway, that's the point."

"Maybe it is. And I have to go on doing it, Nick."

"I understand that." It was a sober moment between them, a moment of peace that sealed a pact of understanding. He took a sip of his tea, and then looked down at her again. "What are you going to do, though, if someone does find out? If they unearth the past? I assume you've faced that possibility."

"Yes and no. The only way I make myself get out there is to pretend it won't happen. If I really thought it might, I'd never leave the house again."

"That might be very pleasant." They exchanged the first real smile in an hour. "I'm being serious though."

"I don't know, love." She sighed deeply and lay back on the rug. "I don't know what I'd do, really. Run, panic, I don't know. Maybe it won't matter as much now that you know. Of course there's still Tygue." She sighed and then remembered something as she looked across at Nick. "Remember that party you took me to in L.A., after I was on Jasper's show?"

He nodded. "That guy who said something that upset you? He knew?" Jesus. No wonder she had freaked.

"Not really. He just picked up on my name. Harper. And told me all about a football player named 'Joe or Jim or someone,' who'd gone crazy, and, well . . . he knew the story, more or less. He asked if I was related to him, as a big joke. And of course I panicked."

"Poor baby. No wonder. Why the hell didn't you change your name after all that, though?"

"It didn't seem right, because of Tygue. Tygue was his son. He was meant to be Tygue Harper. Changing names seemed such a shoddy thing to do to Tom. Not that he'd have known. I don't know. I just always had such a feeling of loyalty about that."

"What about Tygue now though? You can't keep this from him forever. And if someone tells him one day that his father almost killed two men and virtually destroyed himself instead, it'll screw up his whole life. You owe him the truth, Kate. Some kind of truth, at an age where he can begin to digest it. Will he ever see him?"

"Never. That would be impossible. Tom wouldn't understand, and it would break Tygue's heart. That's not a daddy. That's a strange helpless child in a broken man's body. He doesn't even look well anymore. Tygue would have to be a grown man to be able to withstand it. And why should he? He doesn't know him. It's better that way. And by the time Tygue is old enough to understand, by then—" She paused and there was a small sobbing sound. She looked up at Nick, but his face was grave and not tearful as he looked at her. "What was that?" She sat very still. And Nick cocked his head.

"Nothing. Why?"

"I heard . . . oh God . . ." And then she realized. They had both forgotten the car pool bringing Tygue home. The clock behind Nick said five-fifteen. He had been home for half an hour. Long enough to . . . and then without thinking, she wheeled around, and saw him standing there, silent, with tears pouring down his face. Tygue. They both moved toward him at the same time, and he darted away down the stairs, his sobs echoing as he shouted back at them, "Leave me alone . . . leave me alone. . . ."

CHAPTER 29

"Is he all right?" Nick looked at her somberly as she came out of Tygue's room. It was six-thirty, and it had been a long hour. He had hidden from them in the garden, and had been soaked to the skin when they brought him inside, clutching an equally soaked Willie. Kate had put him in a hot tub while Nick made hot chocolate, and she had sat for a long time in his room. Nick had waited on the stairs.

"I think he's okay. It's hard to tell. Anyway, he's asleep." She looked exhausted.

"What did you tell him?"

"The truth. What choice did I have? He had heard most of it already, standing at the door. I don't think he meant to eavesdrop. He says he came upstairs to tell me he was home, and he heard us talking about Tom." She motioned to the open door of their bedroom, and Nick nodded, and followed her inside. They closed the door, and Kate sat down heavily on the bed as Nick handed her a cigarette. She looked more like she needed brandy and a hot bath. All they could think of was Tygue.

"I stirred up some fucking hornet's nest, pressing you about Tom." It was all he could think of as he waited on the stairs. But she shook her head through the small cloud of gray smoke.

"Don't do that to yourself. Painful as it is, I think

you've done us all good. I feel relieved. And Tygue will live through it. This way I can tell him the good stuff too. Tom Harper was a beautiful human being. Tygue has a right to know that, and he can't unless he knows the rest. So now he'll know both. It's a fair trade." She hesitated for a moment and then spoke again, with a sigh. "There have been times when I've wondered about the way I've played God. I kept a very important part of himself away from Tygue. I kept him from knowing who and what his father was. I thought that would be easier for him." She sat down slowly and looked very hard at Nick. "But there were other reasons too."

"They couldn't have been bad reasons."

"Maybe they were. I wanted him to be mine. I wanted him to be totally free of all that. I didn't want him to be . . . like Tom." Nick waited for her to go on, without saying a word. "I didn't want him to fall in love with the image of Tom Harper, the glory of the albums and the clippings and the adulation. Tom loved all that stuff. What man wouldn't? I think maybe I was always a little bit afraid that Tygue might want it too, maybe even to prove something for Tom. To leave the Harper name 'clean.' God only knows what crazy ideas might have gone through his head . . . I was afraid of all those possibilities. It was just a lot easier the way it was." And then, remembering Nick again, she smiled a tiny smile. "But it wasn't right, Nick. It's right that he should know. One day I'll probably even have to tell him about my parents. I let him think the whole world around him had died, except me. But that's not the truth. I suppose everyone has a right to the truth." Nick had had a right to it too. For a moment, she felt as though she had betrayed them all, and she felt a wave of exhaustion sweep over her at the thought. "Anyway, darling, things have a way of working out for the best." She held out a hand to Nick, but he didn't take it and he looked suddenly stricken again.

"Does Tygue think so?" Nick said it bitterly as he looked at her and then out at the Bay. He should have minded his own business.

"He's confused. He doesn't know what the hell to think. The only thing he was positive about was that he wanted to see his dad. I told him he couldn't." She sighed again. "And right now he hates me for it, but he'll get over it. He has you." She smiled at Nick's back, and then moved toward him and put her arms around his waist.

"I'm not his father though, Kate."

"That doesn't matter. You give him more than most fathers would—emotionally and in every other way. And I don't know, Nick. This is our reality. Tom was who he was and he did what he did. For whatever reasons. Maybe it's just time we both faced the truth. It won't kill either of us. So stop looking like somebody died." He turned to face her and tried to smile, but it was not an overwhelming success. He felt as though the world had fallen in on him, and he didn't know what to do to make it up to them. "By the way, aren't you working tonight?" She looked at the clock in surprise.

"I called in sick while you were in with Tygue."

"I'm glad." She smiled up at him and stretched out on the bed. "I'm so tired I could die."

"I can't imagine why, Cinderella." He sat down and started to rub her feet and then her legs. "I mean, after all, you only drove about three hundred miles today, came home and were forced to confront me with all the skeletons in your closet, after which, I was kind enough to tear the guts out of your son, forcing you to rescue the child from the pouring rain, bathe him, comfort him, and generally save the day. Why the hell are you tired?" She was grinning at the description.

"Do I get a national award for all that? It sounds exemplary."

"You really should. And me, I should get a kick in the ass."

"Would you settle for something else?" She sat up as he rubbed her legs and slid her arms around his neck.

"I don't deserve it." He hung his head like a wicked child and she laughed.

"Just shut up and relax." He did and they did, and it was nine o'clock when Kate went in to run a bath. "Will you keep an eye on this for me for a minute? I want to check on Tygue."

"Sure." He stopped her for a moment, for a long tender kiss. She had given him everything that night, he knew that. Her body, her soul, her heart, everything she had to give had been his. As though to soothe his pain for what he'd done. "I love you, Cinderella. More than you know. By the way"—he looked down at her gently and smoothed a stray lock of hair from her face—"far be it from me to snoop into your life or question your motives, but it seems to me that you forgot something tonight." She looked up at him with a confused little smile. She knew he was teasing but she wasn't sure about what.

"I did?" And then she grinned broadly. "Oh damn. Dinner. Oh darling, I'm sorry. Are you starving?"

"No, I'm not starving. I couldn't even eat. I meant something else." He pulled her back into his arms and felt her body bring his to life again as they both smiled and kissed. "You forgot the flying saucer—you know, the magic baby catcher." He looked at her with a grin. He had forgotten it too. Until afterward. Everything had been so topsy-turvy all night. And when he looked at her now, she was frowning with a look of irritation but not panic.

"Shit. My diaphragm." She had left it sitting virginally in the drawer.

"Is that a disaster?" He felt an obligation to ask, although for him it was anything but a disaster. He still wanted her child. Tygue as well as his own. "Would you freak out?"

"No. But I won't get pregnant anyway. It's the wrong time of the month."

"How do you figure that?" Not the way he understood things.

"I had my hair done yesterday."

"Huh? You're crazy. And you haven't answered my question."

"What is it?" But she was teasing him and he knew it.

"The question is . . . oh to hell with you. Get pregnant, so what. I'll drop you off at the unwed mothers' home, and go to Tahiti with Tygue."

"Be sure you send me a postcard. And don't bother watching my bath." She grinned as she turned it off, and grabbed a white terry-cloth robe to go check on Tygue. "I'll be back in a sec."

"Do that." He said it with a smile. And she did. She was back in a second but without a smile. She walked back into the bathroom with her robe flying wide, showing her long thin naked body, and her face deathly white.

"Tygue's gone."

Nick felt as though the earthquake had hit. She silently handed him a note, and as he read it, she bent over the john and threw up.

CHAPTER 30

"No, we don't know where he went. All we know is what he left in this note." Nick looked across at Kate. They had discussed it all before the police arrived. They were not going to say anything about Tom. It wouldn't help.

"Let's have another look at that note."

The note was painfully simple. "Iym goang to fine mie fathere." Nice plain seven-year-old English. He was going to find his father. The plainclothesman looked up at Nick and Kate.

"You're not his father, Mr. . . . er . . . Waterman?"

"No. He's Mrs. Harper's son. But Tygue and I are very close." After he said it, he felt like an ass. But who was thinking straight? Kate was beginning to look strangely translucent and gray. She had barely spoken to the police, and Nick was afraid she was going into shock.

"Do you know where his father is? Seems like it would be pretty simple to give him a call." Kate looked agonized, and Nick shook his head.

"I'm afraid not. The boy's father died before he was born."

"Was he angry at you then?" The cop came back at him quickly and this time Kate revived.

"No, I think, if anything, he was angry at me. I think mostly he's just under a lot of new pressures.

We just moved to San Francisco, and he's in a new school, and . . ." She faltered and Nick squeezed her hand.

"Does he have any money?"

Kate shook her head. "I don't think so."

"Did he take anything?"

"Yes. His teddy bear." Her eyes filled as she said it. "It's a large brown bear with a red tie." She looked down at Bert, who wagged his tail and approached, and she only cried harder.

"What's the boy wearing?"

She didn't know. And she would never be able to guess. But she went to the hall closet and discovered his slicker was gone.

"A yellow slicker. And probably jeans and cowboy boots."

"Anyone in town he would go to?"

"Felicia!" She ran for the phone, but there was no answer when she dialed. Somberly, she gave the officer Licia's number. And Tillie's. And Joey's back home. And . . . "And I think he might have tried to get to Carmel." She looked miserably at Nick.

"Does he know anyone there?" The policeman looked up.

"No. But he likes it." Damn. What could she tell him? He went to find his retarded, crippled, once-famous father, whom he didn't even know was alive until this afternoon? "What are you going to do?" She squeezed Nick's hand as the police closed their little brown books.

"Comb the area until we find him. Now we need some pictures." They brought out dozens of them. Color, close-up, distance, in every possible outfit, on his pony, with his dog, at Disneyland, on a cable car with Licia. They shoved the makings of an album into their hands. "We'll only need one or two." Kate

346

nodded numbly as they went out into the rain. "We'll call you every hour to report."

"Thank you."

"Hang tough." They looked encouragingly at Nick as they left. Expensive house. And the kid looked happy enough in the pictures. They obviously weren't abusing him. Maybe he was just one of those funny little kids who needed to run away. They'd seen that kind before. The girls tended to stand dramatically in the doorway, giving their parents every opportunity to beg them to stay home. The boys just packed up and split.

"Oh God, Nick, what'll we do?"

"Just what they said, darling. Hang tough."

"I can't . . . oh God . . . Nick, I can't. He could be kidnaped. Run over. He could be . . ."

"Stop it!" He grabbed her by the shoulders and then pulled her tightly into his arms. "Just stop it, Kate. We can't do that. We have to know he'll be okay." Kate nodded numbly as she cried, and then clutched hopelessly at Nick. There was something agonized in her eyes that tore at him, and finally as she sobbed, he began to understand. There was more than just fear and worry in her heart.

"It's my fault, Nick . . . it's all my fault."

"I said *stop it*, Kate. It's not your fault." He wanted to tell her it was his own fault for bringing up the whole mess that afternoon, but it was pointless for either of them to blame themselves now. What they had to do was get Tygue back and tell him about his father, talk about the past, try to explain Kate's reasons for keeping him in the dark. And they would love the boy more than they had before. He needed that. Tonight proved it. But breast-beating was a futile act. Nick held tightly to Kate and gently pushed her chin up with one hand until her drenched eyes met his.

"It's no one's fault, darling. We can both torment ourselves with that for the next hundred years, but maybe it was just meant to come out. Maybe he had to know."

"I know he did. I should have told him years ago and then this wouldn't have happened."

"But you didn't, and you can't know now if that made any difference. Maybe he couldn't have handled it till now. Whatever the case, you just have to let the past be. You didn't tell him. Now he knows. Those are the facts we have to deal with."

"But what if something awful happens to him?" Her voice was a plaintive wail again as her eyes flooded again.

"Nothing will. We just have to believe that, Kate."

"I wish I could." She blew her nose loudly and closed her eyes.

The police had called every hour, as promised, but they still had no news. It was after midnight when they reached Felicia.

"Oh my God." Felicia gasped and sat down as Nick explained. Kate was in no condition to talk. She had stopped crying, but she only sat there, staring, and thumbing through the pictures. Nick had finally stopped trying to take them away from her. "Should I come over?"

"It might help. You've been through worse things with her before."

"Yeah. And Nick"—she hesitated for a moment, and then decided to say it—"I'm glad you know. She needs to be free of all that. She can't hide forever."

"I know. But this is a rough way to go."

"Maybe there's no other way." Nick nodded silently and they hung up. Felicia came right over, and they sat there together, drinking coffee and going crazy until five. And at five-thirty, the police called again.

Nick braced himself for the same dismal news. No news.

"We've got him."

"Where?"

"Right here." The cop grinned down at the kid.

And Nick closed his eyes and shouted into the room, "They've got him." And then into the phone again, "Is he okay?"

"Fine. He's tired, but fine. Willie the Bear looks a little forlorn though." The kid was very quiet. Probably sobered by the experience.

"Where was he?"

"Sitting around the Greyhound bus station, trying to talk someone into taking him to Carmel. His mother was right. They usually are. We'll have him home to you in ten minutes."

"Wait. Can I talk to him?" He was going to put Kate on, as she stood there next to him sobbing and laughing and squeezing his arm while Felicia looked on through her own tears.

The policeman came back on in a minute. "He says he's too tired to talk." Ornery little bugger. But that was their problem. He'd make out the report, give the kid a speech about the evils of running away and the dangers of bus stations, and take the boy home.

"What do you mean he was too tired?" Kate looked stunned after Nick hung up, and then she understood. "He's still pissed."

Nick nodded. "I assume so."

He assumed right. When Tygue got home he was subdued, and he waited until the policeman had left before speaking to them. He had dutifully hugged his mother when he came in, but it won her no warmth and no comfort, only the puddle Willie had squeezed onto her shirt. He was still soaking. Tygue had dried off in the bus station. It was amazing he had gotten there at all. He said he'd had a nickel and had taken the bus. Bus drivers all along the way had given him directions.

"Do you have any idea what could have happened to you?" She was starting to scream at him out of relief. He hung his head, but he did not look contrite. And then finally he spoke.

"I'm going to do it again."

"*What?*" She shrieked as Nick tried to calm her down.

"I'm going to find my father. I want to see him." And then she sat back with a sigh and looked at her son. How could she tell him without breaking his heart that there was no father to see? There was a man, and he had been his father, but he was gone now. And Tygue couldn't see him.

"You can't do that." She said it very softly.

"I'm gonna, Mom." He looked at her with determination all over his face.

"We'll talk about it."

She put him to bed and this time he stayed there. But it had been a very long night, and as Felicia drove home at six-thirty in the morning, she had a feeling that it wasn't over yet. Maybe this time. But Tygue meant what he said. He was going to see his father. She hoped Kate understood that. But at that moment, Kate was already sound asleep in Nick's arms. She got three hours sleep. Stu Weinberg called at nine-thirty.

"Hm?" In the deep haze of sleep, she couldn't figure out who it was. Nick had promised to leave a note out for the car pool, and they would all sleep late. All day, if she could. Nick had said he'd deal with Tygue until she got up.

"Did I wake you?"

"Hm? What? . . . No . . ." But she was already

drifting off again. Nick walked into the room and shook her shoulder.

"Wake up. You're on the phone."

"Huh? Who is this?"

"It's Stu Weinberg, for chrissake. What the hell is going on there? Did you go to a wild party last night?"

"Yeah. Very." She sat up in bed, squinting, feeling sick. Her head churned as though she had the worst hangover of her life, but at least now she was functioning. "How's the book?"

"Making you and me both a fortune. In fact, that's why I'm calling. You've got another tour."

"Oh no. Did Nick fix this one too?" She tried to smile, but her face wouldn't comply. What was Nick up to now? But Weinberg insisted Nick had nothing to do with this one. And he sounded sincere. "Then what is it?"

"A week in New York. Your publisher wants you there for promo to keep the book hot on the lists. It's a must, kiddo, especially if you want to hit them pretty soon with the one you're working on now. You'd better stay in their good graces."

"I can't now." There was too much to cope with at home.

"Bullshit, Kate. You have to. You have an obligation to these people. They're making your career." He began to tick off the shows they had booked her on. Too many, maybe. It was going to be an incredible week.

"I told you. I can't."

"You're going to have to. I told them you would."

"How could you do that?" She was ready to cry. And she was still so unbearably tired from the night before.

"I did it because you have no choice. Ask Nick. He knows what this means."

"Never mind that. All right, I'll see. From when to when?"

"You leave in three days. You'll be gone for a week."

"I'll do my best."

"You'll have to do better than that." He was relentless. "I'll call you later to confirm it."

"Okay." She was too weak to argue. She lay back on her pillow and tried to think.

"Who was that?" Nick looked down at her with concern.

"Weinberg."

"Something wrong?"

She nodded. "He called to tell me that my publisher booked me on tour in New York. For a week."

"When?" Nick looked stunned.

"I leave in three days."

"Sonofabitch. I'll kill him." Nick sat down and ran a hand through his hair. "You can't go."

"He says I have to. And he didn't do it. I told you. My publisher did." And besides, dammit, Nick couldn't tell her what she could and couldn't do.

"I don't care who did it. You know goddamn well you can't go now. You told him that, didn't you?"

But she hadn't. Even with everything that was happening, she hadn't. Stu had made it sound as if her career were on the line, as though she had to "or else."

"What the hell did you tell him?" Nick looked down at her, shocked.

"I told him I'd see what I could do."

"You mean you're going?"

"I don't know. I don't know, dammit. I can't even think. How do I know what I'm doing three days from now?"

"If you have any sense, three days from now you'll

352

be trying to straighten out this mess with your son. That ought to be the number one priority."

"It is, but . . . godamnit, leave me alone." Would they never get off her back? Nick with his righteous indignation and ideas of perfect parenthood, and Tygue with his overwhelming needs and demands. Jesus, she had a right to some kind of life too. She had a right to the success that was coming her way.

"Falling in love with yourself, aren't you, Kate?" It took every ounce of control not to slap him. "It's not so much fun being a mommy now, is it?"

"Will you leave me alone, damn you?" She was shrieking and her voice didn't sound like her own. "What do you want from me? Blood?"

"No, some reality. You have a child who is facing a major crisis in his life. He doesn't need you to go gaily off on tour."

"Well, what about what *I* need? What about my career? What about what I've given him all these years? Doesn't that count for anything? Don't I get a little time off for good behavior?"

"Is that how you feel about it all, Kate? Is that how you feel about him? About me?" For an insane moment, she wanted to say yes, but she didn't dare.

Her voice was suddenly very quiet. "I just need some time to think. That's all. Just let me work this out for myself." She sat down on the bed and ran a hand through her hair.

"I just don't think you've got much choice."

"I've never had much choice. Maybe right now I need to be able to choose, to make my own decisions."

"You've made decisions before, Kate." Why was he pushing so hard? Why didn't he get the hell off her back? But she didn't say any of what she was thinking. She was suddenly lost in her own thoughts.

"Yeah. I've made decisions before." Like the decision not to tell Tygue about Tom. That had been some great decision, as it turned out.

"What's eating you, Kate? Are you feeling guilty again? Is that it?"

"Dammit, Nick, yes!" She jumped to her feet as she shouted at him again, and this time her eyes were blazing with fury. "Yes, I feel guilty. Okay? Does that make you feel better, to hear me say it? Yes, I feel like this whole mess with Tygue is my own goddamn fault. And you know what? It doesn't make me love him any more than I did before. It just makes me want to run away. Because between his being pissed off at me and not understanding anything I've done, and you shoving it in my face, I want to get the hell away from both of you. How does that sound to you, mister?"

"Just dandy." He turned on his heel and left the room, and she slammed into the bathroom, to emerge ten minutes later looking tidy but still wan. Tygue was still asleep, but Nick was sitting at the breakfast table with a cup of coffee. She poured herself one and looked over at him. He looked like hell too.

"I'm sorry I yelled."

"It doesn't matter." His voice was subdued now too, but he looked at her as though examining a visitor from another planet. "Are you going?"

"I don't know."

"It's happening to you, Kate."

"What is?" But she knew what he meant.

"The star trip. The Me-Fabulous-Me syndrome. You have to do what you have to do for your career. Do you have any idea what's happening to that kid right now?" Nick was seething again.

"Do you have any idea what's happening to me? How many ways I'm being pulled?"

"I'm sorry. But you're a grownup. You can deal with it, Kate. He can't. I know you've had a lot of rotten breaks, but that's no reason to pass them on to him. He can't help it. And he is totally confused right now about his father."

"And I can't change that. I can't wave a magic wand and make Tom whole again. He's not. And Tygue can't see him. It would be terrible for both of them." She was shouting again.

"I understand that"—he made an effort to lower his voice—"but Tygue doesn't. I just can't believe you'd go to New York now."

"I didn't say I would."

"No, but you will."

"How the hell do you know?" She wanted to throw her coffee at him, as he sat there glaring at her, angry and self-righteous. She hated him.

"I know you'll go because you've already been suckered into that whole horseshit game of success. The shows, the interviews, the money, the best sellers, all of it. I can see it happening to you, Kate. And I'll tell you something, I'm goddamn sorry I had anything to do with it. I'm sorry they put you on the show."

"What does that have to do with it? Look at the money I've made in the last four months. It comes to over a quarter of a million dollars. Me, I made that, all by myself, with one lousy book, with or without your lousy show. Tygue will go to college because of that, he'll go to a good school before college. He'll have everything he needs."

"Except his mother."

"Fuck you."

"You know something? I don't give a damn what you do. I just don't want to have to sit here and watch when you tell him you're going to New York."

"Then don't. I'll tell him while you're out."

"You're going, aren't you?" He pushed and he pushed and he pushed . . .

"Yes!" It was a long angry wail that seemed to fill the whole house. They were both startled, mostly Kate. She hadn't even been sure she was going. At least, she liked to think that. Actually she had known all along. As soon as Weinberg had told her how important it was for her next book. She wanted that one to do even better than the first. It told her a cold hard empty thing about herself as she sat in the kitchen alone, after Nick had quietly left the room. Maybe he was right. Maybe it was starting to happen to her. The success trip. But not at Tygue's expense . . . no . . . not Tygue.

She tried to explain it all to him that afternoon, but Tygue didn't want to talk. She tried to make him understand about Tom, about the books, about her work, about what had happened to Tom, about . . . but he was only seven. He didn't understand very much. And all he could think about was his father. She gave him an album of Tom's old clippings from the golden years of success. Tygue left to devour those in his room. And Kate called Tillie.

Tillie would come to stay in the guest room for the week she was gone. It would ease the burden on Nick, whom Kate barely saw before she left. He came home late both nights, when she was already asleep. And he was out all day. She tried to explain what she felt to Felicia, but she was unsympathetic too. No one understood. Even Tillie seemed cool when she arrived, but perhaps she was only intimidated by the city. Kate was grateful she had come. And Tygue seemed thrilled to see her. In fact, Kate felt suddenly shut out: Tygue was happier to see Tillie than he was to be with her.

"Want me to take you to the airport?" Nick looked at her coolly.

"I can grab a cab. I want to leave Tillie my car here at the house. But it's no big deal."

"Don't be a martyr. I'll drive you."

"I couldn't stand the speeches." There was a chill between them that had never been there before, and it terrified her, but she wouldn't let that show.

"I've made all the speeches I'm going to make. Except for one. You look tired, Kate. Try not to overdo it in New York."

"It's been a rough couple of days. For everyone." She looked over at him and something softened in his eyes.

"Just don't forget that I love you, Cinderella." It was the first time she had seen him soften like that in several days. "What time's your plane?" He smiled a slow smile and she told him what time she had to leave. They both looked at each other with regret. "Damn." She slipped into her dress. He zipped her up instead of down, and five minutes later they left. It was a quiet trip out to the airport and she was sorry they hadn't had time to make love. It would have done them both good. A reminder of what they had. A peaceful bond before being cannonballed into the madness of New York. But when he kissed her, she knew how much he cared. She waved to him as she boarded the plane, and felt as though she had never been as lonely in her life. She drank a great deal too much wine before reaching New York, but it took the edge off her loneliness, and she slept the last two hours. It was a hell of a way to get to New York. Tired and rumpled and hungover. A honeymoon this wasn't. It was for real. And she was alone in the big city. She knew it as she stood on the sidewalk fighting for a cab. The limo they'd sent for her hadn't shown up, and she couldn't find one of her bags. It was a perfect beginning. But things got better after that.

In desperation, she shared a cab into the city with a very nice-looking, well-dressed man, an architect from Chicago, somewhere in his late forties. And he was staying at the Regency too.

"How convenient. Do you always stay there?" He made no effort to discover her name, and made pleasant conversation all the way into the city. She looked over at him casually. His hair was gray, his face well-chiseled and fine-featured but worn. His body looked taut and young though. He was attractive, but in a very quiet way. He looked nothing like the healthy, athletic men of California. He looked cosmopolitan and a little pale, but interestingly so.

"I stayed there the last time I was in town."

"I manage to get here about once a month." He glanced at her casually and smiled. They chatted about the buildings, the view, San Francisco, and inadvertently she let slip that she was a writer.

"What a marvelous profession. You must love it." He looked at her with frank envy and she laughed. He made it sound even better than it was.

"I enjoy it a lot." And then, somehow, he drew her out and she found herself telling him about her next book.

"You know, it has a feeling, not a similar plot pattern, but just a family resemblance in terms of mood, to a marvelous book I just read, *A Final Season*." She began to laugh.

"Have you read it too?" He looked amused as she grinned.

What the hell? Why not admit it to him? "Well, not recently. But I wrote it." It took a moment to register and then he looked at her in amazement.

"Did you? But it's a wonderful book!" He looked stunned.

"Then I'll send you a copy of the next one!" She

said it teasingly but he immediately whipped out his card and handed it to her with a smile.

"I'll expect you to keep that promise, Miss Harper."

And now he knew her name. She put the card away just as they reached the hotel.

CHAPTER 31

It was a far cry from her trip to New York with Nick. Gone were the limousines, the hansom cab rides, the secret adventures, the lunches at Lutèce and dinners at Caravelle. And gone the buffer of his loving. This time she was confronted with New York in all its bold brassy reality, pushing, shoving, fighting for cabs, fighting stiff winds as newspapers and litter swirled around her feet. And the bookings her publisher had made were almost inhuman. She had three radio shows to do the first day, no time for lunch, and at four that afternoon she taped a television talk show, where the host had paired her with a sportswriter who was openly condescending. She was numb with exhaustion and anger when she reached the hotel at six, and it was the wrong time to call Nick or Tygue. Nick would be setting up the show, and Tygue would still be in school. She called room service and asked for a glass of white wine, and then sat back quietly to wait until she could call Nick. Even the room was less pretty this time. It was more elaborate, in white and gold, but smaller and colder, and the bed looked sad and empty. She smiled as she remembered the love-making of their last trip.

She sat back on the couch with her glass of wine and tucked her long legs under her. She was three thousand miles from home, alone in a strange hotel, and she couldn't talk to anyone she knew. She felt unloved and suddenly frightened, and she desperately wanted to go home. This was it. The wild fabulous high rise of fame. But it was a lonely, empty building and no one else seemed to live there. She longed to be back in the house hidden in the hedges on Green Street. If he even wanted her back. Maybe it was almost over. It felt as though they had just begun, and she and Tygue had only just moved to San Francisco the month before, but maybe it would all be too much for Nick. Maybe her career would be too great a conflict for him, with his own work, or maybe he just couldn't accept her. Kate started to call room service for a second glass of wine, and then with a frown she put down the phone. This was ridiculous. She was in New York. She was a star. She grinned to herself at the word. All right, so she wasn't a star, but she was successful. She could go anywhere she liked for dinner. She didn't have to sit in her room. It was absurd. She reached into her handbag and pulled out the sheet of paper where she'd written a list of restaurants Felicia had given her. The first on the list was someplace called Gino's. Licia had told her she could go there alone, and that it was crawling with models, ad men, and writers, a smattering of European society types, and "beautiful people." "It's a good show. You'll love it." And it was only two blocks from her hotel. She could walk.

She ran a comb through her hair, washed her face, and put on fresh makeup. She was ready. The black dress she had worn all day would do fine. Felicia said it wasn't dressy. By New York standards, anyway, that meant blue jeans, Guccis, and mink, or your latest Dior. As she picked up the long red wool coat off the back of a chair where she'd flung it, she remembered the grueling heat of only two months before. She

361

looked down at the black lizard shoes, and then around the room again . . . so empty. God, it was so empty. It was going to feel good to get out. Even the view didn't delight her this time. The whole city looked very tall and frightening and dark. And it was chilly and even windier when she stepped outside. She turned up the collar of her coat and turned east toward Lexington Avenue. She had rejected the doorman's offer of a cab, and walked rapidly away. She had already picked up the pace of New Yorkers. Run, dash, fly, bump into someone on street, grunt, shove, and run past. She laughed to herself as she thought of it. She had only been in town for a day and she already felt corroded by the pace. Her mind wandered back to Nick as she walked, and she was annoyed at herself. And at him. What right did he have to make her feel guilty about her success? She had worked hard for it. She deserved it. And she wasn't short-changing Tygue, or Nick, for that matter. All right, so the timing wasn't perfect for a trip, but Christ, she'd only be gone for a week. And she had a right to this . . . she had a right to it . . . the words kept echoing in her head as she turned south on Lexington Avenue, her high heels beating an even staccato against the subway grill beneath as she avoided fleets of pedestrians clattering by. She was almost thirty years old now, and she had a right to this . . . right to this. . . . She almost missed the restaurant, and looked up in surprise as two men bumped into her. They were just leaving Gino's. They didn't even say sorry, they merely looked her over, seemed to approve, and walked on, stepping off the curb to grab a cab from two other men. Standard New York. In California, the men would have been knocking each other cold for something like that. In New York, the two men who'd lost their cab simply hailed another, and grabbed it, just before the woman who'd flagged it first from the curb. Kate smiled to herself as she slipped inside Gino's double, yellow, swinging doors. It would take years to develop a style like that on the streets of New York, or maybe it happened very quickly. Maybe one got that way without noticing it. It still seemed funny to her.

"Signora?" A dapper Italian in a gray pin-striped suit came to her side with a smile. "Table for one?"

"Yes." She nodded with a smile. She could hardly hear him in the din as she looked around with amusement. The walls were a hideous coral color, covered with zebras chasing each other diagonally up and down the walls. Plastic plants flourished in several locations, and the lighting was dark. The bar was jammed seven deep, and the tables were covered with white cloths and well populated by "*le tout* New York." Just what Felicia had promised. Models still wearing the day's makeup and the latest Calvin Klein, ad men looking suave, married, and unfaithful, actresses and society matrons of some note, and a certain uniform look to the men. There were two kinds: European and American. The Americans all looked very Madison Avenue, in striped suits, horn rims, white shirts, and ties. The Europeans had them beat by a mile—better tailors, better shirts, softer colors, more scandalous eyes, and their trousers were all the right length. The laughter of women darted in and out of the conversations of men, like chimes in an orchestra, and thickly woven into the background was a constant caw and clatter provided by the waiters. They made as much noise as possible with their trays, all but destroyed the crockery as they sent it sailing into the hands of the busboys, and shouted to each other as loudly as they could from as far away as they could manage in the crowd. The kitchen itself would have produced lightning and thunder, and for lack of that they did the best they could with the materials at hand. They managed very nicely with metal pots and heavy utensils. And all of it combined to produce Gino's, a rich tapestry of sounds and sights, and the luscious smells of Italian cuisine.

"We'll have a table for you in a moment." The maître d' in the gray pin-stripe suit looked her over in a manner worthy of Rome and waved her graciously to the bar. "A drink while you're waiting?" His accent was perfection, his eyes were a caress. She had to force herself not to laugh. Gino's was a heady experience. It catapulted her instantly from her earlier mood of gloom to a feeling of fiesta.

With only the slightest hesitation she walked to the bar, ordered a gin and tonic, and heard the man just in front of her order Campari. Obviously an Italian. She could tell by the way he said "Campari soda" and then carried on a few sentences of conversation in Italian with the bartender. Kate looked him over from just behind him, where she stood. He smelled of a rich European men's cologne . . . something French . . . she couldn't remember it, but it was familiar. She had tried it out once at I. Magnin's, thinking of buying it for Nick. But it wasn't Nick, it was too rich, too sophisticated. Nick's lemons and spice suited him better. But not this man. The collar she saw was a warm Wedgwood blue, the back of his suit looked like a blazer, and it too had an Italian flair to it, from what she could see. The hair was gray, the neck slightly lined . . . forty-five maybe . . . forty-eight . . . and then suddenly he turned to face her and she felt herself blush and then gasp in surprise.

"Oh, it's you!" It was the man from the cab she'd taken from the airport. The architect from Chicago. "I thought you were Italian." And then she was even more embarrassed to have admitted considering the matter at all, and laughed again as he smiled at her.

"I lived in Rome for seven years. I'm afraid I'm addicted to scungili, antipasto, Campari, and all things Italian."

His front view was even more impressive than the rear view had been, and she realized now that he was much better-looking than she had first thought him. She hadn't paid much attention to him in the cab.

"How is New York treating you, Miss Harper?" He smiled at her over his drink and made room for her at the bar.

"All right, for New York. I worked my tail off today."

"Writing?"

"Nothing as easy as that. Doing publicity."

"I am impressed." But he looked more amused than impressed, and his eyes somehow embarrassed her. It was as though he saw too much through the black dress, yet he said nothing inappropriate. It was just a feeling she got. There was something raw and sexy beneath the well-tailored clothes and the businesslike manner. "Will I see you on TV?"

"Not unless you stay in your hotel room and watch daytime television." She smiled at him again.

"I'm afraid not. I've been doing my New York number too. We started with breakfast conferences at seven today. They work like madmen in this town." And then together, they looked out at the room. "They do everything like madmen. Even eat." She laughed with him and for a few minutes they just watched the scene. Then she felt his eyes on her again, and she turned toward him. She said nothing. They only looked at each other, and he smiled and held up his drink.

"To you, Miss Harper, for a book that meant a great deal to me. How did you ever get those insights into what makes men tick? The crawl for success, and the heartbreak if you stop just shy of the top—or get there, and fall off." He looked into his glass and then back at her, and she was surprised at the seriousness she saw in his face. The book really had meant something to him, and suddenly she was glad. He understood. It was as though he understood Tom.

"You handled it very well. Even from a man's point of view. I would think it would be difficult for a woman to really understand what it's like. All the macho nonsense about making it, and then the heartbreak of it when you don't."

"I'm not so sure it's all that different for women. But I watched my husband go through it," she said, looking into her drink. But she was very aware of this man's gentle voice, like a soft summer breeze in the winter storm of the noise around them.

"He must be very proud of you now."

She looked up at him unexpectedly and shook her head. "No. He's dead." She didn't say it to shock him. She just said it, but he was stunned nonetheless. And then she was the one who apologized. "I didn't mean to say it that way."

"I'm sorry for you. But now I understand the book better than I did. That makes a lot of sense. Did he make it, in the commercial sense of the word, before he died?" It seemed to matter to this man a lot. And Kate had decided to be honest with him. He was a stranger, and she had had two drinks. The wine at the hotel, and now the gin. She was feeling unusually honest, and cut off from everyone she knew. Here, no one knew her. She could say anything that popped into her head.

"Yes, he made it. And he blew it. That's what killed him. He had to have another chance, 'or else.' He got the 'or else.'"

"Heart attack?" It was his worst fear.

"More or less." And then she realized what she was doing to this man, and looked up quickly. "No. Not a heart attack. Something else. His soul died. The rest just sort of went with it. But no, it wasn't a heart attack." He looked only slightly relieved.

"I wonder what the answer is. To refuse to play the game? To refuse to run the race for success? But it's so damn tempting, isn't it?" He looked at her with that warm, sexy smile, and she smiled back.

"Yes, it is. I'm beginning to understand that better now myself. You always end up having to choose, having to make decisions about what matters, hurting somebody. Somehow one shouldn't have to make those choices."

"Ah, Miss Harper, but one does." He smiled ruefully.

"Do you?" She was shocked at her own question, but she liked talking to him. He was worldly and bright and very good-looking, and he wanted to talk about the things that were bothering her now.

"Yes, I have to make those choices. I have a wife who says she needs me in Chicago. For dinner parties, or something like that. A son who thinks I'm a capitalist asshole, and a daughter with cerebral palsy. They need me. Probably very much. But if I don't run after the almighty dollar, then my wife can't give her dinner parties, and my son can't sit on his lazy ass and espouse his saintly causes, and my daughter . . . well, she needs it most of all." He grew very quiet and looked into his drink, and then back at Kate again. "The bitch of it is that my reasons for running all sound good and righteous and proper, but the truth of it is, that isn't even why I do it anymore."

"I know." She understood. Only too well. "You do

it because you enjoy it. Because you have to. Because now it's part of you, and . . ." She said the last words very softly, as though to herself. ". . . because you have a right to it. To the good stuff. To the excitement, the success . . ." She looked up at him again and he held her eyes for a long time with a small ironical smile.

"That's why I loved your book. Because you knew."

And then she smiled too. "The funny thing is that when I wrote the book, I knew all about it. Or I thought I did. But I knew it from seeing it, not feeling it. I knew it from where your wife sits. Now I know it differently. Now I'm confronted by the same things myself."

"Welcome to the land of the successful failures, Miss Harper."

"Do you consider yourself a failure?"

"Depends on how you look at it. I suspect that to them, my family, I probably am. I don't know. To the business community, I'm certainly not a failure." Far from it. He had won several major international awards in the past five years. But he didn't tell Kate that, he merely smiled the small ironical smile. "One pays a very high price, just like all the songs say."

"Is it worth it?"

"Ask your husband." Ouch. She almost flinched at the words. "You ought to know the answer to that."

"I suppose so, but I see it differently now. I'm enjoying what I'm doing. I don't see why you can't have both. A real life, a family life, a life with some meaning and integrity, and a successful career."

"I suppose so." He waved to the barman to refill their drinks and she didn't object. "But it depends on what you call successful and what you call a career. Your career is by no means of small proportions, I would think. In a sense, you're a celebrity. That must take its toll."

"And you?" She wanted to know more about him. She liked him.

"I'm not a celebrity. I'm just an architect. But I play in the big leagues."

"Are you happy?"

"No." He said it very simply as though it were something he accepted, not something he cried about. "I suppose it's very lonely for all of us." He looked at her pointedly.

"And your wife?" Kate's eyes bored into his with the question.

"I suppose she's unhappy too."

"Doesn't she say?"

"No. She's a very well-behaved woman. And"—he hesitated for only a moment—"I don't ask her. We knew each other as kids, and we got married young. We had both just finished college. I was going to be a commercial artist. She wanted to play around with fine arts. Instead, my father suggested I go to graduate school at Yale. I did and studied architecture, got my degree, and that was the beginning. We both forgot about the dreams. The small dreams anyway. The big dreams came easy. Too easy." And then he looked up at Kate with a broad smile that belied everything he'd said. "And now you know my entire life story, Miss Harper. From beginning to end. The dismal failure of my marriage, the pains of my soul, even my fears about a heart attack. You can use it all in your next novel." He finished his drink and then looked up at her again with irony and laughter in his eyes. "And I'll bet you don't even remember my name."

She still had his card somewhere but she hadn't looked at it. And now she gave him an embarrassed smile. "I hate to admit it, but you're right. Besides, I'm awful with names."

"So am I. The only reason I remembered yours is because I liked the book. Kaitlin, isn't it?" She liked the way he said it.

"Kate."

"Philip. Philip Wells." He held out a hand, and she solemnly shook it.

And then suddenly the headwaiter in the pin-stripe suit was standing discreetly next to them. "Signore, signora, your tables are ready." He waved toward the center of the room, and Philip looked at Kate.

"Could we consolidate them into one? Or would I be intruding on your time alone?" It never even occurred to him that she might be meeting someone, but she liked the idea of eating dinner with him. She didn't want to eat alone.

"No, that would be very nice."

The headwaiter nodded instant acquiescence, Philip paid the bartender for their drinks, and they moved on toward the main dining area in the center of the room, between the diagonally fleeing zebras. Kate looked up at them with a dubious expression and winced as Philip held out a chair for her and laughed at the look on her face.

"I know. Aren't they awful? The best of it is that every time they've redecorated, they've gone to fabulous expense to reproduce the exact same decor. Right down to the plastic greenery and the zebras. They're probably right. The natives expect them."

"Do you come here that often?"

"I'm in New York fairly often, and I always come here when I am. I told you, I'm addicted to all things Italian." Especially the women, but he omitted telling her that. She suspected it anyway. He didn't look like a man who was faithful to his wife, and he had told her enough to let her know that he was unhappy. That was the usual prelude. But she didn't care. She liked him anyway. And he was an intelligent person to talk to. It was better than watching television in her room. Much better. And besides, Nick wasn't home either . . . she felt the same gnawing worries again as Nick crept into her thoughts.

"When did you live in Rome?" She forced herself to think of Philip and not Nick, at least for the duration of this meal.

"We came back ten years ago. We were there while the children were small. My daughter was born there. It's a marvelous city."

"Do you go back often?"

"Once or twice a year. I have more business in Paris and London than I do in Rome." She could see what he meant about being successful. Paris, London, Rome, New York. It sounded exciting. She wondered if she'd ever have to go to Europe to tour for the book. Nick would probably kill her. If he was still around.

The conversation moved on easily through dinner. No more baring of souls or heartrending secrets. She told him amusing stories about San Francisco, and he told her tales of his adventures abroad. There was a great deal of teasing, right through dessert. They finished the dinner with zabaglione.

"You should come to San Francisco. We have a restaurant there with zabaglione that makes this one look sick." The rest of the dinner had been fabulous, but at dessert she missed Vanessi's oozing rum-kissed treat.

"I might surprise you." She laughed at the thought. That would be a surprise. But she knew he didn't mean it. "Actually, I haven't been out there in about twenty years. Most of my business is in the East or in

371

Europe. We do very little work on the West Coast, and usually when we have something out there"—he looked at her in embarrassment—"I send out one of the underlings."

"That's nice. Don't you consider California worthy of you?" She was teasing, and he laughed.

"I confess. I guess I never did. Business isn't as high-powered there."

"Maybe that's a virtue."

"I never thought so. But maybe you're right." He smiled at her warmly and reached for the check, as she frowned.

"I don't think we ought to do it that way, Philip. Let me pay my half."

"How modern! Don't be absurd." He smiled benevolently as he put several bills on the plate.

"Please don't. After all"—she grinned at him mischievously—"I have an expense account."

"In that case, I'll let you pay for drinks. Can I lure you up to the Carlyle for an hour of Bobby Short?" It was a tempting invitation, but she looked at her watch with regret.

"Would you settle for a quick drink at our hotel? I'm afraid I have to be up and out at an ungodly hour tomorrow. I have to be at the studio by seven-fifteen."

"I have to be at a breakfast meeting on Wall Street at seven-thirty myself. The hotel sounds fine."

And it was better than fine. It was lovely. A pianist was playing, and the room was uncrowded and surprisingly romantic for a hotel bar.

"I didn't remember this bar was so nice." She looked around in surprise and he laughed.

"Is that why you suggested it? You thought it would have neon lights and a jukebox?"

She laughed at the thought. "What a shame it

doesn't. Wouldn't that be fun at the Regency?" They both laughed and sipped their brandies. She had had a lot to drink, but she didn't feel drunk. They had shared half a bottle of wine with dinner, but they had eaten well, so the food had balanced out the wine. Only the brandy was finally beginning to make her feel a little bit high, but not very. It only heightened the softness of the music, and the warmth of Philip's leg next to hers.

"What are you doing at the studio tomorrow?"

"Giving guided tours." She said it with a serious expression and he laughed at her.

"I'm serious. I'm fascinated by all this celebrity stuff."

"Don't be. It's exhausting. And most of it's very dull. I'm beginning to find that out. I was here in August and it all seemed very glamorous. Two months later, it's terribly tedious and a lot of hard work."

"Do you have to prepare for the shows?"

"Not really. They ask me ahead of time what I'll be willing to talk about. And you have some idea of what each show wants. But that's about it. After that it's ad-libbing and being charming and terribly witty." She said it with a face Tygue would have made, and Philip laughed at her.

"I see you take it very seriously. By the way, Kate, could I talk you into lunch tomorrow? Mine has been canceled and I'm free."

"I wish I were too." She said it mournfully and he looked disappointed. "I'm going to some kind of women's literary luncheon. Can you think of anything worse?"

"Can you get out of it?"

"Not if I plan to publish my next book." He smiled regretfully. And he couldn't offer her dinner. He had a big business dinner he had to go to, and she was having dinner with her editor and her publisher anyway, and some guy from the New York office of her agency.

"How long will you be in town?"

"Till the end of the week."

"Good. Then we can do it another day. Day after tomorrow? Lunch?" He was even free for dinner, but he thought he'd wait to suggest that at lunch. Lunch was always a good way to start things. They could work their way toward the evening slowly.

"I'd love it. Where shall we meet?" She was actually beginning to feel drunk now, and was suddenly anxious for bed. She looked at her watch and was horrified to realize that it was after one. They had spent a long time together. And she was going to get only about four hours sleep. Very New York.

He looked at her with a smile and put down his empty glass. "Let's see . . . what's fun for lunch? Quo Vadis?"

"Where is it?"

"Just up the street. It's very pleasant." It also had the advantage of being a block away from the hotel, in case their lunch together went unusually well.

He held her arm as they walked to the elevator, and his eyes watched her hungrily as she got off at her floor. He held the door open for just a moment and looked at her. There was no one else in the elevator, and they were automatically run after midnight. "Good night, Kate." His voice was a caress, and she almost shivered. "I'll miss you tomorrow."

"Thanks."

He let the door close then and she felt foolish. "Thanks." How unglamorous. How unsophisticated. How stupid. Christ, he was way out of her league. She had never met a man quite like him before. He was more European than American, and very, very smooth.

And then she laughed as she let herself into her room. In some ways, he was very much like her father. And not at all like Nick. That was a relief at least. She was so damn sick of Nick and Tygue and Tom and all they wanted from her. Sick of the guilt trips and confusion and conflicts. She lay down for a moment on the bed, promising herself she'd get up in a minute and take off her clothes. But she never did. They called her from the desk at six, and she had to rush to get ready. They wanted her on the air at seven-thirty for a show where they were going to get her name wrong and liberally misquote her book.

CHAPTER 32

Kate didn't get back to her room at the hotel again until after eleven that night. She hadn't had a moment to herself all day. That damned women's luncheon, the shows, the dinner with the people from the agency and the publishers . . . it seemed endless. A carousel crawling with asparagus and smoked salmon, and heartburn, and she was sick of it all. She had missed the chance to talk to Tygue again, but every time she'd been near a phone, it had been the wrong time for him with the time difference. And now it was after eight in San Francisco and he'd be asleep. And she couldn't even talk to Nick. He was doing the show. And by the time he finished it, she'd be asleep. There had been no messages from him anyway, and that was message enough. She knew he was still angry. She vowed to herself just before falling asleep that she'd find time to call both him and Tygue the next day. No matter what. She needed to talk to them, or they'd never forgive her.

But she was gone first thing in the morning again, and she ran all morning until she reached Quo Vadis at noon. Philip was already waiting for her, and she was breathless as she swept out of the cab and into the restaurant. It was freezing outside, and her cheeks were bright from the cool air. She looked striking in the red slacks with her mink coat, and her eyes looked like emeralds. It was the first time she had worn the mink since she'd put it away when she moved to the country. It was the coat Tom had told her she'd wear to the hospital to have his son. And it was a beauty. Long, rich, and full in lustrous bittersweet chocolate-brown fur. Its classic lines were still very much in style. She looked dazzling, and Philip could hardly wait to get his hands on her.

"Am I late?"

"Not at all. I just got here." He helped her off with her coat and felt engulfed in her perfume. It made him want to nuzzle her neck, but not now . . . later. Their eyes met, and with a faint blush she looked away. "So how is New York? I didn't even see you at the hotel yesterday." The headwaiter led them to a quiet table, and Philip took her hand. The gesture surprised her a little, but so did her reaction. There was something very electric about this man, and her response to him made her feel oddly naïve.

"I was never at the hotel. I ran around all day. And when I got home, I went right to bed."

"What a splendid idea." He looked at her teasingly and she laughed as he reached for the wine list. He ordered a dry white Bordeaux that was tart, strong, and wonderful. She had never drunk anything like it. Along with everything else, Philip knew his wines.

They had lobster for lunch, and *mousse au chocolat* for dessert, followed by small delicate cups of espresso. And then he surprised her by ordering something called "*poire*."

"What is it?" It arrived looking like water, but even one sip scorched her mouth with a hot, pungent taste of pear. He smiled at the look on her face.

"It's pear brandy. And I can see, Mademoiselle Harper, that you need to spend some more time in

Europe. Have you been recently?" She smiled at the distant memories. She hadn't been since her last trip with Tom.

"Not in a very long time. I went quite a lot with my parents. But that was part of another lifetime. I haven't been in"—she thought for a moment—"more than seven years. And I was awfully young. No one was offering me pear brandy." And Tom certainly wouldn't have known about *poire*. He was perfectly happy with German beer. She hadn't even gotten him to try *kir*, or Cinzano, or some of the local wines as they traveled around Italy and France. Beer.

"Drink it carefully, by the way. It's strong stuff." He said it in a conspiratorial tone and seemed to edge closer to her on the banquette.

"How can I drink it any way but carefully? It burns the hell out of my mouth." She sipped again, and almost winced, but Philip didn't seem to be having any trouble with it. He smiled at her as he lit a Dunhill Monte Cristo. Philip Wells was a man of taste. She was sitting back against the banquette, watching him carefully light the full tip of his cigar, when her glance strayed just past him, and she thought she heard herself gasp. But she hadn't, there was no sound. She was only staring . . . but it couldn't be . . . it . . . but it was. She hadn't seen him in twelve years, but it had to be. Her father.

"Is something wrong?" Philip looked at her inquisitively through the delicate blue smoke. "Kate?"

She nodded distractedly, but didn't look at him. "I'm sorry. I see someone I know." Had he changed? No, she didn't think he'd changed a great deal. His hair was whiter, and maybe he was a little thinner. But he was sitting very close to a young woman almost her age. Where was her mother? Who was that girl? And why the hell did she care after all these years? She forgot all about Philip, but he was concerned as he watched the color drain from her face.

"Kate, do you want to go?" He signaled the waiter for the check without waiting for her answer. But she only shook her head, and then slid quickly off the seat.

"I'll be right back." That was crazy. She couldn't go over there. He'd laugh at her. He'd tell her to go to hell. He . . . but she had to . . . had to . . . had to. . . . She felt her feet moving rhythmically, and then suddenly she was standing there, looking at him, and saying one word. "Daddy?" There were tears in her eyes, and he looked up at her, shocked, and rose slowly to his feet, with only a glance down at the woman beside him. He was as tall and distinguished-looking as ever and his eyes were riveted to Kate. She had grown to be quite a woman. But he did not hold out his arms. They only stood there, separated by a table and a lifetime.

"Kate." She nodded in silent answer, as the tears ran down her cheeks. But she was smiling, and there were tears in his eyes too. He didn't know what to say. "I read your book."

"You did?" He read her book but he didn't call or write or reach out to her when . . . he had read her book. Why?

"It's a beautiful piece of work." Another fan. Only he wasn't supposed to be that. He was supposed to be her father. "Kate, I . . . I'm sorry about all that. We . . . we thought it was best if we didn't"—he almost choked on the word as she stared at him—"if we didn't interfere. We thought it would only make it harder. It would have been awkward." Awkward? Christ. All these years later and still an excuse. They had read the papers, they knew what was happening to her, and they never held out a hand. Slowly, her

379

tears stopped. And she could see her father had more to say. He was looking well. She could see that now. He had aged, but he had aged well. And she had been right. He did look like Philip Wells. For a moment, she found herself thinking that her father was a successful failure too. Who was that girl sitting next to him and what was he doing in New York?

"I live in New York now." He looked down at the girl and then back at Kate. "Do you?" He was visibly uncomfortable, and in her guts, Kate finally felt something very old slip from its moorings and drift away. Finally. It was really gone.

"No. I'm just here on business. For a few days." It would save them the embarrassment of having to see her, or finding excuses not to. It must have been awkward having a famous daughter who had the bad taste to turn up. She suddenly looked down at the woman lunching with her father, and found herself looking into a young, rich-girl face. "I'm sorry to interrupt your lunch. We just haven't seen each other for a while."

"I know." The girl spoke very quietly, as though with understanding. She wanted to tell Kate she was sorry, but it wasn't her war. It was theirs.

Her father was looking at her uncomfortably again, as he still stood there, the centerpiece in the drama between the two so much younger women. The woman at the table was three years younger than Kate.

"Kate, I . . . I'd like to introduce you to my wife. Ames, this is Kaitlin." Kaitlin . . . he still called her that. It rang emptily now. Kaitlin. It was a name on a book. Nothing more. But this woman . . . this woman was his wife? The words suddenly got through to her.

"Your wife?" Kate looked at him in astonishment. "You and mother are divorced?" God, whole lives had

380

gone on, on their separate continents. But he was slowly shaking his head.

"No, Kate. She died." He said it so softly she could barely hear him. And for a fraction of a moment she closed her eyes, but when she opened them again she did not cry. She only nodded.

"I see."

"I tried to find you, to let you know, but there was no trace of where you were." And then he had to ask. "Is . . . did Tom . . ." But she shook her head and cut him off.

"No. He's still alive."

"I'm sorry. That must be very hard. Or don't you . . ." He still remembered everything he had read in the papers. But he couldn't . . . they had said . . . they had decided to stick to . . . but had they been wrong? He could feel the reproach of his young wife as she sat next to him. He and Ames had argued about it often, especially after she had read the book.

"Yes, I still go, Father. He's my husband." And you were my father. That was what the words said. And then she looked down at Ames again, with the faintest of smiles in her eyes. "I'm sorry to do this to you. It's a hell of a way to have lunch." Ames only shook her head. She wanted to reach out to Kate, to be her friend. God, what bastards they had been to her. She had never been able to understand it when he tried to explain it to her. If he ever did that to their son, she'd kill him. But he'd never do that again. He knew that too. This child would be his forever.

"I . . . you had . . ." It was unbearable, standing there, asking those questions, but they seemed to be frozen into a Greek play, a tragedy, with a phalanx of waiters off in the distance somewhere as the chorus. "You had a child?"

"A little boy. He's six." It was her first real smile.

And then she looked pointedly at her father. It was as though she already knew. "And you?"

"We have . . . we also have a son. He's two." Poor little bastard. For only a second, she hated this man, and then she looked at Ames and knew she could not.

"Would you . . . would you like to sit down and join us?" He waved helplessly at the unoccupied chair, but Kate shook her head.

"No, but thank you. I really . . . have to go." She stood there for a moment, not sure whether to reach out to him, or just leave, and then slowly he held out his hand. It was like a scene in a very bad movie. Across a span of twelve years he held out a hand, only to shake hers. No hug, no kiss, no tenderness, no warmth. But it was fitting. They were strangers now.

"Good-bye." She looked at him for one last moment, and said it in a whisper as she started to walk away. And then she looked back, and saw his wife crying. She wanted to tell her it was okay, but that was his problem, not hers. She walked quietly back to Philip and he stood looking at her with concern. He had paid the check ten minutes before, but he had sensed that a drama was unfolding and he hadn't dared to approach. He had suspected that the tall, distinguished man who had stood there looking so unhappy was a past lover, and it was clear that the meeting hadn't been a joyful one. The woman seated at the table was obviously upset. His wife? It stunned him a little that Kate had had the balls to go over and talk to him, if that was the case. He hoped it wasn't, as he thought of Margaret in Chicago.

"Are you all right?"

"Yes. Can we go?"

He nodded and took her arm. It was a relief to get out in the chilly wind. It whipped her hair and squeezed fresh tears from her eyes. But they were clean tears, tears from the cold, not old, rancid tears that had waited years to be shed.

"Kate?"

"Yes." Her voice was very deep and hoarse as she looked up at him.

"Who was that, or shouldn't I ask?"

"My father. I hadn't seen him in twelve years."

"And you just ran into him like that? In a restaurant? My God, what did he say?"

"He told me that my mother had died, and he has a two-year-old son. He's remarried." Philip looked at her with horror. It was an incredible story.

"That woman was your sister, the one who was crying?"

Kate shook her head. "His wife."

"Jesus." And then he looked at Kate again, and simply took her in his arms. They walked a few steps away from the restaurant, and slowly, painfully, she started to sob. She had nothing to say, but she had to get it out. It was twenty minutes later before he walked her slowly back toward the hotel. And the bitch of it was that he had to be somewhere at three. He would be late. The lunch had taken much longer than planned.

"He didn't even ask to see me again." She said it like a heartbroken child, but he looked down at her, sensing something else too. A woman who understood.

"Did you really want him to?"

And then she smiled up at him through her tears. "He could at least have asked."

"Women. You wanted him to ask so you could tell him to go to hell, right?" She nodded and wiped her eyes with the handkerchief he handed her. It was fine Swiss linen monogrammed with PAW. Philip Anthony Wells. "Listen, I hate to say this." He hated it more than she knew. He had had such sweet plans for after lunch. "But I have a meeting at three, and,"—he looked at his watch with a grin—"it's five past. Do you think you'll be all right, and we'll kind of put back the pieces over dinner?" He gave her another quick hug and she smiled. There were no pieces to put back. She had done that years ago. With Tom's help. She was only crying at the funeral. But for her they had all been dead for so long. Maybe Tom had been right after all. The old bastard was a hypocrite. There he was married to some kid in her twenties, and with a son.

"Can you make dinner?" She had forgotten all about Philip and looked up in surprise.

"Sure. I'd love to." She needed someone to talk to, and he was easy company. "I'm sorry you got mixed up in all this. I don't usually drag my life around in front of strangers."

"I'm sorry to hear that."

"Why, are you fond of dirty linen?" She smiled at him as they walked briskly toward the hotel.

"No, but I didn't think we were still strangers. I hoped you thought of me as a friend." He put an arm around her shoulders again and she sighed.

"I do." And then he surprised her and simply stopped, there on the sidewalk. He looked down at her, and holding her tightly in his arms, he kissed her. She started to pull away, but what surprised her more was that she didn't want to. She found herself responding to him, kissing him back. Her arms were around him now too, and she felt him press his body close to hers. She wanted to feel more of him, but she couldn't through their coats. And she was sorry when he took his lips from hers.

"Dinner at seven?" They were almost under the

canopy of the hotel as she nodded, with a serious look in her eyes. She was shocked at what she had just done. There was something powerful and magnetic about Philip Wells. She wondered if he did that often. But she knew he did.

"Seven will be fine."

"Then I'll leave you here." He kissed her very gently on the cheek and started toward a cab stopped at the corner of Park Avenue. He looked back over his shoulder once with a smile and a wave. *"Ciao, bella.* See you tonight." And then he was gone, and she stood there, too stunned even to feel guilty. Then she walked slowly past the doorman and into the hotel. And as she waited for the elevator, she heard someone call her name. A man at the desk was gesticulating wildly as she turned around.

"Mrs. Harper! Mrs. Harper!" She walked toward him, confused. And he was almost breathless with excitement when she arrived at the desk. "We have been trying to reach you everywhere. Mr. Waterman had us calling every restaurant in New York."

"Mr. Waterman?" Why? Maybe because she hadn't spoken to him in three days. She looked down at the message they handed her. "Call Mr. Waterman immediately. Urgent." It gave her home phone number.

She waited till she got to her room to call back. Nick answered the phone.

"Hi. I got the message. What's up?" She sounded strangely unconcerned to Nick, who didn't realize it was only that she was numb. She had been through too much in two hours. Her father, Philip, and now this wildly urgent call from the Coast. All of that and daytime television too. It was more than she could cope with. And all the wine she'd drunk at lunch didn't help. But she was sober. That she was.

385

"Where the hell have you been?"

"Out, for chrissake. Shows, interviews, lunches, dinners."

"With whom? Nobody knew where the hell you were." He had called her publisher and the agency.

"I'm sorry. I was having lunch." She felt like a truant child apologizing to an irate father. But she was beginning to pick up something more in his tone, and she sat up straighter in her chair. "Is something wrong?"

"Yeah." He took a deep breath, and closed his eyes. "Yes. Something's wrong. Tygue is gone again."

"Oh God. Since when?"

"I don't know. Maybe last night. Maybe this morning. Tillie put him to bed last night, and I checked on him when I got home. He was fine, but he was gone this morning. He could have left anytime."

"Did he leave a note?" But they both knew where he was going.

"No. Nothing this time. Can you come home?" It stunned her that he would even ask, and her heart melted. He sounded frightened and exhausted, and all she wanted in the world was to see him again. She had had enough of New York.

"I'll get on the first plane out. Did you call the police?" It was almost a familiar routine now.

"Yes. Same old routine. I know we're going to find the little bugger on the way to Carmel somewhere."

"Yeah." She knew he was right.

"I want to drive down there myself."

"Now?"

"I'll give the cops a few more hours, and wait for you. We can go down there together."

She smiled softly as she listened to him. Nick. It was like hearing a whole family in one voice, and she knew they'd find Tygue. They had to. He had to be all right. "What are you going to do when we find him? We can't go through this every two days."

"I'll think about it on the flight." He was right, of course. He had been right all along, about her going to New York. She should never have gone. If it hadn't been . . .

"Hey, Kate . . ." She waited as tears filled her throat. It had been a rough day. "Baby, I'm sorry I gave you such a rough time before you left. I know you're going through a lot." And then the sobs engulfed her again. Everything was happening at once, it was all swirling around her like a nightmare. "Come on, baby, it's all right. We'll find him. I promise."

"I know. But I shouldn't have come here."

"Was it rough?" She nodded, and then squeezed her eyes shut, thinking of Philip. Christ, what if Nick found out? She prayed that he wouldn't. She'd only kissed him. But . . . she thought of the dinner date they had for that night. At least she wouldn't be there now. The fates had intervened. She forced her mind back to Nick.

"Yeah, it was rough. And I . . . I just saw my father."

"Just now? You were having lunch with him?" Nick sounded stunned.

"No, he was in the same restaurant. With his wife." She said it very softly.

"Your parents got divorced?" He was almost as stunned as she had been, and he didn't even know them.

"No, my mother died. He's remarried to some very young girl and they have a two-year-old son."

"Sonofabitch." Just hearing about it made Nick want to kill him, but Kate got control of her voice and dried her eyes.

"It doesn't matter anymore, Nick. It's all over."

"We'll talk about it when you get home. Call when you know your flight."

She did, and left the message with Tillie. Nick was busy talking to the police, but there was nothing new. Tillie was beside herself, but Kate felt strangely calm. She knew Tygue was all right. He had to be.

And she left a note for Philip Wells in an envelope at the desk. "Sorry to do this to you, but an emergency has come up and I have to go back to S.F. Will send you that copy of the new book when it comes out. And I'm awfully sorry about the dramatics today. Bad luck. Take care, and thank you. All the best, Kate." It was a perfectly innocuous note.

CHAPTER 33

Nick was waiting at the gate when she arrived, staring tensely at the faces drifting by. And then he saw her, and pulled her tightly into a vast hug. She clung to him for a moment and then sought his face.

"Did they find him?"

He shook his head. "No, but we will. I want to hit that road to Carmel. I don't think they realize how intent he is about that."

"Did you tell them?" He knew what she meant, and he shook his head.

"I didn't think I had to. We'll find him."

"What if we don't?"

"'Then we call out the FBI or whoever we have to. We'll find him.' They picked up her bag, and walked quickly to the car, saying little. But it felt good just to be near him again. To have his arm around her, to be home. She sighed deeply as she got in the car. "You okay, babe?" He looked at her nervously, and she smiled.

"Sure." And then he stopped with the keys in his hand and he reached out for her very gently and held her close.

"I'm sorry I've been such an asshole. I just love you two so damn much."

"Oh Nick." She was crying again. It seemed to be all she had done all day. But there was just too much happening. "I've been so crazy. And you're right, that star trip is crap. It just went to my head for a while. The money, the excitement, it's such a goddamn ego trip."

"There are nice sides to it, sweetheart. You don't have to throw the whole thing away."

"Right now I want to."

"That's stupid. If it weren't for all that, we'd never have met." He released her gently and started the car as she sat back comfortably on the leather seat. Even the car smelled familiar, like home, and it was full of their things. Tennis rackets, the Sunday paper they had shared only four days before. It was so good to be back. With him anyway. Now they had to find Tygue. She talked to him about her father on the trip south. "I don't know how you managed not to slap the sonofabitch."

"I didn't want to."

"Didn't he at least say he was sorry?"

"Not really. He tried to explain it. He thought it would be 'awkward' if he got in touch with me when everything was happening with Tom. I don't know, love, it's a whole other world. He lives in New York now."

"Good. I'd kill the motherfucker if we ever ran into him."

There was a long silence then as they careened down the freeway. And then suddenly Nick had a thought. "You know, maybe we should take the coast road. That might just be it."

Kate lit another cigarette and then handed one to him. It felt as though they had been driving forever, and it had been only an hour. Eight hours before, she'd been having lunch in New York. It was only six o'clock as they hurtled down the old coast road. There was no sight of him yet. And then suddenly, Kate pulled at Nick's sleeve.

"Over there . . . back up, Nick. . . . I saw a flash of yellow jacket." It was already almost dark, but she could have sworn it looked like Tygue's jacket. Nick moved over onto the shoulder of the road and shot into reverse.

"Here?"

"Over there, near those trees." She unlocked the door and jumped out. She ran quickly over the twigs and leaves toward the clump of trees where she had thought she'd seen the jacket. And there he was. Standing there. Watching her. Not sure of what she'd do. He seemed to shrink backward for a moment, and then he just stood there and sagged. She went to him very slowly and pulled him into her arms. She didn't say anything to him. She didn't have to. He was crying softly in her arms as she stroked his hair. She was thanking God that she had come back from New York and Nick had thought to take that road. Anything could have happened. The force of it came crashing in on her again. She hadn't let herself think of it in the hours on the plane. But there had been a sense of mounting panic as they drove along. Now it was over.

She heard Nick walk up behind them, and he put his arms around them both and spoke softly to Tygue. "Hi, Tiger. You okay?" The boy nodded and looked up at Nick.

"I wanted to go to Carmel. And nobody's stopped for me for hours." Poor little thing. He was tired and cold, and probably hungry. When he looked up at his mother, the defiance was gone, but the pain was still there. "I have to see him. I have to. He's my father."

"I know, love." She ran a hand across his hair again, and nodded. But there was no smile in his eyes. "I'll take you to see him." Nick looked surprised but said nothing. "We'll go tomorrow." The boy nodded too. There were no shouts of joy, no glee, no excitement. They were simply doing something they had to do. Like Kate shaking hands with her father before she left New York. Sometimes just knowing wasn't enough.

"What do you want to do, Kate? Do you want to go back to the city or spend the night in Carmel?"

"Don't you have to do the show?"

He shook his head. "Called in sick again."

"Jesus. Won't Jasper get pissed? You want to try and get back?" He shook his head. He'd deal with all that when he went back to his office. This mattered more.

"No, but I think we ought to call the police. They're going to be revving up their engines now that it's dark. It's only fair to let them know." She nodded and looked at Tygue.

"Okay. Let's stay in Carmel."

And there was no way of avoiding it. Nick pulled up in front of the hotel where she had stayed with Tom. But she just didn't care anymore. There were no landmarks, no shrines. It was too late for that. Much, much too late. Tygue was asleep in her arms, and she looked at Nick. She wanted to tell him how much she loved him, but she didn't know how. He just watched her, and finally smiled. But there was worry in his eyes too.

"You're really going to take him?"

She nodded. She had to. For everyone's sake.

"Do you want me to come?"

"I'd like you to be there. But I don't think he should see you. It'll confuse him, scare him. Tygue will be enough."

"I wish you didn't have to go through that."

"It'll be okay."

He kissed her then, and came around the car for Tygue. He carried him inside the hotel, and the boy didn't wake up again. They notified the police that they had found him. And Nick quietly made an appointment with the lieutenant for the following Monday. He wanted to make sure that Kate wouldn't be hassled with social workers and investigations. This was a family matter, but dragging the police into it twice on a statewide alert was going to cause some embarrassment. He wanted to handle it before it got out of hand.

"What did they say?" Kate looked nervous as she sipped a cup of tea in their room. She had just checked on Tygue again. He was still asleep. He would be all night. He was too tired even to eat. He had come a long way in a short time. Hadn't they all. She stifled a yawn.

"They said everything was fine. Don't worry about it. And you should get some sleep."

"I'm fine."

"You look it." She was a pale grayish green, and there was no makeup left except smudged mascara beneath her eyes. He sat down next to her on the bed and held her close. "God, I'm glad you're back, Kate. I've been worried sick about you."

"I thought you hated me when I left."

"I did." He smiled down at her. "But I did some thinking. What we have is too special to throw away."

Jesus, and she almost had thrown it away, with that jerk in New York. It was horrifying to realize that she might have been in bed with him at that very moment if she hadn't had to come home. In a way, Tygue's flight for Carmel had been a blessing. She closed her eyes as she lay in Nick's arms. Only for a moment.

She just wanted to lie there and feel him next to her. Her eyes closed and when she opened them again, it was morning.

She looked around, stunned, as the sun poured into the room. "Nick?" He laughed at her from the other side of the bed. He was already drinking a cup of coffee. "What happened?"

"You passed out, Cinderella. Zap. Gone."

"That must have been fun." She grinned at him and stretched. He had taken off her clothes.

"Yeah, best it's ever been." They exchanged a playful smile, and she reached out for his coffee.

"Where'd you get that?"

"Your son and I had breakfast, my love."

"When?"

"About an hour ago."

"Jesus, what time is it?"

"Almost nine o'clock." She nodded, and then they both sobered. They knew what lay ahead.

"How's Tygue?"

"Okay. Quiet. He was hungry as hell." She bent over to kiss Nick quickly and then went into the other room to see Tygue. He was sitting quietly near the window with his bear. She walked over to him softly and sat down.

"Hi, love. How's Willie?"

"He's okay. He was kind of hungry this morning though."

"He was, eh?" She smiled and pulled Tygue close. He felt so soft and warm in her arms. It reminded her of all the years when they'd had only each other. "Are you ready for today?" He knew what she meant. He only nodded, holding tightly to Willie. "It won't be much fun. In fact"—she made him look at her—"it may be the hardest thing you ever did. He's not like a daddy, Tygue."

"I know." Tygue's eyes were even larger than hers. "He's kind of like a little boy. But a sick little boy. He can't walk. He's in a wheelchair, and he doesn't remember things." She was almost sorry that she hadn't brought him earlier, when Tom had looked bronzed and healthy. Now he always looked so tired and unhappy. It would be harder for Tygue. "And I want you to know . . ." She hesitated, fighting back the tears. "I want you to know now . . . that before he got like this, he loved you very much. Before you were born." She took a deep breath and held her son tight. "And I want you to know that I love you too, with all my heart, and . . . and if it's too hard you don't have to stay. Is that a promise? You'll tell me if you want to go?"

Tygue nodded, and gently wiped the tears from her face as she fought back more. All she could do then was hold him.

"Is Nick coming too?"

She pulled back to look at him. "Do you want him to?"

Tygue nodded. "Can he?"

"He can't see T . . . Daddy, but he can be there."

"Okay." And with an imploring look, he turned his face up to hers. "Can we go now?"

"In a little bit. I'll have some coffee and get dressed." He nodded, and sat where he was.

"I'll wait here."

"I'll hurry."

Nick looked up when she walked back into the room. This was going to be another brutal day. But maybe this would be the last one. He hoped so. "Is he all right?"

"Yes. He wants you there." And then she looked at him again, with those big, bottomless green eyes that he had loved from the first. "So do I."

"I'll be there."

"You always are."

"That's a nice thing to say." He handed her a cup of coffee and a piece of toast, but she couldn't eat. Even the coffee made her feel sick. There was a knot in her stomach the weight of a coconut. All she could think of was Tygue. And his father.

CHAPTER 34

Nick drove up the driveway and pulled into the spot she pointed out to him behind the main house.

"Should I wait here?" He looked as nervous as she felt, and Tygue was sitting silently on her lap, watching everything.

"You can come closer to the cottage. There are other people around. You won't stick out." He nodded, and they all got out of the car. She took Tygue's hand, and smoothed his hair. He was still carrying Willie. Kate had called ahead to warn Mr. Erhard. He said Tom was in good form. At least there was that.

The silent trio followed the pathway, and then Kate pointed to a little white wrought-iron bench. "Why don't you wait there, love? You can see the cottage from here." She pointed again, and he looked. This was how she had spent all those years. He still had to fight back tears when he thought of it.

He looked down at the boy then, and gently touched his cheek. "You're okay, Tiger." Tygue nodded, and Kate took his hand and walked on. Mr. Erhard was waiting in the doorway, and he looked down at Tygue with a warm smile. Kate had already forgotten Nick. She was in Tom's world now. And she was holding tightly to Tygue's hand. She wanted him to know how much they had loved him, how much they had loved each other. She wanted him to see something of

Tom that was no longer there to see. But above all, she wanted Tygue to survive it. She put an arm around his shoulders and forced a smile.

"Tygue, this is Mr. Erhard. He takes care of your daddy. He has for a very long time."

"Hi, Tygue. That's a beautiful bear. What's his name?"

"Willie." Tygue's eyes looked enormous. And Mr. Erhard's eyes sought Kate's.

"We have a Willie too. Would you like to see him?" Tygue nodded, trying to look past him into the cottage, and then Mr. Erhard stepped aside, and Kate walked slowly inside. Tom was staying in the cottage today, despite the good weather, and when she saw him she realized how much time he must have been spending inside lately. He looked ghostly and pale, and seemed to have lost twenty pounds in the past two weeks. But there was a warm light in his eyes today, and he smiled a smile she hadn't seen in years as he caught sight of Tygue. Kate had to clench her teeth so as not to cry. It was Tom who spoke first.

"You have a Willie too! So do I!" He instantly held up his bear and Tygue smiled. "Let me see yours." He very gently held out a big hand and Tygue let him have Willie, and for a few minutes they compared bears, while Tygue stole glances at his father. They decided that Tygue's was in better shape. "Want some cookies?" He had saved some from the night before, and produced a plate for Tygue, as Kate and Mr. Erhard hovered. The two "boys" ate cookies, and Tygue crept quietly into the rocking chair as they talked. "What's your name?"

"Tygue."

"Mine is Tom. And that's Katie." He glanced over at Kate with a broad smile, and she found herself smiling back. "She comes to see me a lot. She's a nice

398

lady. I love her. Do you love her too?" Tygue nodded silently and it almost seemed to Kate as though Tom was forcing himself to speak like a child, to put Tygue at ease. As though he could have behaved as a grownup if he wanted to. "Want to see my boat?" Tygue looked up in surprise and smiled.

"Yeah. I've got a boat too." They talked about their boats for a minute, and then Mr. Erhard stepped in.

"Do you two want to take a walk to the pond? We could try out Tom's boat." Father and son looked enthusiastic, and Kate smiled as he wheeled Tom outside and Tygue walked along beside him. He looked almost proud as he walked next to his father. And the half hour at the boat pond brought laughter to everyone. Even Tom looked better than he had at first. And then Kate could see him starting to tire, and Mr. Erhard suggested they go back inside.

For once Tom didn't argue, and he reached out for Tygue's hand as they started back. He was being rolled along by Mr. Erhard, and Tygue was once again at his side. The little boy held tightly to the shrunken man's hand, as Kate watched them. She was glad she had brought him. And when they reached the cottage door, Tom leaned over and picked two bright orange flowers. One for Kate, and one for his son. He looked hard and long at the boy as he handed him the flower and held his hand.

"Why did you come to see me?"

Kate felt her heart stop, but Tygue looked at him and didn't waver.

"I needed to see you."

"I needed to see you too. Take good care of Katie."

Tygue nodded somberly and she could see his eyes fill with tears as quickly as her own. Tom had never said anything like that before.

"I will."

"And Willie? Always take good care of Willie." But this time Tygue only nodded, and then unexpectedly he leaned over and kissed Tom on the cheek as he sat in his chair. Tom smiled at him and hugged him for a moment.

"I love you." The words were Tygue's.

"I love you too." And then he laughed, the clear, open laugh of a boy, and Tygue laughed too. It was as though they understood each other, as though they had a secret between them. As though they felt the moment in a lighthearted way that no one else understood. They were both little boys. Tom was still laughing as Mr. Erhard wheeled him inside. "Is it time for my nap?" Mr. Erhard nodded, looking at Kate. It was enough. Better to stop now.

"Yes, it is."

"I hate naps." He made a face and looked at Tygue.

"So do I." Tygue laughed back and picked up his bear again. Tom watched him with a funny look in his eyes, but he was smiling.

"I'll trade you."

"What?"

"Willies. I'll give you my Willie, and you give me yours. Want to? My Willie is so tired of being here." Tygue's face lit up then, as though his father had offered him the most precious gift in the world.

"Sure." He held out his bear with a look of awe, and Tom wheeled over to his own and handed it to Tygue.

"Take good care of Willie."

"I will." Tygue stooped to kiss him again, and Tom only smiled.

" 'Bye." Tygue watched him for a long moment, as though wondering what to say, how to end it, but he only smiled and walked to the door.

" 'Bye."

Kate walked toward Tom, and stood next to him, holding his shoulder with her hand. Together, they looked at their son, smiling in the doorway with his bear. He had seen his father. He had won.

Tom looked up at her with a tired smile. The visit had cost him something, but he looked as though he had won too.

" 'Bye, Katie." Something about the way he said it tore at her heart, and she couldn't say good-bye. Tygue was still watching them from the doorway.

"I'll see you soon."

He only nodded, though, with a quiet, happy smile. He was still watching the boy. And Kate could still feel his eyes on them after they'd left, and were out in the warm autumn sun. She looked down at Tygue, and wiped her eyes. "I'm glad you came."

"Me too." And then, with a smile, he walked over to the bench where they had left Nick. Kate had totally forgotten him. And she followed slowly behind Tygue, trying to recover from the hour they'd spent with Tom. "Hi." Tygue stood in front of him with a broad grin. "I've got a new Willie."

"Looks like the old Willie to me." Nick smiled, trying to search the boy's eyes, but he didn't see anything there but peace and love, and a warm glow. The visit had done him no harm.

"It's his Willie. He gave it to me."

"You mean he has one too?" Nick looked at Tygue warmly as he nodded. "That's neat." And then he looked up at Kate, as she stood near them. She was still holding the two flowers Tom had given them after their walk. "How are you?"

"Okay. I kind of forgot you were here." She smiled, looking wistful and tired, but relieved.

"I know. But I'm glad I am."

"So am I. Nick . . ." She looked down for a moment

and then back into his eyes. "Could we go down to my place for a few days? I mean all three of us. I kind of want to . . ." She didn't know how to say it, but it was as though she had to see that too. As though she needed to get away from the city, and the book, and everything that had been happening. "Can you get away?"

"We're going to have to stop and buy some tee-shirts and jeans, but I can get away. I think it would do us all good."

"So do I."

"Are you lonely for the country, darling?" He looked at her curiously as they walked back to the car. He hadn't thought she was.

"No. I don't know. I just need to be there. Just for a few days."

"Okay." He put an arm around her shoulders, and another around Tygue's, and the three of them walked back to the car. Kate was glad when they drove away from Mead. She didn't want to leave Tom, but it was time that she did.

CHAPTER 35

Going back to Kate's house in the hills for a few days had been a good idea. It gave them all the time they needed to absorb the past week. Nick and Kate needed the time together, and with Tygue. He was whole again, and at peace. He was quiet for the first day, sitting outside with the teddy bear he'd gotten from Tom. But he wasn't unhappy, only pensive.

Kate looked down at her son as they sat in the sunshine the second day. Nick was doing something in the house.

"Maybe I should have told him about my horse," Tygue said.

"He never really liked horses very much." Kate was looking off at the hills, thinking back. For a moment she almost forgot the child. He was looking up at her incredulously.

"He didn't like horses?" Tygue looked shocked, and she smiled and looked down into the sunny little face. He looked better again. Rested and happy, like the boy she knew, not the waif they had picked up under the trees on the road to Carmel. "How could he not like horses?"

"He loved football. That was his whole life."

"That's 'cause he was such a big star." Kate smiled at the pride in the boy's voice.

"Yes, he was."

"Are you a big star, Mom?"

She looked down at him with a grin. "No. I wrote a book that a lot of people are buying, but that doesn't make me a star. Nobody knows who I am." She lay back and stretched out the long legs that had modeled so long ago. "But everyone knew who your dad was. Everywhere we went people wanted autographs, they wanted to touch him, ladies wanted to kiss him." She grinned and Tygue started to laugh.

"Did he let them?"

"Not when he was with me."

"It must be neat though, having everyone love you like that."

"Sometimes. Sometimes it's very hard. People expect too much of you. People won't leave you alone. They won't let you be yourself."

"I wouldn't like that." He picked up a leaf and studied it.

"He didn't either. That's what made him sick. All the people pushing him. And all he wanted to do was play football. For the rest of his life."

"Couldn't he?"

She shook her head. "No, love. You can only play professional football for a few years. And then they make you retire."

"What's that?"

"Stop playing."

"Forever?"

"Forever."

"That's terrible!" He threw the leaf away and stared at her.

"That's what your dad thought too. He didn't want to do anything else. And they made him quit. And then a lot of people bugged him about it. Like newspapers and stuff." It was the best explanation she could give him, and it was true.

"And he went crazy. Right?"

"That's about right."

"Does he remember that he played football?"

"No. I don't think he remembers anything except where he is now, and Mr. Erhard and me. And now he'll remember you." She smiled at him with a mist glistening in her eyes, and she heard Nick come out of the house. He was carrying a blanket and two apples. He handed one to each of them, and looked down at them with warmth in his eyes. "Thanks, love." Kate smiled him a kiss.

"Don't you guys want to sit on this?"

"Nah." Tygue looked up at the blanket disparagingly and then he remembered something . . . those words his father had said . . . "You want to, Mom?"

"Okay." She remembered the words too. . . . Take care of Katie, . . .

The three of them spread out the bright plaid blanket and sat down and munched apples. Kate and Nick shared theirs, and Tygue attacked his with glee. They were fresh country apples. They had gotten them from the market the day before.

"You want to go down to the Adams place later and see what kind of new horses they've got?" Nick looked over at him, as he crunched his way to the core, but the boy shook his head.

"No. They've got better horses in the park."

"In San Francisco?" Nick looked surprised, and Tygue nodded insistently. Kate smiled as she listened to him. They had outgrown this place, both of them had. It made her smile to think that four months before he had never left town. She was remembering his first trip to San Francisco in June . . . and hers the month before that. . . .

"And what are you thinking about, Cinderella?"

405

Nick handed her their apple and she took a bite and handed it back.

"I was thinking about last spring. Neither of us had been anywhere then. And suddenly it all started to happen."

"That's what it does."

"What were you doing last spring, Mr. Waterman?" She looked at him with a curious grin.

"None of your business." He grinned back and finished the apple.

"As bad as all that?"

"Up yours." He said it softly as he nibbled her neck. They worried less about Tygue observing them now. He was used to them. And then Nick had another thought. "Want to go see Joey?" But Tygue shook his head again. He had already said good-bye. He had new friends. A new life.

They spent a peaceful afternoon together, as they had the day before. They bought steaks in town and Nick barbecued them in the late-afternoon sun. That evening they watched television together, and made popcorn in the fireplace, as they had the first few times Nick had come up from L.A. And like the old days, they waited until Tygue went to bed, and then rushed into the bedroom, laughing, hungry for each other, aching to make love.

"My, my, aren't we the anxious one tonight," he teased as she kissed the inside of his thighs and tugged playfully at his shorts.

"You didn't exactly drag your feet getting in here either, Mr. Waterman." She sat down on the floor next to him in her bra and pants, laughing up at him as he smiled down at her. She had seemed younger and freer since they had seen Tom.

"Kate? You're glad we went to see him, aren't you?"

She nodded quietly for a moment. "I feel relieved.

There's no more secret to hide, not from you, not from Tygue. It's all out now. I feel free again."

"But what about him?" They hadn't talked about that yet, but there were still questions that Nick felt he had to ask.

"What do you mean, Nick?" She looked very peaceful as she looked up at him, and he slowly knelt down next to her.

"I mean, what happens to Tom now? You can't very well stop seeing him after all these years, I understand that, but . . . well, it takes a lot out of you, Kate."

"I don't think it will anymore. I'm not carrying the weight alone anymore. I can share it with you and Tygue. I can tell you what I feel, what it's like, what's happening to him, whenever I go." There was a moment's pause and then she lowered her face and looked silently at the wedding band on her hand. And then, carefully, she slipped the ring from her finger and held it tightly in her palm. "It's all over, Nick. I won't be going as often anymore. I'm not even sure he'll notice very much. He may at first, but he has so little sense of time. I think if I go once every couple of weeks, it'll be fair to everyone. What do you think?" She turned her eyes back to his, and they were bright and full, but she didn't look unhappy.

"I think you're a remarkable woman, and I've never loved you more. Whatever you want to do, Kate, however you want to handle it, I can accept it."

"That's all I need to know. It means, though, that we can never get married as long as he's alive. I . . . I couldn't do that to him. I know he wouldn't even know I'd divorced him, but I just wouldn't feel right."

"We don't need the papers, Kate, we have each other. And when the time is right, we can get married. In the meantime. . . ." He grinned broadly; she had

407

just given him the only gift he had ever wanted from her—a promise of marriage, even if a remote one. He looked at her again and there was mischief in his eyes. "In the meantime, young lady, I had no idea that you'd even been considering marriage. I thought you were going to carry on this independent act of yours well into your nineties."

"Well, why not?" She glared at him sheepishly for a moment, and then defiantly. "I can't let you make all my decisions for me, Nick. Even if we do get married one day. I did that with Tom, and it just wasn't right."

"I understand that. I think we've been handling that fairly well."

"So do I." She softened again. "And that's not the only thing you've been handling well."

"Oh?" The mischief danced in his eyes again, and she laughed.

"No, you lecher, I meant Tygue. You've gotten him over all the rough spots. I don't think he resents you even a little anymore."

"I think that seeing his father will help even more."

"Probably. But you've done a beautiful job, darling. I'm afraid neither of us was too easy at first."

"My God, a confession. Quick, the tape recorder . . ."

"Oh shut up." She reached over playfully and tweaked the hair on his chest. "And by the way, I'm closing the house."

"What house?" Life with Kate was full of surprises. For all he knew, she was closing the San Francisco house and moving them all somewhere else.

"This house, silly. I don't need it anymore."

"You mean you're giving up your ace? The retreat where you can always flee from me?"

"That's not how I looked at it." She tried to sound

insulted, but she was already giggling. "How did you know?"

"Because I'm not as dumb as you like to think I am."

"I would never think such a thing."

"Good. Then tell me the truth about why you're closing the house, and explain to me what you mean by 'closing' it. You mean giving it up completely?"

"Completely. We don't need it. We never come down here, we're not going to, and I wouldn't want to anyway. This is a part of my life that's over." And then her face grew sober again, and she slowly opened her hand and looked at the wedding ring she had slipped from her finger moments before. "It's over. Just like this."

And then, wordlessly, she put the ring down on a table and came into his arms. She had never been as free with him as she was that night. It was as though something in her had been uncaged, and she gave herself to him in ways she never had before, her body arching and writhing in ecstasy beneath the expertise of his hands and his tongue.

The next morning, they had a quiet breakfast alone in the kitchen before they woke Tygue and told him that he was leaving that morning with Nick.

"Without you, Mom?" She expected a few moments of protest and was surprised by the look of delight on his face.

"Don't look so heartbroken about it, you creep." But in fact she was relieved. It was as though their little family had solidified in the past few days.

"How long do we get to be alone?" His eyes danced at the prospect and Nick laughed.

"As long as it takes me to pack up this house. Speaking of which, young man, I want you to go through your games and toys this morning and decide what you're giving away and what you want in San Francisco." There wasn't too much left in his closet and cupboards, but enough to keep him busy for a couple of hours.

They all rolled up their sleeves and started packing that morning, but by late afternoon Kate was working alone. After lunch, Nick and Tygue had piled into the car and driven back to San Francisco. And Kate was surprised how comfortable it was to be alone in the house. She did a lot of thinking as she packed up the boxes she and Nick had gotten at the supermarket before lunch.

He had been right, she *was* giving something up by letting go of the house. But it was something she didn't want anymore anyway, an emergency exit, a place to hide, a place where she could keep herself from Nick. She had liked knowing that she had that, but she didn't need that anymore. If she needed to get away from him, or express her independence, she could do it with words, or a long walk, or·a trip alone somewhere for a weekend, but not by coming back to the place where she had lived for seven years, mourning the past. There was nothing left to mourn. And if she found herself frightened or bothered or bugged, sometime in the future, she could handle that too—without running away. It was a nice thing to know about herself.

It took her three days to pack up the house. She gave a lot of things away, labeled some boxes for Tillie, and left them in the garage. And she collected what amounted to a small truckload of odds and ends and useful items that she arranged to have sent up to the city. After that there was nothing left. She sent a letter to notify the landlord that she was leaving, and wondered if it wasn't time for him to retire there anyway. Maybe he would finally use the house himself one of these days. It had served her well. It had kept her secret safe for all those years. She remembered how happy she had been when she first got there. Happy just to be away from the hell she had lived through, happy as she lay on the grass in the springtime, feeling Tygue grow inside her, and so happy when he had been born and she brought him home. She stood in the bedroom on the last morning, and remembered looking out over those same hills, all those years ago, with Tygue in her arms. And then solemnly, she turned on her heel, and walked out of the house.

CHAPTER 36

"I'm home!" It was four o'clock in the afternoon when she arrived. And everyone was there, even Bert, wagging his tail in the front yard as she got out of the ugly little rented car. Tygue was clattering around on a new pair of roller skates and Nick was just getting some papers out of the car. It seemed as though everyone converged on her at once, talking and laughing and hugging and kissing. Nick was holding her so tight she could hardly breathe.

"Woman, if you go anywhere in the next six months, I'll go stark staring crazy, and furthermore, I'll . . ." He grinned. "I'll set fire to your new book!"

"Don't you dare!" She looked at him in horror. She was hungry to get back to that too. She hadn't touched it in weeks.

"If you do that, I'll burn all your jockstraps, and . . ."

"What's a jockstrap?" Tygue said it at the top of his lungs and they both laughed. They laughed for the rest of the afternoon. Nick urged Kate to disappear for a "nap," and Tillie shepherded Tygue off down the block to break in his new skates. And when he got back, Nick and Kate were both roaming around in their bathrobes, making tea.

"Want to come to the show tonight, Kate?"

She looked up in surprise. "Like this?"

"No, I kind of thought you'd get dressed." He looked prissy and she made a face at him.

"I mean, you want me on it without my hair done and all that?" She looked horrified, and he sat back in his chair and laughed.

"Listen, Miss Ego, you happen to live with the producer of that show. I wanted to know if you'd like to come and hang out at the studio and keep me company while we tape it."

"And not be a guest on the show?" She looked shocked, but her eyes were dancing.

"What do you think you are, some kind of celebrity or something?"

"Hell, yes, Mr. Waterman. I'm a best-selling author!"

"Oh yeah?" He slipped his hand into her robe, and then leaned across the table to kiss her.

"You're impossible. But since you invited me"—she looked up with a smile—"I'd love to come keep you company while you tape. Will it bother anyone there?"

"That's their problem. I run the joint. Remember?"

"Oh that's right, you do."

"Sounds to me, young lady, like it's time you came home and settled down. You've forgotten how things run around here."

She let her fingers play along the inside of his arm, and he got goose flesh and looked at her with a gleam in his eye.

"If you do that for much longer, I'm going to get a lot more serious than you bargained for."

"In the kitchen?" She was grinning again. It was just the way they had been in the beginning. The honeymoon was on again.

"Yes, in the kitchen, Cinderella. I will make love to you anytime, anywhere, any way, for the rest of your life. I love you."

She kissed him very softly on the mouth, and they made love very quickly, in the kitchen, before Tygue got home. And they laughed like two outrageously naughty children as they hurried back into their robes, and tried to look as though they'd been drinking tea.

"You've got your robe inside out," she whispered to him as they giggled, and he laughed even harder when he looked at her. She had her belt tied through the sleeve.

"You're a mess."

It went on that way for weeks. Clandestine meetings in what she jokingly called "the attic," making love in the upstairs den, sharing long lazy breakfasts in the kitchen, taking Tygue to the zoo. She watched him tape the show almost as often as he did it, and he sat peacefully in his favorite leather chair as she worked on the new book. It was a kind of Siamese-twin existence but they loved it. They both knew it couldn't go on forever, not like that—she'd have things to do for the new book, and he had a lot of extra work he wanted to do for Jasper's show. But right now they both needed what they were getting. Each other.

"Don't you ever get tired of sitting up here while I clack away on this silly book?"

"Darling, any woman who is making the kind of money you are does not write silly books."

"To what do I owe this renewed respect for my talent?"

"Your last royalty statement. I saw it on your desk this morning. Christ, what are you going to do with all that money?" He was glad she was doing so well. He knew it meant something to her. Security for Tygue, things for herself, gifts she'd like to buy him. But it also meant that she felt independent, and he knew that she needed that.

She was sitting back in her chair, looking at him,

wondering what she would give him for Christmas. It was only a month away. "What do you want for Christmas, by the way?" She lit a cigarette and took a sip of cold tea. He had been reading the paper while she worked.

"You know what I'd really like for Christmas?"

"What?" She was grinning, thinking that she knew what he'd say.

"Don't look like that, you dirty old woman. What I'd really like is to see a little color in that pale face of yours. Want to go to Acapulco or someplace for the holidays?" She looked surprised at the thought.

"I've never been there. That might be fun." She was turning the idea over in her mind as he looked at her, but he didn't answer her smile.

"Kate?"

"Hm?"

"Are you feeling all right?" Worry had crept into his face.

"Sure. Why?" But they both knew why. She was tired all the time, her appetite was lousy, and she was always pale. The rings under her eyes had become part of the decor. She was pushing hard on the book though. She had blamed it on that.

"Would you go to see a doctor?" It was the first time he had asked, and it frightened her that he was that worried.

"You mean it?"

"Yeah. I do."

"Okay. I'll see. When I finish the book." And what was he going to tell her that she didn't already know? That she had been under a lot of pressure? That her whole life had altered and her son had run away twice? That she was finishing a five hundred-page book? None of it was news to her. So what was the point of seeing a doctor? "He's not going to tell me anything new. He's just going to say I'm working too hard, or I've been through a lot of changes, or some other bullshit like that. Why spend money to listen to that?"

"Do me a favor, and save your money someplace else." He looked at her seriously and stood up. "I mean it, Kate. Promise me you'll go. And not six months from now."

"Yes, my love." She said it too sweetly, and he frowned.

"Promise?"

"Promise, but only if you promise not to worry about it."

"Sure." Both promises were equally empty. She was not a fan of doctors and he was a devoted worrier, at least about her. But none of that changed how she looked. Felicia had noticed it too. But Kate had brushed her off.

"What are you doing today by the way?"

"I'm meeting Felicia for lunch. Want to come?"

"No. I have to talk to a couple of guys at the Press Club over lunch. And then we've got a meeting at the studio. He looked at his watch, and then stooped to kiss her. "In fact, I'm almost late for lunch. I'll be home around three."

"I'll try to be too." She tried. But she didn't make it till five.

She went shopping for an hour, after lunch at Trader Vic's with Licia, and then she'd wandered over to Saks. Just "for a minute" to see what was new. But the store had been crowded and she had gotten tired, and the elevator had taken forever to come, and when it had she was pressed near the back. And when they reached the third floor, they found her crumpled in the rear of the car. She had fainted. They had wanted to call home for her, but she wouldn't let them. She

416

had sat there at Saks for an hour feeling like a fool, with smelling salts under her nose, and she'd taken a cab home. She hadn't wanted to drive. She'd have to tell Nick she'd had a problem with the car. Dammit. And she still felt light-headed and a little dizzy when she got home. She was fully prepared to be amusing and distracting, and get upstairs as fast as she could, to go to bed. He had wanted to take her to the taping of the show, but she'd beg off.

She slid her key into the door, and turned it. The door opened easily, and for a minute she hoped that he wasn't home. But he was. And he was sitting in the living room, waiting for her, his face rigid with rage.

"Have a nice lunch?"

"Very. How was your . . ." But she stopped when she saw his face. "What happened to you?"

"Who's Philip?"

"What?"

"You heard me." He glared at her and she started feeling dizzy again. She slowly sank down in a chair. "Who the hell is Philip?"

"How do I know? Is this some kind of a game?" She felt weak but she sounded angry. She was scared. Philip? Philip from New York?

"As a matter of fact, I'm beginning to wonder the same thing. Is this some kind of a game? Every couple of months I find out something new about you."

"What's that supposed to mean?"

"This." He walked across the room and threw a piece of paper at her. "It was in an unmarked envelope tucked into the front door. I thought you'd left me a note. I was wrong." The paper was a sandy beige, the ink was brown, and the handwriting distinctive. And then she saw the monogram at the top. PAW. Philip Anthony Wells. She felt her heart slide into her heels. Jesus. And the letter itself did nothing to help. "Sorry you had to leave so suddenly. It was a beautiful lunch, a beautiful evening before that. The music was never the same after you left. I've come West, at last, to see two promises fulfilled. Yours, and that of the zabaglione at Vanessi's. Join me tonight? Call. I'm at the Stanford Court. Love, P." She almost gasped.

"Oh Jesus." She looked up at him with huge eyes that instantly filled with tears.

"That's what I said. It's quite a letter. And don't let me stop you from having dinner with him, darling." His voice dripped hurt and anger. He had felt as though someone had punched him when he read the note. "Just exactly what went on in New York?"

"Nothing, I had dinner with him, by accident, at Gino's."

"By accident?" He looked at her nastily and she jumped to her feet and peeled off her coat.

"Oh for chrissake. I couldn't get a goddamn cab from the airport, so we shared one. We happened to be staying at the same hotel. And that night I went to Gino's for dinner, by myself, and he was there. We chatted at the bar, and then we just decided . . ." It sounded terrible in the telling and his face was looking anything but relieved. But she decided to press on. "We just decided to share a table. Big deal! So what?"

"And then what?"

"What do you mean 'and then what?' "

"Whose room did you go to?"

"Mine for chrissake. And he went to his. What do you think I am, dammit? A whore?"

"We were hardly speaking to each other that week, if I remember correctly."

"So? You think I run out and get laid by a stranger every time we have a fight?"

"No, but apparently you have dinner with one."

"Goddamn you!" She grabbed her coat again and stared at him. Now she was blazing. Fuck him. She'd tell him the whole story, and if he didn't like it he could take his whole goddamn life and shove it. "Yeah, so I had dinner with him. And I had drinks with him after that. And I had lunch with him two days later. And if Tygue hadn't run away that day, I'd probably have had dinner with him that night. But that's all I bloody did. No, as a matter of fact, come to think of it, I kissed him. Whoopee. I'm twenty-nine years old and I kissed him. But that's all I did, you sonofabitch, and I don't need you to play watchdog. I can keep myself out of other men's beds all by myself. And as a matter of fact, smartass, I spent days being grateful that Tygue had run away. Because I was just unhappy enough at that point, and insecure enough about us, that maybe I would have gone to bed with him. But I didn't. And I was so glad I hadn't. Because I didn't want to. Because I love you, you stupid sonofabitch, not anyone else."

She was screaming and trembling and the sobs were starting to shake her voice, but she stood up, waving the letter and advancing on him. Nick was feeling greatly subdued by his effect on her. He had never seen her get like that. Never. She looked as though she were going to have a stroke and fall dead at his feet. And he suddenly felt foolish for making such a stink of it. He knew she was telling the truth, he'd just been upset when he came home and found the letter. He knew she was faithful to him, though he was upset by the kiss. But he could live with a kiss, and he was glad, too, that she hadn't done more. But it was too late to be glad. She stood over him waving the letter. "And you know what you can do with this? You can take it to Philip Wells and cram it down his throat. And then you can both go to Vanessi's and eat the

419

fucking zabaglione for all I care. But get the hell out of my life!" And then, sobbing, she reeled around, threw the letter on the floor, grabbed her bag and coat, and walked out. She stopped in the doorway for a moment, afraid she was going to faint again and he looked at her. Something was terribly wrong with her.

"Are you all right?"

"Mind your own goddamn business." And with that she slammed out of the house. Tygue was visiting a friend, so she knew she didn't have to be there, and now she didn't want to be there with Nick. Fucking Philip Wells. She hated them both. And then, she suddenly realized she'd left her car downtown. She set off toward the Bay, on foot, crying like a child. Why had Philip done this to her? And why had Nick read the letter? And why had she kissed him that day in New York? She sat down on a secluded garden wall a few blocks away, and stayed there for a while with her face in her hands, sobbing, and wishing she were dead.

At home, Nick was still sitting in the living room, staring at the letter she had thrown on the floor, wishing he'd handled things differently. He had never seen her that emotional. And then she had stopped in the doorway, looking absolutely green. He had to get her to a doctor. Maybe it was her nerves. The phone broke into his thoughts, and he scooped the letter up on the way. He crumpled it and threw it into the wastebasket next to the phone.

"Mrs. Harper? No, I'm sorry, she's out. Is she what? What do you mean is she all right? She what? . . . Oh my God. . . . No, no, it's all right. I'll take care of it." He sat very still for a moment, and called Felicia. He was lucky to catch her, it was almost six. But she agreed to come over right away. She could hear in his voice that something was wrong.

"Where's Tygue?" She looked around as she came in. The house seemed unusually quiet and dark.

"Spending the night at a friend's. It's not Tygue, Licia. It's Kate. I think something terrible is wrong with her." He sat down in the living room again, and held his head in both hands. Felicia sat down across from him and looked at him for a minute.

"You don't look so hot either. What happened?"

"I made an ass of myself." He walked to the wastebasket and scooped up the letter and handed it to her. "I found that when I came home, in an unmarked envelope. I thought it was for me."

"Oops." She looked up at him with a wry smile, and he wasn't smiling.

"I confronted her with it when she got home, like a total ass. And she told me the whole story. It's nothing. But what totally wiped me out is what happened to her. Jesus, Licia, I've never seen her do that. She just fell apart. She screamed and shook and she looked like she was going to pass out. She's been looking horrendous lately, and she won't see a doctor. She's working too hard, she's not sleeping enough, she's tired all the time, she cries when she thinks I don't know it. I think she's sick. Or something. I don't know what the hell it is." And then he looked over at Felicia with the clincher. "Customer Relations at Saks just called. She passed out in the elevator there this afternoon. I'm worried sick."

"I take it she's not home now?" Felicia looked worried too.

He shook his head. "No. She blazed out of here . . . over this . . ." He waved the letter and then crumpled it again.

Felicia hated to ask. But Kate was not really one for intrigues. Even though the little minx had said nothing about New York. And then she did remem-

421

ber a gleam in Kate's eye when she had asked her about Gino's. But that didn't explain the histrionics and the fainting. "Is it possible . . . could she be with that guy?"

Nick shook his head again. "Not in the state she was in when she left here. And . . . no, I know she's not."

"I don't think she is either. And she's a grown woman. She'll just have to be reasonable and go to a doctor. She didn't eat a thing for lunch. But she's not losing weight." And then she sat back in her chair and narrowed her eyes.

"What is it?" He looked more nervous than ever. Was there something else he didn't know?

"Something rings a bell." She looked back into his eyes. "I'm afraid I have no experience with it myself, but methinks I've seen this one before with Kate. Then, I thought it was just what was happening—because of Tom." Felicia frowned, wondering. It would be a hell of a relief.

"Her nerves?"

"No. Not exactly." She looked at him with a small smile. "Far be it from me to pry into your private lives, but is it possible that she's pregnant?"

"Kate?" He looked stunned.

"Not Tillie, I hope." He shared a laugh with her at the thought.

"I don't know. I hadn't thought of it. I always figured that if something like that happened, she'd know, and—"

"Don't rely on that. Half the women I know never figure it out till they're about three months pregnant. You figure the flight to New York threw you off, the food, your sex life, god knows. Anyway, for whatever the reasons, people seem not to notice a lot these days." Jesus. The very idea of "not noticing" made her break out in a sweat. But Kate was the kind not to. "Any chance that's it? She had some incredible temper tantrums when she was pregnant with Tygue. Usually about the press, so they were justified, on the surface anyway. But when you thought about it later, you knew she'd gone way overboard. She fainted a couple of times too. And for the first couple of months, she looked dreadful. But"—she looked at him somberly— "she was going through a lot then."

"She's gone through a lot in the last couple of months too." He sat back and tried to think. He was still trying to shake off the idea that she was either having a nervous breakdown or dying of cancer. Pregnant? He hadn't thought of it, and then suddenly he remembered.

"Jesus. I forgot. The night Tygue ran away, the first time . . . we kind of kidded about it . . . she forgot her diaphragm." He looked over at Felicia apologetically, for regaling her with the details. "Anyway, it's certainly possible. So much has happened since then, I think we both forgot. Or I did anyway. You really think she doesn't know, if it's that?" He looked suddenly elated.

"She might not. But don't get excited. I may be wrong. By the way, have you got anything to drink?" She lit another cigarette and stood up. "It's been a bitch of a day."

"Yeah." He echoed the sentiment and walked over to the bar. They always kept the fixings for a martini close at hand, in case she dropped by. "Now what do I do?"

"Wait till she comes home, and ask her."

"What if she doesn't come home? What if she goes out with that guy?" He paled at the thought, and then he flushed as he viciously mixed her martini.

"Don't take it out on my drink, Nick. She'll come

back. Did she take the car?" But it was a dumb question. Of course she had. But Nick was looking at her strangely again.

"That's right. She came home in a cab. She must have left her car downtown." Felicia didn't like the sound of that. She must have been feeling like hell to do that.

"I think you're just going to have to wait this one out and ask her. And will you do me a favor"—she finished her drink and set down the glass—"will you please let me know? If she's sick, I want to know about it." He nodded his head miserably, and Felicia stood up. "I hate to do this to you, but I have to get moving. I'm being picked up at eight and I have to do a lot of repair work before then." She was going to the symphony. With someone new.

"Yeah. I'll call you." And then he looked at his watch too. "Damn. I'm going to have to leave in a minute too. I have to do the show."

"Maybe she'll be home when you get back." Felicia patted his shoulder as he walked her to the car, and she wondered to herself what he'd be like in bed. Beautiful and strong. She had decided that before, Kate was a lucky girl. She looked up at him and smiled. "She'll be all right. And hell, you may even wind up a daddy."

"God, Felicia, I'd love it."

"Just do me a favor, and stick around. I couldn't go through the delivery number again." But the gruffness of her voice told him she could. For Kate.

"Don't worry, Licia, this time you won't have to. I just hope it's that." As he walked back into the house, he found himself thinking back, and suddenly he was almost sure of it. He'd have been ready to celebrate as he drove to work, if only he'd known if she was

424

all right. She could have done anything, the way she was acting when she left the house. Anything.

But all she had done was sit on the wall she had found and cry. And at last she sat there and just shivered. She wanted to go home, but not until she knew he was gone. And at twenty after seven, she walked back to the house, went upstairs, took off her clothes, and went to bed. She was exhausted. She didn't wake up until she felt Nick gently shaking her shoulder.

CHAPTER 37

"Kate?" She felt him shaking her softly, and it was still dark outside when she looked up. It was almost dark in the room. There was only one lamp lit, in the far corner, and it gave off a soft glow. "Hi, babe." He rubbed her back softly and she closed her eyes again. His hands felt so good. But she was mad at him. She remembered that as she started to wake up.

"What do you want?"

"To talk to you."

"What about?" She refused to open her eyes, but she could hear a fire burning in the grate.

"Open your eyes."

"Go away." But she was starting to smile now, and he saw it. He bent down and kissed her cheek.

"Stop that."

"I want to ask you something."

She opened an eye. "Not that again." She was frowning.

"No, not that again."

"Then what?"

"What happened at Saks today?" He was smiling down at her and speaking very softly, but his eyes still looked worried. He hadn't been able to think all night, as they taped the show. And he had raced home to see if she was there. He had almost cried with relief when he saw her huddled form under the covers.

He didn't care if she hated him; at least she was home, and not dead somewhere, sick, or mugged, or hysterical. But she hadn't answered him. "Tell me about Saks."

"Is there anything about me you don't know?" She sat up and looked at him in astonishment. "Are you having me followed?" She looked stunned, but he shook his head with a small, rueful smile.

"No, they called. They wanted to make sure you got home all right. So what happened?"

"Nothing."

"That's not what they said."

"All right, so I passed out. I ate too much for lunch." That wasn't what Felicia had said either, but he didn't want to make her feel totally boxed in, so he didn't say it.

"Are you sure it was that?" He reached out carefully and held her face in his hands. Her eyes instantly filled with tears, and she started to relax in his hands.

"What do you think it was, Nick?"

"I think maybe . . . I hope . . ." He looked at her so tenderly that the tears only came more quickly, and he smiled. "Is it possible, Cinderella, that you're pregnant?" He watched her very closely and she pulled slowly away from his hands.

"Why would I be pregnant?" But like Felicia earlier, there was a look about her, as though she were mentally running her fingers through file cards, remembering, matching events, and then suddenly she looked at him with a sheepish grin. "Maybe. I hadn't even thought of that."

"Possibly more than maybe?" He looked at her hopefully.

"Maybe a lot more than maybe. Jesus, I don't know how come I didn't think of that." She had begun to wonder if she had some rare disease. She grinned at him and he kissed her softly, and then hungrily, feeling carefully in her nightgown for her breasts. "I would be about seven weeks pregnant. It was the night Tygue . . . wasn't it?"

"I don't know. Is it too soon to find out if you are?"

"No. This is just about right."

"Want to try again?" She laughed as he lay next to her on the bed.

"Try again, huh?"

"Sure. Why not?"

But they didn't need to. She was pregnant. The test was positive the next day.

"Are you sure?" He was beside himself when she hung up the phone after getting the results of the test. The nurse's voice had been unemotional. "Harper? Oh. Here it is. Positive."

"You're pregnant?"

"Yes I am, and yes I'm sure. That's what the lady said anyway." She slid her arms around his neck and he beamed at her.

"Oh Kate, I love you."

"I love you too." She said it softly, her voice muffled in his arms. "And I'm sorry about New York." She hadn't said that to him the night before, and she had wanted to.

"It's all right. Nothing happened. But if you ever go back there, I'm sending an armed guard." And then suddenly he looked at her seriously, as he held her gently in his arms. "I don't want you to tour while you're pregnant. Not at all. Is that clear?"

"Yes, sir."

"What about your new book? Will you be willing to wait before you go anywhere? It won't hurt your career to wait a few months."

"It won't be out for another year anyway. Perfect timing." She grinned up at him and ruffled his hair. He was taking it all so seriously. She didn't feel as nervous about this pregnancy as she had with Tygue, but that had been a long time ago too. In some ways, this felt new. And it would be so nice to have Nick there. She held him very tight for a few minutes, and they each smiled at their own thoughts. And then he looked down at her again.

"Promise me you won't push while you're pregnant."

"Push what?" She tried to make light of it.

"Kate . . . please . . ." He wanted this child more than anything. She understood.

"Relax, darling. I promise." She could feel him relax as he held her close again, and the phone rang next to them. She looked at him with a grin. "Maybe they changed their minds."

"Tell them it's too late. We accept." She smiled at him and answered the phone, but her face clouded instantly.

"Hi, Stu." She could feel Nick tense beside her.

"That's a surprise. When? . . . I don't know." She looked at Nick and smiled, but he was already panicking. He had started stalking the room, his face filled with despair. It was starting again. Weinberg and his fucking trips.

"You promised!"

"Relax!" She whispered it with a hand over the phone, and tried to continue the conversation with Weinberg. And then finally to him a vague "I'll see." But suddenly Nick couldn't take anymore. He grabbed the phone away from her and put his hand over the receiver.

"You tell him that the person he's trying to exploit is pregnant, and he can take his next fucking tour, or

429

whatever the hell he's calling about, and shove it up his ass." He looked at her in desperation, but she was grinning as she retrieved the phone.

"Sorry, Stu." She grinned at Nick and his face lightened a little as she said the words. "He won't play in the tournament with you. He thinks you're trying to exploit him. And he's pregnant. Very temperamental." Nick rolled his eyes and sat down with a grin. "No, he said you could shove it up your ass. That's what he said. . . . Fine. I'll tell him." She hung up and stood looking at Nick. "You worry too much, Mr. Waterman." She was grinning broadly.

"You're a spoiled brat, Cinderella. Has anyone told you that lately?"

"Not since this morning. By the way, when am I going to get the other glass slipper?" She smiled at him as she sat down on his lap.

"When you promise me that you're not going on tour, and not going to wear yourself out while you're pregnant. If you promise me that, you can have anything you want."

"I may hold you to that."

"You didn't answer my question."

"Was it a question? It sounded more like an order to me." She raised an eyebrow and ran a finger around his ear.

"I'm serious, Kate. This means a lot to me."

"It does to me too. But you don't have to coerce or threaten to get me to take it easy. Trust me a little."

"Not when it comes to your work . . . and our child." He looked at her with a small worried frown. "Is that going to be very hard on you, Kate? Handling both, I mean?"

She shook her head, but she didn't answer for a moment. "No." She hoped not anyway, but if so, they'd work it out.

"Had you thought of . . . of . . ."

But she cut him off before he could say the words. "No, I wouldn't do that." And then she pulled him closer into her arms. "I want your baby, Nick. I think I've always wanted that. Tygue is special, and he has always been just mine. I never got to share him, the waiting, the getting born, all those special moments that come later . . . I never had anyone to share that with. With us, with this baby, everything will be different."

"Including the fact that we're not married." He sounded a little embarrassed as he said it, and searched her face again. "Will that be very hard on you and Tygue?"

"Of course not. Tygue's too young to care, and do you really think I care about what people think about that? Besides, we'll get married someday." She looked down at the pale line on her left hand where the wedding ring had once been. "In the meantime, it doesn't really matter. Unless . . . will it matter to you? On the show, I mean? Could it cause you problems?" She had to think about that too. Her reputation wasn't the only one at stake, but he was already grinning in response.

"In that crazy world I work in? Are you kidding? They'd think we were strange if we *were* married and having a baby. But you know, I thought of something last night." He looked momentarily embarrassed and then decided to go ahead and tell her his idea. "If it does bother you, or Tygue, we could tell people that we are married. Who's to know that we're not? We could say we went off somewhere quietly and got married. And then . . . later . . . we could do just that. Nobody has to know if we're really married or not." But she was already shaking her head with a look of negative determination.

"Nope. No way, Mr. Waterman, I won't do that."

"Why not?"

"Because when we finally do get married, I am not going to sneak off anywhere to marry you, sir. I am going to do it with more pomp and ceremony and noise and style than you've ever seen. And the whole world is going to know. How about that?"

"You know what, Cinderella?"

"What?" She was smiling as broadly as he.

"For that, you get your other glass slipper."

She grinned at him and put her mouth over his for a long tender kiss. "Do you have any idea how much I love you, Nicholas Waterman?"

"Want to come upstairs and show me?"

"Anytime, Mr. Waterman. Anytime."